P9-CET-037

THE NIGHT SPIDER

John Lutz

PINNACLE BOOKS
Kensington Publishing Corp.
http://www.kensingtonbooks.com

PINNACLE BOOKS are published by

Kensington Publishing Corp.
850 Third Avenue
New York, NY 10022

All Kensington Titles, Imprints, and Distributed Lines are
available at special quantity discounts for bulk purchases for
sales promotions, premiums, fund-raising, educational, or
institutional use. Special book excerpts or customized print-
ings can also be created to fit specific needs. For details,
write or phone the office of the Kensington special sales
manager: Kensington Publishing Corp., 850 Third Avenue,
New York, NY 10022, attn: Special Sales Department,
phone 1-800-221-2647.

Pinnacle and the P logo Reg. U.S. Pat. & TM Off.

First Pinnacle Books Printing: November 2003

10 9 8 7 6 5 4 3 2 1
Printed in the United States of America

For David Bauer

*And in fond memory of
Ed and Betty Bauer*

The spider's touch, how exquisitely fine!
Feels at each thread, and lives along the line.
—Pope
Essay on Man

News fitting to the night,
Black, fearful, comfortless and horrible.
—Shakespeare
King John, Act V

Part
One

1

New York, 2003

Sally Bridge was exhausted.

Wisteria Chance was a premier bitch.

Her Beetle Davis was a totally unconvincing beetle.

Sally had cast aging Broadway star Wisteria in the planned production of the musical *Bug Off. Bug* had played to full houses for the past three months at smaller theaters throughout the Northeast. It was now scheduled to open at the Cort Theatre on West 48th Street in less than a month. Sally, who *was* Bridge's Casting Call, had done what everyone agreed was a great job of casting some major Broadway players in the roles of various insects. This hadn't been easy; ego sometimes stood in the way of accepting such roles. After all, no one had ever won a prestigious award for portraying an insect. This wasn't exactly Shakespeare. Sally had often thought of suggesting they retitle the play *McBug*.

Most of the cast had overcome early reservations about their roles, especially when they found how delightful the material—an insect version of classic Hollywood—actually was. But Wisteria's reservations had grown into tentative-

ness, then outright hostility. Sally cringed and laughed at the
same time, remembering how the haughty Broadway doyenne
had stood before the footlights during dress rehearsal, threatening to walk out on her contract and hurling insults at the
director and Sally, her antennae vibrating furiously as she
waved her legs and arms.

The hell with it, Sally thought, closing and locking her
apartment door behind her. She'd eat leftover Chinese takeout from last night, settle down in front of CNN with a glass
of white wine, and look in on some of the world's real problems.

Sally was young to be so successful, only thirty-two, and
attractive enough to cast herself in some of the leading roles
that crossed her desk. But she'd learned early on that she
wasn't a real actress, didn't have the fire and ruthlessness
and pure commitment. This tall, blond beauty with a busty
build and Helen Hunt features loved the business though.
And she had a touch for casting and a line of bull for dealing
with agents. She also had a genuine affection and empathy
that helped persuade actors and actresses to accept the roles
she offered.

Her apartment was a junior one bedroom, which meant it
was an efficiency with a dividing wall. Though small, it was
well furnished, on the thirtieth floor with a great view of
Central Park, and the rent was reasonable. Tables, chairs,
and lamps were antique and flea market eclectic, mostly
chosen by a decorator friend. The soft leather sofa was from
Jennifer Convertibles and could be made into a bed for
guests. The framed theater posters and playbills on the walls
were supplied by Sally, over the objections of her decorator.

The important thing was, Sally really liked the place. And
she knew that was important, because she tended to get
emotionally involved with where she lived the way other
people did with their pets; it would be difficult for her to
leave this comfortable corner of the world where she felt secure and could watch the seasons change in the park.

The warmed-up egg foo yung was still good. The muted

sounds of traffic filtering up from the street were relaxing. There was nothing too disturbing on the news. The wine made her even sleepier, and she dozed off in the middle of an SUV commercial and woke up near midnight slouched in a corner of the sofa, her cheek lightly glued to the soft leather by dried saliva.

"Yuck!" she said aloud. She forced herself up off the sofa, used the remote to switch off the TV (another SUV commercial—or the same one), and lurched zombielike toward the bathroom.

She brushed her teeth, which woke her up somewhat, but decided to shower in the morning. It took her only a few minutes to undress, slip into her knee-length sleep shirt with the likeness of Marlene Dietrich on it, and switch off the lamp by the bed.

Her mattress was only six months old and soft yet supportive. *Pure comfort* . . . At least there was some reward for exhaustion. She listened to her long sigh drift out into darkness. A brief vision of an SUV, crawling like an intrepid insect up rough and rocky terrain toward a mountain plateau, and then Sally was asleep.

Not yet opening her eyes, she awoke slowly, becoming gradually aware that she couldn't move. The dream she'd had was half remembered, movement soft and subtle about her body, around, beneath, so gentle . . . It was enough to disturb her sleep but not quite wake her.

Until now.

Sally was lying on her back in the dim bedroom, her arms at her sides. One palm was pressed flat to her hip, the other turned outward so that her arm was twisted and ached at the shoulder. She tried to move the arm that hurt, and it didn't budge. *What the hell? How did I get so twisted up in the sheet?* The night was warm and there was no blanket or bedspread over the sheet. She should be able to at least goddamn move!

Her eyes were open to slits now, and she could barely lift her head from the pillow to squint and try to see her feet, which were pressed so tightly together that it hurt her ankles. Her calves, thighs, and knees were pressed just as firmly to each other. The area of taut white sheet she could see was wound about her so tightly that her breasts were compressed.

Still, half awake, she was more puzzled than afraid.

Then her heart leaped and began to pound. Movement! Off to the left! Something large and quick! Had she imagined it? She swiveled her head this way and that on the perspiration-soaked pillow, craning her neck so it ached.

But she saw nothing alarming other than the window next to the one that held the humming air conditioner. It was open!

I locked it! I know I locked it!

She wasn't alone!

Then the mattress creaked and sagged and the form she'd glimpsed was looming above her, straddling her, lithe and angular, large and powerful and dim as the dusk. She tried to scream but her throat was paralyzed. Something was jammed in her mouth, then slapped across her lips, binding them shut. Pain flared in her right side, a deep stinging sensation almost like an insect bite. *Bug off!* she thought inanely, her mind jumping to the play and casting problems even as she tried to scream against the pressure in and against her mouth, even as she tried to move her arms, her fingers, *anything!*

Another stinging sensation in her side. Another. Each more painful than the last, and she could only lie mutely and endure, her eyes bulging, her entire body vibrating in agony inside its shroud. Sally knew she was going to die.

End this! she screamed silently. *End it, please!*

But she was helpless, staring up at the angular dark form above her, into unblinking black eyes that gazed into hers and searched patiently inside her for her pain, for her death. Not to find her death but to avoid it. For a while. Forever.

End it! Please!

2

NYPD Homicide Detective Paula Ramboquette pulled the unmarked car to the curb in front of the Layton Arms apartments on East 56th Street. She'd been in New York almost a year now, and this was the first case where she, and not her partner Roy Bickerstaff, was lead detective. This was because Bickerstaff was retiring and would be gone by the end of the month.

A large, potbellied man who favored cut-rate woolly suits and ineffective cheap deodorant even in summer, Bickerstaff sat still in his seat and waited for Paula before raising his bulk out of the car. He did have a certain sensibility she hadn't noticed at first, and he was a good detective. And God knew Paula had seen worse.

The uniformed doorman had emerged from the lobby and was walking toward them, not realizing the unmarked was a police car like the rest of the cruisers angled in at the curb. He was a short, dark-haired man with an aggressive curved nose that reminded Paula of a beak, and he was waving them away. "This space is for police," Paula heard him say through the glass. "We have an emergency here today."

"Straighten this bird out, Roy," Paula said, thinking Bickerstaff, in his rumpled brown suit, would be quite a contrast with the hawklike doorman in his royal blue outfit with gold epaulets. While the wheezing Bickerstaff opened the car door and squeezed out, she glanced over her shoulder for on-coming traffic, then climbed out on the driver's side.

Despite being sartorially outranked, Bickerstaff had been persuasive. By the time Paula had gotten around the car, the doorman was holding one of the glass front doors open for them. "Ms. Bridge is on thirty," he said politely, as if she were expecting them. Which Paula knew was impossible be-cause Ms. Bridge was dead.

Paula and Bickerstaff crossed a tile lobby with a square blue area rug and gray leather furniture. Everything looked new and unsat on or unwalked on. Back In New Orleans, Paula had worked the Garden District and was more used to decaying elegance than this kind of contemporary tidiness.

They zipped up to thirty in a polished steel, hexagonal el-evator that reflected them so many times it made Paula feel as if she were standing in a crowd. Not much high-speed el-evatoring in the Garden District, either.

It was easy enough to find Sally Bridge's apartment on the thirtieth floor. Hers was the one with the door open and the blue uniforms lounging nearby in the hall.

"Ms. Bridge still at home?" Bickerstaff asked, still caught in the doorman's mood of civility.

"You mean have they removed the body?" one of the uni-forms asked. Then answered his own question. "No, she's still at your disposal."

Bickerstaff gave the man a glance and waited like a gentle-man for Paula to enter before him. Old school.

And it was Paula who led the way past the techs dusting for prints and into the bedroom where the body lay. As they entered the room, she noticed that the door frame near the latch was splintered. The door had been forced.

The assistant ME was still there, a seedy little guy even more rumpled than Bickerstaff. Paula had seen him around and remembered him because his name was actually Harry Potter. And he looked like Harry Potter, grown up and gone to . . . well, pot. Put on a little weight, lost most of his hair, wore a different style of glasses. Still had the calm, intelligent look, though.

Paula had pinned her shield on her lapel in the lobby, and now identified herself and Bickerstaff.

Potter straightened up from the body on the bed and stared at her. "What kinda accent is that?"

"Cajun," Paula said. "Is this Ms. Bridge?"

Potter nodded. "The late. She departed this world sometime last night, past midnight."

"We all want to die in bed," Bickerstaff said.

"Not like that."

"Sex crime," Bickerstaff said, as they all stared at the dead woman on the bed. She still had on a short nightgown, though it had worked up over her breasts, and the bed was stripped down to the mattress pad. Bloodied white sheets were in a pile at the foot of the bed. Bickerstaff bent over the stained linen. "The sheets were stabbed lots of times like she was."

"Over three dozen times, actually," Potter said. "At least that's what we've found so far. And she doesn't appear to have been sexually violated. Though we'll have to check more closely for semen."

"There's different kinds of sex," Bickerstaff said.

Paula took a closer look at Sally Bridge. She'd been an attractive blond woman in her thirties. This was evident even though there was a rectangle of silver duct tape over her mouth and her features were contorted in horror. A well-built woman. Probably men had thought her sexy in a blowzy way. Her almost nude body was smeared with crusting blood, but something other than the obvious didn't look right.

"Stabbed all those times," Paula said, "there should be even more blood."

Potter nodded approvingly at her. "There was plenty of blood. Most of it was stemmed by and then absorbed by the sheets. I had to unwind them to get to the body."

"Unwind?"

"Yeah. She was wrapped tight like she was in some kind of shroud. Sheets are full of holes, too, like your partner says. She was wrapped alive, tape put over her mouth, then she was stabbed repeatedly with a narrow, sharp instrument. Few of the wounds are fatal. I'd say she bled to death, and it took her a long time."

"Different kinds of sex," Bickerstaff repeated.

"The killer wrapped her up alive?" Paula asked.

"Wrapped her tight as a tick."

"Was she drugged?"

"We'll find that out later."

Paula moved closer to the body and took it all in: the blood smears, the pale flesh, the narrow slits made by knife thrusts, the eyes like dull marbles that barely reflected light, that seemed to draw light in and make it darkness. Sally Bridge's arms were still at her sides, her legs pressed tightly together. The way Potter had unrolled her. Never in her life had she dreamed strangers would look at her this way.

"So what are those angular marks on her flesh?" Paula asked.

"Creases. That's how tightly she was wrapped."

Bickerstaff said nothing, standing and watching with his arms crossed while Paula studied the bloodied mattress pad, still neatly held at the corners by elastic. If there'd been much of a struggle on the bed, the pad would have been pulled loose.

"Odd she didn't put up a fight," Bickerstaff said. "Looks like the killer kicked open the bedroom door or slammed his shoulder against it. You'd think the noise would have woke her up and—" He was staring at something on the floor.

"I wondered when you were going to notice," said Harry Potter.

Paula walked over to look where Bickerstaff was staring. There was a faint and partial bloody footprint on the carpet. The surprising thing about it was it appeared to be the back three-fourths or so of a bare foot.

"Hard even to figure the size," Bickerstaff said, "but it's a right foot and almost surely a man's."

"Maybe he stripped nude before the murder so he wouldn't get blood on his clothes," Paula said. "We need to Luminol this place, try to bring more of the footprint out. Then check the tub or shower stall drain, see if the killer cleaned up before putting his clothes back on."

"The way she's wrapped up tight as a tamale," said Harry Potter, "her killer probably would have gotten little if any blood on him. You can see near the footprint that there's blood where some of it soaked through the sheets and ran down to the floor. But that's the only blood I saw on the carpet."

"More might show up under the lights," Paula told him.

"Have you talked to the uniforms who took the call?" Potter asked.

"Not yet," Bickerstaff said.

"One of them forced open the door. The super was supposed to repair a leaky faucet in the bathroom. He got no answer when he knocked, so he let himself in and started to work. Bathroom backs up to this room. When he wanted to see if there was an access panel in here to get to the plumbing, he found the door locked. Knocked and got no answer. Thought not much of it till the phone rang and Sally Bridge didn't pick up. Super figured she might be in the bedroom and need some kinda help, so he pounded on the door, still got no answer, and called the cops. He's got keys to the hall doors, but not the inside doors, so they had to break in here."

"You been playing detective?" Paula asked the little ME.

"I got eyes and ears."

Paula glanced at Bickerstaff.

"I'll go talk to the super," he said, and lumbered out of the room.

"Crocker's his name," Potter said.

"Crocker," Bickerstaff repeated without glancing back. "Like Betty Crocker."

The ME stared at Paula.

"He does that all the time," she said, "to help his memory." She then added, "He's about to retire," knowing that probably had nothing to do with Bickerstaff's memory method.

"Mmph," was all Harry Potter said, nodding.

Paula went to the window where long sheer drapes were dancing rhythmically in the summer breeze. In the room's other window an air conditioner was humming away. Who'd open one window on a hot night, then switch on an air conditioner in another?

"Was this window open?" she asked.

"That's just how I found it," Potter said.

Keeping her hands away from the brass handle, Paula gripped the wooden frame and lowered the window until it was almost closed. It worked smoothly and silently.

She was about to turn away when she noticed through the inner glass that a small crescent of glass had been neatly cut from the bottom of the top window. It was centered precisely over where the lock would be if the window were closed and secure.

"I'll be damned," Potter said, looking where she was staring. "The killer got in through the window."

"And out," Paula said, "seeing as the door was locked and had to be forced by the cop who got the call. Unless the killer had a key and locked the bedroom door on the way out."

"If he had a key," Potter said, "he probably wouldn't have come in through the window. And anyway, he'd have no reason to lock the bedroom door behind him when he left."

"You oughta *be* a detective."

"So I've been told," Potter said. "But not often."

Two white-uniformed men appeared in the doorway. EMT had arrived to remove the body. The paramedics were both hefty guys with black curly hair, and could have been brothers.

"Okay to take that now?" one of them asked, motioning toward the dead woman.

"If she says so," Potter said, pointing to Paula.

"Police photographer been here?" Paula asked.

Potter nodded. "Left just before you arrived."

"She's yours," Paula told the paramedics.

"What kinda accent is that?" one of them asked, as they bent to their task.

"Cajun."

"Alabama?"

"Louisiana."

"Cajuns make great music," Harry Potter said.

"Jumbalya," said the paramedic.

"That's food," said the other.

"A song, too," Potter said. He began to sing. It didn't sound like singing.

"Yuck," the paramedic said, working his gloved hand beneath the butchered body. "Crawfish pie."

Harry Potter packed his instruments into his bag and said good-bye. Paula was glad he was finished singing.

As Sally Bridge was leaving her bedroom, Bickerstaff returned.

"Got the officers' story," he said. "And Crocker the super's. And the doorman said nobody suspicious entered or left the building all evening."

"Our killer came in through the window," Paula said.

Bickerstaff raised his bushy brows. "No shit?"

Paula walked with him to the window and opened it wider, still careful not to touch the glass. They both looked down. Paula got dizzy up high and had to back away a few steps.

"Hell of a climb," Bickerstaff said.

"But the street's pretty deserted after midnight, and once the killer got a few stories up he'd be in darkness and nobody'd notice him."

"But it's damn near a sheer brick wall. How'd he climb it?"

"Maybe pulled himself up on some kind of line," Paula said. She examined the windowsill for marks where a grappling hook might have been attached. The sill was unmarked, and nothing else in the room seemed to have been disturbed other than Sally Bridge.

"The super said she lived alone," Bickerstaff said.

"I gathered."

"She was a casting director. Even did some work on Broadway."

"Really? She have a boyfriend?"

"She was between them, according to the super and the doorman. They both said she was always working and didn't have much opportunity for romance. She used to joke about it, how she needed more time to meet interesting men."

"She found time last night."

"And she isn't joking," Bickerstaff said. "Or even slightly interested." He nodded toward the bloody sheets. "Maybe because she's on the rag."

Police humor, Paula thought. She could live without it.

3

Retired NYPD Homicide Captain Thomas Horn didn't have a hell of a lot more to do these days than eat toasted corn muffins, which was what he was waiting to do on a warm, gray Monday morning in the Home Away Diner on Amsterdam on Manhattan's West Side.

Horn, still in his early fifties, had retired early because of what happened to the World Trade Center. He'd been on his way to interrogate the CFO of Jagger and Schmidt Brokerage at the firm's office on the forty-second floor of the north tower. The man had almost certainly defrauded the firm's clients of several million dollars, some of which was part of the police pension fund.

Since it was such a clear, beautiful morning, Horn had decided to leave his car where he'd parked it after pulling to the curb. He went into a jewelry store to look at gold hoop earrings for his wife, Anne. She'd said she wanted such earrings, and there in the store's window was a sign stating they were on sale. HALF OFF HOOPY-DOOP EARRINGS, the sign had declared in large red letters. GOLD AND SILVER.

On impulse Horn decided to buy a pair. On impulse he

decided to walk the rest of the way to the World Trade Center.

Horn spent more time than he planned in the store because there were already three customers ahead of him. Then the earrings he wanted weren't on display and the jeweler had to go into a back room and locate them. These little things added up, changing his world.

Though he was in the store less than an hour, a lot had happened during that time. The earrings had saved his life.

After leaving the store slightly before ten o'clock, earrings in his suitcoat pocket, he'd strolled about a block when he saw several people pass him going the other way and knew from their faces and the way they were walking that something was wrong. He hadn't suspected it was at the World Trade Center, but he picked up his pace.

From conversation overheard along the way, he learned that a plane had struck one of the towers. Now he began jogging in the opposite direction of those passing him, seeing something beyond fear on some of their faces. He saw terror and, in some cases, people staring blankly ahead under the anesthetic of shock. Faces and hands were cut, clothing was torn. *What the hell?* He wanted to get to the damaged building, urge people to stay in the area and not to panic. His mind went back to the time when, as a child, he'd heard about a plane striking the Empire State Building. A catastrophe but one that was manageable. As a cop he'd learned that most catastrophes could be managed.

"Do yourself a favor and turn around, buddy," a heavyset man in a business suit told him without pausing as he passed. "Both those towers are gonna fall."

Both those towers?

Horn had stopped and stood still, puzzled. He noticed the day had dimmed and looked up to see a dark pall hanging low over the tops of buildings. Burning jet fuel, no doubt, from the collision. It must be worse than he'd imagined. He began running again, toward the towers.

And heard a roar like a thousand jetliners coming in for a landing.

A cloud of smoke that was a solid wall rounded the corner at the end of the block and rolled and rushed toward him. Horn's heart skipped a beat as he looked up to see that the top of the cloud had curled like an incoming wave and was *above* him. He was going to be engulfed by it!

Something smashed loudly into a nearby parked car. Debris began falling. A woman on the opposite sidewalk disappeared beneath a crashing mass of tangled wreckage. Instinctively Horn dropped and rolled toward another parked car, trying to get beneath it to shelter himself from what was raining down.

And remembered nothing else.

He'd awakened in a hospital bed with his shoulder aching and bandaged. Doctors told him he'd been struck by falling debris, and a steel reinforcing rod had speared his right shoulder. *Rerod*, construction workers called it. Rescue workers had to bend it to get Horn to fit into the ambulance so the six-foot-long rod could be removed at the hospital. He was sure he'd been able to get under the car, so they figured the rerod must have somehow been shoved in after him by the terrific impact of crashing steel and concrete.

Three weeks later he was an outpatient with an almost useless right arm, and scars suggesting he'd been shot through the shoulder and the bullet had exited out his back.

A month after that he was retired. Pensioned off.

Through grueling physical therapy he'd recovered most of the use of his right arm and hand, and a modicum of strength. There was no way to recover his work, his life in the NYPD.

The Job had been more than a job; it had been what he

was about, who he was. But what Horn wasn't about was self-pity. He knew now he'd have to become someone else. Trouble was, he couldn't figure out who.

"Corn muffins, Horn."

He looked up from his steaming coffee cup.

Marla, the waitress who usually served Horn on the mornings he came into the diner for breakfast, had placed a plate with two toasted muffins before him. She was fortyish, maybe older, slim, and attractive, even in her dowdy black-checked uniform that made her somber brown eyes look even darker. She didn't wear much makeup and didn't seem to care much about her mud-colored hair, which she wore pulled back in a ponytail.

"Sorry," he said, "I was daydreaming."

"Want juice this morning?"

"No, this is fine."

"You gonna tell me crime stories today?"

"No, I'm slacking off. I'm not some old fart living in the past."

She grinned. "You hardly qualify for old fart status." She walked away, then came back with a coffeepot and topped off his cup. "Even if you sometimes think so."

He glanced around. The breakfast crowd was gone and there were only a few other customers in the diner, down near the other end of the counter. Maybe he *would* talk with Marla. She made him feel better, that was for sure. Sometimes her incisive questions surprised him—her curiosity about the criminal mind and the mind of a cop, about serial killers, which had been Horn's specialty when he was active.

But when he was about to call her back, the bell above the door tinkled as another customer entered. Marla would have work to do, and Horn didn't want to pass the time of day with her anyway if the customer sat down within earshot.

Horn sipped his coffee as he turned and glanced to watch where whoever had entered would settle.

He was surprised to see heading toward his booth Assistant Chief of Police Roland Larkin.

"Now you're retired," Larkin said with a grin, "I see you're working on clogging your arteries." He shook his head. "You were eating those toasted muffins when we were young and riding together in Queens."

"Not like these," Horn said. "These are toasted just right and are delicious."

"And have soaked up all the grease and every flavor from the grill." Larkin extended his right hand palm down and Horn shook it with his left. Old friends.

"Why don't you sit down and have some of your own, Rollie?"

Larkin slipped the button on his suitcoat and slid into the seat on the other side of the table. When the coat flapped open, Horn saw he wasn't carrying a gun. Too important these days. Larkin looked good, Horn thought. Tall and lean, even if a little paunchy, his gray eyes slightly more faded, his hair grayer, his usually rouged-looking cheeks a little more florid. He was the kind of tough but compassionate Irishman who would have made a good priest and had made a good cop.

Marla came over with a menu, all waitress now, as if she'd never seen either man before.

Larkin handed the menu back and told her just coffee.

"You come in here often?" Horn asked, knowing Larkin lived across town.

"First time. Just to talk to you."

"How'd you find me?"

"I'm a cop. I followed the muffins."

Marla brought coffee, then left and began working behind the counter, not far away.

"So how's retirement?" Larkin asked.

"It hasn't dulled my senses." Horn took a bite of toasted

muffin, chewed, and swallowed. "How come you looked me up, Rollie?"

Stirring sugar into his coffee, Larkin leaned over the table and lowered his voice. "Need your help, Horn. Something's going on."

"What something?"

"Last week a woman named Sally Bridge was found murdered in her apartment. She'd been wound up in her bedsheets and stabbed thirty-seven times."

"Lot of stab wounds." Horn took another big bite of muffin.

"Not many of them were fatal. The killer wanted to inflict maximum agony before she died."

"Husband?" Another bite of muffin, what was left of the top removed and buttered. Horn chased it down with some coffee.

"Bridge was single. And we don't have the killer."

"Victim have a love life?"

"About what you'd expect. She was between rides."

Horn spread butter on the uneaten half of his muffin, watching it melt in. "What is it about this murder, Rollie, other than the thirty-seven stab wounds?"

"The media haven't tumbled to the fact yet, but it's the third one like this in the last five months."

"Ah!" Horn rested the knife on his plate. "Serial killer."

"Uh-huh. Same guy for sure. He climbs the building and enters through the bedroom window. Then he winds the women up in their bedsheets like they're wrapped in some kind of shroud. Does it so expertly it looks like they don't even wake up all the way until he slaps a piece of duct tape over their mouths. Then he goes to work with the knife, all stab wounds, no slices, missing the vital organs. Victims finally give out from the pain, die of shock or blood loss."

Horn was staring into his coffee cup. "You said he climbs the buildings?"

"Yeah. The women live on high floors, think they're safe.

But our boy's a hell of a climber. Uses a glass cutter to get to the hardware if a window's locked."

"Victims the same type?"

"They're between twenty-five and forty-six years old. Attractive, well built but maybe a little on the chunky side. All were single. A call girl, a computer programmer, and a casting director, in that order."

"Sexual penetration?"

"Not unless you count the knife, all over the body. Narrow blade, about ten inches long, with a very sharp point."

"Unusual killer," Horn said.

"And the time between the second and third murders is less than between the first and second."

"And scales buildings."

"Must."

"You've got a problem," Horn said.

"To be honest," Larkin said, "why I came here was to talk you into making it your problem."

Her case. Paula knew this one was going to be something of a test, with Bickerstaff headed for retirement in Minnesota where he was going to ice-fish. *Jesus! Ice-fish!* From what he'd told Paula, that meant sitting all day shivering in front of a hole in the ice trying to catch a fish instead of pneumonia. Paula had never had the patience for any kind of fishing.

She watched the unmarked she'd just climbed out of turn the corner at the end of her block and disappear, leaving a faint wisp of ghostlike exhaust smoke in its wake. Then she entered her apartment building, checked her mail—bills, ads, bills, coupons, bills—and rode the elevator to the fifteenth floor where her one-bedroom apartment was at the end of the hall.

Not a bad place, she thought, as she fitted her key to the dead bolt lock. Secondhand furnishings, framed museum prints, and an old tile bathroom with yellowed porcelain and pipes that clanged but otherwise was in pretty good shape. Kitchen from hell, though the owner was supposed to replace everything in it soon. Sure. More than one burner on the stove would work then.

Paula tensed and stood still. Something was wrong—the dead bolt was already unlocked.

She raised her right hand and eased the door open a few inches, nervously touching the butt of her 9mm handgun beneath her blazer.

"You Ms. Rambo-cwet?" asked a male voice.

Paula pushed the door open the rest of the way.

A portly man with wild gray hair and a dead cigar in the corner of his mouth stood solidly in the middle of her living room. He'd left footprints on the carpet and was wearing dirty white coveralls. A large box-end wrench was stuck through one of many cloth loops on his coveralls, dangling at his waist as if it might be drawn as a gun.

"Rambo*cet*," Paula corrected. "Like *"get"* only with a *hard C* instead of a *G.*"

"If you say. I'm Ernie Flatt—regular *F*—of Flatt Contracting. The super let me in. I'm here workin' on the kitchen."

"Really?" Paula said, stepping all the way into the apartment and closing the door. "And I was thinking of working on dinner in the kitchen." *Heating water for tea to go with Thai takeout, anyway.*

Ernie smiled around the stale stub of cigar that was stinking up the living room even though it wasn't burning. Smoking the things had left his teeth a jagged jumble of yellow. "Oh, I don't think you'd wanna do that. I got the water off."

"Could you turn it back on?"

"Only if you want wet floors. I got the sink pretty much tore out."

Paula walked over and looked into the small kitchen.

She almost gasped. The old porcelain sink was dangling sideways on the wall. There were dark holes where the leaky faucet and handles had protruded. Holes in the wall. Exposed plumbing. Layers of old paint and faded wallpaper, like an archaeological dig; a rose pattern could be seen where the wood cabinets had been removed. Plaster dust and dark slats of lath were scattered on the floor. Paula's dishes, a mismatched service for six, were stacked precariously on the table, along with her used toaster and new Braun coffee brewer.

"God!" she said. "I wish somebody'd told me you were coming."

"I ain't God, and just be glad I came," Ernie told her, holding his ground. "You realize how long a waitin' list I got?"

New York, Paula thought. Everybody was always poised to turn the tables on you.

"Yeah, maybe you're right," she said, rolling with the punch.

Ernie smiled broadly, cigar stub twitching. They were friends. "I'll be outta here in a week or so, things go right. And I'll be workin' days while you're workin' yourself. Whatddya do?"

"Do? Oh, I'm a cop."

"No shit?"

"I wouldn't lie to you, being a cop."

"No uniform, though."

"Plainclothes. Detective."

"Hey! Interesting!"

"It sure can be, Ernie."

"Well, I was gettin' my tools together. Just leavin'. I was gonna leave you a note, explainin' that a bomb or somethin' hadn't gone off in your kitchen. I'll be outta here in a few minutes."

"How about if I want to take a shower?"

He cocked his head at her, speculating. *Ho, brother!* Then he understood. "Sure, sure. I left you water service in the bathroom. Just in the kitchen's where I'll be workin'. You'll see when I'm done. You'll love it."

He waved, swaggered back into the kitchen, and Paula heard tools clanging around.

She barely had time to take another look at the mail she'd brought upstairs and throw away everything but the bills, when Ernie emerged from the kitchen lugging a large dented black toolbox.

"See you tomorrow," Paula said.

"Yeah, if I'm still here when you get in from chasin' the bad guys." He paused with the hall door open. "I been listenin' to you, and if you don't mind my askin' . . ."

"Cajun," Paula said. "I'm from Louisiana."

Ernie grinned, wagging the cigar stub in his mouth. "Didn't sound like the Bronx." He left and closed the door behind him.

Paula immediately walked over and locked it. People were something in this city. But then, people had been something in New Orleans.

She started to remove her shoes, then remembered the state of the kitchen and left them on. At the kitchen door, she was relieved to hear a soft but deep humming sound. Thank God, or Ernie, the refrigerator was still operating.

Paula made herself a J&B and water (from the bathroom washbasin) on the rocks, then went back into the living room, sat down on the sofa, propped her stockinged feet up on the coffee table, and used her cell phone to call the corner deli.

In her cozy if abused apartment, with only the humming refrigerator and muffled traffic noises nibbling at the silence, she sipped her drink while waiting for supper to be delivered, thinking about the bulging, agonized eyes of a dead woman with thirty-seven stab wounds. What had those eyes seen in the last long minutes and hours before her death? What emotional storm had raged behind them?

Christ! Thirty-seven!

Paula's case.

4

Thomas Horn lived in a three-story brownstone on the West Side near Columbus Avenue. It had a basement with street-level barred windows, fancier wrought-iron bars on the first-floor windows, and wonderfully elaborate, if less formidable, bars on the second- and third-floor windows. There were green wooden shutters on all of the windows facing the street and green wooden flower boxes with geraniums and ferns on the first-floor windows. These windows were on either side of four concrete steps that led up to a stoop and stained oak double doors. The tall, heavy doors had small, triangular leaded windows in them. The worn concrete steps were flanked by black wrought-iron railings that echoed the elaborate bars on the upper-floor windows. The effect of all this was that of an urban fortress that had somehow fallen to Martha Stewart.

In the beamed and wainscoted living room Horn sat in his usual green leather chair near the seldom-used fireplace and watched his wife, Anne, slump down on the sofa and ease off her practical low-heeled black pumps. Working women's shoes. Horn sometimes thought it a shame that a woman with ankles like Anne's had a job where she walked quite a bit and needed such comfortable shoes. She was in hospital administration at Kincaid Memorial Hospital and was, in fact, chief administrator of the imaging and radiology department. A responsible job that paid well and, until recently, had provided her with satisfaction.

An attractive women with long blond hair, a model's complexion, and clear blue eyes, she raised one nylon-clad foot and massaged it with both hands. Horn loved her.

She smiled at him and said, "Something's on your mind."

He wasn't surprised she could tell. "Why don't we have a drink, then go down to the Regency for dinner and talk about it?"

"It requires a drink?"

"'Fraid so."

"I'll go change."

She was smart enough not to press. Not yet. Something Horn very much liked about her was her feel for timing. He watched her climb the carpeted stairs in her bare feet, holding her shoes in her right hand. Timing wasn't everything in life, but quite a lot.

When Anne came down fifteen minutes later she was wearing faded jeans, sandals, and a white blouse. Her hair was piled loosely on top of her head, she wore little makeup, and looked about forty though she was actually fifty.

She came over and lightly pecked Horn on the cheek. He'd made her a martini and himself a Glenlivet on the rocks. He sat down in the green leather chair, and she sat in a corner of the overstuffed sofa on the other side of the oriental rug whose pattern reminded Horn of some kind of large game board.

"So how was your busy day?" he asked.

She shrugged. "How was your day of hard-earned leisure?"

Christ! Did she somehow sense what he was going to tell her? "I'm getting used to it."

She smiled. "Are you now?"

Change subject. "Anything new on the Vine lawsuit?"

"Nothing I feel like talking about. I want this evening to be only about us."

So they sat and enjoyed their drinks and talked about anything but the Vine suit against Kincaid Hospital, and whatever it was Horn wanted to tell her. Their conversation flowed easily, old friends as well as lovers. Their shared past was the strength and foundation of what they had today.

Twenty minutes later they were strolling along the sidewalk toward the restaurant.

Horn loved walking in New York. The sights, sounds, and smells of the city were his oxygen. The exhaust fumes, even the sweet smell of the garbage wafting from black plastic bags not tightly sealed, soothed his spirit. If he shared the thought with Anne she'd laugh and tell him it was probably the scotch that made him feel that way about carbon monoxide and garbage. Horn had to smile. Anyone in his right mind would agree with her.

The Regency was a medium-priced casual restaurant that served great Italian food and tolerable red wine. Horn and Anne decided on a sidewalk table shaded by a large blue canvas canopy. They were near a dividing wall and well back from the street, so they could talk more or less privately if they didn't raise their voices.

The waiter came with ice water and menus. Anne ordered a salad and angel-hair pasta, Horn the house specialty, baked lasagna, and a glass of merlot.

The wine arrived, along with bread and Anne's salad. He sipped, she ate, he talked.

When he was finished telling her about his conversation with Rollie Larkin, she put down her fork and patted her lips with her napkin. "You're going back to work." Parallel vertical lines appeared above the bridge of her perfect nose. *Subway tracks*, Horn used to call them, because they signified she was thinking deep thoughts.

"Only for a while, with special status for the serial killer case. I'll be in charge, and I got Rollie to assign to me the two detectives who have the case now."

"You start when?"

"Tonight. The detectives are coming by the brownstone at about nine o'clock so we can talk."

"As if I didn't have enough to worry about," Anne said.

"I know, darling." He sipped merlot. "The Vine case."

A ten-year-old boy, Alan Vine, had become comatose on the operating table six months ago at Kincaid Memorial. The boy's parents were convinced that a mix-up in body scan images had caused the mishap, meaning Anne's department, and ultimately, her responsibility. She, and the hospital, knew better. The boy's condition was most likely caused by his rare reaction to his anesthetic. "Blaming the victim," the family's attorney said as often as possible. Which, in a perverse way, was true; in this case there was no one else to blame. Not the anesthesiologist who'd performed as he should, not the medical technicians who'd conducted the scan, not the doctors who'd interpreted the images. And not Anne.

Then why did she feel guilty?

"Thomas, you don't call me *darling* unless you don't mean it." She was the only one who used his given name. Everyone else Horn knew simply called him by his last name. Horn had never minded.

"But I do mean it. Hell, it isn't hard to know you're under stress and this is a bad time for me to become active again. That's why I set it up with Rollie that I'd mostly be advising these other detectives."

"Do you know them?"

"No. One's a woman who hasn't been in the department very long. The other's old school and is going to retire soon, if I don't talk him out of it."

"And I'm sure you will."

He didn't answer, and Anne went back to work on her salad.

"I talked to Ashleigh today," she said. Ashleigh was their

married daughter in Connecticut. "Dan Jr. tried to set fire to the garage."

Horn raised his eyebrows. "He's only five years old!" he said of his grandson.

"Ashleigh said she found an open matchbook and some burnt matches on the garage floor. And there were some charred sticks nearby stacked in a pyramid pile."

"Sounds like he was trying to build a campfire."

"In the garage?"

Horn raised his glass and sipped; he looked thoughtful. So his only grandchild was a pyromaniac. "Well, no harm done if they gave him a good talking-to. Boys are naturally intrigued by fire."

"So are men."

He smiled. "You should have some wine with your meal, relax, then after dinner we'll go back home and I'll show you I meant it when I called you darling."

The waiter arrived with their food. He rested his large round tray on a nearby table and with a flourish raised silver lids to expose steaming entrées.

Anne's face gave away nothing, but she ordered wine.

5

"Kinda posh for a former police captain," Paula said, as she and Bickerstaff were about to climb out of the unmarked Paula had parked at the curb in front of Horn's brownstone.

"Nobody ever suggested Horn was a bent cop," Bickerstaff said. "Rumor is he inherited some money, made some smart investments. And he's not exactly a millionaire."

"Yeah, but I bet his wife's not bagging groceries so they can scrape by."

"Matter of fact she does hold down a job. Some kinda executive at a hospital."

Paula had her fingers curled around the door handle but paused. "You like this guy."

"Never met him. But I like what I heard. He's straight and tough and an old-fashioned cop."

"What's that mean—old-fashioned?"

"Means he knows when and how and how hard to push." Bickerstaff sat and wheezed for a while, then added, "I know how you feel about Horn taking over the investigation, but the important thing you gotta know is that from everything I heard about the guy, he's not about to hang us out to dry."

Paula sighed. "So he's got balls. *Cajones.* He'll go to the wall for us."

"Let's get outta the car, Paula," Bickerstaff said, perceptive enough to know when he was being patronized.

He'd already opened his door and was squeezing his bulk out. Egress wasn't his strong suit. He was still working on it after Paula had gotten out of the car. She slammed her door before he did his. Too many doughnuts, the unknowing might say of Bickerstaff, but Paula knew better. He could move amazingly fast when it was necessary and with an economy that made what he did count. *Almost* too many doughnuts.

Neither of them said anything as they took the concrete steps to tall oak doors that had to be original to the house. Bickerstaff pressed the faintly illuminated doorbell button.

There was no sound from inside, but within a few seconds the door to the left opened and a tall man with bulky shoulders and the beginning of a stomach paunch smiled out at them. He had a nice smile that crinkled his craggy features. He was wearing pinstriped gray suit pants and a white shirt, loosened red tie, and dark blue suspenders, but Paula thought he'd look good modeling hunting outfits in an outdoorsware catalog. It was something about his rangy if slightly paunchy build, and his marksman's pale eyes. Your manly guide for hunting moose in the north country.

"Detectives Ramboquette and Bickerstaff," he said, and shook both their hands with his left hand. His own hands were huge and rough as a stone mason's but clean and with closely trimmed nails.

Paula managed to smile back at him, slightly irritated that he'd unnerved her with his size and presence. He wasn't exactly what she'd expected, and his welcome and amiability seemed genuine.

Paula and Bickerstaff followed as Horn led them into the comfortably furnished living room with overstuffed chairs and sofa, an oriental rug on hardwood flooring, a fireplace that had a brass shovel and poker set alongside it but looked as if it was never used. On the mantel was an arrangement of elegant vases and framed photos of a young blond woman holding an infant, and an older blond woman who might be her mother.

"My wife, Anne, and our daughter and grandson," Horn said, reading Paula's mind. He glanced at the photos and held a trace of a smile when he looked back at Paula and Bicker-staff.

"He a relative, too?" Bickerstaff asked, pointing to a framed, wall-mounted black-and-white photograph of a distinguished looking man in coat and tie.

"No, that's a signed photograph of George Hearn. He's a great Broadway actor people who mostly go to movies don't know about. My wife and I are avid theatergoers."

"I have to admit I never heard of him," Paula said. *Jesus! Insert foot in mouth.*

Horn motioned for both of them to sit on the sofa. "You're officially off duty. Either of you want something to drink? I have some good single malt or blended scotch."

"Nothing for me, thanks," Paula said. *At least you won't think I'm a drunk.*

"I'll try the single malt," Bickerstaff said, settling into a corner of the sofa. He was a guy about to retire with nothing to lose. "Splash of water, no ice."

"Done," Horn said. He went to an old-fashioned mahogany credenza and worked for a few minutes with his broad back to them. There must have been an ice bucket there; when he turned around he was holding two drink glasses with cobbled bottoms, a couple of ice cubes in one of them. The scotch without ice was a much deeper amber than the other; Paula wondered if Horn had lightened up on his drink and gone heavy on Bickerstaff's. "To our new working relationship," Horn said, after handing over the glass to Bickerstaff.

The two men clinked glass rims, while Paula smiled and

made a toasting motion with her hand. She felt suddenly out of place in a male world, sitting there alongside Bickerstaff and watching Horn settle his rangy bulk into a green leather armchair opposite them. She was the one wearing the wrong kind of underwear here.

"This," Bickerstaff said, "is wonderful scotch."

"And you," Horn said, fixing his gray-green eyes on Paula, "are Cajun."

"You have a good ear for accents," Paula said.

"Ah, I do," Horn said, "but the fact is I read it in your file. I learned as much as I could about the two of you before deciding if I wanted you with me on this case. I am sure. About both of you. I want you to be sure about me."

"I've heard about you," Bickerstaff said. "I am sure."

"I heard from Roy," Paula said.

"You left the New Orleans Police Department because of a personality clash with a superior who had a record that didn't stack up against yours," Horn said to Paula. "They gave you top recommendations so they could move you along out of town, and you had somebody influential in the NYPD to act as your angel."

"My uncle, Captain Sean Boudine," Paula said, figuring Horn would already know that but wanting to seem open and cooperative.

"Politics out, politics in."

"Isn't that the way it works?" Paula said.

Horn smiled. "'Fraid so."

Bickerstaff sipped his scotch and said nothing, obviously intrigued by their exchange.

"Boudine's a fine man and a good cop," Horn said. "And because of him you managed to move into plainclothes Homicide immediately, though in truth you're in a probation period."

"In truth," Paula agreed.

"And I know you want to retire at the end of the month and go ice fishing in Minnesota," Horn said to Bickerstaff. "I was retired myself and looking forward to deep-sea fishing in the Florida Keys, landing a blue marlin. What I'm proposing is we both push that off into the future, until this case is resolved. When we do get around to catching those fish, it'll be all the sweeter for the both of us."

"Agreed," Bickerstaff said, amazing Paula.

"Have you got any plans that need putting aside?" Horn asked her.

"I'm a working cop," she said. "I plan on being one a year from now. That's about as far ahead as I want to look." *So here I am, sitting around with a guy who wants to squat in front of a hole in the ice and another one who wants to catch a fish with a sword on its nose. Is this a wise career move?*

Horn sipped his drink, then rested the glass on his knee, holding it with the middle finger and thumb of his left hand. "I've read the murder files on all three dead women, as I'm sure you have. I don't think I have to ask if there's any disagreement on whether we have a serial killer at work here."

"You don't," Bickerstaff said.

Horn looked at Paula, who nodded.

"I also see by your records that neither of you ever did any rock or mountain climbing. Neither have I. But it seems a certain degree of skill had to be involved for our perp to reach those bedroom windows. That's something that needs looking into. He's also got some skill with a glass cutter and masking tape. Two of the windows were locked, and he silently—almost had to be silently—cut a crescent in the glass at the latch, using tape so the section removed wouldn't fall to the outside sill or ground. And it looks like some kind of wax or oil was put on the tracks before he raised the windows so they'd move easily and without making much noise."

"An experienced B-and-E man," Bickerstaff suggested.

"Cat burglar," Paula said. "They climb."

"Don't usually kill," Horn said. "Our man has a rare combination of skills."

"The autopsy reports suggest he knows anatomy and how to use a knife," Paula said. "He kept his victims alive so they'd suffer as long as possible."

"Medical background, you think?"

"Maybe. But the postmortems suggest he doesn't have skills at that level. More like a butcher or simple torturer with experience."

"A cruel bastard!" Horn said, with a vehemence that surprised Paula.

"Which brings us to kinky sex," Bickerstaff said. "You think the victims mighta known their killer? That they mighta wanted to be wrapped in their sheets that way for some kinda S-and-M thing, then he surprised them by going too far?"

"There's nothing in their backgrounds to suggest that," Horn said. "So for now, we can rule it out."

Good enough for Paula.

Horn looked from her to Bickerstaff. "You two have got a few days on me when it comes to this case. Is there anything else you think might be worth mentioning?"

"The footprint in Sally Bridge's bedroom," Paula said. "The lab brought it out more. Looks like a man's bare right foot, medium-sized. Not as good in court as a handprint, but a match might help build a case if we catch this guy. *When* we catch him."

Horn sat back and lifted his glass of scotch but didn't sip. He simply stared at it while he rotated the glass and made the light change in the amber liquid. "Yes, he apparently climbs barefoot."

"Or, more likely, undresses before he kills so he doesn't get bloody," Bickerstaff said.

"I'd agree," Horn said, "except there doesn't figure to be much spurting or flowing blood, the way he shrouds his victims in their bedsheets before going to work with the knife. Aside from method, that single partial footprint is the only thing remotely like a substantial clue at any of the three murder scenes." He took a sip of scotch. "Still, we don't want to form too many preconceived notions at this point. We're not dealing with someone who thinks logically in the ways that we do, which is why we need to get inside his mind, gain some idea of his particular and peculiar logic." He smiled.

"You know, they don't all murder their mothers over and over."

"But plenty do," Bickerstaff said.

"Plenty." Horn shrugged. "Maybe even this barefoot, rock-climbing, glass-cutting, sheet-winding killer with a sound knowledge of human anatomy."

"He sounds more individual," Bickerstaff said, "when you put it that way."

"Oh, he's individual, all right. Unique and dangerous."

And that's why he interests you, Paula thought, looking at the expression on Horn's set features. *Maybe you belong in that hunting catalog after all.*

"As far as we're concerned," Horn said, "this investigation enters a new phase tomorrow. I want you two to pore over and collate the information on all three cases, do some follow-up interviews of the people who discovered the bodies; the family, friends or neighbors who knew the victims. Sometimes people have fresh recollections after days or weeks have passed. Don't just look for something new—look for combinations of information that might *mean* something new. Don't toss aside anything. We can get together and decide among us whether it's important. Meanwhile, I'm going to visit the crime scenes, starting with the Sally Bridge murder. A new perspective sometimes turns up something meaningful."

He motioned for both of them to remain seated but stood up and went to one of the bookshelves with doors beneath it. From inside one of the doors he retrieved two cell phones; he gave one to Paula and the other to Bickerstaff. "Pertinent phone numbers are already in the data banks. I have a cell phone of my own. That's primarily how we'll stay in touch. You two will report only to me and be pretty much on your own. We meet back here at the same time, two days from now, and compare notes."

Paula and Bickerstaff took that as a signal that the meeting was over. They stood up, Bickerstaff wheezing as he struggled out of the grasp of the deep sofa cushions.

"Needless to say," Horn told them, "we keep all this from the media. They'll catch up to it sooner or later, but maybe we can choose when and be able to use them in some way."

"That would be nice for a change," Paula said, slipping her cell phone into her blazer pocket.

As Horn ushered them into the foyer, a tall blond woman came down the stairs. Her hair was piled gracefully on her head and she was wearing jeans and a bleached-out blue shirt with the sleeves rolled up. She looked fresh and clean as only certain blond women could. Late forties, Paula thought, maybe early fifties. The older blond woman in the mantel photo.

"My wife, Anne," Horn said, and introduced everyone as the woman walked the rest of the way down the stairs. Paula had the impression she'd timed this casual meeting so she could get a look at them, see what her husband was getting into.

Anne smiled graciously and said she was sorry they were leaving. Horn told her not to worry, they'd all be seeing plenty of each other. Paula noticed that Anne smelled subtly of perfumed soap or shampoo and wondered what the scent was. She wouldn't mind smelling that way.

The handsome, mature couple stood with the door open as Paula and Bickerstaff left and climbed into the unmarked.

"You're going to enjoy this, aren't you," Paula said to Bickerstaff. Not a question. Maybe an accusation.

Bickerstaff shrugged as he buckled his seat belt. "We're gonna do it, Paula. It's our choice whether we enjoy our work."

When the car had driven away and the front door was closed, Horn said to his wife, "I thought you might want to take their measure. What do you think?"

"The man looks like he shouldn't climb stairs; the woman doesn't look big enough to open an olive jar. I don't like the idea of you having to depend on them, maybe for your life."

"The man's a good cop with a lot left in him."

"He looks like he should use what remaining energy he has to work out in a gym and try to lose some weight."

"He's about to retire."

Anne shook her head. "Don't you know what always happens in crime novels and movies to cops who are about to retire?"

"If this were a book or movie," Horn said, "I'd be chief."

She frowned. The parallel lines again, deeper with each year, with each new worry in her life. Her cop husband, her job, the lawsuit against the hospital, and now her pensioned-off husband's involvement in a murder case. "I really don't like the feel of this, Thomas. You sure they're going to be okay?"

"They'll do just fine," Horn said, grinning to show his confidence. "A wheezy fat man with savvy, and a feisty Cajun. I could do a lot worse."

Anne smiled. "Isn't that profiling?"

"Full frontal nudity wasn't possible," Horn said, and kissed away the lines in her cool forehead.

The last glance back at Horn and his wife in the doorway as the car pulled away stuck in Paula's mind. The alpha male with his mate, made clever by experience and still plenty able. Like some rock-hard Cajuns she'd known. Her uncles, who'd roamed the Louisiana swamp with their shotguns modified to fire solid lead slugs, poached for whatever could be sold or eaten, the bigger the better. Hunters, southern version.

Horn was the northern version. Despite his obvious sophistication, the image of him in the deep woods in camouflage, armed with a high-powered rifle, still and silent and sighting through the scope at a distant and elusive moose, persisted.

Poor moose.

6

Central America, 1998

Hector Ruiz carried his ancient but well-oiled Kalishnikov automatic rifle loosely by the barrel, not in any way recommended in arms manuals. His fellow guerilla fighter, Armand Mora, stood beside him in the deep shade of the forest canopy. They were exhausted after spending the night in the forest. Armand had a slight shrapnel wound in his thigh from when a grenade had detonated near him during their fight the day before with government troops who were searching for them and trying to cut off their escape route back into the hills. To make matters worse, an American commando force was rumored to be operating in the area.

Hector was perspiring heavily and the palms of both his hands were scraped. He used his free hand to brush bits of bark and leaf from his clothes as both men stared at the object he had lowered from the tree using a rope.

The object was the body of a dead girl no more than thirteen. She was wrapped in mud-caked leaves held fast by vines wound around her thin form. The leaves and mud were dark, discolored by blood.

Last night Hector, standing watch, had looked up to find the moon and see if it might foretell rain. He'd noticed a dark, still object high in the branches of the tree, and his heart leaped; for a second he thought he might be looking at a government sniper. But there was a looseness about the dark bulk above, as if it weren't lying on or affixed to a limb but might be tied there, suspended.

In the morning he'd climbed high into the tree to satisfy his curiosity, only to raise more questions.

"What must have done this to her?"

"It looks as if she was stabbed to death," Armand said, his dark eyes wide. "Stabbed many times. See the slits in the leaves?"

Hector slung his Kalishnikov over his shoulder and nodded. "She was dangling in a kind of sling made of vines. This poor child . . . who would do such a thing?"

"Not the Americans. Probably the government troops. They're bastards! Think of some of the things they did to those of us they captured."

"But this young girl—"

Hector stopped talking, astounded, as Armand's right ear exploded from his head. Armand's eyes wore the vacant gaze of the dead as he dropped straight down to lie beside the girl.

Hector whirled to run, but the automatic weapons fire that had erupted from the surrounding forest brought him to his knees, killing him before his upper body struck the ground.

7

New York, 2003

Pattie Redmond hung up the phone behind the counter at Styles and Smiles and looked pensively out the window at the backed-up morning traffic on Second Avenue.

The guy she'd just talked to, Gary, was still a question, so maybe she shouldn't have agreed to meet him for drinks tonight at the same place they'd met last night. It was a bar in the Village, where she and Ellen had gone to pass time before seeing a movie. Pattie's mom, who lived up in White Plains, had cautioned her about meeting men in bars enough times. Still cautioned her regularly over the phone. A young girl living alone shouldn't take chances, her mother would tell her. Some things, she would say ominously to Pattie, never change. Like Pattie might meet some nice fella in church, if she went to church.

Pattie had to smile. She was twenty-four—not so young, at least in her mind. Pretty enough, she knew, with her long auburn hair and too-wide mouth with white, even teeth that almost didn't look real. Lips a little too large, like they'd been collagened. Gary said it was her smile that attracted him.

This guy, Pattie had thought last night in the bar, looked like something out of a soap opera. He was tall enough, darkly handsome, and perhaps partly Hispanic—the sexy part. And his suit looked expensive, maybe even Armani. Pattie knew clothes; she'd learned about them working here at Styles and Smiles, which sold men's as well as women's apparel.

Ellen had listened to their conversation and afterward told her that Gary had a practiced line of bullshit. Sure he did. Didn't they all? He was single—said he was, anyway. And he'd been straightforward enough, just walking over and asking if he could buy her a drink. Ellen thought he might have assumed they were prostitutes, the way they were perched at the bar on those high stools and surveying the room, and for a few seconds Pattie thought the same. She'd even found herself toying with the possibilities. In her mind, toying.

Line of bullshit? Maybe. But it turned out Gary was more interested in listening to Pattie's story than in telling his. She hadn't told him where she lived, but she *had* mentioned where she worked. So he'd called and—

". . . forty percent off each of these, or if you buy two?" a short redheaded woman holding a blue blouse was asking. "The sign says buy two, get forty percent off."

"You don't get the forty percent off if you only buy one," Pattie said.

"But if you buy two, do you get forty percent off each of them, or off the total price?"

"It's the same thing," Pattie said. *Isn't it?*

"Or do you get forty percent off one but not the other?"

"Well . . ."

"Or just twenty percent off if you buy only one?"

"I'll tell you what," Pattie said, "you buy both and I'll give you forty percent off each one."

"Isn't that what the sign says?"

"Uh, well . . . yes."

"You people won't get anywhere trying to confuse customers," the woman said. She put down the sweater, turned, and strode angrily from the shop.

Pattie normally would have been seething. But this morning her mind was on other things. She simply smiled and walked over to return the sweater to stock.

She caught sight of herself smiling in one of the mirrors by the changing room. The sensuous and vibrant woman looking at her from the mirror made her feel good. She could understand why Gary had been attracted to her. She really could.

Horn hadn't expected much from his visit to the first two crime scenes, and he hadn't learned much. The apartment of the first victim, call girl Marilyn Davis, in lower Manhattan, was still vacant but had been cleaned. That of the second victim, computer programmer Beth Linneker, on the Upper East Side, had already been leased to a new tenant. Both women had lived on high floors where they must have assumed they were safe from street criminals and crime in general.

In each apartment the killer had entered through the victim's bedroom window. In the Linneker murder, he'd cut away a crescent of glass and used masking tape, a bit of which was still on the outside glass, to catch and hold the detached glass and keep it from falling and attracting attention. Davis's window had been unlocked and open slightly to allow in a summer breeze after a brief shower.

Horn examined each windowsill and found scratches and dents on the wooden one but nothing on the marble sill. It was impossible to tell if the marks were from the killer's entrance, but some of them looked fresh. In both murders the women had been wound in their sheets. Since there was no sign of struggle, this was done while they were still asleep, or so quickly and deftly they hadn't time to resist. Duct tape was placed over their mouths to silence them. They'd apparently been killed with the same weapon that was used on Sally Bridge. Davis, with thirty-seven stab wounds, had bled to death. Linneker had a fatal heart attack—after being stabbed thirty-six times. In neither case had the killer left anything behind that hinted at his identity.

Maybe Paula and Bickerstaff had learned something new in reexamining the two apartments earlier, as Horn had instructed. Probably it had been a waste of time, like so many things in homicide investigations.

Horn figured he might have better luck stumbling across something new and pertinent in Sally Bridge's apartment, which was still an official crime scene.

He got the key from the super but when he reached the apartment found he didn't need it. The yellow crime scene tape had been untied from the doorknob, and the door was unlocked.

When Horn entered he found Paula and Bickerstaff inside.

They'd heard him in the hall and were standing about ten feet apart, staring at the door to see who might come in.

Neither of them appeared surprised, but both seemed relieved. Horn wondered if they thought Bridge's killer might have wanted something in the apartment and returned for it.

"Learn anything at the other two crime scenes?" he asked, noticing that the apartment still smelled of death, the faint coppery blood scent that could almost be tasted.

"Nothing that isn't already in the files," Paula said. "And so far we haven't found any connection at all between any of the three victims."

"Show me this footprint," Horn said.

Paula led the way into the bedroom. The air was stale and smelled more strongly of blood. Bickerstaff stayed in the living room.

There was the footprint by the bed. It was faint but it was there, and Horn could understand how the techs could bring it out so it showed as the enhanced image in the file. The heel and ball of a bare foot, probably a man's, medium size. A few distinctive lines, maybe enough to make a match that would mean something in court.

Sally Bridge's bed hadn't been touched since the murder. It was stripped down to the bare mattress. The pile of bloodied sheets Horn had seen in the crime scene photos had been taken to the lab for testing and evidence entry.

"They ever get a make on the blood type?" Horn asked, staring at the stained mattress.

"O-negative," Paula said. "Same as the victim's; when the DNA match comes in, it figures that all the blood in the apartment will be hers."

Horn wandered over and examined the window where the killer had entered. The glass and handle had been dusted for prints, revealing only that the killer had worn gloves, but Horn was still careful when he slid the window open. It moved easily in its wooden frame.

"The lab said the killer used candle wax on the window frame," Paula said. "Just ran it over the tracks so the window would raise real easy and wouldn't make noise."

"Uh-huh. So we look for a guy who carries a candle in his pocket."

"Narrows it down," Paula said, smiling to let Horn know she was joking.

Horn leaned out of the window and looked down.

"Heck of a climb," Paula said.

"I don't think so."

He didn't elaborate, and Paula figured she should hold her silence. She still wasn't completely comfortable around Horn. The stories about his NYPD exploits sometimes contained touches of brutality. That didn't seem evident in the man, despite his size. He acted more like a kindly uncle than a legendary tough homicide cop and political infighter.

She watched as he stared pensively at the window for a while longer before closing it.

"No marks on the marble sill," he said. "Maybe a slight scuff mark from the killer's shoe. But we can't be sure."

Paula said nothing. She wasn't sure of anything yet in this case.

"Nothing for sure on the windowsills at the other two crime scenes, either," Horn said.

He walked back into the living room, and Paula followed.

"You reinterview the neighbors here?" he asked Bickerstaff.

"We just finished up before you got here. There were a few slight discrepancies, but their stories are pretty much consistent with their first interviews. Basically, nobody saw or heard anything unusual."

"We were about to leave when you arrived," Paula said.

"I'll leave with you," Horn said. "After we get done on the roof, we'll find someplace to eat supper and compare notes."

"Roof?" Paula said.

Horn nodded. "Yeah. You know—the windowsills."

"But they were left mostly unmarked when the killer climbed in."

"And out," Bickerstaff added. "The techs found nothing even microscopic that was of use on the windowsills."

"Like a microscopic dog that didn't bark in the night," Horn said.

Paula grinned. "Sherlock Holmes."

"I'd have guessed Lassie," Bickerstaff said.

"Got a handkerchief in your purse?" Horn asked Paula.

She searched but couldn't find one. "Only tissues." Among other items she pulled from her purse while rummaging through it was a white latex glove of the sort used to examine crime scenes.

"That glove'll do," Horn said.

Paula and Bickerstaff glanced at each other.

They followed Horn into the bedroom, where he got a wire hanger from the closet, straightened it, and tied the white glove on one end. He then went to the window and opened and closed it, wedging the hanger between frame and sill so the end with the glove stuck outside about eighteen inches.

"Oughta do," he said.

Understanding now, Paula led the way out of the apartment. She was starting to like this, Horn thinking a little outside the box. Sometimes a little was all it took. Outside was outside.

She could hardly wait to get to the roof.

As soon as they were on the roof, Bickerstaff wedged a piece of tile in the service door so it wouldn't close and trap them up there. Then they went to the low brick parapet at the roof's edge, approximately above the window to Sally Bridge's bedroom. About ten feet from the parapet, Horn held out a hand and stopped them. "Look at the tar and gravel near the edge," he said. "It seems it might have been disturbed."

Paula looked. The gravel adhered to the blacktop roof seemed to have been rearranged recently, some of it even kicked or scraped loose.

Horn went to the parapet and examined it, then leaned over it, staring straight down.

"I see the glove sticking out right under the disturbed gravel," he said, turning away and standing up straight. And there's a spot on the parapet where the tile's been rubbed clean. And look at this."

Paula and Bickerstaff moved closer to see where he was pointing. There was what appeared to be a fresh hole low in the brickwork of the parapet, as if something sharp had been driven into the brick and mortar at an angle.

"A whatchamacallit, maybe," Bickerstaff said. "One of those steel spikes mountain climbers use to fasten ropes to cliff faces."

"A piton," Horn said. He glanced around, then walked over to where a grouping of vent pipes protruded from the roof.

He stooped down next to one. "Look at the way the grime has been rubbed away from the base of this pipe. My guess is our killer drove in his piton near the roof's edge, then ran the roof end of the rope back to this vent pipe. He then wrapped it around the pipe as a safety precaution in case the piton broke free when he draped the other end of the rope down the building wall and began his descent."

Paula stared at the base of the old lead vent pipe. Horn was right. Something had definitely been tied around it, then perhaps tugged at and rotated to test for tightness and strength. "How did you know one of the pipes would be marked up?" she asked.

"Mountain climbers are nothing if not cautious. They believe in backup, just like cops."

Paula was liking this more and more. "So our killer doesn't necessarily climb buildings; he goes to the roof and lowers himself to the bedroom window he wants to enter."

"Probably easier when you stop to think about it," Bickerstaff said. "But how did he get to this roof? If he used the front entrance, he'd risk being seen coming or going. And if you look around, there's no way he coulda got up here other than stairs or elevator."

Horn put his fists on his hips and turned in a slow circle. The adjacent buildings were too far away to leap across.

"Maybe if we look on one of those other building roofs we'll find a board or something that enabled him to cross over to this roof."

"Or maybe he tossed or shot a line over here," Paula said.

"Yeah. Like Spiderman," Bickerstaff said dryly.

"Not exactly," Horn told him, nodding and smiling at Paula. "He might have tossed a grappling hook over here and snagged it on something, maybe one of those vent pipes. Then he attached his end of the line on the other roof and hand-walked to this one, or used a sling or pulley of some sort."

They went to the parapet and vent pipes and searched for

fresh scratches, and found a pipe that might have suffered a little recent damage from a grappling hook catching hold.

"I dunno," Bickerstaff said dubiously, scratching his double chin. "Those marks don't look all that recent to me."

"But look at the tracks in the tar," Horn said, "from where he overshot with the hook and dragged it back to catch on the vent pipe." He pointed to long, parallel gouges in the blacktop that led to and then straddled the protruding pipe. *Subway tracks,* Horn thought, seeing Anne thinking deep thoughts.

"Lowering himself from the roof like that," Paula said, "probably nobody'd notice him in the dark even if they did happen to glance up. Not if he wore dark clothes. I kind of like the theory. And I don't see any other way he'd be able to get to this roof without risking coming and going through the lobby."

"Let's put off supper for a while," Horn said, "and talk to doormen and neighbors in the adjacent buildings. See if anybody saw or heard anything suspicious the night of the murder."

Neither Paula nor Bickerstaff objected. Paula wasn't hungry anymore. Her heartbeat had picked up, the way it sometimes had when she went hunting long ago with her uncles, when they sensed they were closing on their prey.

Bickerstaff simply pulled a candy bar from his pocket and started peeling off the wrapper.

"Since we're gonna eat supper late," he said, "anybody else want one of these? It's a high-energy sports bar."

"Those things are about six hundred calories," Paula said. "They'll even put weight on your eyeballs while they petrify your arteries."

"Maybe. But I carry them 'cause I figure I might need energy when I least expect it." He patted the bulging side pocket of his rumpled suitcoat. "I got chocolate peanut butter with almonds."

Paula held out her hand.

8

Pattie Redmond had used her Styles and Smiles employees' 20 percent discount to buy two of the 40-percent-off blouses, one of which—the gray one—she wore with her navy slacks, the ones that showed off her slender curves. Why not impress the hell out of Gary?

After get-acquainted drinks at the Village bar where they'd met, Gary suggested they have dinner at a Peruvian restaurant just a long walk or short cab ride from Pattie's West Side apartment. Since Gary had never asked where she lived or even known her complete name before tonight, she knew that had to be a coincidence.

Or maybe fate.

Everything had gone wonderfully. Her hair had behaved and the summer breeze hadn't mussed it. The conversation over drinks had been smooth. And she hadn't drooled or spilled anything on her new blouse during dinner. Not only that, Pattie had caught Gary staring at her a few times in a way she knew and liked.

Gary Schnick was his name. He smiled and said that was why he hadn't told her the first night they'd met; his name sounded kind of dirty or like an insult. Pattie told him she found nothing wrong with "Schnick" and he put on a puzzled look and said he'd meant "Gary." So he had a sense of humor. That was essential in a man, especially one with the good looks that suggested he was vain, humorless, married, or gay.

By the time they took a cab to her apartment, she was satisfied he was none of those. She fought him off in the back of the cab, having to struggle exactly the right amount, keeping it all light even if serious. And he gave up at precisely the right time, letting her know he yearned for her but respected her and wasn't some kind of rapist who couldn't control his sexual appetite. Not Gary Schnick.

Still, Pattie didn't invite him in. She wanted to string this out, test him a little. She felt strongly that Gary wasn't one-night-stand material. He was a keeper.

He didn't give her a lot of crap about not being invited in. Not any, in fact. He simply grinned, kissed her on the forehead, and said he'd call her. Then he climbed back into the cab and waved to her out of the rolled-down window as it pulled away from the curb.

Mrs. Ledbetter, the elderly widow who lived on the floor below Pattie and sometimes talked to her in the laundry room, happened to be leaving the building as Pattie arrived and saw the cab drive away.

"So who was that?" she asked. "Antonio Banderas?"

"I don't know any Antonio Banderas," Pattie said, playing dumb.

Mrs. Ledbetter, who knew she wasn't dumb, grinned at her and wagged an arthritic finger. "I'm going to the grocery store to get one of those giant blueberry muffins for a late-night snack. You need anything?"

Pattie thanked her but said she didn't, then punched in the tenants' code and pushed open the door to the outer lobby. She used her key to unlock and open the door to the inner lobby, then crossed the stained marble floor to the elevator. For a building without a doorman, this one had good security. And where she lived, on the nineteenth floor, she didn't have to worry about break-ins by junkies or weirdos. Safety was one of the things Pattie liked most about living here. That and the very reasonable rent.

The elevator smelled like somebody had smoked a cigar in it recently. Pattie tried to hold her breath all the way up but didn't quite make it. The tobacco scent followed her most of the way down the hall as she strode toward her apartment door. Why *on earth* did people still smoke? She hoped the stench wouldn't cling to her clothes and make her smell like an icky tobacco fiend if she wore the same slacks tomorrow.

The apartment was small but she didn't mind. The landlord had recently refurnished it in a kind of modern style, with lots of pastel vinyl and light-colored wood, and while the colors didn't quite match, that was okay with Pattie. At least everything was new or almost new, even if it might not be comfortable. She wasn't mad about the stark wall hangings either, except for a big framed photograph of lightning striking far away on a dark plain. She liked that one.

She closed the door behind her and tugged at it to make sure the lock had caught. Then she keyed the dead bolt and fastened the brass chain. The lamp she'd left on had a 150-watt bulb and made the living room so glaringly bright that the blue vinyl sofa looked wet.

Pattie placed her purse on the table by the door, then kicked off her high-heeled shoes and padded into the tiny alcove kitchen. She wolfed down half of a Krispy Kreme glazed doughnut left over from breakfast, then opened the refrigerator and sipped some milk out of the carton.

She went into the bedroom, walked to the window, and switched on the air conditioner. It settled into a soft hum and started to cool the room while she washed off her makeup and brushed her teeth. She would shower in the morning, before work, she thought. Maybe get up early enough so she had time to wash her hair.

By the time Pattie left the bathroom and turned off the light in the living room, the bedroom was comfortably cool.

Her apartment was a corner unit, so the bedroom had two windows. She went to the one without the air conditioner in it and made sure it was locked. Though she was wearing only the oversized men's Rangers shirt she slept in, she didn't bother pulling the drapes shut. Whoever might be watching, let them look. What did she care? Give the poor lonely sickos a thrill. She was going to turn out the light soon anyway and go to bed. For a few seconds she contemplated getting her vibrator, which she kept hidden in the back of a dresser drawer. Then she decided against it. For all she knew, Gary might phone tomorrow and want to meet her for lunch, or immediately after she got off work.

She turned back the top sheet and light cover on the bed, then sat down on the edge of the mattress and switched off the lamp. In the abrupt blackness, before her eyes got used to the dark, Pattie swiveled on the mattress and lay down, adjusting her pillow beneath her head. The room wasn't yet as cool as it was going to get, so she lay on her back on top of the thin blanket and sheet.

She sighed, comfortable, feeling the cool breeze from the air conditioner play over her bare thighs.

Her intention was to relive in her mind tonight's date with Gary, but the alcohol she'd consumed earlier that evening must have gotten to her. Just as Gary was standing up at the table and smiling to greet her, she fell asleep.

Pattie was rolling down the grassy hill in the yard alongside the house, toward where her father had raked the autumn leaves into a big pile. She was about twelve and knew she'd soon be too old to enjoy this kind of thing.

She came to the bottom of the hill and started to stand up.

But she couldn't stand.

Couldn't even move. Her arms were tight to her sides, her legs bound together so firmly her knees and protruding ankle bones hurt where they pressed against each other.

When something clamped itself firmly and roughly across her mouth, she breathed in hard through her nose and woke up. Her bulging eyes stared into solid blackness.

For a brief moment she felt relief.

Okay, this is the end of the nightmare . . .

Only it wasn't.

The air conditioner continued its monotonous low humming. A car horn honked blocks away. Far, far in the distance a police or emergency vehicle siren wailed like a lost lament. The soft breeze pushing through the open window caused the drape cord to sway so its plastic pull tapped lightly against the sill.

All of these sounds were louder than Pattie's screams.

They had all made do on Bickerstaff's high-energy candy bars and decided to meet for breakfast so they wouldn't be too exhausted to talk. Paula had said good night to Bickerstaff, climbed out of the unmarked, then trudged up to her apartment. She was barely able to stay awake long enough to undress and fall onto the bed.

Horn was right, she remembered thinking just before falling asleep. It was already 11 P.M., and everyone's brains were scrambled from listening to the same stories for the second or third time, going over the same crime scenes, and making the same notes. Tomorrow, Horn had said, was soon enough to start analyzing what they had.

It hadn't taken them long to examine the roofs above the victims' apartment windows and determine the killer had lowered himself to his prey, not climbed up. Other than that, they'd have to talk things over in the morning and compare notes, see if there was something else worthwhile when they put their information together. Other than that . . .

When Paula and Bickerstaff walked in, Horn was already at the diner where he'd set up the meet, a place called the

Home Away, not far from his brownstone. He was slouched in a back booth, sipping coffee, with a plate in front of him that contained nothing but yellow crumbs.

There were only a few other customers, and it was pleasantly cool in the diner. The unmarked's air conditioner wasn't working well, so Paula and Bickerstaff had removed their jackets and, still uncomfortable, had left them in the car. Bickerstaff had tucked his holstered service revolver beneath his shirt, where it was barely noticeable amidst his bulk. Paula had her handgun and shield in her small black leather purse, which she carried just for that purpose. After a few days around ninety, with nights that didn't cool down much, the city's miles of concrete held the heat like a kiln. Summer in New York could be brutal. For some people it was hell.

The two detectives slid into the booth so they were across the table from Horn. Paula thought the mingled scents of fried bacon and slightly burned toast or bagel smelled great, but she wasn't hungry. Bickerstaff's energy bars seemed to have formed an indigestible lump in her stomach.

Bickerstaff didn't feel the same gastric discomfort. "So what's good here?" he asked.

"Toasted corn muffins," Horn said without hesitation.

A waitress with an order pad came over. She was a nice looking brunette with a good figure and kind of sad face.

"I'm not a muffin man," Bickerstaff said.

"Could have fooled me," the waitress said without a change of expression.

Bickerstaff grinned.

"Marla, Marla . . ." Horn said. Then to Bickerstaff: "Marla has a droll sense of humor, among her many other attributes."

Marla seemed unaffected by the compliment.

Bickerstaff simply grunted, then ordered scrambled eggs, bacon, and coffee. Paula just went with coffee.

"You must come in here pretty often," she said to Horn.

"Probably too often. It's the muffins."

"They must be something." Paula glanced at the waitress, making sure Horn saw her.

So she'd built up the nerve to joke with him. Horn liked that. It could be they were becoming a real team.

"Let's go over what we learned last night," he said.

They did this through breakfast, then over second cups of coffee.

"Seems to me the only new thing we learned is that the killer lowers himself from the roof to get to the victims' windows," Bickerstaff said.

But something had struck Paula after hearing overlapping accounts of the murders. "The first victim was stabbed thirty-seven times, the second thirty-six, the third thirty-seven."

"Sounds like my first wife," Bickerstaff said. "Thirty-seven, thirty-six, thirty seven."

Christ! Paula thought. She and Horn both frowned at Bickerstaff.

"According to the ME, the sick bastard knows exactly where to stab them over and over without killing them, so they suffer maximum pain," Bickerstaff said with exaggerated somberness, obviously realizing he might have gone too far humorwise. "Turns out the way he does it, the number of stab wounds they survive is in the mid-thirties."

Paula felt slighty ill.

"A surgeon?" Bickerstaff asked.

"Not likely," she said, "according to the ME. The murder knife isn't surgical, and a doctor would probably cut rather than stab."

"So?" Bickerstaff raised his bushy eyebrows as he delicately picked up a last crumb of bacon from his plate and popped it into his mouth. Paula noticed that though it was cool in the diner, there were still dark crescents of perspiration beneath the arms of his wrinkled blue shirt.

"He's killed plenty of times before," Paula said. "Not only these three times. He must have, in order to learn precisely how, where, and the number of times to stab his victims to inflict pain without causing immediate death."

"Or even unconsciousness," Horn said, smiling at Paula.

She was pleased by his approval but at the same time irritated. Horn had known where she was going and was there ahead of her, waiting for her to catch up. He must have thought of the likelihood of previous victims and already talked to the ME about it.

"I called the ME from home this morning," he said, knowing what she must be thinking.

"What about the partial bare footprint?" Bickerstaff said. "What the hell is that all about?"

"Our barefoot boy didn't get undressed to prevent himself from getting bloody," Horn said. "In all but the Sally Bridge murder, the sheets wrapped around the victims absorbed most of the bleeding and prevented him from becoming bloodstained. At least bloodstained enough that it was worth the risk to take extra time undressing, washing up afterward, and dressing. And there was no sign of blood in the bathroom or kitchen drains."

While they were thinking about that, Horn finished his coffee and set the cup down slowly but firmly in its saucer so it wouldn't clink. If the cup was going to be picked up again soon, it wouldn't be by him.

"So what're our marching orders for the day?" Bickerstaff asked.

"You and Paula see if you can find some cold cases in the area during the past three or four years that are similar to the three murders we've got."

"Murders when he was learning," Paula said. "Perfecting his act."

Horn nodded. "And it wouldn't hurt to check some other cities. Our killer might be a transient."

He slid his bulk out of the booth and stood up straight, a big man with dark slacks, white shirt with tie, and suspenders. The shirt had long sleeves, but they were neatly rolled up to about six inches above his wrists. Paula thought he looked like an ominous blackjack dealer and wondered if he always dressed that way.

"What I'm going to do today is consult some experts," he said.

"Medical experts?" Bickerstaff asked.

"No," Horn said, "I'll be looking for somebody who climbs mountains."

They'd just stepped outside the cool diner into the bright, warm morning, when Horn's cell phone chirped.

He fished it from his pants pocket and stepped a few feet away. Paula could see his face while he listened to whoever was on the other end of the connection, the phone made miniature in his huge hand. His expression might as well have been sculpted in marble. The call could be his wife reminding him to pick up some salami on the way home tonight, or it might be news of catastrophe. You couldn't know which by studying Horn's features.

It wasn't the salami.

He slid the phone back in his pocket and returned to where Paula and Bickerstaff stood in the shade of the diner's rust-colored awning.

"Another killing," he said, and gave them a West Side address. "We'll take your car. Use the siren so we arrive before the crime scene gets as cold as the victim."

9

When they approached the address of the reported homicide, Paula saw only one police car parked directly in front of the building. No unmarkeds of a make and model like hers and Bickerstaff's. No ambulance or other emergency vehicles. Only a hint of the horror above.

"We got the call early," Horn said from the backseat. "So we can examine everything fresh and unedited."

Paula was impressed. She had to admit it was nice working with someone with pull. Bickerstaff, quiet beside her, simply stared straight ahead. "There," he said, pointing to a parking slot that turned out to be a loading zone featuring a homemade sign saying DON'T EVEN THINK OF PARKING HERE.

Paula parked there anyway and pulled down the visor to display the NYPD placard. Inanely, she wished she had a sign saying DON'T EVEN THINK OF TOWING THIS CAR.

When they were out of the car, Horn led the way. He was swinging his long arms, head thrust forward on his bull shoulders. He seemed eager.

An overweight uniformed cop stood near the building entrance and straightened his posture when he saw them approach. Horn flashed his shield in the way of a man who'd made the motion thousands of times.

"Nineteenth floor, sir," the cop said to Horn. "Apartment 195."

"Anybody up there but the victim?"

"My partner Eb guarding the door. We got a ten-three when we got the call, then phoned in and were instructed to secure the scene and wait for you."

Horn nodded and pushed inside, holding the door open for Paula and Bickerstaff. There was no doorman. Except for the uniform outside, nothing in the lobby seemed out of the ordinary. The elevator door opened and two women got out jabbering to each other about someone's wedding. Not a word about anyone's death.

The three detectives made it into the elevator before the door slid shut, and Paula punched the button for nineteen.

When the door glided open they saw Eb halfway down the hall. He was young and tall and looked as if he'd spent most of his brief life lifting weights. When he pushed away from leaning against the wall, Paula noticed his uniform appeared to be tailored.

When Horn showed his shield, Eb said, "Door's unlocked, sir. Vic's name's Patricia Redmond. When she didn't show for work this morning, her employer called and had the super check on her. He found her . . . like she is." An expression of distaste, maybe fear, crossed his handsome features, which appeared to be unmarked by previous experience. "My partner Carl and I checked to make sure she was dead, like we were instructed when we phoned in to the dispatcher. Then we secured the area and kept a low profile till you guys showed."

Paula wasn't sure a low profile was a six-foot-two uniformed cop stationed in an apartment hall, but it seemed to have worked. An elderly woman emerged from an apartment down the hall, did a double take when she saw the uniform and knot of people near Patricia Redmond's door, then got in the elevator and descended. Seemed to have worked so far, anyway.

The door was cracked open half an inch. Horn used a knuckle to ease it open all the way. He instructed Eb to stay on guard in the hall, then led the way into the apartment.

Immediately, Paula caught the faint but unmistakable scent of fresh blood and sensed the unearthly stillness that gathered like coagulated time in the wake of violent death. She and Bickerstaff looked at each other, then at the broad back of Horn moving almost grudgingly toward the bedroom. She knew both men felt as she did, that they were unwilling trespassers in a place made terrible and sacred by the killer.

Horn had been to this place many times following the footsteps of numerous killers. While he moved slowly, he didn't hesitate as he entered the bedroom, leaving enough space for the other two detectives to come in behind him without inadvertently touching anything.

Paula heard her own involuntary gasp as she saw Patricia Redmond beyond Horn's left shoulder. Bickerstaff swallowed, phlegm cracking in his throat. Horn, still facing away from them, held out a big hand and motioned for them to stand still.

To his credit, Paula thought, he didn't voice what he was thinking: that they should be careful here and not disturb any evidence. A virgin crime scene had to be treated with respect.

Patricia Redmond was lying on her back in the center of her double bed, shrouded in tightly wrapped blood-soaked sheets. Even the bottom sheet, with elasticized corners, had been pulled up from the mattress and used to shroud her. She must not have been able to move anything but her head, fingers, and toes. The toes of her left foot, nails enameled a brilliant red, extended beyond the edge of the taut sheets, tensed and curled like talons. At the other end of the shrouded form was her head. Her shoulder-length dark hair was wild, suggesting she'd thrashed her head around violently as she'd suffered. The white of the one eye visible beneath the tumble of hair could be seen all the way around the pupil, as if she'd taken a terrified peek into the void an instant before death. Her mouth was agape, forming a round depression in the gray duct tape that covered it. To Paula, nothing had ever looked more silent. *Where are the screams she tried to form? What happened to the stillborn screams of these women?*

"Pattie," Bickerstaff said, breaking Paula's mood.

"What?" Horn asked.

"I bet the people she knew called her Pattie. She was probably a pretty thing." Bickerstaff shook his head. "Fuckin' shame!"

"The victim was stabbed repeatedly," Horn said, slipping into cop talk to put a protective shell around his emotions and to signal Bickerstaff and Paula to do the same.

"I'll bet somewhere around thirty-seven times," Paula said, noting the many slits in the bloody sheets. Each cut must have seemed like a world of pain in suspended time. Paula hoped her stomach, her emotions, were going to hold up here.

Careful not to tread on any impressions on the throw rug, Horn moved across the bare wood floor to the open window. He peered up beneath the shade. "The glass has been cut so he could open the window and climb in. Looks like soap or candle wax on the tracks to smooth the way and mute the sound."

"Our guy," Paula said. Not that there'd been some doubt.

Horn led them back into the living room. Strangely, it was like leaving a church.

"We'll let the ME and techs go over the place," he said, "see what they come up with before we conduct a thorough search. Assign some uniforms to question neighbors in this building, and don't forget canvassing adjacent buildings. Then you two interview the best possibilities in a second pass and compare their stories with the first versions."

Bickerstaff was staring down at an angle through the living room window. "Cavalry's here. Ambulance, two squad cars, and the ME."

Paula walked over and looked down at the small shiny vehicles parked at careless angles in front of the building, like toys hurriedly shoved there by a child. Tiny, foreshortened human figures were scurrying toward the entrance. "They're on the way up."

"Fine," Horn said. "We're done here, for the moment, anyway."

"Let's go up to the roof," Bickerstaff said. "Maybe he dropped his wallet."

It's happened before, Paula mused, as they exited Pattie Redmond's apartment and made their way toward the elevator.

Not this time, though.

But the roof gave them what they expected to find. There were scuff marks in the heat-softened, graveled tar directly above the victim's window. The tile-capped parapet was marked by what might have been a rope rubbing on it. And there, low on the parapet, was a deep and freshly forged hole where a piton might have been driven into the mortar.

"He was here, all right," Horn said.

"Notice the pigeon droppings here have been stepped in," Paula said. Further evidence.

Horn looked over at her approvingly, but Bickerstaff said, "Sherlock Homing pigeon."

The roof of the building next door was only about ten feet higher than the one on which they stood, and only about ten feet away, sharing what amounted to an air shaft. At that edge of the roof they found more scuff marks, and, in farther, a vent pipe that was marked by what might have been some kind of grappling hook that secured a line.

Horn smiled grimly. "We certainly have his MO nailed."

"Now all we have to do is nail the bastard himself," Paula

said, surprising herself with the vehemence of her words. Horn didn't seem to notice, which didn't fool Paula. Bickerstaff was grinning at her.

The three detectives spent another ten minutes on the roof, carefully searching for anything of possible use.

All they came up with were a tangle of old antenna wire and a crumpled chewing gum wrapper.

"Juicy Fruit," Bickerstaff said, staring at the smoothed-out wrapper in his hand.

"The sun's faded the lettering," Horn said, "and the antenn wire's rusty. This stuff's been here awhile and doesn't help us."

Bickerstaff nodded, then wadded and flipped the gum wrapper away.

They went back through the service door and into the building. As they were descending in the elevator, it stopped at nineteen to pick up Eb, the uniform. He nodded to them, and when he stepped in, Paula looked beyond his bulk and got a glimpse of the techs and emergency personnel milling around in the hall. The ME was there, too. Harry Potter again.

He caught sight of Paula and smiled and winked at her as the elevator door slid shut. There was no reason death shouldn't be a little bit fun.

10

Pattie Redmond's fellow clerk at Styles and Smiles wasn't a guy who minded people seeing him cry. His name was Herb, and dressed in black as he was, he looked too thin to be alive as he stood near a rack of swimwear and unabashedly let tears track down his sallow cheeks.

"She was a sweetheart," he said of Pattie Redmond between sobs.

"They say the good die young," Bickerstaff said.

Paula rolled her eyes. She felt sorry for Herb and wished Bickerstaff would keep his sarcastic platitudes to himself.

"Ain't it the fucking truth!" Herb said, dabbing at his eyes with a handkerchief.

"Did she have any—"

"Nobody in their right mind could help loving Pattie," Herb interrupted her.

"We don't think whoever killed her was in his right mind," Bickerstaff said. "You got any idea who he might be?"

Herb shook his head, sniffed, and folded and replaced his handkerchief in the pocket of his black silk shirt. He drew a deep breath and let it out slowly, gaining control of himself but not completely or permanently. He stood there as if he were balancing on a wire.

"She confide in you much?" Paula asked.

"Quite a bit." *Sniff.* "We were friends."

"Just friends?"

Bickerstaff gave Paula an incredulous glance.

"You can count on it," Herb said. *Sniff, sniff.* Out came the handkerchief again. He dabbed at the tip of his nose while holding his free hand out away from his body as if to provide a counterweight and keep from tilting.

"So she might talk to you about the men she dated?" Bickerstaff asked.

"Now and then. She wasn't the sort to dish."

Bickerstaff looked puzzled. "Dis?"

"Dish. The dirt."

"Ah!"

"She was kinda excited about this guy she met last week. Gary something. According to Pattie, they met some place in the Village. I'm not sure exactly where."

"So you can't think of Gary's last name, and you don't remember where she said they met."

"She never told me Gary's last name. The place in the Village she did tell me. Sounded something like a stream or river, but not those."

"Like Mississippi or something?"

"No, no."

"Creek?" Paula ventured.

"Brook!" Herb almost shouted. "Brook's Crooks. It's near McDougal, I think."

"I know where it is," Bickerstaff said. To Paula: "It's a respectable enough place, hangout for yuppies who work nearby on Avenue of the Americas. They go there and pick each other up, try to mesh their pathetic lives."

Herb gazed at Bickerstaff with wounded eyes. "God! Such a cynic!"

"You've just seen the surface," Paula said.

"I doubt if it was Gary," Herb said, "considering how kind and gentle Pattie said he was."

Bickerstaff simply looked at him, and Herb turned away.

About ten years before, on the Upper East Side, some people were killed with an ice ax of the sort mountain climbers used. Back then the NYPD had called on a mountain climber of note named Royce Sayles to identify the weapon, then to help the police locate the killer. Sayles had then testified in court and helped to gain a conviction. The murderer turned out to be an attorney who was well-known for championing controversial liberal causes. The *Times* was convinced the police arrested the wrong man. Horn had thought they might be right, but there hadn't been another ice ax murder on the East Side.

It wasn't difficult for Horn to locate Sayles. He lived in the same apartment near Riverside Drive and, in fact, was now married to the young widow of one of the ice ax victims. Lucky in love and rent stabilization, Horn thought, as he parked his low-mileage, ten-year-old Chrysler in front of an attractive apartment building with a white stone facade and fake Doric columns flanking the entrance.

A uniformed doorman held the outer lobby door open for Horn and called up to tell Sayles he'd arrived, then directed Horn to the elevators. Directions were needed; the elevators were around the corner in the main lobby and had doors of such convincing faux marble that they blended perfectly with the red-veined marble wall. Only a single brass button gave them away.

Horn had called ahead and Sayles was expecting him. When Horn stepped out of the elevator on the tenth floor, the mountaineer was standing across the hall holding the apartment door wide open in welcome.

Sayles was average size and still looked fit, though Horn remembered him with dark hair and now it was gray. His blue eyes were the same, brittle bright with quiet daring and surrounded by heavily seamed tan flesh. He was wearing pleated gray slacks, a pale blue-on-blue striped dress shirt open at the collar, and a maroon ascot with white polka dots. He looked good in the outfit. Horn wondered how he got by with it, thinking maybe it was the thirty-two-inch waist on a man who was probably in his sixties.

The apartment had tall windows and was bright, what decorators would call airy. On both sides of the windows were bookcases stuffed with volumes of every size and stacks of dog-eared magazines that appeared to have been pored over. The top magazine on one of the stacks was *The Economist.* The furniture was traditional and expensive. The walls were white, and on one of them was a vast framed landscape oil of a mountain range. There were framed black-and-white photographs of mountains on the other walls. A tall, black-laquered desk that looked to be of Chinese origin was the only incongruous thing in the room.

"Seventeenth century," Sayles said, noticing Horn looking at the desk. "Beautiful and practical. I obtained it years ago. Spent a great deal of my youth in the northern provinces of China."

"Really? I didn't know." Horn didn't recall that morsel of information from ten years ago.

"The desk is the only furniture in the room Andrea didn't choose. She indulged me when I insisted on keeping it."

"Andrea?"

"Sorry—my wife. I'd introduce you but she's visiting her family in Vermont. You being a policeman of some note, I thought you would have known all that before coming here."

"I didn't know about Vermont," Horn said. *Or China. That's two.*

Sayles smiled and motioned for Horn to sit in a comfortable-looking cracked brown leather armchair. "Get you something? A drink? I feature fine scotch."

"Excellent," Horn said, settling into the chair. For a second he thought he might never stop sinking into the soft cushion. He watched as Sayles got a bottle and some glasses from an oak credenza and poured two glasses of Macallan.

"If you want ice or water I'll have to go to the kitchen," Sayles said.

"Straight up's fine."

After handing Horn his glass, Sayles sipped from his own and smiled with satisfaction. Then he settled into a matching armchair facing Horn's.

"He lowered himself from the roofs," Sayles said.

Horn grinned. "Ah, you're ahead of me. First up the mountain."

"Wasn't hard to figure out. And because of the climbing aspect, I was interested and followed the murders in the smaller papers before the major media tumbled to what was happening. Two of those buildings would be almost impossible climbs from ground level. And time consuming. Hard to believe anyone could have spent time scaling them, even at night, without being noticed. But going down instead of up, that's another matter. Wearing dark clothing or dressed to approximate the colors of the buildings, gaining entrance to those windows without being detected would have been within the capabilities of an expert climber. Except for one building, where the Bridge woman died."

"That one was more difficult?" Horn said.

"Oh, that one would have required superb skills. Not to mention iron nerve." Sayles flashed a sad smile. "I might have been able to do it when I was a bit younger."

Horn sipped his scotch and was further impressed. "A climber that skilled . . ."

"Not just skilled," Sayles said. "Gifted."

"With that ability," Horn continued, "wouldn't he be well-known, at least to other climbers?"

"He would," Sayles said. "And that's your problem. I know of no one climbing now who might have exhibited such technique and ability."

Horn found himself slightly irked by the note of admiration in Sayles's voice. "What about a good climber with new or revolutionary equipment? Might we be seeing evidence of that and not so much his climbing skills?"

Sayles considered for a moment, then shrugged. "Equipment could account for some of it. With the new lightweight harnesses and slender but almost unbreakable lines, the new friction belayers that allow someone to virtually walk down a wall, abilities are enhanced, especially in descent. But I was also thinking about other problems your killer had to contend with. He had to be silent. He had to be fast. He had to be as invisible as possible from the ground or surrounding windows, and he had to gain access quickly. And, of course, he had to duplicate his feat in the opposite direction when leaving the scene of the crime."

Horn nodded over his Macallan. "He showed some of the skills of an expert B-and-E man. A cat burglar. By the way, this is terrific scotch."

Sayles cocked his head to the side and smiled. "Isn't it, though? The papers I read are calling him a spider. The Night Spider. I suppose because he drops on a line to his victim's window, then envelopes her, saps her of life, and leaves behind the shrouded and inanimate husk. Much like a spider."

"I haven't read the papers today," Horn said. He wasn't surprised the advance news hounds had caught the scent. The Sally Bridge murder had stirred a lot of interest because of her show business connections. And the NYPD could leak like a spring shower. "Night Spider," he said. "I suppose that's accurate enough."

"Soon they might be calling you the exterminator," Sayles said.

"I hope so."

"Like Arnold Whatsisname."

"I was thinking James Bond."

Sayles grinned as if thinking, Damned if you didn't find a sense of humor in the most unlikely places, even in a retired homicide detective who'd seen hell.

Horn said, "We think the . . . er, Night Spider entered buildings adjacent to the victims', crossed gangways or air shafts to the roof, then dropped down on a line to the victims' windows."

"Sounds plausible."

"Wouldn't that entail a lot of equipment?"

Sayles ran a finger around the rim of his glass and thought about it. "Not really. As I said, climbing ropes are thin and lightweight these days. And the hardware's sometimes made of unbreakable but light polymer materials." The glass rim sang. "Your killer might have simply wrapped the slender line around his waist, had whatever else he needed, including a telescoping or folding grappling hook, in his pockets or taped to his inner thighs. The military developed top secret stuff for Ranger and Special Forces mountain units." Sayles sat back and took a sip of scotch, his blue eyes watching Horn over the glass rim as if peeking above a foxhole. In this case, he was waiting for another question to be lobbed. It struck Horn as it had years ago what a wily and willful man Sayles was. He knew how to reach mountain peaks, how to get to know the right people, and how to handle media. And now he was living well and more or less anonymously on the momentum of his early success.

"The military," Horn said. "A climber as skilled as you say might have been in one of those units, and with the right equipment could be the climber who reached those windows."

"I doubt if even Special Forces can climb like that." Sayles squinted and seemed to look inward. "But I've heard of a secret Special Forces mountain unit in the military that works in conjunction with the CIA in black operations."

He didn't have to tell Horn what black operations were—missions done secretly and at times without the knowledge of even the president. For many people in power, some things were better not known.

"The men in those units are the cream of the cream," Sayles said. "They go on missions that can't fail and can never be made public. That's the only place I can think of where you might find somebody not known to the outside world who can climb like . . . well, a spider."

"An outfit like that," Horn said, "doesn't usually publish its roster."

"If such a unit even exists," Sayles cautioned. "I told you, it's only rumors that I've heard, and now I'm repeating them to you." He reached into his shirt pocket for a pen, then pulled a small writing tablet from the drawer of a nearby table. After setting down his glass of scotch, he scribbled something on a sheet of paper and ripped it from the pad. Then he stood and crossed the room in three long strides, bending at the waist and holding out the piece of paper for Horn.

"A name and a phone number to call," Sayles said. "No promises, but the man who answers might be able to help you. You can mention my name."

Horn accepted the paper and slipped it into his pocket. "A name and number. That's just what an old cop like me needs and wants. The NYPD thanks you again for your services, Mr. Sayles."

"I don't like murder or the people who do it," Sayles said. "They make the ordinary risks we take in life seem meaningless."

Ordinary risks like climbing mountains? Horn started to struggle up out of the comfortable chair, but Sayles waved him back down.

"Don't leave till you've finished your drink, Captain Horn. Then please have another. I took note years ago that you were an unusual and interesting man. Very different from most policemen. I enjoy talking with you. About climbing, police work, theater, human nature, whatever . . ."

"Not Captain any longer," Horn said, settling back down. "I retired, then temporarily unretired to handle this case."

"Temporary, is it?"

"Yes. To keep a promise to my wife."

"Once a captain always one," Sayles said. "It's much more than a title, especially in your line of work."

Sayles had it right. But husband was one of those titles, too. Horn had another drink.

* * *

Nina Count, anchor of *Eye Spy* six o'clock news on cable, put down the notes she'd been studying and looked up at Newsy Winthrop. Nina was tall and blond and icy, all angles from the neck up, curves from the neck down. Said neck was elegantly long, and she consciously accentuated it with V-neck blouses and blazers with long lapels. She was known for her dedication to ratings and her insistence on excellence from the people around her. These people included Newsy, who was thirty-five and hungry for approval and a promotion, who was a small and dark man, with round-rimmed glasses that rode low on his perpetually greasy nose. He had the face of a ferret with spectacles and the soul of a wolverine. Nina was prominent and lusted after because of the long shots that showed off her shapely legs. In New York, her legs were famous.

She was aware that Newsy was her legs—her practical and efficient legs.

It was Newsy whom she sent on errands and assignments, who did her bidding and returned with hard facts—hard enough, anyway. Quick and precise and pithy Newsy. Invaluable. *Behind every successful woman . . .*

"This is some potent shit," she said, after motioning for Newsy to close the office door. "These women were all murdered by the same sicko who came at them in their sleep like a nightmare."

"The Night Spider," Winthrop said.

"That's what the *Times* calls him. I wish we'd thought of it first." Nina glanced again at his notes. "It looks like most of what you got here is from the *Times*."

"That's where most of it is," Newsy said. He grinned, a dark lock of hair from his widow's peak dangling over his forehead. "From a mole in the NYPD, to the *Times,* to us."

"Why don't *we* have somebody in the NYPD?"

"We do now."

Nina smiled in a way that made Newsy's stomach flutter. Not an unpleasant sensation.

"But the *New York Times,* Nina. They've got resources and lots of ways to check their facts. I figured, even though most of what I gave you's on record, you'd at least have it right and all in one place and be up to speed on the case."

"Thomas Horn's acting as an advisor to the police," Nina said. "That's a crock of shit. If Horn's involved, he's in charge."

"How come you say that?"

Nina snorted. "Horn was probably in charge of the delivery room five minutes after birth. He's a smart, tough cop. Old school and with no quit in him."

"I've heard of him," Newsy said. "S'posed to be a real piss cutter. Beat up a couple of mob guys in Brooklyn about five years ago. Took their guns away from them first. But lots of times you hear that about old cops and it's bullshit."

"Seven years ago," Nina said. "And it isn't bullshit this time. But Horn has a softer side when you get to know him. He's not just a goon set to catch a goon."

There was a look in Nina's eyes Newsy wasn't sure he liked. "You know him well enough to say that?"

"Well enough I might be able to get his cooperation. Use him as a source."

Newsy's face split wide in an admiring grin. "You get the lead investigator as your source, we'll have the competition by the balls. But how about what we've got so far? Good enough for the six o'clock? There's some tape of the crime scenes, just the buildings from the outside. Cops are keeping a pretty tight lid on this one. You wanna go for the six, I can get you the tape."

Nina gave him her sincere on-camera smile. Newsy knew it was canned as shucked corn, but he liked it anyway.

"We're not only gonna put it on the six," Nina said, "we're gonna lead with it."

11

"Sure, I know her," said the bartender at Brook's Crooks. "I got a photographic memory for faces. That's Pattie."

Paula caught Bickerstaff's expression in the mirror behind the long, curved bar. It was one of pleased disbelief, as if he were ice fishing and had just yanked a ten pounder up through the hole. Sometimes luck was on the side of the good guys.

"She's not a regular. Only been in a few times when I was here." The bartender looked concerned as he glanced up from the photograph lifted from one of Pattie Redmond's credit cards. The place wasn't yet crowded but somehow managed to smell like stale beer. "That ain't a good shot of her, though. Pattie's a real attractive woman. She could make it as a regular."

"What do you mean by 'making it as a regular'?" Paula asked the bartender, a skinny, buzz-cut guy who had a silver ring through one nostril and looked too young to be serving liquor. He was wearing a black, sleeveless Brook's Crooks T-shirt with a name tag that said he was Lightfinger.

"Not what you might be thinking, ma'am. This is an up-an'-up kinda place. I just meant we got a good class of single women who come in here regular. This is one of the best places to meet them. Then what goes on between people outside of here's something we can't control." He grinned. "You're a cop, and you could be a regular."

Paula, who hadn't been thinking anything disapproving beyond murder, was surprised. "You're saying Pattie wasn't a hooker? Just like some of the other women who hang out in here aren't?"

"He's a bright guy trying to help us without hurting himself," Bickerstaff explained. "I think he's successfully avoided a visit from the vice squad."

Lightfinger, who'd been fidgeting, was suddenly motionless. "You used the past tense," he said to Paula. "Did I hear the past tense?"

"Pattie Redmond is past tense," Bickerstaff confirmed. "She's been murdered."

"Oh, man! Ain't that some shit . . ." Lightfinger gripped the bar with both hands and leaned in on it. For a moment Paula thought he might faint. "Shot or something?"

"Stabbed."

"You got any idea who did it?"

"We're trying to get an idea," Paula said. "That's why we're talking with you."

Lightfinger went to the shelves of bottles on the back bar, poured himself a Jameson, and tossed it down straight as if he needed it in the worst way. Sensitive guy.

When he returned to the bar he looked pale but steadier. "Yeah, Pattie was no hooker. She just came in and had a margarita or two, listened to the music, maybe danced." Lightfinger saw no reason to mention the woman Pattie was with the first time, Ellen something. Not unless he was asked. Why spread trouble like a germ?

Paula tried to imagine the Patricia Redmond she'd seen, alive and smiling and gyrating on the dance floor. She found it impossible.

"She sounds lonely," Bickerstaff said in a tone that suggested he was lonely himself. Maybe he was, Paula thought with a twinge of sympathy. No wife or family to speak of, looking forward to a lonesome retirement.

"I wouldn't know if she was lonely," Lightfinger said. "I think she just didn't know losers when she saw them."

"Your customers a lot of losers?" Bickerstaff asked.

"No, but a lot of my customers are losers."

While Bickerstaff was struggling to make the distinction, Paula said, "Can you recall if she left with anyone?"

"She might've." Giving away nothing.

"Ever see her with a guy named Gary?"

Uh-oh! Gotta avoid being an accessory here. Lightfinger pretended to brighten with recollection and stood straighter behind the bar. "Yeah! Sure! Gary Schnick. I know his name because he's always flashing business cards around. He and Pattie were drinking together last night over in that corner booth." He motioned with a stringy, muscular arm, revealing a coiled snake tattooed on his inner right biceps. "But I can't say I saw them walk outta here together." *Might* not have seen them.

"Could they have left together without you noticing?" Bickerstaff asked.

"Sure. I'd hate to think what happens around here without me noticing."

"You wouldn't happen to have one of Gary's business cards, would you?"

"Naw, I throw that kinda stuff away when I close up. But I remember he's an accountant works out of his apartment. Freelance accountant, he calls himself. Not a bad guy, but tell you the truth he's a pain in the ass around tax time, comes in here mostly to drum up business instead of pussy."

"Accountants." Bickerstaff smiled philosophically and shook his head, the way some people do when they hear the word *lawyer.*

"Gary ever pick up any other women in here?" Paula asked.

"Not as I can recall. But it wasn't from lack of trying."

"Yet attractive Pattie Redmond went for him."

"Like I said, she wasn't a regular. Could be she just didn't see enough of the guy to judge him."

"I'm sure you remember the address on his business cards," Bickerstaff said hopefully.

"No, but maybe he's in the book." Lightfinger turned around and got a Manhattan phone directory from a shelf beneath the beer taps. He laid it on the bar, flopped it open, leafed through some pages, then turned it around for Paula and Bickerstaff to see. As he'd swiveled the directory on the bar, he'd kept his forefinger in the same spot. There was Gary Schnick's address and phone number, halfway down the page.

Paula got out her notepad and copied it.

"He's not a suspect, is he?"

"I dunno," Bickerstaff said. "Why do you ask?"

"I can tell you Gary'd never kill anyone. I mean, I know the guy some from seeing him around here. In my job, you can just tell about people. Guy's probably got the balls of a field mouse."

"We won't tell him where we got his name and address," Paula said, figuring Lightfinger might be afraid of Gary, whatever the size of his testicles. "While I'm writing things down, what's your real name, Lightfinger?"

Lightfinger looked confused. "Lightfinger. Ethan Lightfinger. I'm from Canada."

"Ah!" Paula said, and wrote.

"And I'm not worried you'll tell Gary where you got his name. I'm just trying to help out by letting you know he's not the kinda guy who'd kill somebody. For Chrissake, I told you the guy's an accountant!"

"You think accountants never kill?" Bickerstaff asked.

"Can you name me one?"

Bickerstaff was stumped.

"What about bartenders?" Paula asked. "Can they be killers?"

"Never," Lightfinger said. He swallowed hard. Had to ask. "Can they be suspects?"

"All the time," Bickerstaff said.

They thanked Lightfinger for his cooperation and left. Paula tried hard not to glance back.

Horn read the name Sayles had given him: Goesling. No first name. Horn sighed. Maybe Goesling was one of those people like Sting or Bono who had only one name. But then, would he have chosen Goesling?

Whatever, Horn stood closer to the phone and punched out the number after the name. It had an unfamiliar area code.

Only two rings, then a man's voice said hello.

"Er, Mr. Goesling?" Horn asked.

A pause. "Who is this?"

Horn explained who he was. Then: "Royce Sayles suggested I call you. You do know Royce Sayles."

"Know of him."

"He said you might be able to give me some information about a secret Special Forces unit. It's a police matter, Mr. Goesling. Homicide. More human life might be at stake."

"A secret Special Forces unit? Shouldn't you be calling the military?"

"I thought maybe I was."

"No."

"But you do know what I'm talking about? A top secret elite combat unit that engages in black operations?"

Again a pause. Longer.

"Tell you what," Goesling said, "I'll call you back. Not right away, maybe."

"Sure. Listen, I understand you have to be—"

But the connection was broken, the empty line droning in Horn's ear.

Goesling had been cryptic, all right. And maybe not much help. His weren't the loose lips that might sink ships.

Horn replaced the receiver harder than was necessary. *Not military, my ass!*

He hadn't asked what Horn meant by *black operations*.

Horn had made the call from a public phone rather than his brownstone. Everyone had caller ID these days.

Caller ID probably would have designated that his call had come from a public phone. Yet, when Goesling told Horn he'd call him back at some point, he hadn't asked for a number. He probably already knew Horn's number.

This stirred the hair on the back of Horn's neck.

Neva Taylor stood brushing her hair and staring out her apartment window. At last she had something she'd always wanted: a view of Central Park.

The apartment itself was smaller than she'd imagined for herself. Her promotion after landing the Massmann Container advertising account hadn't come with a commensurate salary that allowed for the penthouse she was certain was her eventual destination. Neva, a tall redhead who'd been a cheerleader as well as president of the Women's Political Forum in college, was long on ambition and knew how to attain her goals. It didn't hurt that she had large green eyes, a film-star figure, and was stunningly attractive even without the minimal makeup she wore. Her 147 IQ didn't hurt her chances, either. Add to that artistic talent and a marketing degree, and here she was, a rising star in one of the biggest advertising agencies in the country.

So she was only temporarily satisfied with this fortieth floor, one-bedroom co-op in the Weldon Tower, one of the most desirable addresses on the Upper East Side. She wouldn't have been satisfied with it at all except for the Central Park view. In fact, she'd purchased it because she knew she'd have an inside track in the future when one of the penthouse apartments came on the market. She figured that in less than two years she'd be able to afford one. She already had the unit she wanted picked out. It was a spacious three-bedroom, and it had the same view as the smaller, lower unit she'd bought. Sooner or later the present owner, a man who managed a chain of exclusive jewelry stores in New York and Philadelphia, would move. And Neva was prepared to make him an irresistible offer if he wasn't inclined to move. She'd be able to afford it. Neva planned early and with confidence.

She turned away from the sweeping green rectangular vista below and surveyed her living room, then the view over a serving counter into the modern kitchen. Neva had moved in only six busy weeks ago, but still the place had a comfortable lived-in look. The living room had a sofa and chair, dark blue to contrast with the soft gray carpeting, an asymmetrical mahogany coffee table from Bloomingdale's, brass lamps with fluted white shades, red throw pillows, and accent pieces that included a large Bingham print mounted on the wall behind the sofa.

Near the table in the entry hall hung an unlettered rendering of the Massmann *Container Industry* full-page ad, a succession of foam cups, each larger than the other, about to collapse together in the manner of subsequently larger fish following and about to devour each other simultaneously. It didn't match the rest of the expensive decor, but Neva didn't mind. The advertising artwork did, after all, represent what was responsible for that decor and the co-op unit itself.

She leaned forward slightly so her forehead rested against the cool glass of the window. This was like a dream, the way her career had unfolded since she'd arrived in New York. Maybe it was true what the gas-bag politicians kept saying, that if you played by the rules, good things could happen. She gazed down at the street that seemed miles below. She was moving higher in the world. She felt herself ascending even as she stood there motionless.

She gave herself a mental jolt of reality. She didn't need the penthouse. Not quite yet. This was a suitably comfortable and impressive apartment. And a safe one. The first three floors of the Weldon Tower featured elaborate stonework and curlicued iron bars over the windows. Then the building stair-stepped upward in three soaring, offset planes, with gleaming windows set like a pattern of rectangular jewels.

At least they'd seemed that way when Neva had first laid eyes on the building in the bright morning sunlight.

No need for bars on her windows to distract from the view. Here she was high above the rest of the city. Here she was secure.

The Night Spider sat on the park bench in the dusk and studied the Weldon Tower through small but high-powered Leica binoculars. What was the woman doing, standing so close to the window, leaning out as if there were no glass between her and the outside world, as if she might be about to take flight? It appeared that her forehead was actually touching the smooth glass pane. Light from a lamp somewhere behind her shone through her flaming red hair, setting it aglow like the lowering sun.

Moving the binoculars only slightly, the figure on the bench took in the buildings on each side of the Weldon Tower. They were considerably smaller, falling short of the Tower's height by about ten stories. That was all right. The Night Spider knew that the back of the Weldon, facing the opposite block, was only thirty-five stories, and within reach from the roof of the building behind it. The lower building was snugged up to the Weldon to form a completely enclosed air shaft that was sheer brick wall above the fourth floor.

To reach the Weldon's roof, the Night Spider would have to scale ten stories of that wall above the air shaft, avoiding windows overlooking the shaft. Ascent before descent and the prize—the confection to be wrapped and consumed from the inside out. He would not let this one lose consciousness except for brief periods; he would patiently, painfully, draw her out through her eyes. Until . . .

He moved the binoculars back to the fortieth-floor window.

The prize was no longer visible.

The Night Spider studied the building a while longer, counting windows horizontally and vertically, occasionally making notes in a small pad on his lap.

"Wacha lookin' at, Mister?"

A blond boy about ten, in jeans and a sleeveless T-shirt, was stooped down and tying his shoe near the bench.

"You should get out of the park," the Night Spider said. "It's going to be dark soon. Not a safe place."

A wide, confident grin. "It's okay, I'm with my mom."

Trudging along the path about a hundred feet away was a large, lumpish woman pushing a blue baby stroller. She was moving slowly and looked tired.

"So wacha doin', spyin' on people?" There seemed no hostility or disapproval in the boy's question.

"Peregrine falcons," said the Night Spider.

"So what're those?"

"Birds that hunt other birds. They live in angles and on ledges of buildings high up and snatch other birds right out of the air."

"Sounds neat."

"It is neat. That's why I'm a bird watcher. In case your mother asks what the stranger you were talking to was doing. Bird watching. It's my hobby. I especially like peregrine falcons."

The boy raised his eyebrows curiously. "So these falcons just fly over an' grab the other birds, like pigeons or somethin' just flyin' along, an' then eat them?"

"That's pretty much it. They do it fast. Things flying along up high aren't as safe as they think."

"And you watch it?"

"That's why I'm here. I watch it and write down what happens."

The boy started to say something more, but his mother called sharply and he waved a hand and bolted away to join her. His sneakered feet made soft slapping sounds on the paved path.

The Night Spider watched the slight, receding figure for a while, then raised the binoculars back to his eyes.

Found the correct window.

. . . aren't as safe as they think.

12

"Schnick as in prick," Bickerstaff said, as they climbed out of the unmarked.

"Try to behave," Paula told him.

Gary Schnick's building didn't have a doorman, but when Paula and Bickerstaff entered the spacious, rather shabby lobby, a fat man in gray overalls watched them with a sideways gaze from where he sat on a sofa. The lobby had a cracked gray-and-white-tile floor, red concrete planters with obviously fake ferns in them next to the scattered furniture, and an odor that suggested insecticide.

Paula and Bickerstaff studied the bank of tarnished brass mailboxes.

"He's in 106," Paula said, spotting Schnick's name above one of the boxes in the top row. Something white was visible through the slot; Schnick hadn't picked up his mail today. Above the name slot was an intercom button, but Paula could tell by the many layers of paint over it that it didn't work.

"Help you?" a smoker's hoarse voice asked behind them. "I'm the super."

It was the guy in the overalls, looking much bulkier now that he was standing.

"We're looking for Gary Schnick," Bickerstaff said, showing his badge. "So far we found his mailbox."

The obese super's complexion turned the drab gray of his uniform. His reaction interested Paula. Bickerstaff, too. They moved closer to the man.

"I can tell you he's not home," the super said. Paula noticed he smelled like stale sweat and cigars.

"What else can you tell us?" she asked.

The super's doughy face widened, and flesh beneath one of his eyes began to tick. His mouth worked for a few seconds but no sound came out. Clearly there was an inner struggle going on here.

"Gary didn't mention any police," the super finally said.

"So what did he mention?" Bickerstaff used his quietly menacing voice. Watching all those Clint Eastwood movies paid off.

"Said where he was gonna be," the super spoke up immediately. "Told me to call him if anybody came around looking for him. Didn't mention any police, though."

"Police you got," Paula said. "What's your name?"

"Ernie Pollock."

Bickerstaff made a show of writing it down. "Okay, Ernie, what can you tell us about Schnick?"

Pollock sucked in air, expanding his already immense torso. "Nice guy, is about all. I don't hardly know him well enough to tell you more'n that. He does some kinda accounting work in his apartment. He offered once to do my taxes. I told him, hell, they ain't that complicated. My girlfriend Linda does 'em for me. She says we'd get married, only it'd cost us."

"Seems to cost everyone," Paula said. "Ever known Schnick to have overnight female guests?"

Pollock rubbed his sleeve across his glistening forehead. He was sweating as if he were working at it. "Once in a while, is all. But, hell, he's young and single. There was never anything like a parade up there."

"He ever cause any kind of trouble?"

"Not in the slightest. I said he was a nice guy. I'm kinda the unofficial doorman here, and he springs for a nice gift at Christmas, which is more'n you can say for some of the other cheap bastards that live here."

"Now the big question," Paula said. "Where might we find Mr. Schnick?"

Pollock suddenly turned even paler, fixing his gaze beyond Paula. "There," he said hoarsely. "Right there."

Paula turned around to see a short, dark-haired man about forty, wearing wrinkled khaki pants and a perspiration-soaked blue shirt with a red tie plastered askew across his chest. His face was pudgier than the rest of him, which was actually kind of thin. Paula thought Lightfoot was right to wonder what Redmond had seen in Schnick.

When he saw Paula and Bickerstaff with Pollock, Schnick's jaw dropped and he broke stride, actually did a little skip. His body language became pure babble. First, he almost whirled and bolted, but then he took a stride toward them trying to look casual. Then he shuffled his feet and veered away from them. No, he was back on course now. He knew he had to keep coming toward them, but his body wouldn't accept the message.

"He always do the hokey-pokey when he comes in?" Bickerstaff asked.

When he drew closer, Schnick nodded at Pollock. "Ernie." For a second he seemed to consider walking on past, toward the elevators.

Bickerstaff stopped him with one hand placed lightly on the shoulder; he flashed his shield with the other hand.

"They're cops," Pollock said unnecessarily.

Paula tried to catch Schnick when she saw him turn a pasty color. He was so slippery with sweat that he oozed through her arms and sank to his knees.

Ow! Jesus! She'd bent back a fingernail.

Schnick's eyes rolled back, and she managed to hold on to a handful of damp hair and ease his descent, but with the sore finger she couldn't stop him from going down the rest of way to lie curled and unconscious on the cracked tiles.

Horn settled into his usual booth at the Home Away. Anne had wolfed down her toast and orange juice at home, then hurried off to her job at the hospital.

It had become their weekday-morning ritual. Horn would rise first and put on the coffee, then share caffeine and conversation with Anne during her breakfast. It used to be that those times were comfortable, their conversation easy and about the trivial but necessary things a man and his wife discussed. But since the lawsuit Anne hadn't been sleeping well and was almost always irritable in the mornings. Horn found himself looking forward to her leaving, so he could finish getting dressed, and then on some mornings, walk over to the Home Away to have his own leisurely breakfast while he read the *Times*.

There was something about her distance and distraction, their increasingly frequent separation—both physical and mental—that bothered him, but maybe not as much as it should. In some ways it made him feel like a young cop again, on the Job, doing something worthwhile with his life.

Searching for a killer.

Though the booth Horn sat in wasn't that near the window, morning sunlight reflected off the windshield of a parked car and angled in low to cast a rectangular pattern over the table and the newspaper spread alongside his coffee cup. The sun's warmth felt good on his bare forearms as he read. Part of him was thinking how pleasant sitting there was, how this wasn't a bad way to spend a morning.

The news was front page above the fold, emphatic for the *Times*. The caption read SERIAL KILLER MIGHT BE OPERATING IN NEW YORK. The text was factual and matter-of-fact, and referred to the killer as the Night Spider only once. It had always amused Horn how the *Times* always politely referred to male suspects as *Mr.,* and he almost expected to come across *Mr. Night Spider.*

He finished reading the piece and pushed the paper aside. Then he picked up the *Post* he'd also bought after seeing its headline: NIGHT SPIDER NAILS ANOTHER. The following story contained pretty much the same general information as the one in the *Times,* though the prose was more sensational. In bringing to the attention of the citizens of New York that a prolific and particularly horrific serial killer was in their midst, it used the term *Night Spider* twenty-three times.

In both papers, the story was at the very least unsettling.

"I see we've got another one of those guys killing his mother over and over," Marla said, as she topped off Horn's coffee.

"They don't all do that," Horn said.

"I know. It's a lot more complicated than that. I read in the paper you came out of retirement to handle this case. What made you do it?"

"I guess because I was an oldest child," Horn said.

"No, you weren't the oldest."

Horn was surprised. Marla was right; he was the middle of three brothers and the only survivor of the three. "So pop psychology can lead us astray," he said.

"You better believe it."

There were no other customers in the diner, and the glass coffeepot she held was almost empty, so she lingered by his booth as she often did.

"So what do you think?" Horn asked.

"About?"

"This serial killer."

"I don't have all the facts."

"None of us do," Horn said. "That's the problem. What do you make of it from what you read in the papers and hear on the news?"

Marla seemed a little surprised he was asking her about

this seriously, but she walked over and placed the coffeepot back on its burner, and then returned. Her manner was slightly different, but it would take a practiced eye like Horn's to notice. She wasn't in her waitress persona now; she seemed involved and thoughtful. There was more going on behind her eyes than over easy and bacon crisp.

"He kills women he doesn't know," she said, "or he'd simply knock on their doors then incapacitate them instead of sneaking through their windows."

"He might have a thing about them needing to be asleep," Horn suggested.

"I know. I'm only hypothesizing. The victims are all attractive women but not of a particular type." She saw the curiosity in his eyes. "Television news had their photos on last night. Nina Count's channel."

"It would be hers," Horn said. "She's a wolf among news hounds."

"Your killer must have some kind of climbing skills," Marla said. Something in the look she gave him revealed she was locked on like radar, now that he'd asked her opinion. She wasn't interested in his asides about a TV anchorwoman. "So he might be involved in rock climbing—that's a growing sport—or mountain climbing. Or maybe entomology."

That brought Horn up short as he was lifting his cup to his mouth. He placed the steaming cup back down. "Entomology? The study of insects?"

Marla nodded. "The media aren't just calling him the Night Spider because he crawls up and down buildings. There's the way he swathes his victims, like a spider using secretions to wrap and disable a victim before draining it of fluids. And the wounds are stabs rather than slashes, almost as if he's emulating a spider slowly sapping the life of helpless prey caught in its web. The killer doesn't seem to be in a rush. Neither is a spider. It feeds at its leisure off insects it's trapped and wrapped, until they weaken and die and become useless husks." She smiled without humor. "If I were a bug, I wouldn't want to be at the mercy of a spider. It doesn't know mercy, and neither does your killer."

"You're saying the killer somehow identifies with spiders?"

"Exactly. I wouldn't hazard a guess as to how or why, but it looks that way. And for that he needs familiarity with spiders. Like an entomologist."

Horn sat back, studying her. It wasn't just what she'd said but the way in which she'd said it. "You weren't always a waitress, Marla."

"Who was? I had a life before this."

"What kind of life? You don't look that old."

She laughed. "The past is dead and gone. And I'm . . . let's just say in my early forties."

"Sorry. I didn't mean to stray where I shouldn't."

"That's okay. I understand. It's the cop in you."

"Marla—"

The bell over the door jingled, and she hurried toward the front of the diner to wait on a guy in a business suit mounting a stool at the counter.

Horn used his cell phone to contact Paula and Bickerstaff. It was Bickerstaff who answered.

"You still interrogating Gary Schnick?" Horn asked.

"Paula's in the room with him now. This guy didn't do it. Two of his neighbors saw him arriving home last night a couple of hours before Redmond's time of death. He doesn't know that yet, though, so we're letting him ramble."

"He might have returned to her apartment later."

"Could have, but I doubt it. Nothing in his apartment suggests he knows anything about climbing, and his hands are soft from years of pushing pencils and tickling tax returns. This character's no more a mountain climber than I am. Doin' it without Viagra's the extent of his vertical challenge."

"You press him hard?"

"We did. He had a rough night and looks about ready to

fold. Paula's easing up now. He didn't even ask for an attorney for about two hours. Then he got some schmuck tax client of his that knows nothing about criminal law. I think they're bartering, trading services so they can screw the IRS. We were about to release Schnick. His lawyer will be shocked."

"You want to cross him off our list entirely?"

"Almost entirely. I *know* this guy's telling the truth, and Paula feels the same way. This is not a hard case. He actually fainted when he knew we were gonna confront him about Redmond's murder."

"Before you uncage him," Horn said, "have Paula find out if he knows anything about insects."

"Incest?"

"In*sects*. Bugs."

Bickerstaff was silent for a moment. "Like was he ever an exterminator?"

"Or a scientist. An entomologist or biologist."

"We checked out his background," Bickerstaff said. "Nothing like that in it. No sheet on him, degree in accounting, been a CPA for the last ten years. Course, there's always hobbies. Maybe he had a butterfly or beetle collection. You know, one of those guys sticks pins through bugs to mount them on a display."

"Yeah," Horn said. "Find out about that. Make sure before you put him back on the street."

"Will do," Bickerstaff said before hanging up. "Bugs . . ."

"Spiders," Horn said into the dead phone.

As he slid the phone back in his pocket, he saw that Marla had finished waiting on the executive type at the counter and was returning to his booth, carrying the coffeepot as an excuse. She was eager to talk to him about this case. He wondered why.

The cop in him.

13

Arkansas, the Ozark Mountains, 1982

Seven years old and he was terrified.

But he was used to being frightened, existing with the living lump of fear in his stomach. There was no light or movement of air where he was, only heat and darkness. His mouth was dry, and the corners of his eyes stung with perspiration. Listening to the sounds coming from the other side of the locked closet door, he wondered why his mother did this. Did all mothers do it?

He understood some things from hearing his mother and father arguing, yelling and losing their tempers, like he did at times. Their faces would be red, their eyes bulging. Their mouths were ugly and shaped like the ones on the stone things he'd learned about in school, the gargoyles. They would scream at each other sometimes until they got too tired to go on. Did they feel as he did afterward, empty and lost? He thought they did.

He knew his mother had once been a snake handler in the name of God. At least that's what his father had said. Both his father and mother said God a lot when they talked or yelled at each other. What a snake handler was, the boy didn't know. It had to do with a special kind of church, he was once told by his father. He was then given a look that made it clear he wasn't to ask about it again.

His father was away most of the time because he was in the army, leaving the boy in the care of his mother. She would beat him with one of his father's belts at times when he was bad, which he deserved though it made him mad for long times. Teaching him respect, she would say, or sometimes shout, losing her temper. Teaching him respect. Respect in this world that was hard.

He wished the noise on the other side of the door would stop so he could be let out of the closet, so he could finally have something to eat. He wasn't sure if his stomachache was from fear or from hunger.

Here were the spiders!

After a while in the dark closet they always came. He knew the place he lived was old and all by itself in the woods, and he'd heard his father say the rotted wood house was full of termites. That's why it had so many spiders, they ate the termites. And there was no shortage of flies and roaches for them to feast on, according to his father.

Then why did they still bite?

The first spider was like the touch of a feather on his left arm. He knew better than to knock it off with his hand. The spiders could bite quickly.

He made himself lie still while the soft exploring tickling sensation traveled up his arm toward his shoulder. There was another tickle on his right ankle. His left arm. His cheek. His mouth was open wide but he knew what would happen if he screamed. So he screamed silently because he had to. He couldn't be seen or heard in the dark closet.

Oww! A bite on his left arm. He made himself stay perfectly still. Painful experience had taught him that was his only defense. Lie still. Let the spiders have their way.

There was one on his right cheek. He hated it when they got near his eyes. It wasn't a terrible sensation, more like somebody slowly dragging a piece of thread across his flesh, but he didn't like to think about being bitten in the eye. He did take the risk of clenching his eyes tightly shut. Then he closed his mouth and gritted his teeth, protecting his tongue.

More tickling on his chest and stomach. He wished he was wearing more than his underpants. Lying on his side on the bare wood floor, he wanted to curl up, to sob. But he knew he couldn't risk crying. It made his body shake. Made them bite. Very slowly he allowed his knees to draw up. He couldn't help trying to make himself smaller—small as a spider—so he could crawl right out through the crack of dim light beneath the door.

He told himself it wasn't all that bad, the slight tickling all over his body. He told himself it could even feel good. He was getting used to it and so were the spiders. They didn't bite him so many times now.

But he knew they might if he moved suddenly, or if he didn't. He knew they might.

"In the name of our Lord!" shouted his mother's voice from outside the dark closet.

The spiders were still.

"Amen in the name of the Lord of the earth!" shouted the people who were out there with his mother. Her flock, she called them.

"Praise be it, the poor shall inherit the earth, and after them the animals and then the smallest of the Lord's earth, the kings of heaven!" The boy listened. *What did it all mean?*

"Praise be it!" shouted everyone beyond the door. "The kings of heaven!"

"The flesh of the rich shall be rent with disfigurement and the pain of their sins! The green of their money and gleam of their possessions shall be as the black of dust. The small and the crawl shall reap the reward. And the reward shall be ours and then theirs."

"Ours and then theirs! Ours and then theirs!"

The chanting had started. He knew that soon they would be singing. And dancing. Wild voices.

"The psalm of the mandible!" his mother said. "The psalm of the hive and the wing! The small and the crawl!"

"The small and the crawl."

The singing began. The boy felt his heart jump and jump. The dancing started, the shouting and tromping on the old plank floor—the rhythm of God, his mother had called it—making the whole house shake. The old house shake. The pots and pans rattle in the kitchen. His room, the closet, everything felt it. Everyone felt it. Maybe God felt it and paid notice. Or Satan. His mother talked and screamed so much of Satan while she made the house bounce, the whole house shake, while she beat and beat with the belt.

She loved him. The boy knew she loved him. She would kiss his forehead and make him feel better when he cried; she told him nothing was his fault. And sometimes at night she would read to him from the Bible till he went to sleep.

If she loved him, why did she lock him in the closet? Why did she beat him with the belt?

What did it all mean?

In the dark, the spiders began to move.

14

New York, 2003

Anne nodded good morning to people she passed in the wide, cork-tiled hall of Kincaid Memorial Hospital as she made her way to Radiology. Hospitals were depressing to some people, but she'd always liked the efficiency and order of them, the practiced routine, even the antiseptic scent. Except for the patients, everyone knew more or less what to expect in such an environment.

At least it had been that way until lately.

She glanced in through glass doors lettered RADIOLOGY to see how many people were in the waiting rooms. This was the time for morning-appointment imagery and, sometimes, the last pre-op X rays or scans for patients scheduled for early surgery.

About half the chairs and upholstered benches were occupied in the waiting area. It appeared to be a busy morning.

Ida, Anne's fastidious, graying assistant, was already at her desk when Anne pushed through the unmarked gray door that led to the reception area of her private office. Sun was pouring through the window and the printer was clicking and humming industriously. The morning light was golden and seemed thick and tangible.

When Ida saw her, she stopped typing and turned away from her computer keyboard. She and Anne had worked together for five years. They'd reached the point where they communicated silently if there was anyone nearby they might not want to overhear them. With a sideways motion of her head, Ida let Anne know that someone was waiting in her office. Anne knew it would be hospital personnel or somebody she was expecting. Probably the rep from Central Medical who wanted to talk to her about the new PET scan equipment the hospital had on order.

But her caller was a tall, long-jawed man with flowing gray hair and wearing an elegant brown silk suit. Dr. Herbert Finlay, Kincaid's chief of administration—hospitalese for CEO. He was half sitting with his rump against the edge of Anne's desk and leaning back. His arms were crossed so his marble-sized gold cuff links glinted in the sunlight streaming through the window. When he looked up from studying his polished oxblood loafers and saw Anne, he smiled.

Anne wasn't fooled by the smile as she said good morning.

"I hate to make it not such a good morning," Finlay said, standing up straight and turning to face her as she laid her attaché case on her desk and pulled out her chair. She hadn't sat down.

"The Vine complaint?"

"I'm afraid so, Anne. It's no longer a complaint. Now it's a lawsuit. Our attorneys called. The family filed this morning."

Now Anne did sit down. She felt flushed, resentful. And, God help her, at the same time guilty. *I've done nothing. Why can't I shake this? Why can't I escape the guilt?* "Do they really think a momentary, after-the-fact mix-up in CAT scan images caused their son to be comatose? The operation was completed when the mistake was noticed and mentioned. It might have been a serious screwup, but in this case it wasn't. It simply wasn't a factor."

"It doesn't matter what the family thinks," Finlay said. He was standing with one hand in his pocket now, weight on one foot. A familiar casual pose. Finlay's posturing often irritated Anne. "It's what the family *says* that's important."

"The boy had a reaction to the anesthetic," Anne said. "It's rare, but it happens. If they want to sue someone, it should be the anesthesiologist."

"You know anesthesiologists here aren't on staff, Anne. They're contract workers. Besides, hospitals have deeper pockets."

"Justice!" Anne said disgustedly. "My husband used to be in the justice business, and he tells me it's rare and often occurs outside the system."

"Yes, I suspect he's right."

"Outside the family, no one feels worse about the boy than the people who were in the OR during the operation. No one feels worse than I do. But it isn't a perfect world. Those infrequent side effects listed in fine print actually do happen to some people." *Listen to me . . . Don't I sound like a coldhearted bitch? But I'm not! I'm not! I went to visit the boy! He didn't know I was there!*

"I don't need convincing, Anne. And I certainly don't hold you or anyone else on staff even slightly responsible."

"We offered the family a fair settlement even though it isn't the hospital's liability."

"That was a mistake," Finlay said. "The Vines' attorneys are now characterizing our offer as an admission of guilt."

Anne sank farther back in her black leather desk chair and sighed. "Once the lawyers get hold of something like this, compensation can become financial rape. What does Legal say about it?"

"They haven't had time to study it yet." Finlay smiled slightly. "Their preliminary observation was something like yours." He uncrossed his arms and smoothed his coat sleeves down over the bulky cuff links. Anne now saw that they were in the form of elaborate lions' heads and had tiny rubies for eyes. "Something else you should know, Anne.

The complaint names the hospital, attending surgeon and additional OR personnel, and you."

She looked up sharply. "Me?" She'd expected to be named in a potential lawsuit but hearing that she had been was still a shock.

"As the chief administrator of radiology, you would be technically responsible for anything that happens in your department, including imagery mix-ups. At least the Vines' attorneys hope the law will define it that way."

"You didn't mention the anesthesiologist," Anne said.

Finlay shrugged like an actor onstage, a gesture he'd long practiced and made elegant. "The other side wants to remain on good terms with the anesthesiologist."

"Of course! They don't want what happened to be his fault."

Finlay used his shrug again. "Legal maneuvering, Anne . . ."

She rocked this way and that in her chair for a moment. *The other side. Battle lines had been drawn.* "The sad part is I actually feel as if I've done something wrong, that I should pay for it."

"You mustn't feel that way. It was the anesthetic reaction, Anne. We all know that."

"You mean the anesthetic administered by the doctor who wasn't even named in the suit? Who's cooperating with the plaintiffs so he won't be sued himself? Who'll probably be out of the country during the legal proceedings?"

"We'll subpoena him, Anne."

"We probably won't have to. He'll probably testify for the prosecution."

"These matters usually don't even reach court. Legal will handle it. You'll see. I just thought I ought to let you know about it soon as possible so you can be careful of who you talk to, what you say."

Anne nodded. "Thank you for that."

"We'll all have to be on our guard," Finlay said. He went to the door, then turned and smiled before going out. "Let's try to make it a good morning anyway."

Alone in the office, Anne folded her hands in front of her on top of her attaché case and felt like sobbing, unable to help what she was thinking. She wondered what kind of morning it was for the four-year-old boy who'd been moved to Roosevelt Hospital and was lying in a coma. Was Alan Vine seeing the same brilliant sunlight streaming through *his* window? Was he thinking how wonderful it would be to climb out of bed the way he used to and jump and run in its golden warmth?

Was he thinking anything at all?

After leaving the Home Away, Horn walked and talked. Unlike many people acting similarly in New York, he was using a cell phone. It was almost ten o'clock, and pedestrian traffic on the wide sidewalk was relatively sparse. No one paid any attention to the big man with the tiny phone tucked to his ear. The sun was higher and brighter, and passing in and out of the shadows of buildings brought noticeable contrasts in temperature.

"What about Gary Schnick?" Horn was asking Bickerstaff.

"We cut him loose. He couldn't kill anything but time, and he's got an alibi for the night of one of the Night Spider murders. He was with a woman in her apartment in Queens. She swears to it. He was with another woman in *his* apartment the night of one of the other killings, but she's married and a little shy about talking. This guy, I tell you, is a pussy magnet."

"That's not his reputation."

"His reputation is wrong. My impression is, he's one of those guys who doesn't kiss and tell so he gets a lot of stray."

"You sound jealous."

Bickerstaff laughed. "Maybe ten years ago. Now what I wanna do is catch this asshole we're after so I can go fishing."

"You really see it that way?" Horn asked.

"About fishing?"

"No. That the bartender at Brook's Crooks regards Schnick as an obvious loser, but women see him as just the opposite."

"It only takes one woman to see him as the jackpot: the woman we're talking about."

Horn supposed that was true.

"Where's Paula?"

"I'm on the line," she said. "Thinking about Bickerstaff's pathetic sex life."

"You two get anything fresh from Redmond's neighbors?" Horn asked.

"Nothing yet," Paula said. "But there's something that mighta been missed on the roof—"

"At least Paula thinks it's something," Bickerstaff interrupted.

"There's an irregularity in the blacktop where there's no gravel mixed in. Looks to me like the heel print of a bare foot."

"Or a dent in the roof underneath the tar," Bickerstaff said. "Or it's where somebody dropped something, or maybe some kid ran barefoot a long time ago."

"It looks fresh," Paula persisted. "I photographed it."

Horn dodged a posse of chattering teenage girls taking up half the sidewalk and waited for Bickerstaff to chime in, but Bickerstaff remained silent.

"That's good work, Paula," Horn said. "What I want's for you two to stay on the neighbors, maybe shake something loose."

"The neighbors are scared," Bickerstaff said. "Especially the women. It don't help us that this guy's killings are all over the news now. I'll bet the prick loves it, reads all the papers and watches all the TV news."

"It's almost a sure bet he enjoys it," Paula said.

Horn filled them in on what he'd been doing, including his phone call to the number Sayles had given him.

"The military has a way of clamming up," Bickerstaff pointed out. "Secret weapons and all that."

"I don't know," Paula said. "Could be promising."

Horn was only half a block from home. "I have to hang up. Let me know if you come across anything else that might mean something." The *else* was for Paula and her potential bare heel print.

"I'd just as soon stay off roofs for a while," Bickerstaff said, catching Horn's meaning. "I might catch vertigo, like in that movie."

"You've been dizzy since I've known you, Roy," Paula told him.

"Stay on it," Horn said. "We'll meet later and discuss."

He replaced the phone in his pocket and started up the steps to the brownstone's door.

A male voice made him pause and turn. "Thomas Horn?"

Horn looked down at the man from his vantage point two steps higher. He was average height but with a compact, muscular build that somehow made him appear smaller. His gray suit was well tailored, blue tie neatly knotted at the collar of his white shirt. He had precisely cut and parted dark brown hair. The bland, innocuous features of a man whom you wouldn't mind dating your sister. Harmless looking, with his balanced stance and amiable smile.

"Thomas Horn?" he asked again.

You know I am.

"I'm Luke Altman. Can we talk?"

"What would be the subject of our conversation?"

"Mountain climbing."

Horn decided not to invite Altman in. He stepped down off the concrete steps and faced him on the sidewalk. Altman was surprisingly tall and broad, when you got up close to him. "Are you with an agency, Mr. Altman?"

"Yes. A government agency."

Not good enough. "That would be the CIA?"

The friendly smile. "Or something like it. We were curious about your inquiry concerning Special Forces mountain-terrain groups."

"One particular group."

"Yes. That's what made us curious."

"Why I want a list of members should be no secret," Horn said, suspecting he was talking to a man who assumed secrets everywhere. "I think the serial killer the news media are calling the Night Spider might be, or once was, a member of a secret and elite mountain-terrain fighting force."

"Why would such a force be secret?"

"To do the kind of dangerous, undercover wet work no country can afford another country to know about."

Altman shook his head. "*Wet work.* That sounds like something out of a spy novel. And the operatives you describe sound like dishonorable men."

"Only the people who send them on missions could make them act dishonorably. They'd be soldiers, defined by their orders."

"Wouldn't they also be assassins?"

"At times, I suppose. Very efficient ones. And skilled climbers. It's possible that among these almost exclusively honorable men is one who lost his way—one who learned too well how to stalk and kill, and came to like it. It happens. I've seen it with cops."

"So have I, with soldiers. I served in the marines, and there's no finer outfit than the corps. But still, experience can shape the man."

"If I'm to stop this killer, Mr. Altman, I need to see the roster of that elite unit. Past and present members."

"That would be a difficult thing to supply even if there were such a unit."

"You're telling me there isn't?"

Again Altman's car-salesman smile. "I'm defined by my orders, too, Captain Horn. And they are to inform you that there is no such unit. Oh, we know about the rumors, and that's exactly what they are—rumors."

"The CIA actually sent you here to tell me that?"

"I didn't mention the CIA."

"You're telling me you're not a spook?"

"Spook? Oh, you mean a spy. A secret agent. That's a quaint term."

"It's a quaint business."

"If only that were true, especially these days. But, no, I'm not a spook. I can see where it might be fun, though. Maybe in the next life I can be a romantic figure like that. But back to your question: Yes, my superiors did send me to tell you that. Also to show you the light so you'd stop assuming this secret elite fighting unit exists."

"I guess if I knew for sure," Horn said, "it would no longer be a secret unit."

"That would follow," Altman said. "But it doesn't exist, so there's no list of names for you to possess. Therefore, we'd like it if you forgot this particular avenue of your investigation."

"*We?*"

"My superiors. The ones who sent me here. If I were the sort of agent you assume, I would assure you that if there were anything amiss in this imaginary unit, my department would deal with the problem and maintain secrecy. With that assurance, you could eliminate an unnecessary phase of your investigation."

"What if I persisted?"

Altman shrugged. "Then you'd waste your time."

Horn studied him, knowing Altman, behind his smile, was studying him right back. He changed his mind about inviting Altman in. The more he could keep him talking, the more he might learn.

Pulling his key ring from his pocket, Horn turned and took the steps to the stoop and the brownstone's front door. "Why don't you come inside, Mr. Altman?" he asked over his shoulder, as he keyed the lock.

But when he turned around, Altman was gone. Here and then gone.

Horn couldn't help smiling as he opened the door and went inside.

Presto-change-o!

So like a spook.

15

He had to walk fast to keep up with her, this long-legged, boldly striding woman who'd tripped a tendril of his web, who'd sent a subtle tremor of interest and intrigue across the void between them.

He'd seen her across the street. That was all it took, really, a glimpse, a connection.

He always knew when he found the one. She would suddenly become the only woman before him even if she happened to be part of a crowd. Deep in the sacred cruel center of his being there would be a stirring, then an irresistible tugging at his mind and heart toward his core. Ancient voices and instincts would take over. Predators' instincts. His mind, his desire, his every fiber, would focus sharply on his prey.

He was never wrong about these women. It was almost as if they emanated signals. Toward the end, when he was very near them, through all the odors of their fluids and fears, he could smell their need.

Theirs had been a holy covenant from the beginning, from every beginning, and finally they understood that and surrendered to death. He always could see by their eyes that they understood.

At first they weren't trapped—constricted and helpless—and his. That took time, delicate spinning, and careful preparation. He would learn more about them, including where they lived and whether it met his expectations. That wasn't much of a problem, as most single and attractive women in New York lived in apartments, and usually on high floors for their so-called security. He traded on his victims' false sense of security. It lulled them like a drug until they realized in their silent terror that it had failed.

She's slowed by that knot of pedestrians near a street vendor. Fall back, keep pace, not so close . . .

This one was tall and had red hair. How it must confuse the police that his victims were of no particular type, or no particular type they could perceive, anyway. Even he couldn't predict which would be the chosen one, so how could they? It was as if he sent out trailing threads of the mind that were extremely sensitive to willing victims—and there was something in these women that made them want to be his. He could feel the tremors of connection, and he knew that on some level they could feel them. But they didn't understand until it was too late, until he was on them and they realized that their destiny and his destiny were locked together. When he saw them on the street, on a bus or subway train, in a restaurant, or through a window, he knew everything in their futures was his will because, on a whim, he could take away their futures.

Over time he followed and watched them, wrapped them secretly and softly in layers of knowledge that would make the consummation of their affair sweet and inevitable. Eventually . . . eventually . . . Everything would be revealed to them and to him through their pain, through their passage. Through their pain.

It was necessary for them. For him.

*   *   *

Seeing the tall, fiery redhead walking angrily toward them prompted people on Third Avenue to move out of Neva Taylor's way.

She was plenty pissed off. Handleman, the asshole account executive at Massmann Container, had made it clear that if she wanted to grow their advertising arrangement, she might consider sleeping with him.

He'd been shrewd, saying nothing, doing nothing, that could in any way be actionable if she were to formally complain. And of course if she did accuse him of sexual blackmail, he'd simply and successfully deny it. Even Neva had to admit it would be wrong to prosecute a man without sufficient proof of wrongdoing.

This left her helpless.

On the other hand, she hadn't been so much as touched by the creep. And she still had the account.

That was small solace at the moment, as she strode past the Citigroup Building Barnes and Noble; across the intersection, while staring down a cabdriver about to make a right turn; and past a shop, where she might normally pause to look in the window.

She barely saw or heard the people around her as she relived in her mind the humiliating and infuriating events of an hour ago. The unctuous Handleman, with his transparent verbal fencing, trying to back her up, trying to draw blood. It was as if he knew that if she weakened, he'd have her. He understood women like her, he was implying. He knew better than she what she *really* wanted, and they both knew what that was. And she could have it and gain much on the side.

Neva stopped and stood still. She drew a deep breath and held it while people walking in the opposite direction stared.

Then she exhaled and made herself walk more slowly, made herself think as well as feel.

Handleman's desk had been cluttered with framed photos of his family, an overweight wife and three or four chubby kids who looked too much like Handleman. Neva considered a counteroffensive. She might intimate to Handleman that if he persisted in his subtle but unmistakable advances, she'd take their little dance outside the business world and into his personal life, make trouble for him with his family.

Jesus! What am I thinking?

She put any idea of a counteroffensive out of her mind. If Handleman kept it up she'd tell her boss, who'd believe her but probably couldn't do anything about the matter, either. Then, if necessary, she'd force the issue, get Handleman to discuss it. Neva knew this about herself: There was no kind of trouble she'd ever been in that she hadn't been able to deal with and, at times, turn to her advantage.

She stopped at the next intersection to stand and wait for the traffic signal to change. Around her the city roared and played out lives. Cars and trucks on Third Avenue blasted their horns. Tires hummed on hot concrete. Sidewalks trembled with the rushing of subway trains beneath. The air was full of dozens of smells and noises and conversations and exhaust fumes, and Neva loved it.

When she'd arrived here from Cincinnati five years ago, she'd somehow known that this city was hers on a plate. The tempo and tumult of Manhattan made some people nervous, but from the very first day, Neva found it all strangely soothing.

It was working on her that way now.

Maybe she'd have a better sense tomorrow afternoon of where the Handleman dilemma was going, when she had another meeting with him scheduled.

Also attending the meeting would be his superiors at Massmann Container. They didn't figure to be leeches like Handleman, and she could size them up, see who might help her if Handleman forged ahead despite her warning signals and tried to get physical. Probably she could figure out who at the meeting disliked Handleman.

Surely somebody else saw through him as she did. And she couldn't be the first woman he'd tried to pressure.

When Neva reached the Weldon Tower, she was still irritated by this development in what had promised to be a smooth and profitable contract agreement with Massmann Container.

The doorman, whose name she'd found out was Bill, nodded and smiled at her automatically as he held open the door for her, then did a kind of double take. What must her face look like, she wondered, after the dark thoughts she'd been harboring. She said hello and smiled back at Bill, noticeably melting him, as she entered the lobby and made her way to the elevators.

Don't be such a worrier, she told herself as she stepped into an elevator that had been at lobby level. She pressed the forty button harder than was necessary. *You can handle a creep like Handleman. You're a lot brighter than he is. Hell, you're even in Mensa. Maybe if you can't deal with a problem like this, you don't deserve the Massmann account.*

After entering her apartment she carefully locked the door, then kicked off her high-heeled Guccis and walked into the kitchen. She used the ice maker to dump some cubes into a glass, ran some tap water over them, then padded back into the living room to sit on the sofa, sip, and cool down.

She was exhausted, not only from a difficult day's work but from her simmering anger after her meeting with Handleman. Sometimes Neva wondered if it was all worth it, if maybe she should accept one of the almost annual proposals of marriage she received and settle down with a husband in the 'burbs, mow the lawn, and raise some kids. Sometimes she wondered; not often.

In one way or another, every man she met turned out to be a disappointment. She was sure there was one somewhere out there who was compatible with her, who was her equal and saw life as she did, as a challenge. He didn't have to be rich or handsome; he only had to understand her. *To be able, at times, to master her?* If ever she met a man like that, she might reshuffle her priorities. Such men were *not* like public conveyances that came along every so often and pulled to the curb for you. Neva was, in a secret, private part of her mind—sometimes secret even from herself—waiting for such a man, would know him when he arrived in her life. And then . . .

There'll be a time for that kind of living, she told herself. Take life in sequence, that was her plan. And always she had a plan.

Tired as she was, Neva decided not to go out this evening. She'd phone down to the deli she'd discovered two blocks over and have them deliver some of their spicy chicken with rolls and slaw. She was sure she had a wine that would be good with such a meal. After a leisurely dinner alone she'd have some more wine while she watched the Yankees game on television until she was deliciously sleepy.

Bedtime then, probably about the seventh inning. This had been a stressful, tiring day. If necessary, she'd go in to work late tomorrow morning in order to get a good night's sleep.

Neva wanted to be at her best tomorrow.

That was, after all, what she was about—her tomorrows.

In the darkness, Horn lay silently in bed beside Anne and listened to her breathing, knowing she was awake. He'd met with Rollie Larkin that evening to brief him on the status of the Night Spider case. Rollie had been polite and understanding, but they both knew that, so far, Horn had failed.

The Night Spider was still operating, victims were stacking up, the media were turning up the heat, and the pols were increasing pressure from above. "Dealing with the pressure's my job," Rollie'd told Horn, "but you could make it a hell of a lot easier by getting a solid lead on this bastard." Rollie's unsubtle way of urging Horn to do *his* job. At the same time he was reminding Horn the pressure didn't stop with Assistant Chief of Police Roland Larkin.

"You checked out Luke Altman?" Horn asked.

"Yeah. It was pretty much like checking out Casper the Ghost. The Luke Altmans in our computer banks, as well as the Fed's, didn't pan out to be anyone who could be your spook."

"He didn't say he was CIA," Horn reminded Larkin.

"If he had, he wouldn't be CIA, we can assume."

"More assumption," Horn said. "There's too much of it in this case. I'll be glad when we get beyond the point of assumptions."

"To when a jury assumes the bastard's guilty."

Horn smiled. "For now, I guess we have to figure Altman is CIA, and his purpose was to assure me the agency had or was investigating any such secret Special Forces unit and would deal with the killer if they found him there."

"If the Night Spider is a member of the military," Rollie said, "my guess is he'll meet with an accident. Maybe die a hero."

"And if he's a former member?"

Rollie gave the cold grin Horn recalled from their earlier days in the department, when they were street cops. "Then he's ours."

The meeting had run long, and by the time Horn arrived home, Anne was already in bed. He'd undressed quietly, crawled into bed beside her, and listened to her shallow, irregular breathing. Not the deep, rhythmic breathing of sleep. Yet she'd said nothing to him.

"You awake?" he asked softly. Seeing if she'd pretend sleep.

"Yes." She didn't move, lying curled on her side facing away from him.

"Something's wrong."

"Yes. I'm in bed, it's nighttime, and I'm not asleep."

"Something more?"

She sighed and turned over onto her back, staring up at the ceiling in the dim light. "The Vine family's filed suit against the hospital, naming almost everyone involved in their son's operation, including me."

Horn had expected this and been afraid of it. "How'd you learn?"

"Finlay told me."

"He named in the suit?"

"No. And I think the hospital's plan is to contain the damage to Radiology, which means I could be the scapegoat."

"Sounds that way." Being honest. "What do the hospital's attorneys think?"

"They're still studying the charges. The family's already turned down a proposed settlement, and a reasonable one—if there can be such a thing if your four-year-old son's been placed in a vegetative state."

"So the hospital will probably fight it out in court."

"They'd like not to. The publicity would be brutal. And the family's never going to accept. They don't really want money. They want revenge."

"How do you know that?"

"It's what I'd want." The sheets rustled as she half turned on her pillow to face him. "Thomas, I can't help feeling guilty about what happened to that child."

"Sure. But you're *not* guilty of anything."

"I'm in charge of Radiology. It happened on my watch, as the politicians say."

"But what happened to the boy wasn't radiological. The hospital should be able to establish that in court."

"Like you often point out, Thomas, there are no guarantees in court. Anyway, it isn't that I'm afraid of punishment. It might even make me feel better."

"But it wouldn't be fair. It wouldn't be justice."

He could barely see her smile in the dimness. "You've been a cop too long to expect justice. And I've been a cop's wife too long. There's a shelf life to these things."

"Expecting justice, you mean?"

"I mean there's a shelf life. A time comes when hope finally surrenders to apprehension and loneliness."

Horn gave a noncommittal grunt in reply and rolled onto his stomach. Now he was the one afraid of where words might lead, who wanted to feign sleep. Talk was to be feared. It could be a downhill road to catastrophe, where speed increased and there was no turning around.

The silence in the bedroom roared, allowing only troubled dreams.

Neither Joe nor Cindy Vine had slept much last night. Cindy had been crying again, off and on, waking Joe the few times he'd made it to sound sleep. They sat at the tiny gray Formica table in their Lower West Side apartment. Cindy's breakfast was orange juice and black coffee. Joe's was a Bloody Mary. They often argued about which was healthiest. They often argued about everything.

"I'm scared, Joe." Cindy used the back of her hand to wipe orange juice from where it had dribbled on her chin. The hand dropped down to grip the empty glass and hold it tight to the table. He knew it was to keep him from seeing the trembling in her fingers. She would have been an attractive woman if it weren't for the worry on her face, the bags beneath her large brown eyes that were always bruised-looking. And her hair. She did little with her hair these days, the thick and soft brown hair that used to bounce when she walked.

"You're scared of something new every day," Joe said. He was in his early forties, medium height and build but muscular in the white T-shirt he'd slept in. He had on brown slacks and was barefoot. His own hair was short but ragged. It looked as if it needed to be shaped by a barber. "I'm scared, too. For Alan."

"You think I don't care about our son?"

"I didn't say that."

"You meant it."

"Bullshit," Vine said sullenly, staring down at his tomato-juice-stained glass. There was a limp stalk of celery in it that he hadn't touched.

Cindy was too tired this morning to muster a continued offense. "We're taking on one of the biggest hospitals in the city. We maybe shoulda accepted their offer. We're gonna get them pissed off, Joe."

He stared at her and something in his eyes withered her.

"*I'm* pissed off at *them!* They're gonna find out I'm not the kinda guy they want pissed off!"

So much goddamned pride! "We don't have a million dollars to fight a court battle, Joe."

"Our attorney says he'll take payment on a contingency basis. Didn't you hear him?"

"Yeah, but I didn't hear him tell us that if we lose, the court won't say we have to pay the hospital's legal costs. It happens that way sometimes in these lawsuits, Joe. Read the papers. It's on page one when somebody sues a big institution and wins a million dollars. But it's on page nine if they lose and have to pay a quarter of a million in court costs."

"Sigfried says it's okay, we can't get burned." Sigfried was Larry Sigfried, their attorney who'd been recommended by a patients' advocacy group. "Besides, they might come up with a better offer than the first one."

Cindy didn't reply. Joe saw that she had her head bowed and was crying. *Christ! At breakfast!*

He didn't like the feelings of guilt she stirred up in him. She was hurting, as he was, and he was the stronger. He knew he should take care of her, not be furious with her. And that was how it had been in the beginning, when Alan was first diagnosed. They'd shared their trouble, mistakenly thinking it would draw them closer instead of wearing them down. She needed him now more than ever, and he knew it. But Joe Vine was so full of rage! So fucking full of rage!

He stood up suddenly, knocking his chair backward onto the floor, and stalked from the kitchen. Wondering where this train was taking them. To what wilderness? Life was so full of disillusion and sadness and anger, of pain that persisted and hope that dissolved.

He paced to the window and looked out at the sun casting angled patterns on the buildings across the street.

Another goddamn morning. He hated mornings.

They meant he had to bear another day.

16

When Horn walked into the Home Away that morning, Paula and Bickerstaff were already there, occupying the booth where they'd sat before, where private conversations wouldn't be overheard. He wondered how many trysts, confessions, and conspiracies had taken place in the booth over the years.

Horn said good morning then slid into the booth, taking the smooth wooden seat across from the two detectives. Marla came over and placed a cup of coffee before him. Paula and Bickerstaff already had coffee. There was a scattering of crumbs on the table. A plate with a fork on it smeared with egg yellow was in front of Bickerstaff, a smaller plate with half a slice of buttered toast in front of Paula. Marla topped off the coffee then began picking up plates and clearing the table of silverware except for spoons, stacking everything on a tray she'd placed on an adjacent table.

"Toasted corn muffin," Horn told her.

"I know. It's on the grill."

After Marla brought Horn's breakfast, along with a napkin and flatware for him, she considerately went back behind the counter to read a newspaper and wait for another customer. She would pump Horn for information later. He wondered again what her background was, and what had brought her here to the kind of job that sometimes provided escape and anonymity. Hell of a city, Horn thought. Half the people waiting tables were also waiting for a break so they could rise to success as actors, writers, dancers. The other half, if they weren't simply working a job to pay the bills, had never gotten their break, or had been broken themselves.

Horn slathered butter on a muffin half, watching it melt almost immediately and penetrate the toasted surface. "I was paid a visit by a guy named Luke Altman." He glanced up from the muffin at his two companions, who made faces and shrugged to indicate Altman's name hadn't struck a chord.

Between bites, Horn described his meeting with Altman.

"Guy has to be CIA," Bickerstaff said, when Horn was finished talking.

"As much as said so," Paula agreed. "That's as much as you get from them, because a spook never says anything right out. Sounds like your phone call to the number Sayles gave you stirred up something."

"The question is," Horn said, "did what it stir have anything to do with the Night Spider murders?"

"You'll never get the answer from Altman," Paula said. "You'll probably never see him again. CIA spooks are like that. We had one in New Orleans turned out to be watching a potential terrorist. He set up the guy for us, then totally disappeared. We had his man on narcotics possession. Third time. He'll be in jail another twenty years. End of terrorist threat. The CIA let us and the local courts do their work for them."

"Tom Sawyer," Bickerstaff said.

Paula stared at him. Was something going around that kept people from saying things directly?

"You painted the CIA's fence."

"I get it. Twain."

"It happened more than once?"

Horn interrupted before Paula and Bickerstaff got into what he'd come to recognize as another of their frequent dustups that were mostly, but not all, good-natured ribbing. "The CIA and FBI catch a lotta crap from people who don't know what they're talking about. They have their screwups, but they're a helluva lot more effective than some people seem to think. Point being, if Altman is CIA, the possibility the Night Spider's in the military could be bad news for Night Spider."

"Point being," Paula said, "we might just be duplicating their efforts if we don't veer from the military angle and concentrate on the civilian population."

"Just what Altman said," Horn pointed out. "More or less. Also pretty much what Assistant Chief Larkin said, when I met with him last night." He looked at Paula and Bickerstaff, anticipating their questions. "Larkin says we've made a splendid beginning, which means he wishes we were further along."

Paula took a last sip of coffee and made a face. "Everybody's so fucking cryptic."

"It's the times," Bickerstaff said. He craned his neck so he could peer toward the front of the diner, then summoned Marla over from where she was reading her paper.

Ordered a toasted corn muffin.

Monkey see, Paula thought.

After Paula and Bickerstaff had left Horn to another cup of coffee and, they were sure, another muffin as soon as they drove away, Marla sauntered over and topped off Horn's cup.

"Making progress?" she asked.

"We won't know for sure until we know for sure."

"Is that another old cop saying?"

"Yeah. It means we can't know what's valuable until it turns out to be gold."

"Like in life."

Horn grinned. "Very much so."

"Seriously, are you getting anywhere?"

He filled her in, telling her only what he thought she should know. He didn't mention his conversation with Altman.

As he talked, she looked at him in the sunlight that revealed every moment of his age. Still a handsome man, but he was older than she was and married. Yet Marla couldn't deny the attraction that was growing in her. And she knew, in the way the heart sensed these things before the mind, that he was attracted to her. She also knew the attraction shouldn't lead anywhere, should remain—as such feelings usually did—between people who were already attached—sort of low-grade infections of heart and groin, held in check by common sense.

"I asked you about yourself the other day," Horn said, sitting back and relaxing in the booth. "You seemed hesitant to answer."

He can read my mind, the way lovers do. "Still am, I guess."

"Then I'll drop it."

She knew she should turn away and walk back behind the counter, but for some reason she couldn't move. The soles of her shoes might as well have been glued to the floor.

"I was a psychoanalyst in my previous life," she said.

He looked up at her, surprised. "Can I ask why you changed careers?"

"You mean, was it booze or was it drugs?"

"Or sex," he said, playing with her now, letting her know that whatever had brought her down, he wasn't going to judge her.

Giving her a way out.

"Don't get your hopes up," she said with a grin. They were customer and waitress again, trading friendly barbs to pass the time, to show they were buddies.

"Should I call you Dr. Marla?" He was still joking; it was in his eyes.

"It's Dr. Winger," she said. "But just Marla will be fine."

Horn sat staring up at her. *Jesus! She means it!*

Marla gave him a parting grin and made her way back behind the counter, feeling safer there, less vulnerable. She needed the counter as a barrier. *Why did I reveal myself? Who will he tell? There's no going back now . . . no going back . . .*

She looked over; he was still watching her, sipping his coffee. Her face was calm, professionally blank, but her heart was banging and banging away. Her blood was rushing and she felt flushed, felt as if she'd just accepted a dangerous dare. *Why did I open up that way? Why did I confide in him?*

But Marla knew why. It was because she trusted him. It made no sense. It was trust based on emotion and not logic.

Worse still, she realized with a pang that seemed to cleave her heart, he was the only person in this fucked-up world she did trust.

What she feared most, because of where it might take her, where it might leave her, was trust.

17

Bosnia Herzegovina, 1997

Lieutenant Amin Arrnovich lay on top of his sleeping bag in the warm night, his hands cupped over his ears. His sergeant, Kalisovek, would bark an order now and then whenever the firing stopped. And, except for brief moments, it seemed that it never stopped. The chatter and clatter of automatic weapons fire seemed almost constant. Short bursts, but so many of them.

There were no screams.

That's what surprised and disturbed Arrnovich, that there was not a human voice, only the language of guns.

It wasn't that the villagers didn't deserve what they were getting. After all, six members of Arrnovich's unit had been murdered during their sleep the night before only half a mile from here, their throats slit as they slept. There had been no screams then, Arrnovich told himself.

Command had warned of an American strike unit in the countryside, but there was no doubt in his mind it was men from the village who had killed his sleeping and defenseless soldiers. It would take men who knew the terrain to move with such stealth in the dark, then disappear completely. It had to have been the villagers. That was why men of combat age were nowhere to be found. Only women, children, and old men remained in the small village. Forty-three people. Arrnovich personally had carefully counted them. Mustn't leave anyone out.

There must be no witnesses to what he'd been ordered to do.

This afternoon, when Arrnovich had reported to the major what had happened, the reply had been swift. The order had come down through the ranks almost immediately.

The order to do what was happening now beneath the tilted half-moon on this unseasonably warm night.

The villagers had been herded to where a tank with a bulldozer blade had gouged in the earth a five-foot-deep trench. They'd known what was going to happen. They'd also known the inevitability of it. There was no way to escape.

For a moment, one old man with a gray beard seemed to consider bolting for the nearby woods. He caught Arrnovich's eye, then looked down at his worn-out boots and continued walking, his arm strapped tightly around the quaking shoulders of the young girl next to him. His daughter or grand-daughter? Arrnovich hadn't looked closely at the girl's face. He didn't want to remember her.

The shooting stopped.

The abrupt silence seemed to make the night suddenly cooler.

Arrnovich didn't want to be seen like this, lying on his bag rather than facing what he himself had ordered. It was bad enough he'd chosen not to be present. Picking up his rifle and using it as a prop, he dragged himself to his feet.

The bulky form of his sergeant appeared in the night. "It's finished, sir."

Arrnovich knew the only way he could be sure his men would carry out the order was to have the villagers led into the trench. His troops would fire down at the huddled, frightened figures in the dark pit, killing not people, but mere deep shadows that stirred.

"Should we fill in the trench?" the sergeant asked. He was

a large man with a burn-scarred face. His voice was so calm, after what he'd just done, what he'd seen.

"Wait until dawn," Arrnovich told him, "when we can see what we're doing." *But early, so aerial reconnaissance won't be aloft yet and see and photograph what we've done here.* "I'll give the order when the time comes. Post guards near the trench till then, in case . . ."

"Yes, sir. In case some of them are alive and try to crawl out."

"Exactly, Sergeant." *You will someday make a better officer than I.*

The sergeant told him good night, then withdrew.

Arrnovich didn't worry about waking early enough to order the trench filled, then have brush spread over it so it couldn't be spotted from the air. He knew he wouldn't sleep. Tomorrow he'd have to count dead the people he'd counted alive today. He had to make sure every soul was accounted for.

Secrecy demanded it.

In the morning, when a thin layer of light was appearing in the dark sky above a distant line of trees, Arrnovich went to the trench. His eyelids seemed to be lined with sand, and there was a bitter taste in his dry mouth.

Nearby in the dimness loomed the huge form of the tank with the bulldozer blade mounted on it. It seemed to be looking on like some primal and innocent monster from the time of dinosaurs, the time before good and evil and guilt. The guards stood by silently while Arrnovich smoked a cigarette to cover the odor already wafting up from the tangle of corpses. He would wait until it was bright enough to see into the trench before conducting his final count.

In truth, it wasn't as bad as he'd imagined. These were simply lifeless rag dolls, not the enemy, not real people. Not anymore. Dolls carelessly flung.

He moved to the very edge of the trench until the earth might have crumbled beneath his boots, risking falling in with the dolls. He made himself do that.

Then he began to count. It wasn't easy because many of the dolls were intertwined. There was a female holding a younger figure that looked much like her. There was a doll with a gray beard that looked like the old man Arrnovich had cowed into submission with a glare last evening.

There was a wild-haired young woman who was shrouded in dark cloth, as if she'd tightly wound herself in a blanket to ward off the bullets.

Arrnovich counted. . . . *Forty-three, forty-four.*

Hadn't there been forty-three yesterday?

He was sure there had been. He counted again, from another vantage point, even more carefully.

Forty-four.

All right, forty-four. So be it. In such carnage, what did it matter if there was one *more* corpse than anticipated? Certainly everyone left in the village was now in the trench. That was the important thing.

Arrnovich squinted up at the brightening sky. It was going to be a cloudy day, but still the NATO planes would soon appear.

He gave the order to fill in the trench, then lit another cigarette.

The roar and clatter of the tank's engine filled the morning, and the behemoth lurched forward. Its steel blade sliced deep into the sloping pile of dirt. An acrid scent of burning diesel fuel hung in the air. The powerful engine roared louder as Arrnovich tucked his cigarette into the corner of his mouth; he breathed in smoke, breathed it out.

He watched the loose earth tumble into the trench, covering what he had done. It was all deep and dark now, dust into silent dust to become insignificant in the immensity of time.

After today, he would try never to think of it again.

18

Nina Count was here because it was Newsy's day off, insofar as somebody like Newsy ever had a day off.

She goosed the accelerator of her Ford Expedition so the big SUV shot forward and nosed into a parking space about to be backed into by a blue minivan with commercial lettering on its door. The station would have provided her with a car and driver, but Nina preferred to jockey her big, heavy-duty SUV, with its roof rack, winch, and fog lights. It helped her to foster the image of a real, working journalist, not just another TV talking head. Trouble in the boondocks? Nina was ready.

The minivan jerked to a stop, blocking traffic. Horns began blaring, ripping whatever calm silence Manhattan traffic had left of the quiet morning. A bulky, T-shirted man with a dark, seriously receding hairline got out of the minivan and began shouting at Nina, adding to the din. The morning belonged to the city now.

Nina placed her station logo and call letter plaque in the windshield and the man stopped shouting. She extended a nyloned leg, letting it linger, then climbed down from the SUV's seat.

Mr. Receding Hairline saw who she was. It amused her to see his flush of recognition. His anger, his testosterone fit, passed from him before her eyes.

"Nina," he said, almost actually grinning, "you oughta drive more careful. I'd hate to turn on the TV news and not see you."

"Why, how kind of you to say!"

"We watch you—like, the whole family—just about every night."

She smiled, walked over to the flustered man, and apologized for taking his parking space. "Press business," she explained.

He assured her he understood, all the time rooting through his pockets for something she could write on. Finally, he extended a plastic ballpoint pen and a folded bill of lading so she could sign the blank back of the form. *Next time, you get my parking space,* she wrote, then scrawled her name. The guy absolutely loved it. He looked like he was going to have an orgasm.

He was still standing there, oblivious of the angrily blasting car and truck horns, as she strode into the deli where Newsy was waiting for her in a booth by the window. He'd phoned and asked her to meet him there. It always amazed Nina how much business and personal intrigue were talked in New York's delis and coffee shops.

"You handled that neatly," Newsy said, as she sat down opposite him. He'd only been drinking coffee, waiting for her before ordering breakfast.

"I don't usually eat in hellholes like this," she said, glancing around at the crowd pressing against the pastry display case in the warm deli. Men and women in business suits, tourists in denim and polyester, a few teenage kids stopping on their way to school, a couple of worn-down, cheaply dressed women who looked like weary hookers after a hard night, all pressed forward for bagels or Danish and coffee.

"It's not a bad place at lunchtime, when you can sit and listen to conversation. It's surprising what you hear. People let their guard down when they eat. It's like they can't chew and be careful at the same time."

"Sound does carry well here," Nina said, keeping her own voice low. "It's like dining inside a drum. What have you got for me?"

"You want a cup of coffee? Maybe a cheese Danish. They're great. Well, edible, at least."

"I want out of here soon as possible."

Newsy smiled. "Okay, Nina. Here's what leaked my way. Ever hear of Royce Sayles?"

"I take it you don't mean Rolls Royce automobile sales."

"Nope. Sayles helped the cops here solve a series of murders about ten years ago."

"Before my time as a New Yorker," Nina said, thinking anyone in the TV news business who was here ten years ago would be in imminent danger of being fired. "Should I take notes?"

"Naw, I got it all written down for you." Newsy pulled a quarter-folded sheet of paper from his shirt pocket and laid it on the table in front of her. It reminded Nina of the bill of lading she'd signed outside for the minivan driver. "You can read it when you get to the station. I know you're rushed."

"What am I going to read?"

"Ten years ago some fruitcake was killing people with what turned out to be an ice ax. The cops went to Sayles for help in finding the killer because he was a reasonably famous mountain climber."

"There are only a few of those," Nina said.

"Anyway, Sayles ID'd the weapon and helped the law track down the killer, who turned out to be an amateur rock climber." Newsy took a long sip of coffee then placed his foam cup squarely before him. "Where this goes, Nina, is I learned Thomas Horn went to see Sayles a few days ago, spent a lot of time with him."

Nina thought about that. She liked it. "So the police are

consulting a mountain climber again. Makes sense, considering the killer has to be able to climb the sheer faces of buildings to get to his victims' windows."

Newsy leaned forward and spoke softly. "I figured maybe we show some mountaineering equipment, including an ice ax. Gives us an excuse to roll out the old tape on the ten-year-old killings. Juicy stuff, if I remember correctly."

Nina was sure his memory would be accurate, if selective.

"Put something together on it when you come to the station tomorrow," she said.

She stood up. "Thanks, Newsy."

"I thought you might want it on the six o'clock," he said. "If so, I can ride down to the station with you and get huffing."

Nina thought that was a fine idea. "Bring your coffee, but put a lid on it so it doesn't spill all over the upholstery. I've got a pad and pen in the glove compartment. We can write as we drive."

Newsy liked that. News on the go, that was his life. Let the pretty faces and Nina, with her famous gams, do the on-camera work. He knew he was the guts of the station news. News on the go. That was Newsy's dark religion.

After work, Marla walked from the Home Away down to Flicks and rented Hitchcock's *Vertigo*. She'd already seen it several times but it still fascinated her. As a former psychoanalyst, she knew that its science was a bit improbable—the merging of necrophilia with fear of heights—but still it was sound enough.

Marla knew why she liked the movie so. It puzzled her, with its many layers of meaning, its star-crossed promise of love, and its fascination with death.

She had her evening planned. There was a Lean Cuisine in the freezer, which she'd prepare in the microwave in her apartment's tiny kitchen. After dinner she'd settle down in front of the TV, plug in her movie, and switch on the VCR. Bernard Herrmann's hypnotic score would take her away from her cramped, twentieth-floor apartment with its view of an air shaft, and its background noise of cooing and flapping pigeons that couldn't be dislodged from the ledges outside her windows.

When she'd had supper and the movie was over, Marla sat slumped on the sofa and listened to the whir of the rewind. She thought about how much she'd love to have a drink. But she knew she wouldn't. Not ever again, if she could help it.

No, *not ever again!* She *could* help herself. She'd been dry for the last two years.

She got up from the sofa. She went into the kitchen, re-filled her glass of ice water, and got a wedge of lemon to squeeze into it. She plunked the rind into the glass with the cubes and clear liquid. It looked almost like a real drink now, the way the refracted light from the ice cubes played over the curved, clear glass. It looked like a lot of bars and nights that could have gone better, and some that couldn't have gone much worse.

When Marla returned to the living room, *Vertigo* was still rewinding. The counter on the control panel was showing a blur of descending numbers, indicating the machine's breath-less speed.

Marla sat on the sofa and stared at the swift backward flow of numerals, the reversal of tape and time. Cause and effect be-coming effect and cause. Consequences known ahead of time. *If only it could be that easy . . . editing life like editing tape.*

She sipped her water with its faint tang of lemon and thought about bourbon and soda. About Thomas Horn.

All the things she couldn't have.

Horn sat next to Anne in fourth-row-center orchestra, and watched the closing first act number of *Mortgage and Mar-*

riage. Anne seemed to like the elaborately staged musical; Horn figured it would have a brief run. The male lead was miscast and had little voice, preventing the female lead and supporting actors from salvaging the play. The poorly choreographed dance numbers were a waste of wonderful talent, seeming more like exercise classes than Broadway dance numbers. *The reviewers tried to warn us,* Horn thought. The *Time*'s theater critic had been right. It happened.

The dancers in the chorus struck awkward poses while the athletic young man who played the bank's loan officer did a series of back flips across the stage. Then the theater went dark.

Intermission, thank God!

When the houselights came up, Horn stood and stretched. Anne looked over at him and smiled. She *did* like this monstrosity of a musical. So did the people around them, who were talking and laughing and saying how good the first act was. It made Horn wonder. He whispered in Anne's ear, then edged out into the crowded aisle to make his way to the lobby and join the line outside the men's room. Unlike the stage, it was a place where people knew what they were doing.

As he emerged from the auditorium into the cooler air of the carpeted lobby, a man standing near the bar detached himself from the knot of people waiting to order drinks and came toward him.

Horn was astounded to see it was Luke Altman.

"Great first act," Altman said, smiling.

"I've got to think," Horn said, "that you being here is more than coincidence."

"I thought *Breaking the Code* was still playing."

"A spook with a sense of humor."

"Not so unusual. Nothing's funnier than geopolitics." Altman reached into the pocket of his dark blue suitcoat and pulled out a letter-size white envelope. "While I happen to be here enjoying the show, I might as well give you this."

Just as if you didn't follow us here from home or the restaurant.

He handed the envelope to Horn, who accepted it and slid it into the inside pocket of his sport jacket.

"It's a list of names," Altman said. "Former members of that special unit you mentioned during our last conversation."

"Why have you changed your mind?" Horn asked.

Altman shrugged. "Because I did a more detailed check on you, Thomas Horn. You're a very capable fellow. And looking over your record, one can only conclude that you never give up. That even a stake through the heart wouldn't make you give up. Since you'd probably get what you wanted, eventually, we thought we might as well give it to you up front and prevent you from making a lot of waves."

"So you're taking the easiest course."

"Oh, no. You wouldn't want to know the easiest course."

"You said former members."

"Present members needn't concern you. They've already been considered and cleared." He smiled. "These men wouldn't have the time or opportunity to commit civilian crimes."

Horn knew he was probably right.

The lobby lights blinked. Act Two of the debacle was about to begin.

"We'd better get back to our seats," Altman said. "I want to see if the cute young couple gets loan approval from the banker who does back flips."

"I don't look for a happy ending," Horn told him. "At least not one anybody'd believe."

"It's your business to be cynical," Altman said. "In my business we hope for long runs." He turned and strolled toward the carpeted stairs leading to the balcony.

Horn knew this theater; there was a side exit on the landing.

He took what little intermission time was left to continue to the men's room. He found an empty stall and had a preliminary look at Altman's list.

Only nine names. Apparently, the members of this special

unit stayed in the military, or often didn't survive long enough to complete their hitch.

It occurred to Horn that his wasn't necessarily the most dangerous profession.

He was the last one in the theater to return to his seat, just before the houselights died and the curtain rose. He caused quite a stir, trampling toes and asking to be excused over and over.

As the auditorium faded into darkness, he saw Anne glaring and smiling at him simultaneously, as if he were at the same time annoying and amusing.

He ignored her and what was happening onstage and thought back on his conversation with Altman out in the lobby. Altman had a subtle sense of humor you usually didn't find in a spook. Give the bastard that.

And nothing else.

19

Paula noticed a space across the street from the Home Away and didn't have to double-park. Driving Manhattan's narrow streets had proven no problem for her, despite the fact that in New Orleans, once out of the French Quarter, she'd seldom had to worry about both sides of the car.

"You might remark on it," Paula said.

Bickerstaff went all innocent. "Remark on what?"

"My luck at finding parking spaces in this rabbit-warren of a city."

"Oh. Sure. But who needs 'em? Why don't you just double-park all the time like me?"

"So some citizen won't be tugging on my sleeve asking me to move so he can get his car out."

"Yeah, I guess there's something to that. Anyway, I was thinking about other things and didn't notice."

Paula wished he'd think about dropping off his suit at the cleaners. On damp days it was beginning to give off an unpleasant musty smell. "You were thinking about ice fishing, I suppose."

"You're unnecessarily cruel to me, Paula. I was wondering about the list the spook gave Horn. We start trusting information from the CIA, we might be headed off in the wrong direction."

"If you can't trust your government, who can you trust?"

"We both know the answer to that."

Paula dropped the visor showing the car was NYPD so they wouldn't get a ticket. Then she and Bickerstaff got out and crossed the street to the diner that had become their unofficial headquarters since Horn had gotten involved with the case.

Bickerstaff held the door open for her, probably because he thought it would annoy her.

The diner was warm, like the morning outside, and most of the customers eating breakfast were at the counter or tables nearest the door. Paula saw Horn seated in his usual booth, in a small alcove a comfortable distance from the other customers. He had his head down and was reading a folded newspaper, a cup of coffee and his half-eaten breakfast before him on the table. *Damned corn muffins!* Paula knew that because of Horn she was going to try them one of these mornings—animal and vegetable fat, and probably even mineral fat, if there were such a thing, racing straight to her hips.

She had to admit the toasted muffins smelled good, along with the fresh coffee. She and Bickerstaff said hello and slid into the booth to sit opposite Horn.

He set aside his newspaper. Paula saw that he'd been reading a theater review.

He used his forefinger to prop his reading glasses back up on the bridge of his nose. "*Marriage and Mortgage,*" he said. "Stay away from it."

"Amen," Paula said.

"The play," Horn said. "That's what Anne and I saw last night. It was torture."

"What did the spook think of it?" Bickerstaff asked, making Paula wince. How could Bickerstaff be such a good cop and come up with such inane questions?

"The idiot liked it. What do you think that says about him?"

"That he really is CIA," Bickerstaff said.

Marla the waitress came by; Paula ordered coffee and juice, Bickerstaff bacon and eggs. Paula caught the way Marla looked at Horn as she topped off his cup. Probably nothing, but still . . . Marla wasn't all that old, and not bad-looking. And Horn was a handsome guy for his age. Well, a handsome guy, period, if you liked the Cro-Magnon type with brains.

"Here's the list," Horn said, when Marla had drifted back behind the counter. He'd taken folded white slips of paper from his pocket. "I made copies for each of you."

Paula and Bickerstaff accepted their copies and unfolded them. Nine names, with addresses and phone numbers.

"These names are all former members of a secret Special Forces mountain unit that conducted black operations in the war in Afghanistan as well as various other trouble spots around the world. I've already done some preliminary checking. Three of the men are deceased, two are permanently impaired by war wounds, and one is grotesquely overweight. It happens that two of the remaining three live in the New York area. The third lives in Philadelphia, not all that far away. The plan is for you two to split up today and see what you find out about the two in New York. I have connections in Philly and will have that one looked into to see if our guy there rates our continued interest. Each of the slips of paper I gave you has a circled name. Those are the men you drew when I handed out the lists just a moment ago. Look at who and where they are and let me know if there's a problem."

Paula looked. Her circled name was Will Lincoln, with an address in Queens.

"No problem," she said.

"Not here, either," Bickerstaff said.

"This might all be going nowhere," Horn told them, "but be careful with these two guys. We don't want them to know they're being investigated until we learn a little about them.

Check to see if they have priors, maybe talk to some of the neighbors. You're either going to get a solid citizen who's done his duty for his country, or you're going to be stepping into a tiger pit. And you probably won't know the difference until it's too late."

"My guess is we'll be able to eliminate all three of the remaining names," Bickerstaff said.

Paula grinned. "He doesn't trust the CIA."

"I don't trust anyone," Bickerstaff said sadly. "Neither should you, Paula." He glanced out of the corner of his eye and bit off whatever else he was going to say.

Marla with the coffee.

Anne left the bright morning as she walked through a side entrance to Kincaid Memorial Hospital. It was considerably dimmer and cooler inside than out. She strode down a long hall, still under construction, to the spacious and tiled main lobby. It seemed there was always construction going on in Kincaid. Expansion was turning the place into a maze. She wondered how anyone who hadn't learned their way around the hospital ever found anything.

There were several people standing near the circular reception desk; three volunteers were giving out information and validating parking tickets. In the center of the lobby was a fountain. It was behind the bronze nude figures of a man, woman, and child clutching each other's hands that the mayor had tried to have removed a few years before because it was "Too suggestive."

Skirting the flower shop and escalators, Anne went past the main elevators to a Hospital Personnel Only elevator and pressed the Up button. A breast cancer surgeon, Dr. Rebecca Fore, strode past in a neat gray business suit and nodded a good morning to her.

Anne watched the dark-haired, attractive woman, who was about her age, walk away and wondered if she, Anne, should be doing Dr. Fore's kind of work instead of hospital administrative duties. Something that saved people's lives. *I could have gone to medical school. I had the grades. Even, at times, the desire.*

But she knew better. Surgeons were a special breed. A rare combination of arrogance, compassion, and intelligence that translated into artistry with the scalpel. And they didn't wear down in an occupation that would burn out the average person in a few years. Anne knew she was not of that breed.

"Anne Horn?"

She turned to see a heavyset, bearded man in jeans and a black T-shirt lettered GOT METH? She didn't recognize him.

"Yes?"

He smiled almost pityingly; it had been so easy. "This is for you."

And he handed her a subpoena.

Paula drove Bickerstaff back to the precinct house to pick up another unmarked, then went to the squad room and ran checks on Will Lincoln in Queens. Several of the other detectives said hello. Sergeant Crawford brought her a cup of coffee without being asked. But no one inquired about progress on the Night Spider murders. Even if they weren't directly involved in the investigation, they knew how it was going from the way the media were raking the NYPD. They thought Paula might be sensitive about the subject. If they said something she took the wrong way, she might also take their heads off. And of course Thomas Horn was running that show, and no one wanted to cross him by ragging one of his own. Paula thought that might be why nobody'd called her Rambo.

The battered old Dell computer on the corner desk, complete with aged yellow Post-its stuck to the frame of its monitor, gurgled and winked and did its thing. Paula sat forward to be closer to the monitor.

Lincoln turned out to be William Ambrose Lincoln,

thirty-six, married, with two children from an earlier marriage. He'd had no previous trouble with the law. On a whim, Paula fed his name into the Internet.

And hit big.

This was great. The guy had his own Web site. It had to be him, even listed his phone number, and street and e-mail addresses. A business Web site; he wouldn't want to have a potential buyer not be able to locate him.

Interesting site. It turned out Will Lincoln was a sculptor. There was a photograph of him. He was balding but with lots of wavy dark hair around the ears and neck, had strong features, and looked a little like a younger Warren Beatty. And there were photographs of his work. Abstract creations of welded steel. One piece was barely recognizable as a horse. The rest of it was a mystery to Paula. She tried to find something in the tortured, angled metal that suggested sadism and serial murder, but if such a message was there, she couldn't decipher it. Lincoln's work must be good, though, because his Web site included lists and dates of exhibits he'd had around town. There was one now, at a gallery down in the West Village.

A sculptor, Paula thought, leaning back from the computer and taking a sip of the horrible coffee Crawford had brought her. Somebody with imagination and time. And climbing experience. And trained to kill efficiently and silently.

Paula's senses became more alert. *William Lincoln, the more I learn about you, the more intriguing you become.*

"You want some cream for that coffee, Paula?" Crawford was asking.

"No. It might only make it worse."

"I am wounded," Crawford said in a hurt tone.

"Have some coffee. Make it fatal."

Crawford slunk away.

Paula's pulse quickened as she logged off the computer and left the precinct house to drive to the Village.

20

Neva Taylor dreamed.

She was floating in soft liquid but could breathe freely of perfumed, intoxicating air. A lake, she guessed. A very special lake from her childhood, somewhere secret in her memory. It all seemed so normal, as if she were suspended just below the surface at a depth determined by someone nearby. Someone in control.

Someone watching her.

In her dream she turned lazily and saw through the shimmering brightness a face behind a glass pane. Was she in an aquarium like that one in Florida where tourists paid to watch shapely women costumed as mermaids swim underwater? *Stroke* . . . half fish . . . approach the glass . . . *stroke* . . . smile . . . *stroke* . . . half turn, a rhythmic exercise in youth and grace and flirtation, in voyeurism and need. To drift . . . to float . . . Everyone's final dream . . .

The lone face on the other side of the aquarium glass was unclear in the wavering distance, but the eyes were fixed and dark and brilliant and demonic.

Everyone's final dream!

A rasp drawn sharply and roughly over steel woke her.

Her own shrill gasp, as her breath caught like a burr in her throat. Her eyes wide, she lay in late-morning brightness and numbing terror, the recently painted white ceiling close to her like a lid on a box.

Trapped?

Still gasping for breath, she became aware that her fingertips were digging painfully into the mattress. Finger by finger she willed her hands to relax.

Gradually the sunlight blasting through the separation of the drapes overwhelmed her fear. Nothing could happen to her in such a golden wash of light.

Her strained neck ceased to hurt. Her head sank back into her soft pillow and she made herself smile. A dream, a nightmare. That was all she'd experienced. No connection to the real world, unless one chose to believe certain suspect psychics.

Barely moving her head, she let her gaze slide across the reassuring familiarity of her bedroom: her dresser; a glimpse of the opposite wall and plastic light switch in the mirror; her chair, over the back of which the dress she'd removed last night lay draped; the top half of the door frame, white enameled with perfectly mitered wood, form and function and reason neatly joined.

Not a dream but the real world.

Relieved, comforted, she turned her head slightly so she could see the clock radio. *My God, almost ten o'clock! Overslept. Late for work. Not like me! Not at all like me!*

She swiveled her body and sat on the edge of the mattress, her toes sensitive to the coarse texture of the throw rug by the bed. She was tired, as if she'd had a shallow sleep, as if something had disturbed but not quite woken her. It was like some dark dread on the edge of her consciousness. *Father dying; not dying while I slept, only when I woke, but dying all the time until the end.*

Stop it!

She shook off her nameless apprehension and stood up, brushing the palm of one hand over her eyes. *Floor tilting. Slightly dizzy.* The bedroom was too warm, the air stale. The acrid scent of her own perspiration was unpleasant.

Neva walked to the window and threw open the drapes. The sudden assault of full sunlight made her wince. She unlocked the window and raised it about six inches to admit what she hoped would be a morning breeze, but turned out to be a sluggish shifting of warm air. Life, never quite living up to expectations.

As she turned to trudge into the bathroom, she noticed faint, curved scratches on the outside of the upper window and stopped to look at them more closely. They were deep, more like gouges. She didn't think they'd been there before, but she couldn't be sure. They made her think of a giant bird attempting to get in by slashing at the glass with its beak; she couldn't imagine what had really caused them.

Nothing to worry about, she thought. Like the real worry of becoming unemployed if she didn't get to the office and deal with whatever problems awaited. The scratches were on the outside of the glass and didn't go all the way through. Not even worth a mention to the super.

By the time she was standing with her head back and her eyes closed beneath warm needles of water in the shower stall, she forgot all about her indefinable dread and the scratches on her window. Her lithe body swayed; soon she was fully awake. The music of her morning was the soft hiss of the shower and gurgle and trickle of water swirling and racing down the drain.

Her mind played over her ambitions and more practical dreams. She was young, healthy, and beautiful, and, as an old boyfriend used to say of her, "had her shit together."

She'd have put it a different way, but it was true.

Paula parked her unmarked across the street from the New Genesis Gallery in the Village. The gallery didn't look promising from the outside. It was on the ground floor of a crumbling brick building with green double doors that needed paint badly. A sign on one of the doors instructed her to use the other. Near the corner of the building was a show window in which were displayed several paintings and other works, but Paula couldn't see clearly beyond the glass because of the sun glinting off it.

As she watched, a short woman in a dark raincoat emerged from the gallery clutching a brown package. She walked slightly hunched and seemed furtive as she hurried toward the corner.

Paula opened the car door, got out into the heat, and crossed the street. Her feet were hurting today, as if her shoes were too tight. Probably swollen.

The interior of the gallery was a surprise. The walls and ceiling were cream colored, and the floor was a subtle design of dark and worn but clean tiles. Oil paintings, with a few watercolors, hung on the walls. All were renderings of bridges . . . the Brooklyn, the 59th Street (the one Cajun Paula still called the Queensboro), the Golden Gate . . . several Paula didn't recognize, including a couple of covered bridges.

Placed around the gallery were steel sculptures. She recognized some of them from Lincoln's Web site. One she hadn't seen on the Web seemed to represent a woman being crucified. Abstract. Interesting. The figure definitely had breasts.

A door located next to a tall painting of a bridge that disappeared in mist opened and a woman stepped into the gallery. She was dressed in black—surprise. She moved gracefully inside flowing slacks and a sleeveless black blouse. Paula noticed she had nice arms—no cottage cheese—so she must be younger than she appeared. She was a dark-haired woman, attractive, but with seamed, tanned features, as if she'd spent too much time outdoors in a land of blistering sun.

She smiled inquisitively at Paula in the manner of someone about to ask if she can be of help.

Paula started to flash her shield but the woman's hand

darted out and closed on her wrist, freezing her outstretched arm while she studied the badge in its leather folder.

"It's genuine," Paula said.

"I see it is."

"So am I."

"Then you'd be the only one I know." The woman released her grip on Paula's wrist. "I hope you're here about the asshole who keeps spray-painting obscene graffiti on the building."

"No, I'm here about a different asshole."

"Okay," the woman said. "I know plenty of them. I'm Careen Carstair."

"You own the gallery?"

"Part owner. And manager. And buyer. And sometimes seller."

"Everything in here by Lincoln?"

"Just the sculptures."

"How much would this stuff be worth?" Paula motioned with her hand to take in the entire gallery.

"It's worth what it brings on the market. The paintings go from anywhere between a thousand and twenty thousand; the sculptures less because the artist isn't as established. Will Lincoln's still building an audience. That's an interesting accent."

"Cajun. He live in the Village?"

"No. Over in Queens. Will's a straight-arrow family man. Got the wife and kids and house in the 'burbs. I can't believe he's the asshole you're looking for."

"No," Paula said. "But tell me about him. I like his work. Might buy something if it's on a cop's salary."

"Which one do you like?"

"Lady Christ on the cross."

"Why am I not surprised?"

"My palms bleeding?"

Careen smiled. "A cop could afford that piece only if he or she were the wrong kind of cop."

"Known Will long?"

"About three years. This isn't his first exhibit here."

"Can you tell me anything interesting about him?"

"He's self-taught. Been sculpting since he got out of the service, he said."

"Service?"

"Military. I don't know what branch. Works out of a garage studio next to his house. If you're looking for dirt on him, you'll be disappointed. He's about the most normal guy I know in this business of bullshit and ego and, sometimes, talent."

"You think Will has talent?"

"I wouldn't display his work if I didn't."

"That him over there?" Paula pointed to the photo from the Web site. It was framed and mounted on the wall near the door, along with information about the artist.

"That's him. He's better looking in person."

"Really? Does he fool around on that wife of his, trapped in Queens with the little ones?"

"Why? You interested?"

"Maybe," Paula said. "It's that crucifixion piece."

"I wouldn't say Will's kinky," Careen said. She winked. "Or that he isn't."

Paula cocked her head and gave Careen a woman-to-woman look, then lowered her voice. "You know something juicy?"

"Nothing I'd tell a cop."

Paula decided not to push. "Enough about handsome Will and back to business. Have you seen a man around here, might be homeless, the way he's dressed? About sixty, red hair and beard?"

"Does he spray-paint?"

For the next fifteen minutes Paula made a show of asking questions and making notes about her fictitious redheaded man. She wasn't sure if Careen was fooled, but maybe it didn't matter. If Will Lincoln was the Night Spider, maybe a little pressure the other way wouldn't hurt. Maybe it was about time he started worrying about being stepped on.

So nice-guy family-man Will might have a kinky extra-marital sex life. Having done duty in the Quarter in New Orleans, Paula could envision it. Maybe he was into S&M, water sports, or bondage. Or worse.

Much worse.

21

It hadn't taken long for Horn to find out about Rett Jackson, the suspect in Philadelphia.

Horn's source with the Philadelphia police called him back within an hour and told him Jackson had finally fallen victim to an old war wound. The previous year he'd had a steel rod inserted in his spine, as well as a complete knee replacement. All were delayed problems resulting from injuries sustained when the man in front of him stepped on a mine, blowing shrapnel and bone fragments into Jackson's lower body. Horn was informed that Jackson had walked with the aid of a cane since his hospitalization.

Not a climber. Not nimble enough to dangle on a line and use tape and a glass cutter, then silently raise a window and steal into a victim's bedroom without waking her.

So there were only two suspects left on the list Altman gave Horn. It seemed the CIA agent's assurances that the Night Spider was unconnected to the secret Special Forces unit were correct.

Horn was sitting in the leather armchair in his living room contemplating this when the jangle of the phone broke into his thoughts. Not the cell phone, but the landline phone he'd used to talk to his source in Philadelphia. As he lifted the receiver, he wondered how long phones would still have cords in this rapidly changing world.

"This is Nina Count," the caller said, after Horn had identified himself. "Do you remember me, Captain Horn?"

"I wouldn't forget you, Nina. And I see you often on cable news."

"Which is why I'm calling. To ask for confirmation, as you've been good enough to come out of retirement to ramrod the investigation into the Night Spider murders."

"I'm not so sure 'ramrod' is the word." *But close.* "I'm acting in more of an advisory capacity."

"Ah, the official line. You're being modest, Captain Horn." *And you're fishing.* "What is it you want confirmed, Nina?"

"That you've consulted with the famous alpinist Royce Sayles."

"Is 'Alpinist' a real word?"

"I don't know. That's not what I need confirmed."

So full of drive and duplicity, these media types. Nina Count among the worst of them. "I didn't think you'd drop the subject." *And you know the answer or you wouldn't be asking the question.* "Yes, I did consult with Sayles about the Night Spider case. You can say he was helpful."

"Are you making any real progress on the case?" she asked in a confidential tone that meant nothing. "I mean, will you confide in me instead of handing out the usual media bullshit you give the other news hounds?"

"Why would I treat you differently?"

"You like me."

That was true, Horn had to admit to himself. Nina had more daring and imagination than any of her competitors. She'd once crashed one of the mayor's private dinner parties and sent back the wine. Horn thought she would have made a great cop. "I think you're full of more piss and vinegar than the rest of them, Nina. Like a crazy aunt I was fond of as a kid. But you didn't answer my question, and I'm going to be as persistent in asking it as you would."

She laughed. "Okay, nephew. You should treat me differently and confide in me because I'll confide in you. We should work together."

"If you have something to confide and don't, Nina, you might be guilty of concealing evidence of a crime. I wouldn't want to see you get in trouble with the law."

"I don't have anything to confide yet, but I might. And you know us members of the news media, how we don't have to divulge our sources or tip our hands."

Horn thought about this. "Nina, are you planning on being up to something?"

"I am, Captain Horn. And when you see what it is, you'll want to talk with me in the worst way."

"To read you your rights?"

Again the laugh. "I know my rights. Watch my news reports. Tell your friends and relatives. I can always use the ratings."

"Nina, ratings aren't worth your life. This Night Spider psycho is more dangerous than you know."

"You're worried about my safety?"

"You bet I am."

"When you're ready," she said in an amused voice, "let me know and we'll cooperate and nail this sick fuck."

"Nina—"

"Loved talking to you, Captain."

And she hung up and left him with a buzz in his ear.

And a new worry on his mind.

"That was the lawyers," Joe Vine said, hanging up the phone. "The subpoenas have been served."

His wife, Cindy, was wearing her faded red bathrobe and sitting with her knees drawn up in a corner of the sofa. They'd had hamburgers for lunch, and the scent of the fried beef and onions still permeated the apartment. "I wish Alan would get well and come home so none of this was necessary."

"We all wish that," Vine said, irritated. He'd hoped she'd cheer up when she learned the lawsuit was going forward. "Don't you think I wish that?"

"Of course I do. I know you're suffering just like me. But I also think you want revenge."

"Sure, I want them to pay for what they did to Alan. Especially that bitch in charge of the radiology department."

"That's what I mean, Joe. With you it's personal."

"Personal is our son lying in a hospital bed for weeks without moving unless somebody turns him over. Personal is me listening to you grinding your teeth all night while you whimper with bad dreams. And personal is me having to listen to you imply I care more about revenge and money than I do about our son."

"I didn't mean it that way, Joe, and you know it."

"Stop telling me what I know."

She looked away and wrapped her arms tightly around her bent knees, gently rocking back and forth. "I'm afraid for Alan. I'm afraid of what your hate might do to us, Joe. I'm afraid of courts and lawyers. I can't help it, I'm fucking afraid!"

"This might not even get to court. The hospital might try to settle."

"They already tried once."

"Cindy? Stop rocking! You look like a goddamn nutcase!"

She seemed to hear only her own internal rhythm.

"Cindy? Honey? Damnit! Answer me!"

She did, in a mumble he couldn't understand. She was talking more and more like that lately, as if they were speaking underwater and she was drifting away from him.

He leaned closer. "Cindy?"

She mumbled again. It sounded something like "God help us."

* * *

"A subpoena!" Anne cried to Horn that evening as soon as she came home from work. "For Christ's sake, a subpoena!" Stress had clenched her face like a fist. A strand of blond hair stuck out above one ear, while another dangled over her forehead. She slammed the door behind her, shutting out the world beyond the brownstone.

"I've seen them before," Horn said, staying calm, hoping it would be catching. He put the Cuban cigar he'd been contemplating taking outside to smoke back in his pocket, then gently pried the envelope she was waving around from her hand.

He unfolded the document inside, kinked from the pressure of her tense fingers, and scanned it.

"Court date's not for two months," he said, handing the subpoena back to her. "Give yourself some time to think about this, Anne. Plenty of things can happen over two months."

"Such as?"

"A settlement."

"You don't seem to understand that I, the radiology department, the ER personnel, the hospital, have done *nothing wrong!*"

"I do understand. I'm usually the one trying to reassure you of that. Remember, you were telling me the other day about how guilty you felt."

She gave him a weary, disdainful look, then turned her back on him and trudged up the stairs, moving like an arthritic.

"Feeling and knowing are two different things," she said without looking back.

They are, Horn thought. *They surely are.*

He took the cigar back out of his pocket and went outside to smoke and walk, and think.

22

Saint Will.

Paula had spent the rest of the day talking to people in Will Lincoln's neighborhood. Everyone, from Lincoln's barber to the patrons of a corner tavern, Minnie's Place, where he sometimes stopped in for a drink, held a positive view of Lincoln. A sweet-natured, friendly kind of guy, they all said. A regular guy, despite the odd way he had of turning a dollar, buying and collecting scrap metal, worthless junk, and welding it into art.

It wasn't until Paula talked to a Mrs. Dorothy Neidler, who lived in a small clapboard house directly across the street from Lincoln's similar house, that a sour note was struck.

"C'mon in," Mrs. Neidler said, when finally convinced Paula was a genuine NYPD detective and wanted to chat about Lincoln. Paula had the feeling that Lincoln was one of her favorite things to talk about.

The living room looked like a worn-out, badly designed set from a fifties sitcom. Tables and chairs were blond *moderne* and included a kidney-shaped coffee table. The blue sofa and chairs matched each other but nothing else, though

Paula guessed they went okay with the sculpted gray wall-to-wall carpet. Clear plastic still covered the shades of the matching lamps on the matching tables on each side of the sofa. In a corner, near some red drapes, sat a blond console TV with a black ceramic panther on it. The panther was actually a planter that featured plastic flowers and a night-light. Paula wondered, where was the basket chair?

Dorothy Neidler was in her seventies and thin, hunched, bitter, and gray. There were short vertical slash marks above her upper lip that looked like old scars from when someone had sewn her mouth shut. When she moved she left in the air a cloying wake of perfume that didn't quite disguise a sharp medicinal scent.

As soon as Paula had seated herself on the stiff blue sofa, Mrs. Neidler offered her a glass of lemonade. Paula accepted and five minutes later was not at all surprised to find the lemonade almost too sour to drink. But she did drink it, sipping cautiously and not making a face. She said nothing, knowing from experience when to wait. It was obvious that a tale or two bounded around in the older woman's mind, itching to escape to a sympathetic ear. That ear would be Paula's, if she could be patient.

Mrs. Neidler trained faded blue eyes on her.

Paula smiled. Sipped.

"So somebody figured it out," Mrs. Neidler said.

"Only partly," Paula said, playing along, thinking maybe she was dealing with the neighborhood witch, a busybody with too much imagination.

But Mrs. Neidler seemed reasonably normal. She had no overt symptoms of being a neurotic or an irrational gossip, simply a gossip. Her clouded eyes seemed permanently pained and narrowed by what might have been a lifetime of disappointments, but Paula had seen the same look on a lot of older people. It was as if they were bewildered and bitter from having glanced in the mirror one day and noticing that somehow they'd suddenly aged. *Will I have that look?*

Mrs. Neidler shifted about in her stiff blue chair.

Paula sipped silently, knowing the pump was primed.

"Well, maybe I can enlighten you on the other part," Mrs. Neidler said.

Paula leaned forward, not overdoing it. *Sip. Look interested.*

"Those two are having trouble."

"Uh-huh," Paula said. *Sip. Don't pucker!*

"I guess you people know what kind of trouble."

"Some of it, yes." Paula got out her leather-bound notepad and a yellow stub of a number-two pencil. Waited.

"I think he leaves the kids alone."

"That's how we figure it," Paula said, pretending to take notes. Mrs. Neidler was talking for the record now.

"But I've seen the bruises on Kim."

Paula remembered Lincoln's wife was named Kim. "Have you ever actually seen him strike his wife?"

"Are you from South Carolina?" Mrs. Neidler abruptly asked.

"No. Louisiana. Cajun country."

Mrs. Neidler squinted and stared at her as if she'd mentioned one of the other planets. "The men there . . . are they of a violent nature?"

"Some. Like anywhere else, I suppose. You were telling me you thought there might be some domestic violence in the Lincoln home."

"I've seen movement behind their blinds. Silhouettes. I can read that kind of body language, even in shadow. Violence, I'm sure, Officer . . ."

"'Paula' will be fine." Paula smiled and worked the blunt point of the pencil.

"Paula, I'm no stranger to domestic abuse."

"Too many women aren't."

"I've seen poor Kim at the grocery or drugstore without bruises. Then I've heard her and that husband of hers shouting at each other, even from across the street. I could never make out the words, but I recognize the sounds. There's no mistaking them." Mrs. Neidler dabbed at a blue eye that had teared up. "The next day I'd see Kim again. She thinks she covers the marks with makeup, but another woman, one with experience, can see behind the makeup."

"Have you ever asked her about any of this?"

Mrs. Neidler shook her head violently. "Not my place."

Paula thought of differing with her, then changed her mind. "But you've never seen him harm the children?" Two of them, Paula recalled. Girls ages seven and ten.

"Never. But that doesn't mean he hasn't. Go and talk to their teachers. They might tell you. Teachers can tell, even though they're afraid to speak up sometimes." Mrs. Neidler shook her head again and clucked her tongue. "Everybody's suing everybody these days. Have you noticed?"

"Hard not to," Paula said.

"Some teachers'd talk, though."

"School's out for the summer," Paula reminded her.

"Ah, I forgot. Old people do forget."

"They remember, too," Paula said.

"Those two girls, cute as buttons, are away at camp, come to think of it. They're always at one camp or another during the summers. Some people see camps as full-time baby-sitters, have you noticed?"

"I have."

"And that Will Lincoln keeps odd hours. Works late in that garage art studio of his. Lots of times banging away on metal: bangedy, bangedy, bang! Got no close neighbors on either side of his house. I'm the closest one, so I've gotta put up with the noise. Bangedy, bangedy!"

Paula leaned sideways and glanced out the living room's picture window. Mrs. Neidler had a view up the driveway of the modest house across the street. Most of the detached garage, gray clapboard like the house, was visible, including a garage window.

"I see the light on in that garage till all hours. And sometimes I'm up at night—old people don't sleep well, you know. I see him leave the garage, must be by some back way. He sneaks down the driveway past that old eyesore truck of his, to where he leaves his car parked on the street. Then drives away quiet like."

Oh, boy! "About what time of night does he do this?"

"Early morning, really. I'd say about one or two o'clock. Sometimes even later."

"And what time does he return?"

"Various times. Mostly he's gone more'n an hour, though. Ask me, I'd say he's seeing some other woman. Be good if he left Kim, beat up on the other one. She'd be the one that deserves it."

Paula was getting some idea of what had happened to Mrs. Neidler long ago. "Does Lincoln work in his garage every night?"

"Most every one. Sometimes he's in there during the day, but almost always at night."

"Do you think he might go out there to get away from Kim? Feeling guilty, maybe?"

"Haw! Not feeling guilty. Not that one. That one's not at all how everybody sees him." She gingerly touched the pink scalp below her sparse gray hair, as if caressing an old injury. "They never are."

"They?"

"The ones that mistreat women."

"You're right about that," Paula said. "Do you have much contact with Will Lincoln? Do you two ever talk?"

"Not hardly anymore. He saw me looking out the window at him one night about two in the morning. Began treating me cool after that. Not that we were ever chummy. Kim, though, she's not like him. She's still nice as pie to me."

Paula looked up from the notes she was taking. "Do you think you're in any physical danger, Mrs. Neidler?"

"Not hardly. Not with my late second husband's twelve-gauge shotgun in the house. I was Portland County ladies' skeet shooting champion two years running. That was some time back, though."

"And you keep the shotgun nearby?"

"Nearby and loaded."

Uh-oh . . . Paula showed no reaction but made a note of that.

"Tell you what," she said to Mrs. Neidler. "I'm going to give you one of my cards. Call me if you see anything else suspicious. Anything at all. Don't mention our conversation. And if you happen to see me around in the neighborhood, don't let on we're friends."

"Count on me, Paula. I know how the police work."

Paula leaned forward and placed her business card and half-finished tumbler of lemonade on the glass-topped coffee table. She stood up and slid her notepad into her purse. "If you see a strange car parked near here with someone in it, that'll probably be me or another detective."

"Uh-huh. A stakeout. Watching Lincoln's house."

"And yours, too. For protection. Just in case, whether you need it or not." She edged toward the door. Mrs. Neidler seemed reluctant to stand up and show her out. Obviously not enough people were good listeners and she wasn't eager for Paula to leave.

"Please don't get up," Paula said.

But when Paula was almost at the door, Mrs. Neidler wrested herself up from her chair and plodded over to usher her out.

Paula stepped outside onto the porch. It was almost dusk and had cooled into the seventies. The darkening sky had the look of being hazed by smoke, but she could see or smell nothing suggesting a fire.

"You be careful, Paula," Mrs. Neidler cautioned.

"I always am," Paula assured her, glancing back at Mrs. Neidler through the screen door. "Skeet shooting," she said to the aged form in the shadow of the dark screen. "That's marvelous."

"Ladies' champion," Mrs. Neidler said. "Two years running. Some time back, though."

"Still . . ." Paula said, stepping down off the porch.

"Still," Mrs. Neidler said behind her.

* * *

Paula sat in the unmarked, which was half a block down from Will Lincoln's gray house with its green metal awnings, and waited for him to leave. It had grown dark, and lights were on in the house. Paula drove to the end of the block once and did a turnaround, checking the garage. Its single, dark window seemed to peer back at her blankly. There was a rusty old Dodge pickup truck with a low front tire in the driveway: the eyesore Mrs. Neidler had mentioned. The truck seemed not to have moved since Paula had first seen it that afternoon. It looked as if it might not be able to move.

She returned to her parking space, which was midway between two streetlights and in the shadow of a big maple tree. Today she'd brought along a plastic portable device that enabled her to relieve her bladder without leaving the car. She'd never shown this valuable accessory to Bickerstaff, who usually availed himself of concealing foliage or dark passageways. There was no need for such a thing when they ran stakeouts together, and he would wait and watch while she found a public rest room. Such a gentleman.

She'd had to use the portable potty only once tonight, squirming to gain proper position in the car, then congratulating herself on her neatness, when a man emerged from the Lincoln house.

Paula hastily rearranged her clothes and got comfortable again behind the steering wheel, glancing at the luminous hands of her wristwatch. Almost ten o'clock.

She was too far away to recognize Lincoln for sure from his photograph, but the man's height and weight looked about right, and he'd come out of Lincoln's house. He also walked past the pickup truck, on down the driveway, and got into a ratty-looking twelve-year-old Pontiac, tan with a black cloth roof, that was parked near the house. Figuring the decrepit pickup truck wasn't regular transportation, Paula had already checked the license plates of the cars on the street. Like the truck, the rusty old Pontiac was registered to Will Lincoln.

The old car needed exhaust work. It growled loudly when it started, then popped and rattled like a machine gun when it pulled away from the curb. Paula followed in the unmarked. She thought that if this guy was smart, he'd trade both his clunkers in on one reliable vehicle that wasn't a tetanus risk. But the Pontiac quieted down to a steady roar when it got up to speed.

Lincoln didn't drive very far, only about five blocks to Minnie's Place, the neighborhood bar Paula had checked out earlier. She hoped no one in there would mention to Lincoln that she'd been around asking about him. There was a chance they wouldn't. Probably there'd be a different bartender on duty by now and mostly different patrons. And contrary to TV, movies, and popular fiction, lots of citizens actually didn't mind helping the police.

Some citizens, anyway.

Minnie's must not have been crowded, because Lincoln found a parking space almost in front of the entrance. Paula parallel-parked between a van and a compact pickup truck and watched him climb out of the old Pontiac and enter Minnie's.

When he crossed a patch of bright light beneath the bar's illuminated sign, Paula got a good look at him for the first time and knew for sure she'd been following the right man. Dark hair with a bald spot, slim, muscular build, long neck and jaw. There was an arm-swinging swagger in his stride that was a challenge. *Try me. I'm easy to provoke.*

Paula considered going into Minnie's and unobtrusively watching Lincoln, then thought better of the idea. Maybe it would work if she knew the place was packed with drinkers who'd provide some cover. As it was, she figured her wisest course was to stay in the car and wait for Lincoln to come back out.

She settled low in the seat and listened to salsa on the factory-installed radio. The evening was warm, so she

cranked down the unmarked's front windows. The back of
her neck rested against the lowered, padded headrest. She
half closed her eyes, slipping into stakeout mode. Though
she wouldn't sleep, she'd still rest, and a part of her mind
would be alert to the comings and goings at Minnie's Place.

Minnie—if there was a Minnie—must do all right.
Somebody entered or left the bar every five minutes or so.
Mostly men, but a few women. Paula wondered if someone
was making book in there. Or dealing drugs.

Time passed, and more time. Paula, thinking about
Lincoln in there drinking all that draft beer (Budweiser, the
day bartender had informed her), used the portable potty
again. It was getting full and she was beginning to worry.

She'd barely finished and put the contraption aside when
three customers staggered out of Minnie's and charted an
unsteady course toward the unmarked. When they got near,
Paula saw that they all looked like teenagers and were undoubtedly underage. *Minnie, Minnie . . .* At least the boys
weren't driving. They snickered and hesitated near the car.
One of them, wearing a black T-shirt with red lettering that
said *Pervert,* leaned down and asked if Paula was a working
girl. She said she sure was and flashed her badge. The boys
hurried away. She kept an eye on them in the rearview mirror, making sure they really were on foot and not simply
parked farther down the street.

When she looked back, the battered tan Pontiac was
pulling away from the curb.

Paula hurriedly started the unmarked and followed, raising the windows and switching on the air conditioner as she
drove.

Lincoln retraced his earlier drive and returned home,
parking in exactly the same spot he'd left. He climbed out of
the Pontiac and strode up his driveway, moving with the
same confident swagger and walking as if he'd consumed
nothing alcoholic.

Paula waited a few minutes, then drove slowly past the

house. When she glanced up the driveway, she saw there was now a light on in the garage.

She looked at her watch. Almost midnight. Lincoln kept odd hours, as Mrs. Neidler said. Mrs. Neidler, who might well be watching her.

Paula knew what she had to do now. She parked in the shadow of the maple tree again, killed the engine, opened the windows to the cooling night air, and settled in for what she knew might be a long time.

She made it till 3:00 A.M. before deciding she was simply too tired to maintain the stakeout.

When she drove past Lincoln's driveway, she saw that the light in the garage was still burning. With the car's windows down, she could hear the faint, rhythmic banging of metal on metal wafting from the garage. *Bangedy-bangedy-bang!*

It was much the same the next few nights when Paula kept a loose tail on Lincoln. Days were no problem; he seemed to sleep through them. And Paula got a good look at Kim Lincoln as she followed her to the grocery store one afternoon. She got within two feet of her as she shopped. Kim was a slightly overweight woman with drab brown hair and defeated eyes. There were what looked like strawberry birthmarks on her right forearm. No signs of bruises, though. Paula could tell the difference and wondered if Mrs. Neidler could.

Every night Paula watched. Instead of being in bed with his wife, he would simply drive around, or drink beer at Minnie's, then spend long hours in his garage studio shaping and welding hard metal.

Paula thought it was something, what people did for love, hate, and art.

23

Neva was having her dream again, the one where she was gently swaddled and drifting warmly through a dark void. Floating, turning, turning . . . Someone, something, touching her lightly, caressingly. *Prenatal memory . . ?*

I must be waking up, to wonder that . . .

And she couldn't breathe!

She quickly sucked in air through her nose, her sleep-fogged mind whirling before she realized something had been clamped over her mouth. She was lying on her back. Awake!

Her eyes flew open and she tried to sit straight up in bed.

Her head and upper back rose a few inches off the mattress, straining her stomach muscles, and she flopped back down.

She couldn't move! Not her arms or legs or even her fingers, which were pressed firmly to her thighs!

Cold fear closed tightly around her. She was wrapped in fear.

There was a movement of air across her face, and she realized the window must be open. She was sure she'd closed it, since the night was warm and the air-conditioning was working. Again she tried to move, tried to call out. She could only emit a muffled moan, and her internal silent screams built an unbearable pressure that swelled painfully in her throat and lungs.

A faint noise. The floor creaked softly. Something dark, huge, and spindly moved in the dimness. Neva had read the papers, watched TV news. She knew now what was happening. *She knew!*

The cold paralysis of fear turned to horror, then panic. Neva's lithe, powerful body, shrouded tightly in her bedsheets, stiffened and began to vibrate.

The thing in her room moved swiftly around a chair and came toward her. The mattress sagged; bedsprings sang. Neva opened her eyes wide and tried to crane her neck to see but could make out only a large, shadowy form at the foot of the bed. Fear caused her to lose control, and a wet warmth spread rapidly inside the taut sheets. Humiliation touched on her terror.

Then there was weight on her. Heavy, but she could breathe.

Dark eyes stared into hers, reflecting what faint light was in the room. The eyes fixed her in a gaze that oddly mixed compassion with cruelty. Neva and her attacker were alone now, was the unmistakable message in the unblinking stare. Only the two of them in the world. Everything was under complete control, but not hers. Certainly not hers. No one to help or hear or care. She was trapped, held suspended and motionless, while around her time and events continued to flow. No longer did any of it have anything to do with her. For her, everything had been decided. It was now pointless to hope.

Nothing of mercy in those eyes.

Hoarse, ragged breathing.

The real pain began . . .

When Paula swerved the unmarked toward the curb to park across the street from the Home Away the next morning, she saw Horn standing outside, motioning with his long arms.

Paula realized he wanted her and Bickerstaff to stay in the car. She eased closer to the curb but left the engine idling as Horn timed the traffic and jogged across the street toward them. Running pretty well for a retired guy, she thought.

Paula lowered the window, letting warm morning air tumble in.

"We've got another Spider murder," Horn said. "Weldon Tower on the East Side, last night. We hurry, we'll be early on the scene."

Bickerstaff stretched out an arm to unlock the car's streetside back door, and Horn slid into the car. Paula checked the outside mirror for traffic, then tromped the accelerator and they were away. "Use the siren?" she asked.

"Too early," Horn said. "It'll give me a headache."

"I've already got one," Bickerstaff said.

"Just drive like hell," Horn said.

The car swerved and slowed, and then abruptly shot forward around a van that was trying to turn a corner. A ballpoint pen tucked beneath the passenger-side visor slid out and bounced off the dashboard. Bickerstaff grabbed for it but missed, and it fell to the floor. He didn't try to retrieve it.

"You look rough this morning, Paula," Horn said from the backseat. He'd been observing her reflection in the rearview mirror and noticed the bags under her eyes.

"Stakeout till late," she explained, taking a corner too fast and ignoring a pedestrian in a business suit who'd had to skid to a sudden stop in his wing tips. She didn't let up as they flashed past a line of parked cars. There was a ticking sound, as if they'd nicked somebody's outside mirror. *Look rough, huh? Let's see if I can get the guy in the backseat to pray.*

"Maybe it'll pay off," Horn told her, sounding as excited as if he were sitting in that big leather chair of his.

"For God's sake!" Bickerstaff said. "Slow down, Paula! This isn't a suicide run!"

Some satisfaction.

* * *

The Night Spider had returned. He couldn't stay away. He wanted to see Thomas Horn, the man the beautiful Nina Count obviously worshipped. She'd predicted it wouldn't be long before Horn would rid the city of the Night Spider. Inevitably, Nina said, Horn would locate this malicious and dangerous psychotic and stamp the useless life out of him.

Dangerous is the operative word, the Night Spider had felt like telling her. Had even contemplated calling the TV station and *actually* telling her.

But mightn't that be precisely what she wanted? Ratings. Television personalities fed on ratings and didn't seem to care where they came from or how. Nina Count, Nina Cunt, was no exception. Nina, with her long legs and pithy insults. As if she understood him in the slightest.

Everyone was a psychologist these days. Everyone knew from a mere few facts what everyone else was thinking, as if people could be read like books of simple prose. *Psychoanalysis for Dummies*.

He replayed in his mind part of last night's Nina Count newscast. *A mental case like most serial killers . . . sick individual . . . pathetic subhuman . . . afraid of women . . . afraid of* her!

Not likely, thought the Night Spider.

He was *not* like most serial killers.

Nor was he afraid of Thomas Horn.

As Paula turned the corner of Neva Taylor's block, she had to hit the brakes hard to keep from running up the back of a white Saturn sedan with a dented trunk, which was moving slower than the rest of the traffic.

"Idiot!" Bickerstaff said. "Kinda asshole causes accidents."

"Too bad we're not Traffic, we could ticket him," Paula said, forcing herself to be patient.

She saw two police cruisers angled in at the curb in front of the building and steered toward them. There was a uniformed cop keeping people from gathering near the entrance, but a knot of onlookers stood about fifty feet down the sidewalk, talking and pointing and wondering what was happening.

"Looks like the public just caught on to this one," Bickerstaff said. "Media vultures will be here next. Nina Count."

Horn paused getting out of the car. "Why Nina Count in particular?" Horn asked.

Bickerstaff looked surprised. "You must not have caught the news last night. She went off on a riff, got all emotional, put you on a pedestal, and then called the Night Spider every insulting thing she could think of but larva."

"Taunting him," Horn said.

"And how. And it looks like she's trying to set up a *mano a mano* showdown."

Horn smiled. "That would be nice."

"Any way we can arrest the dumb bitch?"

"That would be nice," Horn said again.

"Maybe it's really possible," Paula suggested. "She's interfering in a homicide investigation."

"And half the TV audience in New York watches and sympathizes with her," Horn said.

"Try and get her fired," Bickerstaff said to Paula, "and she'll get a couple hundred e-mail marriage proposals and you'll be eating doughnuts in the Bronx."

"Let's go meet the victim," Horn said. "Do our job and let Nina worry about hers."

"Maybe we can get there before Harry Potter," Paula said, working the door handle and climbing out of the car. Both men looked at her quizzically but said nothing. Paula could be a puzzle.

The Weldon Tower rose over forty floors above its phony Greek Revival lower facade. It had a glass entrance so darkly tinted it was a mirror, a doorman who looked like a general in the army of some small country more given to ceremony than war, and bulky concrete planters that held a variety of colorful blooms, none of which grew taller than six inches. The wide sidewalk in front of the building was wet; it had been hosed off recently, probably before the more important business upstairs was discovered.

As the doorman pulled open one of the mirrored glass panels for them, Horn hesitated. "You two go on," he said to Paula and Bickerstaff. "I'll stay down here for a while and scan whoever shows up."

Bickerstaff knew what he meant. Sometimes when a crime scene was fresh, the perp couldn't resist becoming one of the spectators. There could be an irresistible temptation for such a sicko to return and see what he had wrought. And maybe he'd do something to attract suspicion or give himself away. Bickerstaff recalled stories about a pyromaniac who was apprehended while having an orgasm at the scene of a fire he'd set. Wasn't sure if he believed them, but he'd heard them.

As Bickerstaff and Paula entered the building, Horn moved away and tried to look unlike a cop. He buttoned his suitcoat so the breeze wouldn't flap it open and make visible his holstered revolver. Usually he wore the gun in a belt holster at the small of his back, but he didn't like sitting in a wooden booth or riding in a car with it that way. Not only was it uncomfortable, but he didn't like the remote prospect of the gun firing accidentally and shooting off the end of his spine.

An ambulance showed up, without lights or siren, braked sharply, then angled backward into the curb. Then came the ME, who parked directly in front of the entrance and placed a MEDICAL EXAMINER placard in his windshield, just in case anybody might not know there was a homicide in the building.

Horn looked away from the ME in case he might be recognized and greeted. Then he sauntered along the sidewalk, farther away from the entrance, wishing he had an attaché case like most of the executive types striding past. Maybe he could play the tourist. It occurred to him there might be something that looked like a camera, or maybe even a real camera, in the unmarked.

As he strolled casually toward the car, he saw that a

crowd had gathered on the opposite side of the street. Traffic was slowing down as it passed the building: gawkers on foot and on wheels.

Might need a uniform out here to move things along.

Horn was ten feet away from the car when he noticed a white Saturn sedan with a dented trunk easing along the opposite curb. The car Paula had to brake for to avoid hitting. *At least its second time around the block.* The driver was alone in the Saturn, wearing a baseball cap pulled low on his forehead. Though it was a warm morning he had his shirt collar turned up so only a small part of his face was visible.

But it was when he glanced over at Horn that there was a definite reaction. Dark eyes beneath the cap's bill widened then focused sharply. Horn actually felt a chill.

This could mean nothing, he told himself, deliberately not changing pace as he strode toward the car. The Saturn driver might simply be a guy on his way to work who couldn't tear himself away from breaking news. *But there was recognition in those eyes. Fear and hate.* So maybe it was someone who recognized Horn, someone he'd helped put away. More than two decades in Horn's job and you had enemies.

He should reach the unmarked about the time the Saturn got to the intersection, then he'd get into the car casually, in case he was being observed in a rearview mirror. He'd watch carefully to see if the Saturn turned the corner.

Don't rush . . . Walk slowly, slowly . . . Should be time to catch up and follow . . .

And he was at the unmarked, fumbling for the door handle while he observed the Saturn from the corner of his vision.

The handle slipped from his grip, bending back a fingernail.

The car was locked, and Paula had the keys.

He saw me!

The Night Spider fought the impulse to tromp on the Saturn's accelerator and screech away, try to outrun trouble.

But he knew that wouldn't help. He might have been seen, and, undeniably, something had passed between him and Horn, whom he'd immediately recognized from seeing all those photos Nina Cunt had featured on her nightly newscast that was almost completely about Horn. And about the Night Spider. *What she said about me! What she called me!*

A check in the rearview mirror, without the slightest head movement, revealed Horn trying to open the door of a parked car. No doubt it was an unmarked police car.

The Saturn was at the intersection. The Night Spider waited a few seconds for a cab to get out of the way, then made a right turn. Just before the street scene behind slid from the mirror, he was sure he saw Horn's head tilt slightly. *Watching to see which way I turn!*

Traffic was heavy in this direction, too. A bedlam of sun-warmed steel that yearned to roar and run. Blaring horns, frustrated shouting. Noise and exhaust fumes. *Goddamn city's a madhouse!*

The Night Spider eased the Saturn into the faster lane, which, in Manhattan, meant traffic moving forward in twenty-foot increments instead of ten.

Horn has the same kind of traffic! Won't use the light or siren!

Another lurch forward. Halfway down the block now. *Heart hasn't pounded this hard in years!*

Horn decided to follow on foot. Traffic was slow enough he should be able to catch up with the bogged-down Saturn. At least get close enough to see a license plate number.

He began running in the direction the Saturn had gone, not making very good time in his expensive black dress shoes, not made for speed. Leather soles. As Horn veered around a woman pushing a wire cart stuffed full of plastic grocery bags, he skidded and almost fell.

"Excuse you!" the woman shouted after him.

Horn ignored her and gained speed, lengthening his stride, starting to feel a stitch of pain in his right side.

Old retired fucker, thinking you can still sprint . . .

He kept his gaze fixed on the intersection where the Saturn had turned.

The Night Spider moved his hand to blast the horn, then thought better of it. He didn't want to call attention to himself.

Why the hell aren't we moving?

The little Saturn sat still, hemmed in by a delivery truck on the left, a cab behind, and a dust-covered Lincoln ahead. Exhaust fumes from the Lincoln shimmied in the heat then disappeared like ghosts in front of the Saturn's white hood. The seconds the traffic had been at a dead stop seemed like minutes!

Don't panic. Horn's sitting in the same traffic, blocks behind me.

The Lincoln's brake lights went dark, its rear end dropped about six inches, and the big car shot forward.

Only to come to a halt again less than twenty feet down the street.

The Night Spider thought about edging around it, but there was no room. Not without going up on the sidewalk, which wouldn't take him very far, as crowded as they were with people still heading for work. Kill about a dozen, then the car would come up against mass, would be stopped, and they'd be on him.

Don't panic. Horn's sitting in the same tra—

Or is he?

The Night Spider hadn't actually seen Horn get into the car, only stand by the door. He might have noticed how slow the traffic was because of the gawkers near the Weldon Tower. The Nina Cunt was right that the man wasn't stupid. He might have made his calculations, then decided he had a better chance of catching up with the Saturn on foot.

Might be running now like an aging football back, shoul-

ders hunched, head down, knocking people aside, making time . . . gaining ground!

Traffic was inching ahead again. The Night Spider veered the car slightly so its right front wheel was only a foot from the curb, then braked to a halt near a NO PARKING sign, obstructing traffic.

He switched off the engine, slid over the console to the passenger seat, then scrambled out the right-hand door onto the sidewalk.

"Hey, asshole!" the cabbie yelled behind him. "You gonna leave that there?"

The Night Spider ignored him and joined the throng of pedestrians striding past the stopped traffic. He sped up, but not too much. Just enough so that he was surrounded by people who'd been ahead of the white Saturn when he'd exited it.

Then he turned into the entrance to a used-books store.

Familiar musty smell. Only a few other customers.

He made his way to an aisle where he was alone. *Poetry, Self-Help, Inspirational.* With a quick glance around, he removed his flesh-colored latex gloves and stuffed them in a pocket. After counting to ten, he went back outside to the hot, crowded sidewalk.

No one seemed to be paying the slightest attention to him. Traffic still hadn't moved enough that the cars he'd left stuck behind the Saturn had caught up. Behind him, from up the street, he heard horns honking but couldn't be sure if it was because of the obstacle he'd left in the stream of traffic.

He sensed the tempo and walked faster, feeling safer. Still some danger, though. *Wonderful!*

Immersed in the hurried parade of flawed humanity, he blended. He walked toward the intersection at the same speed as other pedestrians. Turn this corner, then another, and he'd be lost in the crowded mad maze of the city.

* * *

Horn was almost winded. He was about to stop and bend over with his hands on his knees, when he saw the knot of people ahead and caught a glimpse of white fender.

He drew a deep breath and continued at a fast but unsteady walk, feeling his heart hammering as he wondered what Anne would think if he arrived on a gurney at Kincaid Memorial Emergency.

The white Saturn was parked in a traffic lane.

People were standing around staring at it, their hands on their hips, as if it might gain a mind of its own and move. Traffic had built up behind the Saturn, but drivers were grudgingly giving enough ground to let blocked cars get around the illegally parked vehicle.

When Horn reached the car, he paused for a few seconds while he tried to catch his breath, waiting for the ache in his side to let up. Then he flashed his shield and asked everyone to move on and not touch the Saturn. He used his cell phone to call in the plate number.

When the phone chirped ten minutes later, he was told the car was registered to C. Collins, address not far away on the East Side.

Horn didn't even put the phone back in his pocket. He stood there holding it, his chest still heaving as his lungs worked to pull in oxygen. He knew what was coming next.

And it came. Another ten minutes and the cell phone chirped again.

The Saturn's owner, an exotic dancer named Christina Collins, had slept late and hadn't even realized her car was stolen until the police knocked on her door and gave her the bad news. She was terribly upset, Horn was told. She wondered if she'd ever get her car back.

Eventually she'd get it back, Horn thought. And he was sure nothing about it would be different. Not even new fingerprints.

He wondered if he'd ever get his breath back.

24

Horn looked in on the late Neva Taylor and found the now-familiar scene of sadism and death.

Despite the horror on her immobile pale features, it was obvious that Taylor had been a beautiful woman. This was, Horn noted, the first victim with red hair. The killer was continuing what might be a deliberate variation in the types of his victims.

"Same sad story," said the assistant ME, a woman with short blond hair and a wattled neck.

"Was she a natural redhead?" Horn asked.

She leaned close and examined the roots of Taylor's splayed red hair. "What you see's the real thing. And in case you're wondering, pubic hair isn't the best way to judge. Sometimes it isn't the same color as natural hair on the head."

"I wasn't wondering."

The woman smiled at him. "No, I guess you weren't." In a more businesslike tone, she said, "At least thirty stab wounds in this one, skillfully applied to prolong suffering before death."

"Look like the same weapon?"

The woman nodded. "A long, thin blade, very sharp. Plenty of bleeding, but gradual and absorbed by the sheets and mattress. Not the bloody river you'd ordinarily get with that many wounds."

"Must have been a helluva way to die."

"There had to be a lot of pain. But then, that's what the shit-head who's doing these murders is all about, isn't it? Inflicting pain? Torture?"

"That's exactly what he's all about."

"He's good at it."

Horn walked over and examined the open window. There was the expertly removed crescent of glass dangling on a strip of masking tape. The unlocked brass window latch. No noticeable marks on the sill. No blood on the floor. Nothing to suggest the killer had been in the room, except for the corpse on the bed.

A camera flash sent miniature lightning through the room. A police photographer documenting everything visual about the crime scene.

"Smile," he said, as he approached the victim and squinted through the viewfinder.

Nobody did, especially not Neva Taylor.

The woman from the medical examiner's office moved back to give the photographer room. "It's like a spider crawled into the building, immobilized her, and slowly drained her of life," she said to Horn. She must have been reading the papers. "You think this sick asshole really thinks he's a spider?"

"He seems to identify with them."

"I don't see how anybody could identify with bugs," the photographer said, going about his business of launching one flash after another. Zeus with a Minolta.

"I don't see how anybody could ask a corpse to smile," Horn said.

The photographer grinned at him around the camera. "Yes, you do. You've got it harder than I do. You have to look at this kind of stuff without the emotional distance a lens gives you."

"A photographer-philosopher," the ME said, not as if she were kidding but was actually surprised to hear such wisdom from the lips of a guy who shot pictures of crime scenes.

The photographer jokingly aimed his camera at her and she quickly turned her head.

"Your sidekicks are up on the roof," she said, finding herself facing Horn.

"I figured."

"Our kind of job," the photographer said. "There's no place to go but up."

"Unless I throw you out a window," Horn told him.

It was windy on the roof of the Weldon Tower, but it felt pretty good on such a warm day. The city was a vista of beautifully sunlit buildings softened by late morning shadow. It all looked antiseptically clean from here, and not as if anything of horror would be happening behind the thousands of windows.

"You almost need a jacket up here," Paula said.

Horn didn't think so, but he didn't disagree with her.

"We got pretty much what we expected here," Bickerstaff said. He pointed to an adjacent building about thirty feet away. "Looks like that's where he came from. We'll do the usual checking with that building's doorman and tenants."

And probably come up with nothing, Horn thought.

"There's marks from a grappling hook of some kind on the base of that antenna," Bickerstaff continued, "and the roof's surface indicates some activity almost but not directly over the victim's bedroom window. Looks like our guy came down the outside wall between the rows of windows so he wouldn't be seen, then swung or walked himself over about five feet to center on Taylor's window."

"No fresh hole in the brickwork," Paula said, "but we think he wrapped a line around that vent pipe, since it was right where he wanted it."

Horn walked over and stooped down to examine the four-inch pipe protruding from the roof. There was a circular mark on it, maybe a slight indentation, that looked fairly new. Paula was probably right in her assessment.

"How do you figure he detaches the lines when he goes back to the other rooftops?" she asked.

"Sayles told me there are grappling hooks, even knots, that can be detached by whipping or snapping the rope or cable."

"Nifty," Bickerstaff said. "Must take practice."

"And training," Horn said. "That our guy is an expert climber is about the only thing that narrows our search."

"And that he gets in and out so clean," Paula said. "Even a good B-and-E artist leaves a scuff mark or clue here or there. Other than a couple of indistinct footprints, we've been given nothing of much substance to work with."

"Will Lincoln has the skill set," Bickerstaff pointed out.

"And an alibi," Paula said. "Me. I've practically been living with the guy. Last night he knocked down some beers at a bar in Queens, then went into his garage studio and worked until about three in the morning. I saw him pass the lighted window now and then, and I saw him leave the garage and go into his house when he was finished working."

"And let me guess," Horn said. "The ME says the victim died sometime before three o'clock this morning."

"That's it," Paula said. "Closer to midnight. Will Lincoln didn't do Neva Taylor."

"Unless he found a way to leave his garage and return without you knowing it," Bickerstaff said.

"I don't think it was possible," Paula said. "Besides, I'm sure he didn't know I was out there watching him almost all night."

"So Altman was playing straight with us when he gave us the list," Horn said.

Bickerstaff stuffed his hands deep in his pockets, cool on the roof like Paula. "It's almost enough to make you trust the Feds."

"I think I saw him down in the street," Horn said.

Bickerstaff looked at him. "Altman?"

"The Night Spider."

Horn had their attention, judging by the way their jaws dropped.

He told them about the dark-eyed man in the white Saturn, his pursuit of the car, and the chase's ultimate unsatisfactory conclusion.

"Jesus!" Bickerstaff said. "Maybe there'll be prints in the car."

"I'd be surprised if he didn't wear gloves to steal cars the way he does for his ritual killings."

"Clean," Paula said. "He operates so damned clean."

"That's the thing about him," Horn said, admiring Paula's knack for homing in on what was pertinent. And for not shooting off her mouth, holding her thoughts till they were ripe. She was impressing him more and more.

Bickerstaff, still with his hands jammed in his pockets, looked around at the skyline and distant river. "It's peaceful up here."

"Which is why we're leaving," Horn said.

"Like nothing bad could ever happen in this city. But we know better. Hey, Paula?"

"Uh-huh." *Do we ever!*

While Paula and Bickerstaff were still supervising or doing legwork on the Neva Taylor murder, Horn went home and used his desk phone in his den to call Anne at the hospital. She seemed calmer now about the lawsuit, but there was still an edginess to her that bothered Horn. He suspected what it might be but didn't know how to make sure, or even if he could do anything about it if he were sure.

Hard years had taught him hard lessons. One of them was

that the damage to cops' wives was sometimes cumulative, building up over time until the women simply had had enough. Then, usually, they would walk. Maybe they'd wait for the kids to leave home, or for this or that to be resolved, but at a certain time they went. Horn couldn't think of any cop's marriage that had broken up that way and that had been made right. It was as if something inside these patient, long-suffering women snapped and couldn't be repaired.

Horn never thought it could happen to Anne. She seemed to have learned to accommodate his profession—the waiting, the worrying, and the upside-down priorities, and coming in second to dates with drug dealers, rapists, and killers. And she wasn't a wife who sat around and fretted constantly about him; she had a profession of her own, a life of her own, outside their marriage.

No, not outside it. Not completely. He knew that the conflicts and pressures of her job, especially since the Alan Vine tragedy, had always been a part of their marriage. They'd always shared. Everything. *Maybe that was a mistake.*

"The trouble with relationships these days," a grizzled desk sergeant Horn knew often said, "is that there's too much communication." He'd gone on to describe the things he'd done without his wife's knowledge and that he knew she'd done, supposedly without his.

He never seemed to be kidding. Horn knew now that maybe he hadn't been. The sergeant retired two years ago and was living in Mexico with his wife of forty-two years.

And here was Horn, on the job again.

Like Anne, damn it! He had the right!

Mentally setting personal problems aside, still not knowing exactly how he felt about them or what to do, he wandered into the kitchen. Comfort food would help, and he was genuinely hungry anyway.

He saw the blur of rain on the kitchen's dark windowpane and could hear the steady drip of water from a nearby downspout. Lightning briefly illuminated the view of the small garden Anne liked to call a courtyard, and a few seconds later distant thunder rumbled. A summer storm. Airborne gloom. Just what he needed to improve his glum mood.

Using meat loaf take-home from the last restaurant meal he and Anne had shared, he found some cracked wheat bread, got ketchup from the refrigerator, and built a thick sandwich. Then he located a bottle of Heineken dark in the refrigerator and opened it. He got a beer glass down from a cabinet, sat at the table, and ate, listening to the rain and what had become a metallic drumbeat from the downspout.

When he was finished with the sandwich but not the beer, he carried the half-full glass into his den and sat down at the antique oak desk Anne had gotten for his birthday ten years before. He couldn't hear the rain from here. Good. He searched his Rolodex. Nina Count should still be at the station, and he knew she'd talk to him. Knew she was probably expecting him to call.

"Captain Horn!" She sounded overjoyed to hear his voice. "You have something to tell me."

"Not that you'd want to hear, Nina."

"C'mon, Horn, we're old friends."

"I've got a pretty good idea what you're trying to do."

"Of course, and you appreciate it. I'm trying to flush out your suspect for you. And I will. Just give me a little time."

He considered telling her about his encounter with the driver of the stolen Saturn earlier that day but decided it would only whet her appetite for danger and ratings. Besides, she'd find out eventually anyway, being Nina.

"My contacts in the NYPD tell me I've already had some success," she said. "You were involved in a dramatic chase this morning. With a little luck, you would have apprehended the Night Spider. It'll be on tonight's eleven o'clock news."

Christ! She was something! "Good. I'll be able to learn all about it. "

"I'm not completely unselfish about this, Horn. If I'm

successful at what I'm attempting, I get viewers and you get the killer. So we both win. You should be grateful for what I'm doing."

"I would be, if flushing out the killer was all you're trying to do. You're taunting this murderous psychopath, Nina. If He's the Night Spider, you're offering yourself as a juicy fly."

"My God! I never thought of that!"

"Bullshit, Nina."

"Yeah, I suppose so."

"If you'd seen what was left of his flies, you wouldn't be doing this." But he knew better; if she weren't a brash and competitive newswoman she'd probably be a trapeze artist or in some other occupation where you could work without a net.

"I understand the risk," Nina said. "And I really am doing this partly for you. And to get this murderous head case off the street."

"Whatever you learn that's pertinent, Nina, I want to know it almost as soon as you do."

"Of course. The minute anything happens I'll give you a buzz."

He wasn't sure if she was putting him on, so he held his silence. It was obvious that nothing he could say would change her mind anyway.

"Are you worried about me, Horn?"

"Yes," he said honestly. "And pissed off that you're making my job more difficult."

"How exactly am I making it more difficult?"

"I told you I was worried. I meant it."

"Why, Horn! If you weren't married I'd be intensely interested."

"Playful doesn't become you, Nina. And I'm too old for you. Too beat up. And too sane."

He hung up, burdened by the sad knowledge that what he'd said was true.

Something else not to think about while he finished his beer.

But he found the beer flat and too warm to drink. It left a bitter aftertaste.

He closed the office door so smoke wouldn't filter into the rest of the brownstone, then sat back down and got an illegal Cuban cigar from the humidor on his desk. After preparing the cigar, using a cutter fashioned after a miniature guillotine, he fired it up with the lighter he kept in the desk's top drawer. A cigar that cost what this one did, it burned smoothly and drew well immediately.

As he leaned back in his padded chair and smoked, it occurred to him that the problems in his life, the many unanswered questions, were beginning to hinder and entangle him more and more.

Like a web.

25

The doorbell late that night made Horn sit forward in his chair, then snuff out his cigar in the glass ashtray on the desk.

He left his comfortable den and trod through the hall to the foyer. For a moment he wished he were still carrying his service revolver. His uneasiness surprised him, even though circumstances were certainly conducive to apprehension. Not like him, after so many years of doing what he must despite fear that was sometimes terror. Maybe the Night Spider case was getting to him. And this *was* like something out of a mystery novel—a late hour of a stormy night, alone in the house, a stranger knocks on the door.

Rings the bell.

The rain might have stopped.

And how do you know it's a stranger?

Horn put his hand on the doorknob and peered through one of the leaded glass windows. It was still raining. And his caller was a stranger.

He opened the door to a tall, broad-shouldered man in a dark raincoat. He was standing partly in shadow and wearing some kind of cap like a delivery man's, its cloth top covered by clear plastic to protect it from moisture.

"Captain Thomas Horn?" the man asked with a smile. He had wide cheekbones, a hawk nose, and a broad, aggressive chin.

Horn confirmed he was who the man was seeking, his body poised, his gut telling him something was wrong here.

"I'm Colonel Victor Kray."

Horn stared at the man. He didn't recognize him. Didn't believe he was NYPD.

"United States Army," the man added, perhaps understanding Horn's confusion.

"Ah!" Horn said. "Come in, please!" He stepped back, offering his left hand, which the colonel shook. If he really was a colonel. Horn kept his right hand ready to knot into a fist.

Once in the foyer, Kray unbuttoned his long raincoat, and Horn saw the uniform, which featured an impressive array of medals on the colonel's chest. The colonel removed his garrison cap to reveal a head of iron gray hair, short and combed down in something like bangs that were high on his forehead. If Julius Caesar didn't look like this guy, he should have.

"I thought we might discuss a list someone gave you," Kray said, as Horn was hanging his wet coat on a hook. A musty, woolly odor wafted from the coat.

"Do you smoke cigars, Colonel Kray?"

"Only when I have something to celebrate."

"Do you drink scotch?"

Kray smiled. "More often than I smoke cigars."

Horn invited the colonel into his den, got him settled in an armchair near the desk, then poured two glasses of eighteen-year-old Glenlivet over ice, which he got from the small refrigerator that was concealed inside a cabinet just for that purpose.

Colonel Kray sat, sipped, and looked longingly at Horn's dead cigar propped in the ashtray. "Maybe I will," he said.

Horn supplied him with a cigar and, when it was burning, relit his own. He didn't mention that the cigars were Cuban and illegal, not knowing quite how a military man would feel about that.

Kray puffed on the cigar and took another sip of scotch. "The pleasures of civilian life," he said.

"You can smoke and drink in the army."

"Not in a well-furnished den like this one. You're a successful man, Captain Horn. Not just a lucky one."

"That, too," Horn said.

Kray fixed him with a steady stare that was, in itself, a reason for promotion. "What I do now in my duties wouldn't interest you, Captain Horn. But you might find what I used to do important. I've been following the Night Spider murders, mostly through the *New York Times* on-line and Fox cable news. I struggled with the decision to come here but from the beginning knew I had no real choice. I think I might be able to help you."

"I could use it," Horn said, sipping his scotch and watching Kray, admiring his charisma and mannerisms of command that only years in the military could provide.

"In the armed forces of this country there is something called the SSF or Secret Special Forces. Its specialty is fighting in urban settings and mountainous terrain; the two have more in common than many people think. Its purpose is to undertake dangerous missions that must remain top secret whether they succeed or fail. These are brave men, Captain Horn, who can turn the suicidal into the doable, and who are ready to pay the supreme price of death in combat. They're never captured. We don't kid ourselves that some people can't be made to talk."

"*We?*"

"I helped to train these men," Kray said. "And I've led them in battle. They can do what your Night Spider does. There is no vertical surface they can't negotiate, and they know how to come and go secretly and kill silently."

"Our killer works silently enough that he doesn't wake

his victims until it's too late for them. There's never any sign of a struggle."

Kray smiled. "I'd be surprised if there were. The men I'm talking about are amazingly gentle and adept, as well as deadly. They're trained to kill enemy troops while they sleep, one after another. And with this killer you're chasing, the delicacy might be part of the thrill, the ritual, having them sleep as long as possible, then awaken already trussed up and helpless. Or almost. Certainly beyond escaping. He'd be ready to clamp tape over their mouths the instant their eyes opened. That might be what awakens many of them, the tape abruptly altering their breathing."

"Like a nightmare," Horn said.

"Oh, I think it is a fairly common nightmare. For women, anyway."

"How can he be sure they're asleep before entering their apartments?"

"Probably by observing them from outside their windows with a night scope or infrared glasses."

"So he can see in the dark," Horn said, "like a real spider."

"And your killer's a nocturnal predator, like a real spider. Or like a former SSF trooper."

Horn regarded Kray curiously. The colonel had to know what he was wondering.

"I took a chance coming here," Kray went on. "I'm going to have to trust you."

"Why?" Horn asked.

"SSF troopers are the most skilled secret assassins in the world, but after they've served, and after psychological readjustment, they become—almost to a man—fine citizens in the military or in civilian life. But the fact is, one of the reasons I'm here is that I feel partly responsible for having aided in creating such capable killers."

"You said *almost* to a man."

Kray smiled again, sadly, as if he might break into MacArthur's "Old Soldiers" farewell speech. "Nothing's perfect, Captain Horn. That's why the SSF exists. I'd like to think I can depend on you to keep what I'm about to reveal confidential, but I realize the risk; at some point you might have no choice but to pass on the information and its source."

About to reveal? "I can promise you I'll try to maintain confidentiality, Colonel."

"I can't ask for more."

"It's obvious you think one of your SSF troopers might not have adapted well in his return to civilian life."

"I have to admit it's possible."

"Do you have a particular man in mind?"

"No. I'm going to leave that up to you. I'm a soldier, not a detective or criminologist." He reached into a side pocket of his uniform coat and brought out a folded sheet of white typing paper. "I'm going to give you this list of names; all are former SSF troopers."

Perfect, Horn thought. Another list.

"Those in present service don't have the opportunity to commit such crimes."

Horn had heard that sentiment before. It was probably true.

"I'm going to place the list on your desk, then finish my scotch and leave. I'm asking that you forget I was here, or how these names came to your attention."

"Agreed," Horn said.

Kray stood up, squarely aligned the list on a corner of the desk, then tossed down the rest of his drink. "There's no need to show me out." He smiled. "I'll finish the excellent cigar on the street. Cuban, isn't it?"

"Cuban," Horn confirmed.

He thought Kray might do a smart about-face, but the colonel simply turned around in normal fashion, tucking his cap under his arm, and strode from the den.

Shortly thereafter Horn heard the front door open and close.

He walked to the foyer and saw that Kray's coat was gone from its hook. There was only a puddle on the floor beneath where it had been draped to indicate the colonel had ever been there.

Horn went back into the den and picked up the list from the desk. Kray might have no idea that Altman had already contacted the police. These names might be duplicates of the ones on Altman's list.

But they weren't.

Horn didn't recognize any of the names.

He stood thinking. A lot of things were possible. The SSF units might be organized in cells, unaware of each other's existence in order to retain strict secrecy. Or the names supplied by Altman might be cutoff names to deflect any investigation into the unit. If that was the case, Altman might not even be aware of it. Why would the federal government trust Altman?

Because if he was CIA, Altman was *the government.*

Either way, Altman the spook wasn't supplying as much information and cooperation as he pretended.

Horn decided not to inform him of Kray's list and a secret unit beyond the one revealed by Altman and the military.

He placed the list in his desk drawer, then glanced at his watch. 10:30 P.M. Anne was running some kind of late-shift efficiency study and wouldn't be home for several hours.

Horn decided to hell with today and went to bed.

There was no shortage of concerns to keep him from sleep. This morning they had run out of suspects, and now they had a list of too many suspects, all of which probably wouldn't pan out. Demonstrable progress on the case had stalled, another woman had joined the grisly parade of victims, and Nina Count was trying to force a showdown by publicly taunting the killer. Horn thought he could expect another call from Assistant Chief Larkin. And probably, before very long, another murder. It was a bewildering deluge of dread.

He fell asleep worrying about whether Anne would smell cigar smoke from when Kray walked through the ground floor of the brownstone and out into the night.

Kray, who had never been there.

Rainy nights depressed Paula and put her on edge. She was exhausted but knew she couldn't sleep, so she hadn't gone to bed. She'd gotten home late, managing to step in a puddle just outside her building, and scarfed down a deli Chinese dinner she'd picked up on the way. Now she had indigestion, one foot still felt wet despite the fact that she'd taken off her shoes and dried it, and she suspected she might be nurturing an ulcer.

The Job. Was she an idiot to continue doing this for a living? Why did a monster who crept through bedroom windows and tortured and killed women have to be her personal responsibility? What would it be like to keep regular hours? Have a circle of friends who weren't intimate with the darker side of life? Not carry a gun?

What would it be like to have a date?

Sitting on the sofa with her bare feet propped up on the coffee table, she studied her lower extremities. Ankles puffed from too many hours on her feet. Toenails trimmed short and threatening to become ingrown and painful. She could only dream of pedicures, elegant pink toes beneath her black cop's shoes.

Fuck it!

She made the effort to reach out and get a hand around the half-drunk can of beer she'd left on the table. On the TV screen that flickered beyond her tortured feet, a promo for an upcoming movie had ended with a matchstick-thin former model, wearing skintight bicycle shorts, standing and waving triumphantly on the rocky plateau of some mountain even the Night Spider couldn't climb. *Sure.* Cut to lots of quick shots, a montage of one ludicrously smiling face after another, between snaps of fires, murder scenes, and traffic accidents. The eleven o'clock news was coming on.

Leaning back, Paula took a pull of beer, then with her free hand picked up the remote and pressed the volume button so the sound she'd muted would return.

There was a flawlessly coifed Nina Count looking glamorous and serious as the camera moved in on her icy perfection. Her elegant hands were folded before her, bejeweled and beautifully manicured.

"More trouble in the Middle East," Nina said. "Today a Palestinian . . ."

Paula figured the woman probably had pedicured feet that would drive a fetishist wild.

"In local news—"

Paula began paying attention again.

"—serial-killer-hunter NYPD captain Thomas Horn came close to apprehending the murderous psychopath that is the Night Spider. In a dramatic morning chase on Manhattan's East Side . . ."

Paula sat listening to the news anchor's account of Horn's desperate attempt to catch up with the man who might have been the Night Spider.

Nina Count embellished the story so Horn seemed almost a mythical nemesis of the killer, as if it were just the two of them—Horn and the Night Spider—in deadly macho combat. At the same time, the haughty blond anchorwoman made disparaging remarks about the killer, using terms like *sick*, *pathetic*, *sexually stunted*, *cowardly*, *full of doubt and self-hatred* . . .

Paula wondered, what about *psychotic*, *skillful*, and *lethal*?

It wasn't much of a surprise to Paula that a canny newswoman like Nina Count would have the police contacts to learn so quickly about Horn's pursuit of the Night Spider. And ratings being essential to TV news, Paula wasn't shocked to hear Nina trying to develop a story line with recognizable and fascinating characters like Horn and the Night Spider. Viewers would soon become addicts of her nightly installments of the part-soap opera and part-mystery playing out among them in their own city. Never mind that to the people directly involved, it was a tragedy.

But this wasn't the first time television and tabloid news had trivialized terror, torture, and death.

What bothered Paula was how Nina Count talked directly and insultingly, even tauntingly, *to* the Night Spider, the camera in close on her model-like made-up features. Paula understood the message in those challenging blue eyes, the red lips and pink tongue sensuously wrapping themselves around every degrading remark.

Does Horn know what Nina Count is up to?

Tape of a derailed train somewhere was playing now, helicopter shots of angled and stacked boxcars in a wooded area.

Paula pressed the Off button on the remote, leaned back, and closed her eyes.

Horn and Bickerstaff were men. Would they fully realize what was going on with Nina Count? Where she wanted it to lead?

She wasn't sure about Bickerstaff, but Horn might have a chance. The more she saw of Horn, the more she understood how he'd gained the respect of some of the most cynical and brutally practical men on the planet.

And women. We're—I'm—not immune to cynicism. The things we learn about ourselves! The things we don't want to know . . .

Paula finished her beer and placed the empty can on top of a *Newseek* on the coffee table. Finally tired, she slid sideways to curl on the sofa; her bare feet were pressed together and burrowed beneath a cushion for warmth.

She knew she should get up before she dozed off, but she was so comfortable she decided to stay where she was. Nights like this had become almost routine. Around 3:00 A.M. she'd wake up enough to rise and stumble into her bedroom, crawl gratefully into bed, and sleep till the alarm woke her.

That process was preferable to getting up now, brushing her teeth and undressing, and lying in bed for hours before sleep came. She actually got more rest this way.

Experience had taught her. What she learned from experience helped her to survive, while the knowledge of increasing odds against her gradually sank into her consciousness. Would she learn fast enough to continue staying sane and living through the stress and dangers of her work, what she used to think of as her calling?

It was a race between what she learned and the risks encountered in her job.

And every day, in ways large and small and often unrecognizable, she bet her life on it.

26

Arkansas, 1978

They were leaving. He'd thought they never would, but now they were going.

Twelve-year-old Aaron Mandle could hear them from where he lay almost naked in the dark closet. He'd be out soon, away from the closeness and the smell and the heat and the sticky sweat. And the spiders.

He wasn't sure if he wanted to be out. Aaron understood what was with him in the closet and it never surprised him. That was what he was afraid of most—surprises. Bad ones. At least he was safe here from what he didn't know about. From what confused and terrified him.

If only it wasn't so hot in here!

He tried to blink away the sweat stinging the corners of his eyes, which only made them burn more.

"The small and the crawl shall inherit the earth." His mother's voice. "The weak and the small, the things that fly and crawl, the beak and the talon and pincer and claw."

The words were familiar to Aaron, always in his mind to

be heard if he listened, or to come to him unbidden, no matter what he was doing wherever he was. Walking in the woods, studying in school those few days he attended, fishing in the muddy lake for bluegill, lying in bed late at night in his room and listening to the cicadas crying to each other over what seemed like miles beyond his open window . . . *The beak and the talon and pincer and claw . . .*

"The weak shall inherit," came a man's answering voice, then a woman's saying the same words, as if reciting from a book.

Aaron had never completely understood about his mother and her friends, the congregation. Religion. God. And his mother used to have something to do with snakes. Before what she called her awakening. Now it was bugs. Spiders. Religion was one of the things that confused Aaron, what it made people think and do.

"Dust," said the man's voice.

"Dust unto dust," said a woman.

"No, I mean there's a car comin'."

"You watch out for yourself, Betheen," said the woman's voice. "'Specially now."

"Like I always do," said Aaron's mother.

Faintly, away from the heat and the darkness, the screen door slammed. Even muffled like that, it was a sound Aaron knew. The last of the congregation leaving. The people that got loud and talked and sang together like one person, that got so excited on the other side of the closet door they took to screaming things Aaron couldn't understand. Tongues, his mother called it. The talking in tongues. He wondered if, when he got old enough, he would understand.

Aaron waited, but his mother didn't come to open the closet door. He heard her moving around out there, but she didn't come for him.

He ignored the spiders on his leg and right arm, and lay still, listening. The spiders were still as well, as if they knew what he was thinking, what he wanted.

The screen door slammed again.

"Gonna be Master Sergeant Oakland Mandle, address Germany!" said his father's excited voice.

His father! What was he doing home? He shouldn't have been here for two more days. *When he drove the old station wagon home from what he called "the base" for the weekend.*

"What're you tryin' to tell me, Oakland?" Aaron's mother.

"That I got the transfer. Gonna be stationed at the base near Mannheim, Germany. Motor Pool command." His father sounded proud. "So ain't you happy?"

It took a while for Aaron's mother to answer. "I would say not."

His father's heavy footfalls on the plank floor. "We talked about this, Betheen. You knew I was gonna ask for a transfer."

"We talked like we always talk."

"There's no reason you won't like it in Germany." His father was beginning to get mad. Aaron could always tell. He wished he could stop them both from talking to each other, right now, so they wouldn't fight.

"I can't leave here, Oakland." His mother's voice was different, too. Higher, like when she talked to her flock. Or like those times when she didn't love Aaron. "I know now that here's where I belong. In this country. Here. With my congregation."

"What're you tryin' to tell me, Betheen? That you don't belong with your husband?"

"That I'm not goin' to Germany."

"The fuck you ain't!"

"And there'll be no blasphemy in this house."

"This cracker-barrel piece of shit ain't gonna be our house much longer. It's all been arranged by Uncle Sam. Gonna have new quarters in Germany."

"Then you'll live there alone."

"You're comin', Betheen. An' those loonies you call your congregation can go to hell."

"We're in hell, Oakland."

"The fuck's that s'pose to mean?"

"We're in hell but not forever. The weak and the small, the claw and the—"

"Shut the fuck up with that nonsense! Good Jesus! I don't know why I ever put up with it! I'm the one oughta be the fuckin' saint in this house."

"I know what *I* have to do, Oakland. What's my command and my duty. You see, you're not the only one who receives orders and messages. I have my own orders and I must follow."

"Follow who? What kinda messages an' who from?"

"There's legions of the Lord. I'm among those spoken to."

"Sometimes you scare me, Betheen, the crazy way you talk."

Aaron moved closer to the door so he could hear better and because his elbow was getting sore from leaning on it on the hard floor. He must have made a sound.

"That Aaron? You lock the boy in that closet again?"

"Not Aaron, no. Not our son."

"Sweet Jesus! You tellin' me Aaron's not mine? Is that what all this goddamn nonsense is about?"

"I warned you about blasphemy in a holy place."

"You're mixed up in the head, woman."

"I warned you for sure!"

"Havin' one of your spells, is what. This ramshackle dump ain't holy, an' neither are you."

"The web and the law command the chosen."

"Ha! Now ain't *that* some shit?"

"The web and the law. Didn't I warn? Didn't I?"

The floor creaked outside the closet door. There was another small, faint sound.

Something stirred in Aaron, some cold knowledge before fact. Something he didn't want to know.

"Betheen! You damned fool!"

"Not damned, Oakland."

"Best put down that shotgun 'fore I take it away from you."

"Take it away from me an' what, Oakland?" Aaron's mother sounded calm now, but there was still something scary about the way she was talking. "An' you'll do *what?*"

"I'll shove it up your fat ass, is what!"

The roar of the shotgun made Aaron's ears hurt even in the closet.

He jumped to his feet as if his thoughts had yanked him up, and he hammered on the door with his fists. "Out! Let me out!" His voice sounded so small after the gunshot, as if the world must be deaf around him. *The small and the crawl shall inherit . . .*

The closet door opened and light broke in. His mother stepped back, cradling the shotgun as if it were a baby. Her face was hers, only it was like a mask.

There was his father on the floor, one of his arms twisted behind him, his chest all red. Aaron saw white bone, like smooth, polished stone.

He became aware of someone screaming.

He was screaming. It was his own voice he heard!

"You come here to me, Aaron!" His mother. Loud. As if he'd done something wrong and was being called to task.

He shook his head, backing away but staying clear of the closet.

"I know who you are," she said, and swung the long shotgun so it was aimed square at him. "Don't you think I don't know you."

He ran and slammed into the screen door. Bumped into it again and it flew open. And he was on the plank porch and down the three wood steps and running.

The shotgun roared again and he felt a rush of buckshot pass close over his head like a storm.

Glancing back, he saw his mother aim the shotgun again, then toss it aside. Both shells in the double-barrel gun had been fired. Empty-handed now, she came toward Aaron, her steps clumsy and long, her face still a mask. His mother but not his mother.

"I know who you are!" she screamed again. "The dark devil's eye! The secret, sinful issue of the other!"

Aaron didn't take time trying to figure out what she meant. He sprinted hard for the woods.

But she took an angle to cut him off, so he doubled back and ran around to the rear of the house. High grass and brush grabbed at his ankles, trying to slow him down. He'd run like this in his worst dreams, when he'd come awake sweating and trembling. *Is this a nightmare?*

More woods before him now, then mountainside.

And the old barn that was about to fall but never did and never would.

The barn where he felt safe, where the webs and spiders were, where Aaron spent long afternoons with the spiders, touching them, feeling their webs, wondering at their lives, what they knew and why. His mother worshipped them, it was said at his school. His mother was crazy. There'd been fights, some of them bloody, then nobody said that about his mother anymore in front of Aaron. But he knew they said it when he wasn't there to fight.

She might not find me if I go in the barn!

Sucking in harsh, painful gasps, he dashed to the tall plank doors that were open about six inches because their rusty hinges were bent. He squeezed inside, feeling splinters sting his bare chest.

He was surrounded by warmth and rays of sunlight that swirled with dust, with ancient straw and the ghosts of animals. And there were the webs, glistening like decoration in the sun that broke through spaces between old boards. The webs were jeweled with dark creatures and white lumps, with writhing and darting movement. And there were warm shadows behind the webs where Aaron might hide.

He ducked beneath one of the large webs his mother said he must never break, then crawled into one of the empty wood stalls. His eyes burned and his breathing was like crying. Around him was the scratchy strawed earth and old smell of animals.

One of the barn doors scraped on bare ground. A hinge screeched and the barn grew brighter. Less safe.

Aaron saw that his mother had opened the door, saw her silhouette black against earth and sky. Behind her, on the long dirt road from the county highway, he saw dust rising.

Car comin'.

Aaron watched his mother step all the way into the barn and turn her head, looking this way and that. She reached into black shadow and her hand came out holding a long-handled ax.

"You needn't think you gotta hide from me. From your own mother that bore you. I hear you breathin' fire, Aaron. I hear the flame of your breath!"

Like an animal that had caught a scent and knew which way to go, she suddenly came directly toward him, fast.

At first he was too terrified to move. Then she was there, bigger than he ever saw her, blocking his way. He scrambled backward, still in a sitting position. His bare shoulders struck hard board and he couldn't move back away from her any farther.

His mother raised the ax.

Then brought it down.

The pain in Aaron's right foot made him scream so loud his mother backed away a step. He rose and limped past her, his cheek rubbing the softness of her sweating breast beneath her housedress. He smelled her as he squeezed past, and it didn't smell like her.

Whimpering and trailing blood, he ran toward the open barn door. But he couldn't move fast enough. Outside the door in the bright day he saw cars stopping. A sheriff's car with flashing red and blue lights. Long-legged Sheriff Lester in his brown uniform climbing out, reaching back in the car for his big riot gun, like the shotgun Aaron's mother had used on his father.

The pain in Aaron's foot made him slow and sit down on the barn's hard dirt floor. He looked at his poor right foot, the parting of his big toe from the others and the blood and bone of it. His stomach tightened and he felt sick.

His mother was over him again, almost straddling him. Gripping the ax with both hands near the end of the long handle.

"What?" she was screaming. *"What?"*

Aaron realized he'd asked her something and tried to snatch what it was from his spinning thoughts.

"Why?" someone with his voice asked. "Why? Why do you wanna hurt me?"

"That's a fair question, Mrs. Mandle," said the sheriff's level voice behind her.

Aaron's mother didn't so much as glance back at Sheriff Lester. She was staring at Aaron in a way he'd never seen, her wide eyes picking up the light but the rest of her almost black against the sunlight and glittering webs behind her. Like an opening into another world.

"How can you believe in God," his mother asked, "without believin' in Satan?"

She raised the ax high, high over Aaron.

And the sheriff's riot gun made thunder and blew away half her head.

"What I am," said the SSF drill instructor ten years later in the searing Louisiana sun, "is your worst nightmare and the devil you know."

More years later he'd remember how SSF recruit Aaron Mandle, standing rigidly in full battle gear and camouflage paint, had returned his hard stare with one of his own that sent a chill scurrying up the spine.

27

New York, 2003

Cindy Vine thought she might be going crazy. She managed the household budget, and the money was tight. Joe's hours had been cut back, and she'd tried to get some kind of job but couldn't. What office skills she possessed were hopelessly out of date. Computers scared the hell out of her. And nobody gave a damn if she knew how to file and could type fast. They might never have seen a keyboard attached to a typewriter.

Now this!

The hospital had made a settlement offer. Three hundred thousand dollars! Plus medical expenses for Alan.

And Joe told the lawyers no.

The apartment had never seemed so small, the furniture so threadbare, the kitchen so dated, the carpet so worn.

"Why, Joe? For God's sake, *why?*"

He simply stood there in the living room looking at her, wearing the angry but faintly amused expression she was beginning to hate. *You could never understand,* the look said. *You have no choice but to leave it to me. You have to trust my judgment. You have no choice. You have no choice.*

"Joe?"

"Because it isn't enough, Cindy. They owe us more. And I want an admission of guilt. No amount of money's enough without that. I want them to say they were wrong, that they turned Alan into—That they did that to Alan!"

"Their position's that they won't admit wrongdoing even if they make a settlement offer. That's what we were told."

"They can change their position."

She was struggling but staying outwardly calm. During the last six months they'd fought enough about this kind of thing. What good was any of it if it was killing you measure by measure, word by word? How did it help Alan or anyone else? And while it was all being hashed out, the bills continued to pile up. "What did our attorneys say when you told them we were refusing the offer?"

"They said it's what they would've advised."

"They?"

"Larry Sigfried. The other partners. They discussed it and that was their conclusion."

She wasn't sure if she believed him. The room seemed even smaller and warmer. Cindy was light-headed from the heat. She had to sit down. She took three unsteady backward steps to the couch and sat slumped in it, pressing a palm to her forehead.

"Hey, Cindy. You okay, babe?"

She couldn't look up at him. *Am I okay? A three-hundred-thousand-dollar settlement offer. No, thanks. No need to check with the wife. Does he know how much that is?*

Now she met his eyes, his expression mingling concern and truculence. "We already turned down half that much money, Joe. Don't you think there's going to come a time when the hospital, through their attorneys, is going to say that's it, that's our limit, Mr. and Mrs. Vine? We doubled our offer and you foolishly refused. So we'll see you in court."

"No. And lawyers don't talk that way except in movies or television cop shows. I think negotiations are just beginning. And that's how our attorneys see it."

She'd noticed that to Joe the hospital attorneys were *lawyers*, and the law firm representing the Vine family was peopled by *attorneys* and *partners*. "I'm their client, too. Don't they understand that?"

"Cindy, you know how it is. What we told them. If they speak to either one of us, it's like they've spoken to us both."

"Then how would you feel if I turned down all that money without consulting you?"

"I'd understand."

"Would you understand if I demanded to be consulted in the future? Would you agree with that?"

"No." His face was flushed. He was getting angrier. "I don't want any of your goddamn word games, Cindy. Turning down a second settlement offer was the right thing to do, whatever you believe. You don't understand about this kinda thing. Cases like ours are usually settled out of court, but they sometimes drag on for years."

"*Years?* What are we going to eat in the meantime? And what's your plan for paying the bills?"

"We're making it okay."

"Says the man who doesn't write the checks."

"That's right! Says the man!"

"Since you're in charge, Joe, tell me where the money's going to come from. You're down to temporary hours at work, and I've tried and can't get a job. Probably couldn't work one if I did, what's happened's got my brains so scrambled. The checking account's overdrawn again. So tell me, where the fuck will we get the money to buy next week's groceries?"

"We can max out the Visa card."

"We did that."

"The other Visa card, the one that came in the mail last week."

He doesn't understand . . . He doesn't get it . . . Cindy bowed her head and cupped her face in her hands, trying not to sob in frustration. "We owe thousands, Joe."

"And we're angling for millions."

She looked up at him. "Do you actually believe that?"

"Other people in our position have gotten that much."

"But it isn't just the money with you, is it?"

Flushed again. Furious. He wrestled out of the rain-spotted jacket he'd put on this morning and hurled it, wadded, into a chair. Righteous rage. He'd gotten good at it. "Fucking right it isn't just the money! It's justice! For Alan! Have you forgotten about Alan?"

"That isn't fair, Joe."

"Maybe it isn't. But Alan deserves a lot better than he got. I don't know if it's possible, but when this is over I want to think he at least got justice."

"It's too late for him to have justice, Joe. No amount of money will ever even the scales."

"I can't believe that. I have to think some kind of justice is possible. It's the only way I can keep on living."

Vengeance. For Joe. Cindy bowed her head again and said nothing.

There was nothing more to say. He wouldn't listen to reason. And she wasn't even sure if it really *was* reason. Millions of dollars. If Alan lived—and he *must* live—think of the things they could do for him with all that money. She had to admit it made sense to give up hundreds of thousands for future millions. Her thinking had been addled lately, so maybe Joe was right.

"I'm going to visit Alan. Are you coming?" His voice was calm. Gentle. Surprising her.

Cindy sighed. She swallowed the years, the pain, and the compromise that was really simply giving in, giving up.

She nodded and stood up from the sofa. Her body ached and her shoulders slumped. The tragedy of what happened to Alan, then the conflict with the hospital, seemed to make Joe more determined and stronger. But it was wearing her down. Aging her prematurely. She felt so weak, as if something more than bone or tissue was broken inside her. She didn't want to fight. Not anymore.

"It's still drizzling outside, but it's warm," he told her.

"I'll get an umbrella," she said. "And one for you."

* * *

The rain made it easier. The Night Spider stood in the spacious underground garage of the Arcade Building, where the broadcasting studios of Nina Count's *Eye Spy* news show were located. No one was there to see him. But if they had been, they wouldn't have taken special notice, with the weather the way it was. It wasn't unusual for someone to be wearing a light raincoat with the collar turned up. A baseball cap pulled low like a pitcher's who wanted to conceal his eyes from the hitter.

It was his face the Night Spider wanted to conceal. There were dozens, hundreds of pockmarks where skin had sloughed off from the spider bites. It had taken a while for him to become immune to the bites, before he no longer felt ill from the venom used to paralyze helpless prey.

Then he'd no longer minded the bites, or the spiders themselves. You became what you got used to, and, so, were immune. The captive came to imitate his captor and then, when the opportunity arose, became *his* captor, or the captor of a suitable substitute. Concentration camps had made that clear; the imitators who became trusties and camp guards were crueler than the real captors. Crueler or wiser. The Night Spider had read much about concentration camps. They were, in fact, his favorite reading.

He'd even gotten used to what the spiders had done to his face and body, how they'd made him pitted and grotesque. *Pitted and pitied.* People thought spiders were grotesque. They didn't understand because they'd never looked closely enough. *The small and the crawl* . . . You had to kneel down, lie down, get very close to see them in the dark.

Not many people could get close enough to understand, and if he tried to explain it to them, that only made things worse. The only girl he'd tried to date in high school had spurned and denigrated him, humiliated him. Her words had stayed with him like burns. Especially one word: *Hideous!* For weeks after she'd walked away from him, he could hardly bear to look at his own features in the mirror, the pockmarks, the dark eyes full of pain.

Then the pain had changed. There was something else in his eyes.

He met the girl by coincidence in the parking lot of a roadside bar two years after graduation, and he'd taught her what had changed. Followed her home after their so-called friendly conversation, waited for the night to come, then taught her what had changed.

He stepped back into shadow as the sound of a car engine echoed in the garage. Tires swished on concrete, headlight beams danced in the dimness, and the large white Ford SUV that he knew was Nina Count's leaned as it turned a corner too fast.

It pulled into a parking space, and almost immediately Nina and a man got out. Without a backward glance, Nina worked her key fob and the SUV's horn gave an abbreviated *eep!* as the doors locked.

The Night Spider stood still and watched as they walked toward the elevator to the lobby. He could tell by the looseness of their strides that they were relaxed and unsuspecting, even confident. The man, short and with a face like a rodent's; Nina, taller than the man and with her long, nyloned legs glimmering in the dim light. She was even taller than she appeared on TV. Wearing some kind of green cape to protect from the rain. It flowed from around her shoulders to a few inches below her slender waist, almost like graceful, folded wings.

The elevator door glided open and she and the rodent man stepped inside. The man glanced around as the door closed, but the Night Spider knew how shadow and light worked, knew everything about the darkness, and knew he hadn't been seen.

He made a mental note of the black number painted on the concrete wall in front of the white SUV. No doubt Nina Count's personal parking space.

That was the information he'd come for. That and whatever else he might learn. Like the presence of the man with Nina. It would be useful to know who he was and what their relationship was. This was the beginning of the stalk, the first tendrils of the web, the growing knowledge and design of its architecture and of how to spin the rest of it. The first excitement.

He unconsciously reached down and stroked himself. For a moment he considered going to the SUV and leaving some kind of message for her. Not a note. But maybe he could break a taillight or bend out a windshield wiper arm and make it useless. Bend both wiper blades so they stuck out like helpless, feeling antennae.

But it wouldn't be wise to alert her. Not yet. When the time came he might frighten this one with a subtle opening feint, make her pay in dread for what she'd said about him. Then she wouldn't see him again. Not until she was securely snagged by his cunning and it was too late for her. Not until she *knew* it was too late.

Then hunter and prey would become captor and captive.

Her last, endless hours . . .

His soft-soled shoes made no sound as he left the garage, skirting a wall and avoiding the light as long as possible.

Marla said, "Think it'll ever stop raining?"

She'd brought Horn the club sandwich he'd ordered. He noticed she hadn't asked about his dropping into the Home Away for lunch, though before he'd had only breakfast there. He figured she hadn't asked because she already knew the answer.

"Never," he said. He wished it *would* stop raining. Wet weather always made his right shoulder and arm ache. He bit into his turkey club: lots of mayonnaise, crispy bacon, not so much lettuce the thing resembled a salad. It was actually past lunchtime, quarter after two, and he was the only customer. Marla leaned back with her fanny against the table across from his, half sitting, not in a hurry to leave.

"You grumpy today?" she asked, as if it were a serious question.

"A little, I guess. Did I ever tell you about the lawsuit against the hospital where my wife works? Names her as a defendant?" *This is why I came here. To confide. To reach out.*

"Never did," she said.

So he told her. She didn't interrupt him with questions, simply stood staring at the floor and listening. *Had she listened to her patients that way, with that same intent but neutral expression?*

When he was finished explaining, he brought her up to date. "Anne found out this morning the Vine family turned down the hospital's latest settlement offer. She thinks they want to go to court no matter what and try to ruin the hospital and ruin her. For revenge."

Marla crossed her arms and thought for a moment. "She might be right. You have to remember, they think she's responsible."

"I don't see how they could really believe that. They must have seen the medical reports."

"Probably think they've been doctored, if you'll pardon the pun."

Horn finished the first triangular quarter of his sandwich. "Yeah, could be. They're not exactly full of trust at this point, and I guess I can't blame them. Four-year-old kid in a coma he might not come out of. That's a damned hard thing."

"So revenge isn't out of the question, right?"

"I don't know. You're the psychologist."

"You're a cop. Cops know people as well as any psychologist."

"Was a cop."

"Was a psychologist."

He laughed and sipped his Diet Pepsi.

"Let's get to your problems," she said. "Any developments in the Night Spider case other than the new victim I read about in the papers? Neva? . . . "

"Taylor."

"Was she killed like the others?"

"With only the minor variation you'd expect. There isn't any doubt it's the work of the Night Spider."

"What about a copycat?"

"Not likely. He wouldn't know enough about the murder scenes from the news reports to recreate one so faithfully. But why do you ask about a copycat? Does the psychoanalyst in you sense something?"

She smiled. "It's the waitress in me asking the questions, Horn. What's the police profiler tell you?"

"Exactly what you'd think. The killer's between twenty and forty-five years old, organized, intelligent, hates women and probably his mother, and stalks his victims before killing them. Yearns for fame and anonymity simultaneously. A sadist who relishes what he's doing even though he's driven to it and knows it might destroy him eventually."

"You buy into all that?"

"Only some of it."

"Good."

"This the psychoanalyst talking now?"

"Yes. And a woman who lives alone. I'd like to see this dangerous sociopath caught."

"We've got a fresh list of suspects, some of them in the New York area. Detectives are checking the names now."

"Then why are you here?"

"Because we have enough cops on the case to check on and interview suspects in and around New York City." *A lie, but she couldn't know for sure.*

"No, I meant *here.* The diner."

"I don't know. Not for sure. Do you?" He smiled when he asked, signaling to her that he might have been joking.

Might have been.

Marla drew a deep breath, then sighed and straightened up from where she'd been leaning back against the table. "Think it'll ever stop raining?"

28

The windshield wipers made a regular, rhythmic thumping sound that would have reminded Paula of sex if she'd let it. She sat in the unmarked and peered through the fogged-up windshield at the West Village building where the next to last name on her list, a former SSF trooper named Harold Linnert, resided. According to the list given to Horn by Kray, Linnert was fifteen months out of the army, single, and thirty-seven years old.

He lived in a brownstone that reminded Paula a little of Horn's, only it wasn't as well kept. The red front door needed paint and the geraniums in the window boxes were dead, though live ferns hung down in long green tendrils that directed twisting rivulets of rainwater. On the foundation wall behind a row of blue plastic trash cans was some elaborate but indecipherable graffiti sprayed on with faded black paint.

When she'd left the car and reached the brownstone's stoop, Paula saw that the building had been made into a duplex. H. Linnert was on the second floor. Paula pushed the buzzer button and stood waiting beneath her umbrella, watching rainwater run from it and puddle on the concrete near a rubber doormat.

A tinny voice from the intercom said something she couldn't understand. She identified herself as the police, playing by the rules.

A buzzer like a Louisiana locust grated and she pushed open the door.

A small foyer with a door to the left, steep wooden stairs straight ahead. The walls in the foyer and stairwell were a glossy green enamel that could be wiped down. The dampness made them smell as if they'd just been painted. Music was on too loud in one of the units, a Gershwin show tune Paula couldn't place.

She closed her umbrella and trudged up the steps, listening to them creak. No sneaking up on Mr. Linnert. Gershwin had been playing in the downstairs unit and faded to silence halfway up the stairs.

At the top of the stairs, a handsome man with mussed black hair stood waiting for her. He was wearing pleated brown pants and a gray T-shirt. Even standing still he projected a kind of effortless grace, as if he'd just completed a dance step and was poised for another. Paula thought if he had a physical flaw it was that his ears stuck out too far. He had lots of muscle, a waist smaller than hers, and he was smiling.

"I'll take that," he said.

At first she didn't understand what he meant. Then she handed him her wet and folded umbrella. He stepped aside and let her in, placing the umbrella in a stand made from an old metal milk can. He moved with easy precision. Not a drop from the umbrella got on the waxed hardwood floor.

The living room she found herself in was orderly and surprisingly well furnished. Lots of prints—in the sofa, chairs, wallpaper, even lampshades. Here and there were solid-colored red and gray throw pillows. A blue carpet was a shade darker than the walls. It all went together.

"Very nice," Paula heard herself say admiringly. "Obviously you have a good decorator."

"My sister. She watches all those decorator shows on cable and practices on my place. I wouldn't give up my dogs playing poker, though." He motioned with his head to his left.

My God, there they were! Hanging near the door to a hall Paula saw the same hideous print of dogs seated around a table and playing poker that had hung in the home of one of her uncles in Louisiana.

Linnert limped past her, surprising her with his uneven yet still graceful gait, and motioned for her to sit down on the sofa. She did, finding it as comfortable as it appeared. She noticed a fireplace with artificial gas logs burning in it. *What a wonderful place to spend a rainy afternoon.*

He offered her a cup of hot chocolate, which she made herself refuse. *What am I doing, having a cozy confab in a place like this with a handsome bachelor? Is this really my job?* She found herself looking around again at the apartment. *Place is like a damned trap.*

Linnert sat down in a chair near the sofa. She noticed how blue his eyes were. Shooter's eyes. He said, "You mentioned questions."

"Did I?" *Dumb thing to say. Maybe I did.*

"Over the intercom."

"Oh. Yes." This guy had her flustered for some reason— she knew the reason—and she didn't like it.

She gathered her wits and explained to him why she was there, not mentioning, of course, how she'd gotten the information about the Secret Special Forces. Horn had told them Kray was probably risking his career to help them catch this killer.

Harold Linnert leaned back and crossed his legs, then folded his muscular tanned arms across his chest. "A part of my life that's over," he said.

"What do you do now?"

"I'm an architect. An apartment I lease across the hall is my office."

"Skyscrapers?"

He grinned. "Not hardly. I mostly tell people how to reroute plumbing, or which walls they can tear down without the building collapsing around them."

"You good at your work?" *Stupid, stupid question!*

"Nothing's collapsed yet."

"About that other part of your life . . . "

"I suppose you're checking out everyone in my old unit."

"Yes. Routine."

"Oh, sure. May I ask why?"

"We'd rather not say right now."

"Uh-huh. I was positive you were going to say you were touching all the bases."

Paula felt like telling him she didn't have time to play dueling clichés. "I'm interested in your whereabouts on these particular evenings," she said, making her tone official, as if she'd never had an impure thought in her life. She read off the dates of the Night Spider murders.

"On one of those nights I was at the Bas Mitzvah of a friend's daughter, all afternoon and most of the evening. The other nights I'd have to check on." He uncrossed his legs. "But I might be able to save you some trouble. May I show you something?"

"Of course."

He bent forward and pulled up his left pants leg to reveal a nasty, barely healed jagged scar running down the inside of his knee. Stitch marks were still visible. "From radical knee surgery. My surgeon will tell you this scar is from the third of three operations over the past year, the last one about a month ago. I can't put my full weight on this knee, run or take stairs fast, or climb. Haven't been able to for months."

Paula sized up the operation scar. It appeared to be as serious as claimed. She couldn't imagine anyone scaling buildings or hand-walking across ropes or cables with such an injury. "An old war wound acting up?"

"Rugby injury. I was playing in a league. Stepped on a tent peg somebody had driven into the practice field in the park, and forgot when they broke camp. I wrenched my knee and messed it up permanently. Dumb thing to do."

"Forgetting a tent peg?"

"No. Tripping over one."

Paula lowered her notepad and pencil to her lap and looked at him.

He gave her his handsome white grin set off by tanned features. "If you don't believe me, you can talk to my surgeon at Kincaid Memorial Hospital. He'll verify what I've said, tell you it was a classic tent-peg injury. He might even attest to my good character, as I've paid him what I owe."

"You know I *will* talk to him."

"Of course." He braced himself with a hand on one of the chair arms, then stood up with some difficulty. Paula watched as he limped to an antique kneehole desk and wrote something on a white card. His business card, which he handed to her before sitting back down. Paula thought the limp looked genuine enough.

So did the business card, with the address of the apartment across the hall. On the back he'd written the name of a doctor at Kincaid Memorial.

Paula slipped the card into her purse next to her gun. "I do have a few questions about your SSF unit," she said. "Nothing that would cause you to reveal any state secrets."

The tooth-whitener-commercial smile again. "I don't know many of those. Our operations were always narrowly defined."

"What did you think of your commander, Colonel Gray?"

"*Kray*. With a *K*. Hell of a soldier." Blue eyes hard now. Something wild and willful in them. "I'd disagree with anyone who said otherwise."

"Nobody has so far," Paula told him, thinking he might be a dangerous man in a serious disagreement. "Kray seems to have had the respect of his men."

"He earned it."

Paula glanced down at the notepad and papers in her lap. "I have another name on my list, without an address. Maybe you can help me with it. Aaron Mandle."

Linnert sat back and looked . . . Paula wasn't sure of his expression, but it certainly made his blue eyes darker.

"I couldn't tell you where to find Mandle," he said. "Haven't thought of him in a long while."

"So maybe you can tell me something about him. Anything that might help me locate him."

"He was a peculiar guy. But then we all were, I guess. It takes a certain type, in that kind of unit." He looked at her and seemed to be considering what he'd just said. "But Mandle was an oddball even in our outfit. Damned good soldier. Knew how to . . . Knew his work and did it well. I guess you know we were primarily a mountain combat unit. Climbing was almost as important as fighting, and we moved every which way on mountainsides—or, for that matter, on building faces in urban settings—as if we were born to it. In a way, you had to be. It's gotta run in your blood. Mandle always removed his right boot and sock before an operation that entailed climbing. He climbed barefoot, and better than any of us. Had this weird extra-long big toe that allowed him to gain grip and leverage."

Paula remained outwardly calm. "Barefoot, huh?"

"Just one foot. He'd sit down on the ground and whip off that right boot and sock, stuff the sock down in the boot, then sling the boot from his belt by its laces. Carry it that way all through whatever happened next."

Paula was having a hard time breathing. "He ever explain the freaky toe?"

"Nope. Wouldn't talk about it. But he could extend that toe out to the side, almost like a thumb; he really knew how to use it. Used that foot like a hand, if he had to."

"Odd, all right."

"You sure you don't want a cup of hot chocolate? Detective . . . Paula?"

"Paula," she confirmed. "Paula Ramboquette."

"French. Cajun. Ah, that explains your accent!"

"Cajun," she confirmed. "And thanks anyway but no to the hot chocolate. Listen, Mr. Linnert—"

"Harry."

"Harry, was there anything else peculiar about Aaron Mandle?"

"Well, he wasn't easy to talk to. Kept his thoughts to himself. A loner, I guess you'd call him. But when it came to teamwork, he was there. There was no other way. We had to trust each other."

"Male bonding."

Linnert nodded somberly. "You can joke about it, Paula, but it kept us alive. The ones of us that stayed alive."

"I wasn't joking," she assured him sincerely. *Why am I so damned concerned if I hurt his feelings? Why am I so . . . what?*

She stood up. She knew she'd better get out of there or she'd be curled up on the sofa and sipping hot chocolate before she knew what happened.

"Thanks for your time and cooperation, Mr. Linnert— Harry."

"Want me to phone my surgeon and tell him you'll be coming by? Doctor-patient confidentiality and all that."

"No, no. I'll take care of it. I won't have to know any details about the injury. Just his general opinion on how it would incapacitate you. You've been helpful."

"Have I?"

"Well, maybe. We never know for sure until later." *Horn's line.* She moved toward the door and Linnert stood up. Too fast. So smooth.

She felt a mild jolt of alarm.

But he was smiling and merely escorting her to the door. He opened it for her and stood at an angle to let her pass. She felt uneasy with him so close and wasn't sure why.

"I wouldn't mind being interrogated by you again," he said.

"Harry—Mr. Linnert. I appreciate the sentiment, but this isn't the time for it."

"Oh, probably not. Would you leave me your phone number. In case I remember something important?"

She had to grin. "I'm with the NYPD, if you need me."

"And I might need you."

"Harry, Harry . . ."

"Okay, Paula. I give up for now." He shifted position a bit so she'd have more room to get by, giving off a faint cologne scent. She liked it, which surprised her after spending months cooped up in the car with Bickerstaff and his bargain-basement odor.

She stepped past Linnert onto the landing.

"One more thing I recall," he said. "About Mandle. It was strange. There were these big karakurt spiders where we were in Afghanistan, kind of like black widows only larger. They were poisonous, but Mandle didn't mind handling them. And when they stung him, it didn't seem to affect him."

"Strange, all right," Paula agreed.

She thanked Linnert again for his cooperation.

He didn't shut the door. Instead, he stood leaning against the door frame so he could watch her leave. She knew he wanted to keep her in sight as long as possible.

As she took the stairs to the foyer and street door, trying not to run, she was trembling and was afraid Linnert might notice and misunderstand.

So uncontrollable was the trembling that she fumbled for and almost dropped her cell phone even before she got across the street to where the unmarked was parked. She collected her thoughts and climbed into the car before trying to use the phone.

Once seated behind the steering wheel in the fogged sanctuary of the vehicle, she was calmer. As she pecked out Horn's phone number, a lock of wet hair dropped over one eye, momentarily blocking her vision before she brushed it back with her free hand. She realized she was soaked. She'd forgotten her umbrella.

Damn it! She knew Harry Linnert would think she'd done so on purpose.

While the phone chirped on the other end of the connection, she wondered if he might be right.

Will Lincoln finished brazing the last of a dozen narrow copper strips. He was going to use these to create a miniature picket fence that gave the illusion it diminished with distance. Alongside the fence was a foot-tall tree with delicate, shimmering copper leaves that caught light from every angle.

He glanced at his watch, then rotated a dial on the compression tank and watched the vibrant flame of his blowtorch sink to a flicker and disappear. He removed his dark safety glasses and laid them on his workbench next to his half-finished *New Hampshire Lane*, a piece he had high hopes of selling to a wealthy buyer in Florida who had roots in the Northeast.

It was past ten o'clock. The rain had finally stopped, and, according to the latest weather report, was gusting out of the area. Next to the workbench, the window unit air conditioner he'd mounted in the garage wall was humming away, keeping the studio comfortable and dehumidified.

His wife, Kim, had taken her meds and would be sleeping soundly by now. He'd given her the white Ativan tablet along with her 500-milligram blue tablet and knew she'd remain asleep until late morning.

It was safe to leave the garage. As usual, he'd leave the light on and the air conditioner running, so if Kim did happen to awaken and look out the window, she'd assume he was still out there working. Will knew she wouldn't venture outside. She would have to cross puddled, cracked concrete and then a stretch of rain-soaked grass to reach the garage. She wouldn't put on her flimsy house slippers and go out so soon after a soaking rain.

Besides, she wouldn't want to see him. Kim always avoided

him for days after the kind of argument they'd had last night. He'd get the sullen, silent treatment, and that was fine with Will. For the next three or four days, whenever he'd enter a room, she'd find an excuse to leave it. And she sure wouldn't come looking for him.

The thick wooden molding above the air conditioner concealed the hinges mounted on the inside of the garage wall. Will put on the light windbreaker he kept in the garage, then took a last look around to make sure everything was in proper disorder; his tools not put away but still scattered on the workbench, and the tiny portable radio still on and tuned to an all-night classical music station. If he did happen to be caught out, he'd simply say he'd gone for cigarettes and locked the garage door behind him. He kept a fresh pack of Winstons in the jacket pocket just for that possibility. Will Lincoln was nothing if not careful. Caution and stealth were a part of his training that had stayed with him. The daring, he'd always had.

He tilted the still-running air conditioner up and away from the garage's back wall, then supported it with his strong left arm while he crouched low and exited through the opening the humming unit had occupied. When he lowered the air conditioner back into place, there was no sign that there was a way in and out of the garage other than the overhead and front doors, both of which were locked from the inside.

Will cut around the side of the garage, then walked down the driveway keeping well to the right of the old Dodge pickup parked there, where he knew he wouldn't be visible from the house. When he reached the sidewalk, he turned to the right and strode about ten yards to where his car was parked, also out of sight in case Kim were to glance out a front window.

Outside Minnie's Place, Will parked his old Pontiac across the street, noticing that the weather report about the rain stopping was wrong and a light mist had begun to fall. Zipping his windbreaker, he jogged to Minnie's entrance, pushed inside, and stood at the bar even though half the stools were available.

"Fifth of Southern Comfort to go," he said, when Bobby, behind the bar, looked his way. Bobby had already been reaching for the Budweiser tap.

"Not your usual drink," Bobby said, reaching instead to a low shelf and coming up with the Southern Comfort bottle.

"If everybody drank their usual drink," Will said, "we'd all still be drinking water."

"Fuckin' arteests!" Bobby said with a grin, and accepted Will's money.

Will told him to keep the change, which wasn't all that much anyway, then gave a little parting wave to Bobby and whoever else he might know in the dim bar, and went back outside into the misty night. It was actually getting a little cool. He was glad for the jacket.

After getting into his car, he drove only about three blocks and parked two houses down from a small brown bungalow of the sort built in the twenties and thirties: narrow with a steeply pitched roof, a front porch that ran the front of the house, and slits of windows above the porch roof that had been attic vents before the upstairs was converted to bedrooms decades ago. One of the shutters on the front windows was hanging crookedly, and the grass needed mowing, if for no other reason than to make it uniform. It grew in uneven clumps as if a goat had been at it.

Without looking around him, Will climbed out of the Pontiac and strode quickly along the sidewalk, then through the scraggly patch of front yard and up onto the porch.

He rapped lightly on the front door with the knuckle of his forefinger, and the door opened.

"Seen you drive up," said the smiling woman looking out at him. She was about five feet tall, barefoot and wearing a gray robe sashed tight at the waist. As she opened the door wider and moved back and to the side to let Will enter, he saw that the robe was gapped at the top to reveal a lot of cleavage. "You brought us something," she said, noticing the brown paper bag in his right hand.

"Like always."

When the door was closed, he bent and kissed the woman's forehead. She raised both arms and pulled him lower by the back of the neck and they kissed on the lips. She didn't want to let up and he felt the soft play of her tongue and tasted mint toothpaste.

"You gonna stay awhile tonight?" she asked, finally letting him straighten up.

"You know I would if I could, Roz." He was telling her the truth. He liked it here with her, where he'd spent a lot of evenings for the past six months. She never bitched, like his wife. Always did what he told her. Eager to please. Goddamned dying to please!

Still smiling just to be in his presence, she took the paper bag from his hand and set it on the coffee table. He noticed the hurried switch of her broad hips beneath the robe as she went into the kitchen for a couple of glasses.

Rosanne Turner was an alcoholic. Will liked that. It was her vulnerability that had interested him when he first saw her practically drooling in a liquor store. He'd judged her accurately, picking her up right there using a bottle of scotch for bait. Later he'd found out she wouldn't drink anything but Southern Comfort, unless there was no Southern Comfort around. Bobby was right; it wasn't Will's drink. But he'd made it his drink the second time he'd met Roz.

The first night, they'd walked and talked and he'd convinced her he was a gentleman and acknowledged she was a lady. He commiserated with her about the lost daughter her bastard of a husband had talked the court into placing in his custody during the divorce. Fucking injustice was everywhere! He agreed with her that her idiot boss at an insurance company had been wrong to fire her and assured her that her infrequent work as an office temp would inevitably lead to steady employment. How could they not hire somebody like her? Not everybody in the world was too stupid or blind to see what she had to offer.

When they'd reached her house, he hadn't tried to talk his way inside. Instead, he'd left her the bottle they'd both only taken a few sips from, a little nudge to help her tumble off the wagon and onto her back with her legs spread.

Their next date, about halfway into the Southern Comfort, she was wildly enjoying her second addiction.

Roz was back with two juice glasses, both full. His had ice in it, the way he liked it, or could stand it, anyway. Usually he was a straight Bud man.

"Before we drink these," she said, "I want to show you something."

Will followed her into the spare bedroom.

There on a table in the center of the room was one of his smaller works, *Blue Mourning,* a surrealistic bronze of a sobbing man seated on a box.

"I bought it at that gallery in the Village. Three hundred dollars."

He didn't know what to think. Maybe he was angry. He couldn't be sure. "I'm . . . uh, flattered," he said. "But you shouldn't have spent the money."

"I wanted to. You're going to be famous someday, so it's an investment."

Will knew it was an investment she was making in him personally. He didn't like that. They had an unspoken agreement about their affair, and he intended to keep his part of it.

She handed him his glass, kissing him again on the lips.

"You love me?" she asked, backing up a step.

"You know I don't," he said, "and you don't give a fuck."

She downed half her glass and grinned in a way that showed most of her teeth. "I'm gonna show you how wrong you are about that last part."

Fifteen minutes later she was smiling down at him, seated on his bare chest with her thighs spread wide. He could smell her sex and feel her heat and wetness against his skin. A drop of perspiration clung to her left breast as if reluctant to leave it and then plummeted to land on his neck.

"Any place you'd rather be?" she asked.

"Can't think of one."

"You home?"

"Home," he said.

Thinking this was about as far away from home as he could get.

And when he returned home, it would be as if he'd never left.

Linnert looked slightly disheveled the morning after Paula had talked to him. He'd still been in bed when Paula, who'd detoured on her way to pick up Bickerstaff, buzzed from downstairs. His hair was flat on one side, and he was wearing a white T-shirt, brown slippers, and the same pleated pants he'd had on yesterday. She thought he didn't look bad a little messy.

Occasionally, Paula dropped in unexpectedly for a brief follow-up interview to catch a suspect off guard. Sometimes they contradicted themselves, or came up with a piece of information even they didn't know they possesed or was important. Sometimes it gave her a new and completely different view of a suspect. That could be valuable for a lot of reasons.

"I came back because it occurred to me you might provide some insight," she said, as he stepped back to invite her inside.

He grinned as he sat slumped in a chair across from her. She'd noted that he limped getting there. "I'm plenty insightful," he said. He wasn't smiling, but it was in his voice. She amused him. It kind of pissed her off.

"You were SSF yourself. If the Night Spider has a background like yours, what do you think might make him assume he can get away with it?"

"Arrogance, plain and simple. Taking the kinds of risks we did, an ungodly amount of arrogance was required."

"Oh? Are you still arrogant?" *Hah!*

"Yes." He smiled. "A guilty suspect wouldn't tell you that, would he?"

Playing with me. "An arrogant one would. Why are you arrogant?"

"Because it is justified. Besides, women find arrogance attractive."

"Some do."

"You, Officer Paula."

"Detective Ramboquette," she said, standing up and thanking Linnert for his time. Abrupt, but what the hell? He had a way of taking the play away from her, turning her in on herself, and she couldn't quite cope with it—with him.

"Hey! You don't have to leave again so soon."

But she knew she did and that he understood why. Insightful bastard.

Not to mention arrogant.

"Have you had breakfast, Paula?"

"Yes," she lied.

"Paula."

His voice stopped her at the door.

"You forgot your umbrella again."

29

There was no record that Aaron Mandle had ever had trouble with the law. His last known address was three years old and in St. Louis, in a neighborhood where it was dangerous to grow up or to grow old. He'd lived in a six-family apartment building long ago torn down to make room for a highway exit ramp.

Horn had checked with the St. Louis police and was told Mandle didn't have a record there, either. VICAP and NCIC had nothing on him. The man seemed to no longer exist.

But he'd definitely existed in St. Louis. The detective Horn talked to, a guy named Homolka, recalled a four-year-old unsolved homicide: a woman wrapped in her bedsheets and stabbed to death.

The next morning, Horn said, "We're catching his act after he perfected it on the road," as if Mandle were someone who'd recently opened on Broadway.

"Then we don't know how many women he's killed," Paula said. "There might be dozens more, in other cities."

"Not that I could find, other than the probable in St. Louis. But it's still being checked out."

"Wouldn't he have been in the military around that time?" Paula asked.

"Maybe," Horn said. "But if he was in the States, he'd have occasional leave."

"The army should have his fingerprints," Bickerstaff said.

"Should, but they don't."

They'd been in the Home Away for more than an hour, trying to figure out what to do with what seemed to be their best lead. Horn was finished with his corn muffins, and Paula and Bickerstaff had sneaked a stop at a Krispy Kreme and told him they were skipping breakfast today. Horn had congratulated them on their dietary virtuousness, then pointed out the doughnut crumbs on their clothes. There were only three coffee cups and saucers, a small cream pitcher, and sugar packets on the table now. Everyone knew where everyone else stood culinary-wise.

Horn said, "I didn't want to drag Kray into this any further, so I contacted Altman and asked him about Mandle. Should have known it was a waste of time. Far as the government's concerned, the SSF and its roster don't exist and never did."

"Not even to catch a killer?" Paula asked.

"Alleged killer. And according to Altman, SSF members' military records are expunged to prevent any possible compromise even after they become civilians. He said he couldn't help me if he tried."

"And we know we can believe him," Bickerstaff said disgustedly.

"Did he ask how we found out about Mandle?" Paula said. "Altman must know he wasn't a name on the original list of SSF members."

"The phony list," Bickerstaff said.

"Useless, anyway," Horn said. "And no, Altman didn't ask. And I didn't exactly use Mandle's real name anyway. Sometimes it's best to cast a lie to a liar."

Paula stared at him. *Fibbing to the Feds. You're just like*

Altman. Now and then Horn would do something that jolted her into realizing anew how devious and relentless he was. How he was so much more than a simple, by-the-book cop who'd put in his time, kissed ass, and gotten ahead in the department. She suspected Altman seriously underestimated him.

"Since we're not even sure Mandle's his real name," Horn said, "we weren't exactly lying to the federal government."

"Good moral point," Paula said with a smile. "And a relief to hear. If I were Catholic, I'd have an easier time going to confession Sunday."

Horn looked at Bickerstaff.

"Botox for my brow, too," Bickerstaff said.

"A unit like the SSF," Paula said, "do you think the military might even have purged Mandle's civilian criminal record?"

"I doubt it," Horn said, "though it's possible. I think we can work on the assumption that Mandle never had any brushes with the law."

"Then why's he so damned hard to find?" Bickerstaff asked.

"Running from family problems, maybe," Paula suggested, burning her tongue on the coffee Marla the waitress had just topped off. "Ex-wife, child support, that kind of thing."

Bickerstaff chewed on the inside of his cheek. A thinking gesture, Paula knew. More chewing. "Maybe he's got an alias."

Paula poured in more cream and cautiously tried her coffee again. *Much better.* "Or maybe Aaron Mandle's an alias."

"He has a Social Security number," Horn told them. "Of course, by now he might have another, or one for every occasion."

Paula looked across the table at Horn, trying to read him. It was like trying to read slate. "You really convinced Mandle's our Night Spider?"

"He looks good for it to me."

"We've gotta find this prick and shut him down," Bickerstaff said. "If for no other reason than so I can go fishing."

Paula didn't comment. *Trying to get a rise out of me.*

"I told Larkin what we have," Horn said. "He was thrilled, but he's skeptical."

"Can you be both those things at the same time?" Paula asked.

Horn smiled. "It's the very juggling act that gets you ahead in the NYPD." He finished his coffee and rested the empty cup on the white paper napkin he'd folded and placed in his saucer. "Time to do the drone work," he said. "Make more use of the department computers. I'm told nobody can walk, talk, and breathe on the planet these days without leaving a trail of some sort. We have to find that trail, then follow it."

Bickerstaff had already stood up. Paula dabbed at her lips with her napkin and slid out of the booth. They'd learned that the emphatic draining of the coffee cup was Horn's signal that strategy meetings at the Home Away were over.

As they strode from the diner, Bickerstaff waved good-bye to Marla, who was busy behind the counter. She gave him a smile and a nod. Friendly but not too personal. Paula thought that if Bickerstaff had any designs on Marla, he'd better go back to thinking about ice fishing.

Outside in the first clear morning in several days, Bickerstaff said, "You notice that waitress isn't a bad-looking woman?"

"I've noticed," Paula said. "Though not like you, I'm sure." *And Horn's noticed.*

Horn had drawn an El Laquito Especial cigar from his pocket when Marla approached the booth.

He smiled. "I'm not going to smoke this here. Just unwrapping it so I can enjoy it on the walk home."

She was carrying a towel, drying her hands on it though they didn't need drying. He waited for her to warn him about the evils, perils, and addiction of smoking, but she didn't. "How's the Night Spider case going?" she asked.

"You seem particularly interested in this one."

"Sure. I guess I'm hooked."

Horn found himself hoping that was a double entendre.

"Any closer to catching the creep?" Marla asked.

He could smell the fine Cuban cigar and felt like lighting it while he was right there in the booth. "As a psychologist, I would have thought you'd regard the killer as sick. Dangerous, but still a product of society's ills."

"*Creep* fits all right. And I'm speaking personally, not professionally. What I am now's a professional food server."

The strategy meeting had started late that morning, probably because of Paula and Bickerstaff stopping for doughnuts, so it had broken up late. The last of the breakfast crowd had left, and Horn and Marla were alone now, except for the cook and whoever else might be in back beyond the swinging doors to the kitchen.

"You don't trust me, Horn?"

"You know better."

He filled Marla in on the case's progress, while she stood by the booth listening. As he talked, she absently wound the dry dish towel around one of her hands, as if she'd suffered a wound.

"Aaron Mandle," she said, when Horn was finished. "So your suspect has a name."

"It might not be his real name. And if it is, he's very successfully erased any sign of himself and gone into hiding. Knowing a name he's used is one thing. Finding him is quite another."

"You'll probably never find him."

Horn put the unlit cigar back in his shirt pocket. He was surprised by such a definite statement from her, and he sensed there was something more coming. "The police are better at finding people than a lot of folks think, or do you have an insight you might want to share?"

"I do. Aside from what you've just told me, I've done a lot of reading on this case, given it a lot of thought and formed some opinions."

"Why?"

"Because you're involved. If something happened to you, what would we do with our year's supply of corn muffins?"

"Enough about me and my vices," Horn said, hoping he wasn't revealing how pleased he was with the reason for her interest in the case. "Why do you say the killer will be so hard to find?"

"He's a sadistic perfectionist," Marla said, "who murders as an erotic art. And I don't think that's putting it too strongly. My assumption is he's also that careful and detail-oriented in other matters, such as concealing his whereabouts."

"For a careful man, he's found himself a pretty risky pastime."

"It's not a pastime for him. I'm sure he sees it as his calling. Convincing himself that what he's doing is his destiny helps him to rationalize it, to reconcile it with the normal side of the self he shows to the world. His facade."

"We talking split personality?"

"I don't think so. Not even bipolar. I'd say your killer's a sadistic, capable son of a bitch all the time. Only sometimes he acts differently, charms people so he can use them. But he's probably quite conscious of doing that. Not like . . . say, a Son of Sam type who hears voices or messages in a dog's barking."

"Any thoughts about motivation?"

She smiled sadly. "That could be a lot more complicated. Almost certainly he hates women, but that could be for a number of reasons. Possibly there was a formative traumatic event early on, something an important woman in his life did to him. A mother, sister . . . But the reasons can also be cumulative, the turning point some seemingly insignificant act whose importance the perpetrator herself is unaware of. The profundity of these things can be entirely in the mind of the afflicted."

Profundity. "You're some hash slinger."

"You're some cop."

"You've given me a lot to mull over. I thought you weren't into profiling."

She unwound the towel from her hand and smiled at him. "Just for friends," she said. "And because I think it might help."

Horn removed the cigar from his pocket again and examined it, rotating it with thumb and forefinger to check the tightness of the wrapper leaf. "It would help a lot more," he said, "if you told me how to find him."

"You probably won't find him."

"Oh?"

"But even though my opinions are based on estimation, I think I can tell you his vulnerability. He has a sick mind, but one you can get inside of. To a certain extent, you can know how he thinks."

"That's his vulnerability?"

"Not entirely. Everything in his actions suggests he's built for risk. He can't ignore a dare. You might be able to make him come to you."

The bell above the door tinkled. A woman and three preschool children entered the diner in a rush of noise and motion.

Marla excused herself. She glanced back at Horn as she hurried around behind the counter. The woman and her charges were climbing onto stools. First up was the largest kid, a grinning blond girl about four who began to revolve.

Horn laid some bills on the table, then slid out of the booth and walked from the diner, the unlit cigar in his hand. As he left, Marla gave him a smile he'd never seen before.

One he didn't understand.

Outside the diner, Horn stood near a doorway and fired up his cigar. He was strolling along the sidewalk, smoking and enjoying the fact that the sun was paying a visit this morning, when his cell phone chirped.

He dug the phone out of his jacket pocket, then removed the cigar from his mouth and watched the morning breeze claim the smoke he'd exhaled. With his free hand, the unimpaired left one, he held the small plastic phone to his ear. "Horn."

"Captain Horn, this is Nina. Nina Count."

"Am I going to be glad it is?"

"I didn't call to give you any bullshit, Horn. I'm scared."

She seemed to mean it. Her voice was different from any other time he'd heard it, a slight quaver making her sound as if she were cold.

Horn stepped aside, letting a knot of pedestrians who were going in the opposite direction pass by. Then he moved into the display-window-corridor entrance to a menswear store so he could hear better. "I didn't think *scared* was a word you knew, Nina."

"I got up this morning, dressed, and was about to leave for work, when I checked my bedroom window to make sure it was locked."

Horn felt his hand tighten on the phone.

"It was locked," Nina went on, "but I noticed something in the upper right-hand corner. Someone had scratched— etched is more the word—a design there. A spiderweb."

"You're sure."

"No mistake about it. It's rather artistic."

"But it's on the *outside* of the glass?"

"If it weren't, I wouldn't still be in my apartment talking to you."

You might still be in your apartment. Dead. He found his gaze fixed on a pair of two-tone loafers with oversized tassels in the show window and knew he'd remember them the way he'd always remember this phone call. The human mind was something, with its overlapping layers of thought. *Why would anyone wear a pair of shoes like that?*

"What's this mean, Horn?"

"You know what it means. You got the desired result through your newscast. Attracted the killer's attention. Now *he's* playing with *you*. Trying to frighten you."

"He succeeded more than I thought possible." The chill in her voice again.

"You want police protection?"

"Yes."

No hesitation. Horn knew she realized the Night Spider didn't have to spend his time etching windowpanes. He could have used his glass cutter and masking tape to unlock the window, then entered her bedroom while she slept and taken her as one of his victims. Spent his idea of quality time with her.

"Should I stay here, Horn?"

"For the time being. You're probably safe enough. He obviously wants you alive for now so he can continue his terror campaign."

Silence. Then, "Yeah, I guess that's true. How long do you think that part of it will go on? I could make a story out of it." Her fear was slackening somewhat. Thinking ratings again. She wasn't short on guts. "The police protection might make a good angle for my newscast. Or maybe I shouldn't mention it. Do you think I should mention what he did to my bedroom window?"

"You can mention the window, but not the protection. That'd only make your guardian angels' job more difficult."

"Do you really think he'd try for me if he knew I was under police protection?"

"I'm sure of it. In fact, I think it would make an attempt more likely."

"Jesus, Horn!"

He can't ignore a dare . . .

"Nina, there's something we need to talk about."

The Night Spider sat on a bench just inside the entrance to Central Park and watched children using the playground equipment. And watched their mothers and nannies.

Nina Count is afraid. Right now. This second.

He played with that fact in his mind and was aware of warm sunlight on the part of his face that was exposed. He wore a short-sleeved shirt, but with the collar turned up, a Mets baseball cap, and oversized orange-tinted glasses that made the park's foliage a more vivid green, and the flesh of the women and children all the more vital and sumptuous.

Nina Count is afraid. She knows it's begun.

He could have taken her last night, as he dangled like death outside her window, watching her sleep through the web he etched in the glass. He'd used soap on his diamond glass cutter so it was silent. Nina Count hadn't stirred. She lay on her side, partly covered with a white sheet that might become her shroud. One languid bare leg was extended, pale even against the sheet. He guessed she'd be a natural blonde, though these days, with all the improved dyes and techniques, it was difficult to know. He'd find out for sure soon enough.

When he was almost finished with the web, he had to fight the desire to tap on the glass and wake her, give her a glimpse of him outside her high window, so close to her. Only a thin pane of glass between Nina and everything she'd ever feared.

But he'd resisted and quietly ascended to the roof. He used his line, slender but strong, and, from the ground, invisible as a spiderweb, to traverse dark space to the adjacent roof.

He left behind a sleeping Nina Count, who would look out her window in the morning and know he'd been there, so very near her. Terror would leap through the glass to her and cling to her and bore into her like a parasitic insect that would be her companion for the brief duration of her life.

Something to think about.

She's thinking about it now. She must be because she isn't able to think about anything else. Not completely. She's thinking about me at this precise instant.

Because she knows I'm thinking about her.

Through the light and shadow and angles of the narrow streets, the greater and lesser terrors of swarming humanity, the raucous, hard-shelled traffic with cars like intrepid beetles dusty or glistening in the sunlight, her fear wended its way to him.

He closed his eyes behind the bulging, tinted lenses and fed on it.

30

Paula knew deep down it wasn't really necessary to question Harry Linnert again, at this point. But then she knew a lot of things deep down, and there was nothing wrong with a cop playing a hunch.

She was parked across the street from his apartment building, and occasionally glanced at his windows, which were still dark. It was almost eleven o'clock and she'd checked the apartment twice since eight o'clock. So maybe he was out to dinner with friends, fellow architects or Rugby players.

She was about to give up and drive away when Linnert rounded the corner up the block and walked toward his building. He was wearing a tan waist-length jacket to protect from the mist and carrying a small bag of some sort by its handle.

Paula forgot to slump down; he caught sight of her, did a double take, then stepped off the curb and began crossing the street toward her.

Great! Terrific! Better think of some questions.

He leaned down and peered in through the window, which she lowered.

"Paula?" he said. "Officer Paula?"

"Detective Ramboquette," she corrected.

He grinned. "Detective Ramboquette, I'm getting wet." Bearing down on the *et* syllables and making it sound like a poem.

"Get in the car," she said, making it sound damned official.

He settled in beside her and the windows immediately started to steam up. Two people in the car now, double the body heat, but still, Paula had to be impressed.

"More questions?" he asked.

"That's why I'm here."

"Am I still under suspicion?"

There was a hot, musky scent coming off him, one she thought she recognized. "Everybody's under suspicion," she told him. "Where are you coming from?"

"My gym. I've been working out. Trying to get the leg in shape."

"You've been with a woman," Paula said. "I can smell it on you."

His jaw dropped with surprise, then he laughed. "I've been with a Nautilus machine. What you smell's probably the old socks and jogging shoes in my bag." He leaned toward her. "I can open the bag and prove it."

"That's not the way to respond to questions from the law," she said.

"You want to come up to my apartment again and we'll talk?"

"No." *Not again. Not yet, not yet . . .*

"You don't usually get questioned by the law in a cozy unmarked police car with the windows all fogged up." He glanced around. "You know, we could make out in here, Detective Ramboquette, and nobody would see us."

"You're part of an active homicide investigation," she reminded him.

"Is that all that's stopping us?"

She turned and looked him dead in the eye. "That's all."

That backed him up but not much. He was grinning widely,

obviously pleased. "Do we really have to wait until the case is solved?"

"We do."

"You're damned serious about your job."

"Yeah, I am."

He leaned toward her and kissed her lightly on the lips. She couldn't turn away. Could barely make herself move. She was losing control of the situation here and didn't like it.

There was a deafening high-pitched *Whooop!* that made him jerk backward and bang his head against the window.

"What the hell was that?" His eyes were wide.

"Siren," she said. "For emergencies."

She switched on the wipers to allow a view out of the car, and in. Two elderly women who were half a block away were standing and staring at the unmarked.

"Jesus, Paula." Linnert rubbed his head where he'd bumped it, then he started to laugh.

"Get out of here," she said.

"Now? Right now?"

"You betcha."

He stirred, started to lean toward her again, then changed his mind and opened the door. He slid out of the car, still looking at her. When he'd gotten out, he didn't straighten up. "That's it?"

"No," she said. "Don't leave town."

He laughed again and shut the door.

She drove away fast. Her heart was doing a wild dance. *Dumb, dumb, dumb! Definitely, a dumb thing to do!*
But she wasn't sorry.

This looked like it: the Home Away Diner.

Unimposing little place, Nina thought, as she observed it from across the street. Just another corner diner like a zillion others in Manhattan, windows with booths looking out on the street, menu taped on its tinted glass door, yellow and blue Plexiglas sign that bent around the corner, no doubt backlighted in the evening. A placard on an easel near the door advertised daily specials. It was the kind of place Seinfeld and his friends might use as a hangout.

As she waited for a break in the traffic so she could cross the street, Nina wondered if Horn knew what he was doing.

And do I know what I'm *doing?*

She saw her opportunity and hurried across the street as fast as possible. Her high heels were in her oversized leather purse; she was wearing her Nikes. Still, she almost wasn't fast enough. A horn blared and a taxi she hadn't noticed pulled away from the curb and had to skid to a stop rather than hit her.

The driver rolled down his window. "Better get a guide dog, lady!"

Nina gave him the finger and went on her way.

"Hey! Ain't you that TV newswoman?"

"I am," Nina said, smiling and not looking back.

"Fuck you, anyway!"

New York.

As she entered the Home Away, she saw scrawled on the placard that tonight's special was going to be veal parmesan, including roll and salad. Something to know, she thought, in case she was abducted by a motorcycle gang and dumped nearby.

At least it was cool in the diner. There were a few customers, despite the fact that it was the restaurant business void between lunch and dinner. An elderly couple sat in a window booth drinking milkshakes. A guy who looked like a bum was slouched on a stool at the end of the counter, sipping what appeared to be cola with a straw in it. Maybe too drunk to realize he wasn't in a bar.

A man who looked like he was from the Middle East was perched on a high stool behind the counter, thumbing through a *Sports Illustrated*. He stood up when Nina walked in.

"Whatever he's drinking," she said, motioning with her head toward the homeless type using the straw.

The counterman smiled, put down his magazine, and went to the glasses and taps behind the counter.

Nina saw Horn sitting in a back booth. There was a woman with him, a fortyish, slender brunette, nice looking in a classy way, wearing a white blouse and what looked like Levis. White slip-on sandals showed beneath the booth's table. The waitress on her day off. The waitress-psychologist. Jesus!

Horn had told her about the woman—Marla, was her name. He'd wanted Marla to be in on this because basically it was her idea. At least she'd given Horn the idea. What was going on here? Was Horn stepping out on that stuck-up blond wife of his? Screwing the waitress? *Naughty, naughty, Horn! Lucky waitress!*

With misgivings, Nina paid for her Pepsi and walked back to join them.

Toward the rear of the diner the mingled scents of lunch were still in the air: pastrami and overfried onions, maybe a spicy mustard somebody had spilled. After introductions, Nina sat down. Horn and Marla were on one side of the booth, Nina across from them. A souvenir American flag was tacked to the wall behind the counter. On the wall to Nina's left was a large, framed black-and-white aerial photo of the Statue of Liberty. That was about it for motif.

Horn explained the plan. It was simple. Beginning with tonight's six o'clock newscast, Nina, with occasional advice from Marla, was to step up her campaign of denigrating the Night Spider, heavier on direct insult and humiliation. Then she'd go about her business as usual, driving home after work, maybe stopping for a late snack as she often did, renting a video movie at Hollywoodland near her building, then spending the evening in her apartment and going to bed at her usual time.

The difference was she'd be protected, surreptitiously, by an army of NYPD undercover cops.

The difference was a world-class serial killer was going to try for her.

The difference was, she'd be bait.

"Bait," she said, thinking aloud.

"That's what you wanted," Horn told her.

Nina forced a nervous smile. "I can't deny it."

"Are you having second thoughts?" Marla asked.

"Sure. Wouldn't you?"

"Wouldn't have had first thoughts, myself."

"I'll play the victim looking for victimizer," Nina said. "I finish what I start."

"*Are* you looking for a victimizer?" Marla asked, calm dark eyes fixed on Nina.

Nina laughed. *Mind your own business, bitch.* "Not hardly. Though I understand that's how the Night Spider might see me. That is, if I'm playing the role well. The unattainable, therefore, more desirable. The haughty who thinks she's superior. The eternal brat who needs a harsh lesson. The challenge."

Marla was nodding. "You do understand."

"Maybe not everything," Nina said. "I haven't spent a lot of time around serial killers. Not intimate time, anyway."

Horn took a sip of coffee. "You won't see us, but you'll be as safe as possible. Even in your bedroom. Especially in your bedroom. The more unaware of us you are, the better. Nothing in your actions will tip off anyone that you're being guarded. If he goes for you, he won't get you."

"Can you promise me that, Horn?"

He shook his head slowly. "You know I can't."

"All right. So we understand each other. We all know that sometimes the fish steals the bait."

"Not this time," Horn said. "Not if I can help it."

"That's all I ask," Nina said.

Marla pushed aside her coffee cup and saucer and leaned toward Nina. "When you talk about him on the air, question his manhood, suggest he can't find sex any other way, or that he's impotent so he has to use a knife. Cowardly's effective, too, with this kind of asshole. Make it clear you think he's a coward, and that everyone else—all your viewers—think he's yellow. And don't hesitate to say he's mentally ill. Use the word *sick* as often as possible."

"I know how to get to him," Nina said.

"But keep it as a mind-set so your words come naturally," Marla said. "Don't script it or make it too obvious. Remember, you're trying to seduce him. You're weaving a web."

"Like his webs," Nina said.

"Very much so." Marla and Horn exchanged glances.

They both liked the web analogy. And Nina thought there might be something else in that glance. She was always looking for changes in relationships, chinks in armor, potential leverage.

"If everything's done right," Marla said, "this killer will try for you. He can't ignore a dare."

"Everything on my end will be done right," Nina said.

"In a way, your job's easy," Horn told her. "Simply lean harder on the Night Spider and live your usual life."

"There's a distinction between simply and easy," Nina said. She looked at Marla. "You were a psychologist?"

"Yes. A psychoanalyst."

"It shows."

"Now and then. Like old scars."

Nina didn't ask her why she was waiting tables instead of overcharging an endless line of neurotics by the hour. Nina would find out in her own time and way. Scars were part of her business. You had to find them in order to pick at old wounds. "Interesting work, psychoanalysis."

"It can be too interesting."

"That why you gave it up? It became too interesting?"

"Too personal."

"Maybe after this you'll have a career as a profiler." Nina rotated her right wrist and glanced at the oversized watch she never wore on the air. "I've gotta go invent some news."

"And make some," Horn said.

"One way or the other, huh?"

"Not the other, Nina. And you don't have to do this."

"You know I have to *finish* doing it, Horn." She smiled. "Or finish getting you to finish it."

"You set it up that way, Nina. Practicing to deceive."

"Jesus! Poetry from a homicide cop! That's what I find fascinating about you, Horn." She stood up from the booth and looked down at Marla. "Webs again, hey?"

"Hey," Marla said.

"Men."

"Men," Marla agreed.

She and Horn watched Nina stride from the diner, tall even in her sneakers, hips switching and long arms swinging with each stride. Arie, the guy behind the counter, lowered his *Sports Illustrated* and looked. The homeless type at the counter even turned his shaggy head to watch her passing.

"Think she'll actually go through with it?" Horn asked.

"She'll do it," Marla said. "Risk has already become dare."

"And?"

"Nina can't ignore a dare, either."

"Um," Horn said. *Webs again*.

"It's fucking crazy," Newsy said, when Nina told him about her meeting with Horn and Marla.

"Lots of news is," Nina said. "Your job'll be to have everything set up so we have tape for a breaking news segment. We'll be the only outlet in the city with tape."

"What? You wan't me to make sure there's tape of that psycho stabbing you to death?"

"Only *if* he stabs me to death. But that's not in the plan. You can set up in the building across the street and tape him lowering himself from the roof, using his glass cutter, and raising my bedroom window and climbing inside."

"You really think the police will let him get that far?"

"Sure. They don't want to arrest some guy who can say he was just out practicing mountain climbing. If he doesn't actually enter my bedroom, they don't have much of a case. You know how it goes when a pack of publicity-hungry defense lawyers makes over a suspect. By the time the trial's over the guy'll be acquitted and have his own talk show."

"You're taking a hell of a chance, Nina."

"Not if the NYPD does its job." She patted him on the shoulder. "I've gotta get to makeup now, do the session for that promo. We set for the six o'clock?"

"Just about. Nina, listen, I'm gonna give you a gun. It's a little thirty-two semiautomatic, a lady's gun. Will you take it?"

"Sure. Then you can stop worrying."

"I'll worry, Nina. I'll worry."

And he would. Because they *were* friends, he'd worry about her. And he'd worry about what would happen to the newscast if something happened to her.

He'd worry about his job. Unemployment. About his life.

Murder was like a stone plunked in a pond, and Newsy Winthrop could see a ripple the size of a wave bearing down on him.

Psychotic. Impotent. Cowardly. Sick scum. Loathsome. Mental case. Sociopath. Yellow. Unmanly. Insecure. Ill. Ineffectual. Sexually stunted. Unbalanced.

What that bitch had said about him! Who did she think she was? What was her right? What could she know? *How dare the evil cunt!*

The Night Spider watched the six o'clock news's final cut to commercial, then used the remote to switch off the television. He was mashing down his finger so hard on the power button, it suddenly occurred to him the black plastic case might crack. With an effort, he relaxed his fingers and set the remote aside.

He sat alone in the silence and listened to his heartbeat. Loathing Nina Count. *Nina Cunt!* Knowing she'd say the same things about him tonight on her eleven o'clock newscast.

It wasn't fair, the way she misused the airwaves, filled them with her poisonous words like stinging darts. And what did she really know about him? She knew about his soft center, she said. Twice, she'd referred to his soft center.

What soft center?

She'd keep talking about him, *to* him. That was how women like that were, taunting him, thinking he was helpless to act. In her corrupt self-absorption, she assumed there was no way to stop her from talking about him to the world.

To the world!

He sat alone in the silence and hid his disfigured face in his hands.

He sat alone in the silence and sobbed.

Horn had finished giving instructions to the dozen cops besides Paula and Bickerstaff whom Rollie Larkin had put at his disposal.

"It's going to be difficult and time-consuming to find the Night Spider," Horn had told Larkin in his office earlier that afternoon. "Nina Count started out a fool, but she's given us the one strong hand we've had to play. We need to play it all the way."

Larkin had leaned back and puffed on the El Laquita Especial Horn had given him as an obvious bribe. "And if anything happens to Nina Count's precious ass, it will be *all* our asses."

"That's how it is," Horn admitted.

"You're already pensioned off," Larkin said. "Out of it."

"I've thought of that. You have the most to lose, Rollie."

"Other than Nina Count."

"Goes without saying. But we might catch a killer."

Another long puff on the cigar. Larkin's office was getting cloudy. "Talking head, set of boobs and legs, but I guess we have to give her that she's got some balls."

"She's counting on us having some, too."

"You're such a bastard, Horn."

"Can be. Yes."

Larkin had carefully propped the cigar in the ashtray on the corner of his desk. "Go ahead and bet your hand, Horn. Raise the stakes."

"I didn't figure you'd let us down, Rollie."

"And spare me the bullshit," Larkin added.

He was picking up the cigar again as Horn left the office and headed for clear air. In the outer office, Larkin's uniformed assistant had a little electric fan spinning on her desk to dissipate smoke. She glanced over at Horn and held her nose as he passed.

Horn smiled. Everybody in the office had balls.

When everyone knew their role and had left the precinct conference room, Horn went to see Royce Sales. Then he called a friend on the FDNY and drove south to the docks.

He wanted everything done right, so he didn't rush. He didn't waste time, either. Time was running out for the Night Spider or for Nina Count.

31

The insults, derision, humiliation! She'd pay; pay soon and in full!

In full!

He knew what she was doing and so did her viewers. That's why she was doing it, to create more viewers, more fans. Playing the brave and dedicted journalist. Trying to lure him, to trap him, to kill him. Using him to boost her pathetic ratings. *Nina Cunt!*

The police, Horn, they'd be in on it, encouraging her, underestimating the Night Spider, the fearsome and fearful, the horrid and elegant. How could they know? How could they know what they were dealing with, how wrong Nina Count was about him? How it would all turn out? *The small and the crawl shall inherit . . .*

There she was again on the TV screen, cold and deadly beautiful, blond as vanilla ice cream, the long shot, the pale legs.

The empress of ice cream. The cunt! The evil, satanic, hurtful cunt!

He couldn't stand to look at her. Couldn't look away from her.

Couldn't wait much longer.

* * *

My God, it was almost routine.

Nina thought this was going better than she'd anticipated. The advice of Marla the waitress-psychologist was golden; she really knew what Nina should say to get to this guy. If only it weren't for the constant and cold lump of fear in Nina's stomach, the loss of appetite and sleep.

She went through the motions of her day, studiously not looking right nor left to be sure she was protected. Denying herself the reassurance. She went to bed as usual, locking the bedroom window but leaving the drapes parted about five inches, per Horn's instructions.

Horn. He phoned her frequently, checking on her, making sure her resolve wasn't crumbling. Which showed how little he knew about her.

Nina carefully locked her apartment door behind her, then kicked off her high-heeled shoes and strode into the kitchen. She paused at the door, scanning before entering. A habit. Had she recently acquired it?

She wasn't drinking alcohol these days, needed to keep her mind clear. So she went to the refrigerator and ran cold water from the ice maker into a glass. Before taking a sip, she held the glass against her warm forehead. Another tension headache tonight. That was what they were. Had to be.

It's worth it. Every night is worth the fear!

Every night her ratings were climbing. And when this horror was over, some of that success would stick. She'd have the highest-rated local newscast for years, until something else came along that could be ridden like this crisis to her desired destination. She'd possess the fact that she'd trapped this fuck-head killer. Have it on her resume always. That could be good for a lot. Her ticket would be punched for the next ride. A bigger show. Network. Or maybe politics were in her future.

Meanwhile, her days were terrible but mundane journeys of boredom, trepidation, and frequent spikes of terror. The unfamiliar face with eyes observing her, the sudden moves of strangers—almost anything abrupt and unexpected—could strum her taut nerves and make her almost scream.

Routine. Repetition. Moving through it like an automaton.

Work, occasional late-night drink, occasional late-night dinner, occasional late-night dread. Home, watch a little TV, bed. Now and then uncontrollable trembling.

Relax! They're there, they're there! Watching over me like guardian angels with guns.

But she knew someone else might be there, watching her. Someone whose compulsion and psychotic game was watching and waiting. Someone clever enough and lethal enough.

She wished *something* would shatter the routine!

Or did she?

Another night or two, another newscast or two. Audience share was building like loan-shark interest, in quantum leaps.

She'd read in the *Post* how there were office polls that bet on her day of death and on how many times she'd be stabbed.

Oh, Christ!

It helped to fall asleep thinking about ratings.

Sometimes it was the only way.

Horn couldn't think of anything more he might do to protect Nina, yet not alert the Night Spider.

"You're not sleeping well," Anne would tell him, before leaving for the hospital in the morning. At this point, he was sleeping mainly during mornings. And afternoons, when Nina Count was safely ensconced at the TV station. Captain Thomas Horn, working the night shift like a rookie cop or a precinct detective on a stakeout. In a strange way, it felt good. Maybe he wasn't as old as he thought. Maybe age was a matter of thought and not time.

Maybe the Night Spider would try for Nina tonight.

Marla said it would happen, and probably soon. The tension would mount in the killer, the pressure would build. Nina's newscasts turned the valve up slightly higher every evening at six and eleven. Psychosis would become urgent, would vibrate like a boiler building steam, would become speculation then decision. Madness would become movement, like physics of the mind.

Marla said.

Anne said again, after leaning over the bed and kissing him on the lips, waking him all the way. "You're not sleeping well."

"Neither are you."

"It's the damned Vine family lawsuit. They've filed more motions."

"If you ever do go to trial, it'll be months before you see the inside of a courtroom," Horn assured her.

"It can't be too soon for me. I want this over. I want to be vindicated."

"You will be." This wasn't how she was talking before; she would have done anything to avoid a court fight.

"You really think so?"

"Sure," Horn lied. He knew juries could do anything. Make up their own laws, if they wanted. Juries were not in the least predictable, and they were as different from each other as snowflakes.

"I just want it to be over."

He caught motion in the corner of his vision and heard the retreating *tak, tak, tak* of her high heels on the hardwood floor.

Unmoving on the bed, he closed his eyes and considered.

She wants vindication and legal absolution; assurance and recognition that she didn't take away a child's conscious life.

I want to stop a killer by preventing a murder; I want to save an unknown number of lives.

I want to change the future.

She wants to define the past.

But he knew he wasn't being fair. Anne lived a life much

different from his. She moved in a different daily world with different priorities. It wasn't a trivial thing, being sued for professional incompetence.

He listened to the front door open and close.

Knew she was locking it behind her. He at least imagined he could hear the snick of the dead bolt as she stood outside and turned her key. Locking something out, or in?

Security. At least the illusion of it. That's about all you get in this world.

Horn fell back asleep, into dark dreams he knew were waiting. Intermission was over. Back to the nightly horror movie. Latest installment. Made for TV. Ratings. The whole thing was being fueled by ratings. Something blacker than night stirred, then turned toward him. Nina Count was waiting for him in his dreams.

Can you promise me that, Horn?

The Night Spider closed the door and locked it. He was inside his apartment. Safe. No one could stare at him here. No one could wonder about him, or somehow know he was the one. *Marked like Cain . . . marked like Cain . . .*

Their eyes couldn't find him here. He was safe.

But he knew he wasn't safe. And he knew pieces of his soul were being bitten off and spat out for public spectacle. Another evening of broadcast insult and humiliation. Questions—no, *statements!*—about his sanity and sexuality.

He emptied the contents of a large shopping bag onto the carpet, then sat cross-legged before them on the floor.

There was no point in wasting time. There was every reason not to waste time.

And every reason to be careful and daring.

He used his thumbnail to slit cellophane, open packages. Then he studied what was spread out before him on the carpet.

Everything was here. Time to set to work. His time. His time was coming.

He threaded the needle on the first try. He unwound about a yard of slender, strong thread from its spool.

By a thread . . . Her life hanging by a thread . . .

He began to sew, his fingers moving with incredible dexterity and precision, faster and faster, never missing a stitch. His unblinking gaze was fixed on his task. He moved to the rhythm of his breathing, the rhythm of his own dark cosmos. Bony breast rising and falling . . . a soft hissing, like a bellows fanning flame.

By a thread . . .

32

It would be tonight.

The weather report promised cloud cover and a sliver of moon. The Night Spider's plans had been laid, the enemy measured. The resignation at last induced by constant fear. Soon would come the stupor of the prey in the grasp of the predator. The prey was waiting, afraid and impatient, secretly wishing to be possessed at last.

And he knew she *was* waiting for him, growing restless in her anticipation. They cooperated with him toward the end, in their surrender. He knew by their eyes. Sometimes they grew eager. Death was magnetic.

After double-checking to make sure he was fully prepared, he slipped into a light silk windbreaker, dark like his slacks.

Cap pulled down, collar up. *Ready.* He opened the door and went out into the night, part of the night. Hell on the hunt.

For the first time in weeks he felt wonderful!

"Maybe he's got this figured," Paula said. "Maybe he's too smart for us this time and won't show. If he wants to, he can just sit back and let Nina crow."

Horn had expressed the same doubts that afternoon to Marla. Her confidence had remained unshaken.

"He can't stay away from her much longer," he said now to Paula, echoing Marla's words. "He's trying to outwait us, lull us into complacency so he can take advantage of our carelessness. He'll show. If we're patient, he'll cooperate. He has no choice."

Paula wasn't so sure. But Horn was the boss.

This time she was glad she wasn't in charge.

She went to her station on the apartment building's roof, out of sight just inside the slanted and slightly opened service door. When she positioned herself just so, she had an unobstructed view of most of the roof's dark expanse.

Getting as comfortable as possible, she settled down with her steel thermos full of coffee, her twelve-gauge shotgun, and her fear.

She found herself thinking about Harry Linnert, then tried not to.

A cop's life. What am I doing here? Why me? How the hell did it happen?

A surflike rush of breeze flowed across the roof, warm as the night. Paula felt a bead of perspiration trickle down the side of her neck. She sighed and rested her hand closer to the gun.

Horn did his nightly inspection before settling down in his unmarked parked across the street, from which he directed the operation. Everyone was in place: undercover cops on the street, observers and sharpshooters on surrounding buildings, more undercover cops posing as building employees or tenants.

If the Night Spider appeared on the roof of Nina's building, they would know. When he did his spider's drop toward her window, he'd be observed every inch of the way. Gun sights would be trained on him in case anything went wrong. There was no way he could get close to Nina Count. But if he did, there was a cop in her apartment as a last line of defense, a borrowed SWAT martial arts expert who, on signal, would move into Nina's bedroom and be waiting for whatever came through the window, while other cops closed in on the apartment fast.

Horn leaned back against the car's soft cloth upholstery. From where he was parked, he had a clear view of Nina's apartment building.

He couldn't help a slight amount of complacency. Inevitably in situations like this, it edged in. Repetition was to blame. And this was another night exactly like the ones before. It was doubtful anything would occur. But he hadn't let down his guard or weakened his defenses. The same precautions were in place tonight that had been here on the first night of the operation.

He tucked in his chin to speak into his two-way. "We're up and running."

Everyone acknowledged they'd heard.

Horn had the car's windows down, so he lit a cigar and smoked it, using his cupped hand to conceal the glowing ember whenever he raised it above dashboard level. He was satisfied that Nina was safe.

Safe as anyone in her position could be.

Newsy, set up with his cameraman behind the window of the building across the street, waited and watched and smoked a filtered Camel. Like Horn, he had his hand cupped to conceal the glow of the ember.

He couldn't help staring across the street at the face of Nina's building as its lighted windows went dark one by one.

At 11:45 P.M., which was her usual bedtime, just after the news starring Nina, her own window went dark.

Newsy stepped back and to the side so he could light another cigarette off the one he'd smoked to a stub. His palms were moist. He wasn't sure how he should feel or even how he did feel.

He wanted something to happen.

He was terrified that it might.

33

The Benadryl hadn't worked tonight. Nina wondered if she might be building up a resistance.

Several hours ago she'd finally drifted into restless half sleep and fragmented dreams. Then she'd come fully awake, wishing it were morning.

It was 3:03 A.M., according to the clock by the bed.

She lay in the dimness and listened to the muted sounds of the city late at night. New York might never sleep, but tonight it was doing a better job than Nina at skirting sleep's edges. Right now there was only the distant whisper of traffic, barely audible, almost like a faraway ocean that occasionally surged closer, then withdrew. Life and time, coming almost within reach.

Her pulse seemed to throb too strongly throughout her body. She could almost hear her blood coursing through her veins, *could* hear it pounding in her ears. *The blue hammer,* doctors called the pulse. Pounding madly on its muted anvil. The lump in her stomach took on weight.

Fear was a curious thing when it never went away, when it made its home in you. It might always be there, but you never got used to it. Not completely. It would lie almost dormant, then grab you from the inside when you least expected it, almost as if it had a sadistic sense of humor that was a reflection of your own.

A car horn honked blocks away outside, startling her. But only momentarily. Now she felt reassured. At least somebody was out there going about normal activities. On the way to see a lover, to go home from a night job, to burgle a business, to—

She told herself to go back to sleep, she was safe. Horn knew his business, and there were cops all over the place outside and in the building. Even that cute one, Detective Lyons, in her living room, almost right outside her bedroom door.

Staring up at the shadowed ceiling, Nina smiled. Maybe she could invite Lyons into her room and engage him in conversation. Maybe—

A slight sound close by, from a direction she couldn't determine, made her heart leap. This wasn't like the car horn, obviously far away.

At first she lay breathless, unmoving. Then she snaked out a long pale arm, opened the nightstand drawer, and withdrew the small, nickel-plated handgun Newsy had given her. It was surprisingly cool and heavy in her hand. Horn hadn't wanted her to have a gun. He was afraid the wrong party might accidentally be shot.

Well, fuck Horn! Especially now! She thumbed off the gun's safety.

Then her addled mind regained some function: *Lyons! Lyons right in the next room, just on the other side of the door! In a situation like this, she was supposed to summon Lyons!*

She tried to call out to him but made no sound. Terror was a steel claw at her throat. She could barely move. Nina never dreamed it would be this bad, that she'd be paralyzed like this.

Her hand trembling, she held the gun beneath the white top sheet, her finger curled around the trigger.

Her eyes strained to peer through the dimness at the rectangle of paler night that was her bedroom window.

She heard the soft rush of the bedroom door scraping on the carpet, opening behind her.

Lyons on the job! Thank God!

Nina tried to tell him she'd heard a sound, but she could only emit a strangled squeak. She chanced turning her head a fraction, looking away from the window.

Not Lyons in the doorway! Not Lyons!

A dark figure as tall as Lyons but thinner and more angular.

More nimble.

Quicker.

Before she could move an inch, before she could inhale to scream, it had crossed the room and was on her.

On the living room floor, Lyons felt warmth and wetness beneath him and knew this was serious, he was bleeding badly. He was on his back, his hands at his sides.

If he could only reach the gun in his shoulder holster . . . fire a shot . . . let them know . . .

Slowly and laboriously, with all the effort he could muster, he raised his lower arm, then his elbow, and felt for the gun in its leather holster.

Not there . . . Maybe to the left . . . there . . .

His fingertips moved exploringly on the coarse nap of the carpet and he knew his arm hadn't risen at all.

A burning sensation at his throat, and he was having difficulty breathing.

He was inhaling but he wasn't breathing.

The knowledge struck him with cold, numbing immensity. The recollection of his surprise, his throat being slit.

He wasn't breathing!

The dimness grew darker until it became blackness and silence.

He died gazing at Nina Count's open bedroom door.

34

Nina writhed and bucked beneath the taut sheet but could barely move. The Night Spider was straddling her, his knee on one side of her, his foot on the other. One of his hands was at her throat, cutting off breath and sound. She tried to adjust her right hand, with the gun in it, so the barrel was aimed at her attacker. She was sure he wasn't aware that she had the gun. At the cold core of her panic, she knew the gun was her one slim chance for life.

Quickly, roughly, a broad rectangle of duct tape was slapped over her mouth, then made tighter so her front teeth bit painfully into her lips. The powerful hand came away from her throat. Salt taste. Blood in her mouth. She managed to swallow it.

She could breathe now. Instinctively she tried to scream. The muffled moan she emitted devasted her. It was as if the silence of death already had her. Soon would come the agony.

Her assailant's eyes were dark and wide, and fixed on hers. Something about them. They seemed to draw from her, to drain all her energy and will to resist. Their whites gleamed in the dimness of her bedroom, making the irises seem all the blacker. She could make out nothing of his features other than his eyes, and she couldn't look away from the eternity of darkness behind them.

Inside the tight sheet that he was now tucking beneath her left side, preparing to begin the winding, her right forefinger was still curled around the gun's trigger. She straightened the rest of her fingers so her hand was cupped over the small pistol, smoothing its contours so it might not be noticeable.

But she knew the barrel was pointing straight down along her right leg. If she squeezed the trigger, the bullet would probably carve a furrow in her thigh and strike nothing else. She desperately needed to shift the weight that bore down on her, pinning her to the mattress. Her legs were encased in material he was skillfully drawing tighter.

She *had* to find the leverage she needed. If only she could lift her knees slightly!

Nina gathered all that was left of her stubborn desire to survive, all her physical strength, and dug her heels into the mattress. She strained to raise her hips so she could drop them suddenly and draw up her legs, which were bound together so firmly.

She moaned with effort and the thing that had come for her life stopped his tucking and winding and looked down at her, cocking its head to one side. She was up to something and he was curious.

Nina moaned again, almost getting her buttocks off the bed. And suddenly it struck her: *He must wonder if I'm actually trying to help him tuck the sheet tight beneath me!*

She caught the gleam of white teeth in the darkness.

He's smiling! He's enjoying this!

His weight shifted and he rose a few inches. He leaned his strong, spindly body back so she could do whatever she was attempting in her desperate, futile struggle.

He's helping me!

And holding out hope! He doesn't want me to give up just yet! Wants me to struggle harder! To almost make it! Starting his game!

Back and forth, life and death . . .

Toying with me!

Nina managed to bend her legs at the knees the thirty degrees or so she thought she needed, then lowered them abruptly and created slack in the sheet.

Enough to adjust her hand and elevate the gun barrel half an inch.

Maybe enough of an angle! . . .

She squeezed the trigger.

The gun roared, and she felt a burning sensation along her right thigh.

He was off her and poised by the bed even before the sound of the shot stopped reverberating. She could hear his breathing, rapid, ragged, oddly inhuman. He was hissing in the silence left by the gunshot. There was more rage and malevolence in that hissing than she had ever heard.

He tensed his body to spring at her.

Movement! Shouting!

From the living room!

Just outside my door!

The Night Spider leaped not toward Nina but toward the window. He unlocked and raised it in one smooth, unbelievably quick motion. It was as if time sped up and swept him along. Quick as a thought, he was through the window and outside, dragging a hand and affixing something to the sill on his way out.

Horn's cigar had gone out and he didn't bother to relight it. His mouth was dry and with the stale taste of too much tobacco and coffee, and he'd almost dozed off behind the steering wheel of his parked car. Not that there wasn't enough activity to merit his attention. On a busy Manhattan street like this one, even at this late hour, there was occasional pedestrian and vehicular traffic.

Then he'd seen an undercover cop named Givers leap to his feet from where he'd been pretending to sleep as a homeless man in a doorway and race into Nina's apartment building.

As Horn was climbing out of the unmarked, he heard "Shot fired!" on his two-way and started to run across the street. He almost slipped and fell in front of a cab letting out a woman in front of the building. She was bent over wrestling packages from the backseat, and looked sideways at him with surprise and concern as he regained his balance and raced past her.

Givers was stepping into the elevator when Horn burst into the lobby. He saw Horn and held the door open for him.

"You hear the shots?" Horn asked, as they ascended toward Nina's floor.

"Yes, sir. Just one shot."

"Sound like it coulda come from inside the apartment?"

Givers gave it some thought before answering. "It coulda, yeah."

When the elevator door glided open, Horn was first out into the hall. A uniformed cop and Bickerstaff were already at Nina's door. Bickerstaff was kicking at the door with the sole of his shoe. Several other doors were open, tenants craning their necks to peer out. A couple of men in pajamas and an older guy in Jockey shorts and a sleeveless undershirt were standing outside their doors. The one in Jockey shorts had mussed gray hair that stood up like a rooster comb. His grizzled chin was thrust out, his fists propped on his hips. Whatever was going down, he was game for it.

"Back inside!" Horn shouted, waving his shield over his head. "Everybody back inside now!"

There were a few defiant and resentful looks, but everyone obeyed. The guy with the rooster comb was last in.

Bickerstaff had given up on kicking and was lunging at the door over and over, slamming into it with his shoulder. Horn saw that the door was open about three inches. Its latch was sprung and its lock ripped from the wooden frame, but something was stopping it from opening farther. Movement on the left. Paula came chugging down the hall, breathing hard after taking the fire stairs.

Givers and the uniform were helping Bickerstaff now, all three men hunkering down and pressing against the door and each other, trying to direct their strength and weight in one direction. A cop, a raggedy grifter, and a guy who looked like an overweight salesman, all struggling to get into the apartment. Paula, the winded college girl with the shotgun, did what she could to help.

"Something's up against the damned thing!" Bickerstaff said, looking over at Horn.

"Where the fuck's Lyons?" the uniform asked, doubling his efforts to budge the door. Each time he strained forward, his eyes bulged and his beefy face got so red he appeared ready to have a stroke.

Horn ignored his bad right arm and joined Paula in awkwardly trying to help with the door, but there wasn't enough room for either of them to make much difference. He knew that, viewed from a distance, there must be something tragically comedic about their struggle.

Then the door moved an inch inward.

Six inches.

At last it grudgingly opened far enough to allow entry.

Bickerstaff was first in, gun drawn. Givers and Horn followed. Horn heard Paula behind him instructing the uniform to stay in the hall.

Horn had his service revolver out and was crouching low to make a small target as he moved to the side and tried to see in the dim living room. A heavy chair had been pushed up against the door, tilted so its back was wedged beneath the knob. Bickerstaff cursed, almost tripping over the chair.

Horn was wondering about the answer to the uniform's question in the hall. *Where the fuck's Lyons?*

"Shit!" Paula said. She'd stepped in something squishy and almost stumbled over Lyons's body near the sofa. She looked down and saw that her right foot was on blood-soaked carpet. "Lyons is shot! Looks dead!"

Horn was appalled and relieved simultaneously. *One shot fired. Not into Nina.*

Then he stepped closer and looked down at Lyons, at the black formless shape that framed his body like a shadow and had leached and spread. "His throat's been slashed."

"Shit!" Paula said again.

"Bedroom!" Horn said, pointing to the hall off the living room. He led the way.

The bedroom door was open. Horn held his breath but didn't hesitate.

There was a little more light in the bedroom. Nina was on the bed wrestling with the sheets, frantically trying to free herself, sit up, and rip a rectangle of tape off her face at the same time.

"Nina!" Bickerstaff shouted, letting her know she had help, friends, she was going to be okay.

Beyond her a shadow moved at the window, not *in* the room but beyond it. *Outside.* Horn thought it might have been an illusion, a trick of light and adrenaline.

"The window!" Givers shouted. "He went out the god-damn window!"

Nina was aware that the bedroom was full of dark figures darting in different directions like flitting shadows and still shouting. She heard her name. Then:

"The window! He went out the goddamn window!"

One of the figures was at the window, leaning outside to peer down.

"He's dropping like a fucking stone. If I take a shot I might hit somebody below."

Nina tried to get untangled from her sheets. She had to break free so she could rip the tape from her mouth and tell them his line was attached to the sill. They should cut it. Detach it. *Let the bastard fall like a stone! See if he shatters like a stone.*

Horn was standing near the foot of her bed, yelling something into his two-way.

"Blood on the sheet!" a voice not Horn's said. "She's hurt."

I'm hurt . . . I'm hurt!

"Blood on the window frame, too," said the figure who'd been peering down the vertical face of the building. He stared at his wet fingertips, then wiped them on his pants leg. "*He's* hurt!"

The Night Spider had been ready for anything but what happened. After the initial shock of the gunshot, he'd quickly wedged his small but sturdy grappling hook beneath the window's marble sill and unfurled his slender polymer line down the side of the building. As soon as he was through the window and into the night, he dropped, rappeling; he almost ran down the building, controlling his rate of fall by playing line through his belayer.

But a few yards beneath Nina Count's window, he realized he didn't have the strength in his left hand to break his speed as much as he wanted. He was dropping too fast.

He squeezed harder and gained a grip on the line, finally slowing his descent but bringing pain where there had been numbness in his left shoulder.

I've been hit! She shot me!

The bitch shot me!

Fury lent him strength. He knew he could do this now, knew he could elude his pursuers. *They have no idea what they're dealing with!*

His hyperalert senses picked up movement above. When he glanced up he saw something he didn't understand. It was dark, jutted out from the building about two feet, and was almost the width of the building. And it was moving down the building's face toward him like a wave descending on a vertical stone beach.

Falling toward him faster than *he* could safely drop!

Then it was on him, around him, over him, past him.

No, not past him.

A net! They dropped a net down the side of the building!

His bare right foot snagged in the heavy rope net and he lost his grip on the line. *Sudden drop!* His knee twisted, and there was a painful wrench to his injured left shoulder.

He found himself caught in the net, dangling upside down and pressed tightly against the stone face of the building by its weight.

He was staring straight down. Ten stories above freedom. At least ten more stories.

Not freedom, though. There were dozens of figures directly below now, staring up at him.

Struggling to free himself, he was overcome by more pain. Not only his shoulder, but his knee. He refused to let them have him! Not alive! If he could manage to reach his knife . . .

They can't have me! They can't!

He raised his upper body, bent at the waist as if doing a midair sit-up, and tried to grip a cross rope of the net but fell back. Now his right arm was entangled in the net. Pain blossomed like fire in his shot shoulder and damaged knee. So much of his weight was hanging by that ruined leg! The pain made him dizzy, nauseating him. It overcame his will and defeated his strength. His hope.

All he could do was wave his left leg freely, his left arm limp and dangling from his injured shoulder.

He felt a warm trickle down the arm and watched blood drip from his fingertips. It twisted and plunged in a thin scarlet thread parallel to the slender line that no longer led to escape.

At the window of the building directly across the street, Newsy Winthrop was almost jumping up and down, using all the self-control he had to keep from pounding his cameraman on the back. *Mustn't do that! Mustn't jiggle the frame!*

"Getting it?" Newsy kept asking, staring at the Night

Spider snagged like an insect in a net, pinned to the building by converging brilliant spotlights, dangling like the unwilling specimen of a bug collector. "Jesus! Are you friggin' getting this?"

"I'm getting it," the cameraman kept answering, trying to ignore Newsy while concentrating as intently on his work as if he were alone.

"We're the only ones getting it, my man! The only ones who'll have it!"

"Take it easy, I'm getting it all. Don't distract me, man, okay?"

But Newsy wasn't listening.

He was thinking Pulitzer.

35

When finally he'd fallen into bed at 7:00 A.M. Horn went over it in his mind, how everything had almost gone terribly wrong.

Almost.

Aaron Mandle was in custody and under high-alert guard at Kincaid Memorial Hospital. The Night Spider murders had ended, finally and forever. If Nina hadn't ignored Horn's instructions and sneaked that gun into bed, then fired that shot . . .

Horn tried not to think about it but his mind kept returning to the night before like a dog returning to something buried not quite deep enough.

Mandle had almost won. He'd almost killed Nina and almost made his escape. Only the crack of the gunshot in the early morning hours had made the difference.

The hard fact was, Mandle had outsmarted them. Lying in his hospital bed, waiting for the courts to decide his fate, he'd be thinking about that and it would mean a lot to him. He had that satisfaction, and Horn didn't like it.

The sick bastard had surprised them.

* * *

"You didn't expect that," Marla said the next afternoon at the Home Away.

Bickerstaff and Paula were sitting with Horn. They were in their usual booth, drinking coffee. All three looked tired after their long night at the precinct house and only getting a few hours of restless sleep that morning. A plate containing only a pat of margarine and dusting of toasted corn muffin crumbs was in front of Horn. He'd drunk half his coffee before switching to ice water with a twist of lemon, still trying to chase the taste of last night.

"No," Horn said, "we didn't expect him to go in through the door. We anticipated him lowering himself from the roof toward Nina's window. That's when we were going to drop the net on him."

"The net," Paula said, lowering her coffee cup, "was one hell of an idea."

Horn had first gone to the FDNY for a net, but they didn't have anything large or heavy enough. Instead, he got several cargo nets from a shipping company on the docks, and had them bound together to form one long, rolled net that could be dropped from the roof as soon as the Night Spider began his descent. Fortunately, the net had been large enough to reach well below Nina's window.

"When we removed Mandle's jacket," Paula said to Marla, "he was wearing what looked like a doorman's uniform. Gold braid, epaulets, and all. Even had a pretty good representation of a doorman's cap wadded in a pocket. Guy was a hell of a seamstress."

"That politically correct?" Bickerstaff asked.

Paula frosted him with a look.

"Mandle figured we'd expect him to drop from the roof," Horn said, "so he got into the building sometime during the day and hid there. After he'd killed Nina, he was going to make sure there was a big hullabaloo in the building, then simply walk out. There are three regular doormen. The one on duty was replaced with an undercover cop. If he'd seen Mandle he'd have thought he was one of the regular doormen. If a regular doorman had noticed him, he'd have assumed he was an undercover cop."

"He only had to fool them for a minute or so," Bickerstaff said, "then he'd have been outside, and it woulda been gone no forwarding."

"Think it would have worked?" Marla asked, switching the heavy glass coffeepot to her other hand.

"He'd have made it work," Horn said.

"You see Nina Count's network TV interview this morning?" Paula asked. "She had her skirt hiked way up so the bandage on her leg was visible."

"I doubt anyone was looking at the bandage," Bickerstaff said. He added cream to his coffee and stirred. "What a dumb fuck Mandle turned out to be. Why didn't he just lay off Nina and keep killing his victims at random?"

"Ask Marla," Horn suggested.

Bickerstaff stared up at her expectantly.

Instead of explaining, Marla said, "Ever do any mountain climbing, Bickerstaff?"

"Never had the urge. Never wanted to fall a long way and get hurt or killed."

"You ever jaywalk?"

"Jesus, Marla! I'm a cop!"

"Uh-huh. Anybody want more coffee?"

Paula came all the way awake immediately and sat up, the way it happens sometimes when you've slept well and late in a strange bed.

It hadn't taken long, she thought. Just till the night after Mandle was arrested. Technically, that might not mean the case was closed. After all, Mandle hadn't even been arraigned yet. Still, it had been close enough. Obviously.

Paula was in Harry Linnert's bedroom, in Linnert's bed. He was already up and dressed and standing at the foot of the bed with an oversized cup of hot chocolate in each hand. Paula usually drank coffee in the morning, but she could switch to chocolate. She knew a lot of her habits might change, being in love with Harry.

"This kind of service gonna continue?" she asked, accepting one of the steaming cups.

"Probably not," he said. "Enjoy it while you can."

"You're a depressingly honest man, Harry Linnert."

"Uh-huh. And look where it's got me."

She glanced at the clock on the nightstand. "Jesus! Ten o'clock. I never sleep this late." She climbed out of bed, careful not to spill hot chocolate. "You're spoiling me. Ruining me."

"You mind?"

"Not terribly."

Naked—she never slept naked—she pecked him on the cheek and padded barefoot into the living room. He'd opened the drapes. She hoped no neighbor with a telescope had been lucky enough to choose their window.

The TV was tuned to Fox News. One of the anchormen, along with the terribly concerned anchorwoman Linda Vester and a former New York judge who'd beome something of a celebrity, were avidly discussing the Night Spider case.

A conviction was almost a foregone conclusion, the judge barked knowledgeably. The anchorman appeared absolutely giddy as he described the tape of Mandle's capture showing on a split screen. Gorgeous Linda Vester pursed her lips and looked unbearably pained and sympathetic toward everyone everywhere who might be suffering any sort of trouble beyond a hangnail.

Paula became aware of Linnert standing near her, off to the side, paying no attention whatsoever to what was happening on television.

She became suddenly ill at ease in her nakedness. She took a sip of hot chocolate. "I usually don't sleep past eight o'clock. It's uncoplike."

"You don't have to be at work till this afternoon," Linnert

reminded her, "which makes it okay that you're out of uniform."

"That's true."

"So what do you want to do with the rest of the morning?"

She placed her cup on the glass-topped coffee table and smiled as she moved toward him. "Go back to bed." She wrapped her arms around him. Finding herself kind of hoping a neighbor with a telescope was out there.

"This how you celebrate when a killer gets arrested?" Linnert asked, when she'd pulled away from their long kiss.

"Yeah. And there's almost always a killer getting arrested somewhere."

Part
Two

Part 1

TWO

36

New York, 2004

Aaron Mandle had been found guilty on four counts of murder and one of breaking and entering. It took the jury less than two hours to reach a verdict.

When the verdict was read, he didn't blink.

The authorities decided to wait until late at night, when the city would be quiet and the streets what passed in New York for deserted, before transporting Mandle back to Rikers Island where he'd be imprisoned while awaiting sentencing.

The Department of Corrections prisoner transport van, locks reinforced, steel mesh over the windows, rode roughly over pavement seams and potholes and stayed on side streets as much as possible. In front sat two uniformed, armed officers. In back, safely separated from them, sat Aaron Mandle and a hulking black wife-killer named Hugo Ward. Ward and Mandle sat facing each other on side benches, handcuffed and wearing leg manacles.

The huge, muscular Ward was bouncing around awkwardly on the hard bench, having difficulty keeping his balance. Now and then he'd glance over at Mandle, who rode smoothly and easily with the motion. Mandle looked calmly back at him.

Guy likes pussy so much he had to kill it, Ward thought. Fucked up in the head. Ward had done a stretch behind walls and figured a sex maniac sicko like Mandle would wind up somebody's wife. See how he'd like pussy when he became it.

"The fuck's your problem?" Ward asked. The Night Spider guy, staring at him with those creepy dark eyes, was getting to him.

Now the guy was bending over like he was tying his shoe, only there were no laces on these shoes.

Ward thought he might chip a tooth, the way the goddamn armored van or whatever it was kept bouncing around. Night Spider guy kept working with his shoe. Ward was getting curious. And angrier. He might go over there and kick the shit outta the Night Spider guy, handcuffs, leg chains, and all. Maybe become a goddamn hero. "Fuck's your problem? You hear me?"

Mandle was having a little problem working off the shoe without cutting his foot on the long steel screw he'd worked from the underside of the courtroom table where he sat during the course of his trial. It had taken him two days to loosen the screw, and another three days to work it back and forth and twist it and twist it until it was out and belonged to him. He'd sneaked it back to his holding cell, then sharpened its point and gradually honed its threads on hard concrete.

At the time the verdict was read, the screw was tightly concealed beneath his right toe, where it joined his foot. He'd changed clothes for his trip back to Rikers, leaving behind his suit and dress shoes, and again wearing his convict's jumpsuit and prison shoes. Prison shoes in which the long steel screw was more easily concealed.

"I ast you a question!" Ward said. "You fuckin' deaf?" Now the guy was taking off his shoe, peeling off his sock and putting it inside, and stuffing shoe and sock inside his jumpsuit. Ward was getting bummed out.

Weird-looking damn foot! Enough of this shit! Get the fucker!

Ward had risen from the bench and was halfway across the van when he realized the Night Spider guy had gotten up a second before he had and was coming at him. Punched him in the stomach. *No power. No fuckin' problem!*

No, not a punch!

Ward had been knifed before and knew he was cut. He looked down and saw a glint of silver clutched in the guy's right hand. The silver flashed and Ward's jumpsuit material parted, revealing soft dark flesh and scarlet blood. The pointed silver thing drew back, popped flesh again, and Ward felt himself being sliced open from pubis to sternum. It had all happened so fast he was stunned and hadn't had time to react. Now the Night Spider guy was . . .

Oh, Jesus, he's reaching inside me!

Ward went into shock and couldn't make a sound, so Mandle screamed. He jumped to the front of the passenger end of the van and hammered on the wire-enforced rear window that provided a view from the cab.

The penal cop in the passenger seat, middle-aged man with a handlebar mustache, twisted around to see what was happening and could make out only Mandle's distorted face. The thick glass divider muffled enough sound that he couldn't make out what Mandle was screaming.

Mandle saw the driver's eyes flit to the rearview mirror every few seconds. Mustache twisted around farther and worked the sliding panel so he could hear what Mandle was saying.

"Bleeding to death!" Mandle screamed. "He got a razor blade and cut himself! He's gonna fucking die if you don't do something!" As he screamed he moved aside so Mustache would see the carnage in the rear of the van, Ward gutted like a hog, gray intestines spilling out, and all the blood in the world.

Mustache screamed himself. "Oh, Christ! Stop the van! Pull over! Stop the fucking van!"

"Help this poor bastard!" Mandle shouted. "Please help him!"

"You shut the fuck up!" Mustache yelled, as the van swerved and lurched to a stop. Mandle had a chance to check through the windshield as the van's doors opened and the two cops piled out. A fraction of a second was all he needed. Dark street, no traffic, brick walk-ups, and small, closed businesses. Careful not to slip in the blood, he shuffled to the rear of the van.

When the doors flew open he was ready.

He held on to the grip bar and swiveled his body to lift both legs and kick the one who'd been driving, catching him under the chin with his bare foot. Kicked again even as the man's head was snapping back and felt his big toe find the Adam's apple. Saw at the same time the ring of keys on the man's black leather belt.

Mustache had his 9mm out of its holster and was raising it when Mandle swung himself out of the van. The guard got off a wild shot just before Mandle landed almost up against him and head-butted him. Mandle bent low and slit Mustache's throat with the sharp screw. Picked up the dropped 9mm with his right foot, transferred it to his hand, and shot the driver. The driver didn't want to die quite yet, so Mandle hopped over and pummeled his head and face with the handgun. Yanked his gun from its holster to match the one he had.

It took him seconds to get the driver's keys, maybe another thirty seconds to find the one that unlocked the cuffs and leg manacles.

Mandle stole a glance around. No sign of anyone behind him. The van's headlights illuminated the street ahead. No one. A car passed at the cross street, barely slowing down to obey a stop sign. The van's lights would have blinded the driver even if he had bothered to look all the way up the street.

Mandle worked the dead van driver's wallet from his hip pocket and flipped it open. Bills. Maybe fifty dollars' worth. He didn't bother with Mustache's wallet; he had to get out of there.

He sprinted halfway down the block and felt a pain in his right side. Maybe Mustache had aimed well after all, but the wound didn't feel serious. He cut into a dark passageway. He felt good now despite the throbbing pain beneath his ribs. Exhilarated. His approach startled something behind a trash bag. A dark cat flashed out and streaked through the night to disappear down the alleyway.

The Night Spider grinned. *You and me, baby! You and me! On the run. The small and the crawl.*

There were hours of darkness left. More than he needed. Resourcefulness was his training and his life, his survival. He knew he could find clothes somewhere somehow, ditch the Rikers jumpsuit, and fade into the city the way the cat had blended with the night. He had supreme confidence in himself and his destiny. Soon he'd have his wound tended and healing. He'd have food, shelter, cover. A new identity.

Revenge.

37

They were back at the Home Away.

After Mandle's escape was discovered at 3:16 A.M., Rollie Larkin had phoned Horn, who'd already left in a charter boat for a rich fishing area twenty miles out in the Gulf. Bickerstaff, who hadn't been able to sleep, had caught the news on his TV in Minnesota—watching Nina Count in the anchor job she'd landed at CNN in Atlanta—and phoned Paula, who was working a double shift. He left a disbelieving and agitated message on her machine. Harry Linnert, lying alone in Paula's bed listening to it, decided it would do no good to bother her with it till morning.

But Paula learned of the escape when she was paged just after dawn and phoned into the precinct on her cell phone. After cutting the connection, she'd gone into a hotel rest room and been sick.

Afterward, she'd called Horn at the Florida resort and was told he was fishing, and that Bickerstaff had also called Horn. She called Bickerstaff and got his answering machine, because he'd gone out to paddle his canoe in the lake to work off stress. She called her machine and listened to Bickerstaff's message. Then Linnert got on the phone and unsuccessfully tried to make her feel better.

When she hung up, she thought if Aaron Mandle could know all this he'd be delighted.

When Horn got back to shore at two o'clock the next afternoon after not catching a marlin, he returned Larkin's call.

Three hours later, in the air over the Carolinas, he called Paula and Bickerstaff. He told Bickerstaff he should stay retired. Bickerstaff told Horn what he could do with the entire notion of retirement while Mandle was again at large. Horn didn't mind. He found out when Bickerstaff and Paula could make it, then set up the meeting at the Home Away.

Paula didn't know how the others felt, but she couldn't shake the eerie feeling they'd been moved like chess pieces back into the past to relive it, as if destiny wanted to change what had happened last time around. Destiny was always fucking with people.

"There's still no word on Mandle's whereabouts," Horn was saying, seated in the same booth toward the back of the diner. "He disappeared like smoke after killing the other prisoner and the two guards."

"Disappeared with their guns," Bickerstaff pointed out. He'd lost some weight and grown a scraggly beard. He looked healthier. But right now, not happier.

"Looks like what he used on the prisoner and one of the guards was a wood screw about four inches long," Horn said, "honed so the point and threads were sharpened. There was flesh from the prisoner and the dead guard lodged between the screw's threads."

Bickerstaff made a face over his coffee cup. "Where the hell'd he get a long screw he could make into a weapon?"

"In court, it looks like," Horn said. "Gradually worked it out of the underside of the table while his lawyer was mesmerizing the jury and judge and bailiff and millions of TV viewers. It was one of the long screws that helped fasten the legs to the table."

"Jesus!" Bickerstaff said. "That's why he spent most of his trial sitting at the table with his head bowed, so he could work at the screw. Maybe he used a coin or something for a screwdriver."

"Maybe," Horn said. "What matters now is he's on the loose again. And nobody's seen him. Or called the police if they have."

"Difficult to imagine a fugitive who looks like that, wearing a prison jumpsuit, can stay unreported very long," Paula said. But she didn't really believe it. Not about this fugitive. "He has to change his clothes. At least you'd think somebody'd find the jumpsuit."

"He might have burned it," Bickerstaff said dejectedly. "By now, he might be a thousand miles away in a different city."

"There's not much chance of that," Marla said. They hadn't realized she'd been standing so near. "He won't leave. Or if he does, he'll soon come back. This is where it all has to play out for him. His life and death have to create a certain symmetry, or what he's done and is going to do are meaningless. He can't accept that he's without meaning, that he can die or be imprisoned without attaining his own twisted idea of grandeur. He's crossed the Rubicon and believes in destiny. And in vengeance."

They sat staring at her, knowing in a way deeper than logically that she was right.

She smiled tentatively, as if suddenly embarrassed.

Topped off their coffee.

Alice Duggan figured she had the part nailed. For over a year she'd been understudy to the star of the off-Broadway hit comedy *Leave Her, Take Her, She's Mine.* This morning limited auditions had been held for the starring role, since the present star, Marnie Willison, had announced she was leaving at the end of the month.

Alice knew the show's author wasn't keen on her stepping into Marnie's role on a regular basis, but the director and producer wanted her to have the inside track. Alice's agent had taken the risk of hinting that if Alice didn't assume the role, she might follow Marnie in leaving the show, necessitating finding another understudy. An hour ago Alice had gotten word that the strategy seemed to have worked.

She felt great when she left the theater after morning auditions. On the sidewalk were scattered playbills from the show, along with inserts from last night announcing that she was playing Marnie's role for that performance. She saw the fluttering white inserts stuck to the concrete with stepped-on gum, or pinned by the breeze against the theater wall, as a good omen.

After taking the subway downtown to within a few blocks of her apartment near Twelfth Street and Broadway, she stopped in at a drugstore to buy toothpaste and a *Times*. Then, on impulse, she stopped at a sidewalk stand and bought a bouquet of colorful flowers to brighten up her apartment.

Her world was looking up. Hard work might soon pay off. There was always the possibility—in her mind, anyway— that if she grabbed and shook this role as she knew she could, *Leave Her, Take Her, She's Mine* might find a new life and a new home on Broadway.

As she walked along the sunny, crowded sidewalk, kicking out her long dancer's legs in easy, optimistic strides, she had no way of knowing she'd been followed from the moment she'd left the theater.

"The rumor is the star's leaving the show," Anne said to Horn, while they waited for a cabbie to pay attention to Horn's raised left arm. The theater was close enough to Times Square that the crowd disgorged back onto the street after curtain was joined by theatergoers from other plays on their way home. Half a dozen people stood up-traffic from Horn and Anne, also unsuccessfully attempting to lure cabs. A man in a business suit was impatiently waving a folded newspaper as if it were a signal flag being ignored. Nothing seemed to work. Few things were more coy than a New York cab after the theater break.

"The stand-in wasn't bad," Horn said. "Whatever her name is." He watched a lucky couple half a block up the street hurriedly climb into a cab before a nearby woman on the run could reach it.

"Alice Duggan."

"She'll never be a star, with a bland name like that."

"Remember Cloris Leachman." Anne's tone suggested she'd taken his comment seriously. Probably because she was distracted and only half listening. Horn had known all evening there was something other than the play on her mind, and that there had been for some time.

"Let's skip the cab for now," he said. "It's a nice night. Let's walk a few blocks to that coffee shop we used to stop in and wait for the theater crowd to thin, have some cappuccino, maybe a pastry."

She didn't say yes or no, but fell in beside him as he stepped back up on the curb and began walking. He glanced out at the flow of traffic and counted three cabs whose roof lights indicated they were without passengers. Their drivers were ignoring prospective passengers frantically beckoning them.

Horn and Anne both ordered simple decaf. Sign of growing old, Horn thought ruefully. He glanced around at the oak- and fern-adorned coffee shop, and the counter with computers where half a dozen patrons sat gooing up keyboards with doughnut glaze. He remembered a workingman's bar at this site twenty years ago, mob connections, assaults, illegal gambling, a fatal knifing. The city was changing, had always been changing, always would change. A lot of it was for the better.

Over second cups of coffee, Anne decided to tell him what was on her mind.

"Finlay was in to see me today. About the Alan Vine case."

"How's the kid doing?"

"The same."

"And the lawsuit?"

"That's what Finlay wanted to talk about. The hospital made another offer to settle. Half a million dollars."

"The Vine family accept it?"

"We're still waiting to find out." She raised her cup, then looked at it sourly and put it back down. "The hospital's also offered to accept blame. In exchange for indemnification, of course."

Horn knew where she was going. Why she was upset.

"The radiology department's being made the scapegoat in the settlement and will be tagged as incompetent and dangerous. And I'll be wearing an identical tag. It isn't fair."

"No, it isn't. What about personal indemnification?"

"That's part of the deal. The Vines won't be able to squeeze any money out of me. But that's not the goddamn point!"

"I understand," Horn said quickly. "But at the same time, it'll be nice to know you can't be sued."

"I'm going to resign."

Horn wasn't sure he'd heard correctly. Maybe she meant transfer out of Radiology. "You mean quit your job?"

"Yes." She drilled him with a cold stare, anticipating his reaction. "Like you quit yours."

"Mine was a case of involuntary retirement, with a disability pension."

"The result was the same: you left the NYPD. Just as I'm leaving Kincaid Memorial. I have plenty of money saved up outside my 401K. Enough to last till I find other work."

"I was thinking more about you possibly giving up legal protection as part of the hospital staff. You've only heard Finlay's take on the lawsuit and proposed settlement. Maybe you should see our attorney. I can give him a call tomorrow."

"I already talked to him."

There was a surprise. "It's a big decision," Horn said needlessly, while trying to sort all this out and think of what else to say. What exactly was going on here?

"Not anymore. I've made it."

"Then that's that. Money should be no problem. There's no reason for you to be employed other than if you want to be."

He was looking out the window at the string of unmoving headlights. Theater traffic had backed up and spread to the side streets.

A cop's wife . . . he thought, knowing before he knew.

"I'm going to move out of the house," Anne told him. "I've decided to leave you."

38

They were in Horn's den. The Home Away had been too crowded tonight for them to privately discuss the Night Spider case. At least that was what Horn had told them. It didn't set quite right with Paula.

When they'd entered the brownstone, she'd noticed a stack of cardboard boxes in the entry hall, and a glance into the living room suggested furniture and knickknacks had been removed.

Horn settled in behind his desk; Bickerstaff took an overstuffed brown leather chair. Paula sat in a similar chair that hissed and acted as if it wanted to devour her. The floor overhead creaked. *Anne must be home, moving around up there. Doing a lot of moving around.*

Horn opened a wooden humidor on his desk and got out a cigar so dark it was almost green, then cut off its tip with a miniature guillotine. He held another of the cigars out for Bickerstaff, who hesitated, then accepted the offer. The guillotine didn't work so well in his hands. Paula thought he might cut off a finger.

"Paula?" Horn offered, holding up another cigar.

"Thanks," she said, "but I'm a lady." *And I thought smoking in the house was against the rules.*

Horn and Bickerstaff chuckled at that lady remark. Paula didn't know quite how to take it. She traded glances with Bickerstaff, who finally appeared to be catching on that something essential had changed there. He looked away from her and peered cross-eyed at the tip of his cigar as he struggled to light it with a paper match he'd produced from somewhere.

"Anne and I have decided to separate," Horn said between puffs, effortlessly firing up his cigar with a silver lighter. "She's rented an apartment on the East Side and is preparing to move out."

The boxes in the hall. The missing furniture. Paula didn't know what to say. Heard her own voice. "I'm . . . sorry." *Shit! Inadequate!*

Bickerstaff said nothing but paused in his puffing, salivating attempt to get his cigar burning.

Horn gave a shrug that might have meant anything.

"I think I might not've cut the whole tip off thish thing," Bickerstaff said around the dead cigar.

Horn slid the guillotine across the desk to him. "Mind your finger."

Bickerstaff took another swipe at the saliva-moistened tip of the cigar with the little angled blade, then tried again with a match. "Thash better." Paula saw ash drop from the burning tip of the cigar onto the carpet. Overhead, the floor creaked. *God!*

"So we get to work," Horn said. "Summarize what we've learned."

"That'll be easy," Bickerstaff said, holding the cigar between index and middle fingers, "considering it isn't much."

"Evidence suggests both guards were killed at almost the same time," Paula said, "one with the sharpened screw Mandle used to disembowel the other prisoner. The other was shot, then his face and head were bludgeoned, probably with the butt of the gun."

"The guard's gun," Horn said.

Paula nodded. "Mandle's got both their guns."

"Any witnesses turn up?"

Bickerstaff said, "Not anyone who saw the escape itself. It had to have happened lightning fast. A guy named Smith—actually Smith—who happened to be glancing out a window of a sleazy hotel near where the escape took place and said he saw someone in what he called prison garb leaving the scene on the run. Then Smith disappeared. Apparently doesn't want to get involved. Wants to join all those other Smiths out there who aren't really Smiths."

"We've canvassed the neighborhood," Paula said. "Doubled patrols in the area, buttoned up the airports and Port Authority, put a watch in the subway. And, of course, every minute and a half the media are showing that creepy photo of Mandle taken during the trial."

She thought she might have heard the doorbell chime in the bowels of the house, some noise on the stairs. Horn didn't seem to have noticed. Or care.

"Not that it'll do much good," Bickerstaff said, "but we're keeping a watch on the building where Mandle rented an apartment under an assumed name. Maybe something'll draw him back to his familiar neighborhood—a favorite item he left behind, unfinished business, an old love or something."

"Somebody he forgot to murder," Paula said.

Bickerstaff drew on his cigar and looked at it appraisingly the way cigar smokers do, as if pleased by it and wondering what it was going to do next. "It's amazing—" he said. Paula thought he was going to comment on the cigar. "—the way Mandle just dropped out of the world without leaving tracks. He kills three men, then unlocks handcuffs and leg irons and strolls away dressed in a luminous jumpsuit. Right off the end of the earth. So far, a perfect disappearing act. How the hell did he bring it off?"

"It's his training," said a voice from the doorway.

And there was Colonel Victor Kray in full military uniform, his regulation coat slung casually over his arm. The

medals on his chest gleamed as if he'd just polished them—
or had an aide do it.

"I know because I trained him."

"I feel somewhat guilty," Kray said, stepping the rest of
the way into the room. He draped his coat over the back of a
chair but remained standing. "I don't think I fully got across
to you earlier how skilled Mandle would be in the lethal arts.
And that includes the art of subterfuge. If he's hiding from
the police, from the world, he won't be easily found. He's
trained to be elusive in countries where he doesn't even
speak the language."

Horn's only response was to offer Kray a cigar.

"I don't smoke," Kray said. "But I wouldn't mind another
glass of that single malt scotch."

Paula was beginning to feel as if she'd wandered into a
men's club. *What next? A pheasant hunt and billiards?*

Horn got up from behind the desk and poured Kray his
drink. Paula and Bickerstaff declined, and Horn put the bottle back in its cabinet then returned to sit behind his desk.
Though there was a chair nearby, Kray didn't make a move
to sit down. Paula wondered how he could appear so relaxed
while maintaining such an erect posture. *Must be leadership.*

"I came back," Kray said, after sampling the scotch, "to
offer my help. After all, the Night Spider is, in a way, my
creation. I taught him how to move like a ghost and kill, and
then hide."

"And now you think you're better qualified than anyone
to find him," Horn said.

"I think I might be the *only* one who *can* find him," Kray
said. "Or who can effectively help you find him."

"How do you intend to help?"

"In any way you choose. Fill me in on what you know
about his escape, keep me apprised, and as events unfold,
you can contact me and I'll provide any insights I can.

Obviously, you can accept or reject my suggestions. If nothing else, I'll sleep easier knowing I made them. I'll be staying at the Sheraton Towers. Not for an indefinite period of time, but as long as my absence from other duties permits."

Horn thanked him. "I'm sure your insights and advice will be of value."

"And of course," Kray said, "I'd appreciate it if you'd view me as a kind of ace in the hole. To alert media or other agencies of my involvement would be to admit the SSF exists, which officially it doesn't. The relatively few people who know about it get kind of prickly if they're forced to go on record denying they've ever heard of it. Elections, promotions, and all might be at stake. Careers."

"Such as your own," Bickerstaff said.

Kray shot him a look that seemed to physically press Bickerstaff back in his chair. "Yes, such as my own."

Horn said he understood, and that they appreciated the risk Kray was taking. They'd do everything possible to maintain confidentiality. Bickerstaff and Paula seconded the sentiment.

Kray finished his scotch, then smiled graciously and nodded to each of them in turn as he said his good nights. He abruptly did a kind of smooth about-face, scooping up his coat from the chair back as he spun, and showed himself out.

The room seemed to have been made smaller by his leaving. Paula thought you didn't often meet somebody whose absence made almost as profound an impression as his presence. The man did have an effect. She felt as if she'd hear an order to charge up a hill any second, and up the hill she would go.

"Well?" Horn said, after about half a minute.

"He doesn't waste our time with small talk," Paula said.

"He said what he came to say," Bickerstaff remarked in a tone of admiration, "so it was time to leave and he went."

"How very military," Paula said.

Bickerstaff puffed on his cigar. "You think about it, Paula, we've won some wars."

* * *

Horn's first night alone in the brownstone. Scotch straight up. Cuban cigar and the hell with the smoke and lingering tobacco scent. He was still bewildered and smarting from Anne's departure, and knew he was indulging himself in a way that was almost childishly defiant.

Living alone. Old cop aging in an old house in an old part of an old city. It was a depressing thought, but at least it had *some* advantages. Like greater personal freedom.

Damn, the place was quiet!

He'd just returned from a steak dinner at a neighborhood restaurant he'd always liked but Anne despised. Full stomach, good liquor, and a quality cigar. He knew he should feel at least some sense of well-being if not contentment. What he had, what he was left with, was far beyond the means and luck of most people in the world. There was a reason why misery loved company. It was probably comparison.

But he felt no contentment, and it was no comfort that others had more reason for misery. In the land of the blind, the one-eyed man still had only one eye. He remembered a time long ago when fledgling TV journalist Nina Count almost touched a microphone to the nose of a young cop who'd just shot and killed a burglary suspect and asked, "How do you feel? Right now?" Then it became such a cliché that even TV journalists no longer asked the question. It was an interesting question despite its intrusive and often tasteless nature. Horn took a sip of scotch and asked it of himself.

Lonely, was the answer. *Right now, I feel goddamned lonely.*

He realized he hadn't been lonely in years. Really lonely. The kind of lonely that grabs at your guts and makes you afraid to look into yourself.

He also had to admit he was feeling too sorry for himself. If there was any emotion Horn hated it was self-pity. It robbed you of everything worthwhile. It made you vulnerable.

He mentally castigated himself for falling into such a

funk. *Don't be such an asshole. You've got a life to live. A job to do.*

A job . . .

He tried to concentrate on the Mandle case: how the murderous bastard had escaped, what a capable killer he must be. A man trained to kill in the service of his country now killing in the service of his psychosis.

Was it a psychosis? Or was Mandle simply evil? The truth was that Horn had never much bothered himself about the distinction. His job, his calling, was to stop people like Aaron Mandle, to remove them from society. The world didn't set itself right. For everyone who broke things material or human and upset the balance, someone had to repair and restore and realign. Horn wasn't only working for the city; he was working for the victims. Justice was not an abstract to Thomas Horn.

Illness or malevolence or both, whatever fueled his intent, Mandle was certainly doing evil. And if he wasn't found again and stopped, the evil would resume. That was enough motivation for Horn, enough reason to live and to rouse himself and confront each fresh new morning.

Or so he told himself.

He snuffed out what was left of his cigar, drained the last quarter inch of his drink, and trudged upstairs to bed.

Sleeping alone was nothing new. Because of the hours a cop kept and the hours a hospital administrator kept, Horn and Anne had often slept alone.

But going to bed alone wasn't the same thing as going to bed lonely.

Getting up early wasn't the same thing as waking up early, either. Horn had been awake for hours before finally climbing out of bed when dawn light began filtering into the room.

He put on a robe, stepped into comfortable lined leather slippers, and went down to the kitchen. After getting the

Braun coffeemaker clucking and gurgling, he padded into the foyer, expecting to hear Anne's footfall upstairs or see a note from her on the hall table explaining where she'd gone. When she'd return.

Not gonna happen! Stop messing with your own mind!

Time to step outside and get the morning paper, if no one had stolen it. He knew that by the time he stepped back inside there'd be at least a faint scent of fresh coffee in the brownstone. He'd have a cup at the kitchen table while he scanned the news. Then he'd shower, dress, and walk down to the Home Away for a proper breakfast.

When he opened the door, he wasn't surprised not to find a paper on the concrete stoop or within sight on the sidewalk.

But there *was* something on the porch. A chess piece. A plastic red knight about four inches tall.

Horn thought it was interesting the way it had been placed on the porch, tucked up against the inside of the wrought-iron railing so it couldn't be seen from the street. Someone would have to walk up on the stoop and then turn almost all the way around in order to spot it. Or open the door and look out.

He bent over, picked up the piece, and examined it. Nothing unusual. Cheap plastic from a mold. The red knight was from the sort of set that could be bought at just about any store that sold games.

Horn carried the chess knight into the house and placed it on the kitchen table. He poured a too strong, half cup of coffee, then sat down at the table and looked at the knight, wondering what it might mean. Almost surely someone had placed it on the porch deliberately where he—or Anne— would notice it when leaving the brownstone.

Horn sipped and thought, while the bitterness of lukewarm coffee displaced the stale aftertaste of last night's cigar. Some trade.

The thing about the knight, he mused, was that it was the

only chess piece capable of moving *above* other pieces. It could drop straight down to capture an opponent's piece.

Did that really mean something? Was he making too much of this? Had some homeless person or wandering kid simply found the chess knight on the sidewalk and placed it out of harm's way on the stoop, thinking it might belong to whoever lived in the brownstone? A thoughtful gesture. Such things could happen in New York. Along with the brusequeness, mayhem, and murder, such things could happen.

The phone rang.

Setting down his cup, Horn twisted his body and stretched out his left arm to lift the receiver on the kitchen extension. He glanced at the microwave clock as he put plastic to ear and said hello, wondering who'd be calling him at 6:45 in the morning.

It was Anne.

She was screaming.

39

When Horn finally got Anne calmed down enough to be coherent, she told him over the phone that someone had been in her apartment.

"You're sure?"

"I called, didn't I?" Fear was becoming anger. But plenty of fear remained vibrant in her voice.

Horn fought down his initial alarm. Like him, Anne wasn't used to living alone, and she was in a precarious mental state due to the hospital lawsuit, and the loss of her marriage and job. Who could blame her for overreacting to whatever it was that had scared her?

"How do you know someone's been there?"

"Things aren't the same as when I went to bed last night."

It was a sublet apartment on East 54th Street; most of the furniture and incidentals belonged to the regular tenant. "A new place, Anne. Maybe you're not sure yet where everything belongs." *Maybe you made a mistake, leaving. Maybe you belong here.*

"I'm not an idiot, Thomas! It isn't only that items seem to have been moved about. There are things that weren't here when I went to bed." Her voice broke and he thought she was about to lose control again. But she remained calm. "Some things on my dresser. To think someone was right here while I was sleeping a few feet away, unaware. Christ, it gives me the chills!"

But he knew how strong she was. *What had set her off so! Rattled her so that she was screaming when she phoned?*

"What was it you found on your dresser, Anne?"

"I . . . I'm not sure. Yes, I am. It looks like a tooth with . . . maybe part of the gum still attached."

"A tooth? You certain?"

"I think that's what it is."

"Maybe from the previous tenant."

"Sure, Thomas. That happens all the time, somebody moves out and leaves a tooth." *Sarcasm. Good.*

"Could be there was a pet there and it's a dog's tooth. Does it look like an animal tooth?"

"Well . . . I guess it could be."

"What else, Anne? Stay with what's on the dresser."

"Something not so disturbing. A little black figurine."

"What kind of figurine?"

"Cheap, plastic. The neck and head of a horse."

Horn went cold. "A chess piece?"

"Now that I hear you say it, yes, it could be. It probably is a chess knight. I suppose that's something I overlooked last night. I should have known what it was right away." She sounded peeved, as if he'd accused her of doing something wrong. "The previous tenant might have played chess and the piece got separated from the rest of the set. Something like that. Bounced under the bed and the janitorial service found it, and when the maid reached for it she slipped and struck her mouth on the bed frame and a tooth—"

"Anne."

She recognized something in his voice and fell silent.

"So you're cool enough to be sarcastic," Horn said.

"Yeah, I suppose you're right. But damn it, Thomas! . . ."

"Are you on the cell phone?"

"Yes. The phone service in the apartment hasn't been switched over yet."

"Is there a window in the bedroom?"

"Of course."

"Go to it." He waited only a few seconds.

"I'm there."

"Is the window locked?"

"Yes. Just as I left it last night."

"Don't just glance at it. Look more closely. At the glass near the lock."

"Oh, fuck! Thomas?"

"The glass is cut away so the lock could be worked from outside. Right?"

"That's right. But . . ."

"Be calm and listen, Anne. Please."

He heard her sigh, hoped it wasn't a sob. Then: "I'm okay. What now?"

"Lock the bedroom door and stay inside until you hear the police or the voice of someone you know."

"Thomas!"

"Will you do that?"

"Of course!"

"Someone will be there soon, I promise. I'm going to hang up now so I can make phone calls while I dress and drive."

"Thomas, hurry!"

"I'm stepping into my pants. I won't be the first one there, but I won't be far behind."

He called 911 before leaving his house and was out of the building and in his car within five minutes, driving fast and recklessly and one-handed while making his other calls. First, the governing precinct, to light a fire under their collective ass, then Paula. She could phone Bickerstaff.

When Paula had hung up, Horn called the precinct house again to make sure they were on the move. Thinking there might be something to that law against simultaneously driving and using a cell phone in New York. The drivers blasting their horns at him, gesticulating and shouting insults as he sped past or cut them off, sure were in favor of it.

By the time Horn reached Anne's building and got up to her apartment on the twenty-ninth floor, it was crowded and buzzing with activity. His first impression as he approached the open door was that a party was going on there. His wife's new apartment and she was throwing a party and he wasn't invited. *Jesus, what an inane, self-involved thought.*

He walked in past the open door. Strange apartment. Modern furniture except for what Anne had contributed. Some things were familiar, most not. *Did Anne really live here?* He knew almost everyone at the party: Paula, Bickerstaff, a hulking plainclothes detective named Ellison; Johansen, one of several techs swarming the place, vacuuming for hairs and particulate matter; two uniforms, one of whom Horn knew though he couldn't recall his name. He was a big guy with a deep scar on his face. It bothered Horn that he seemed to have lost some ability to put name to face. Advancing age?

Bullshit!

Anne saw him and came to him. "Thanks, Thomas." At first she appeared ready to hug him, then stepped back, merely touching his arm.

"You back to your usual self?" he asked.

She managed a smile that was a little weak at the corners. "Pretty close. Thanks in large measure to you."

Beyond Anne, Horn saw Paula standing in a doorway. She nodded and beckoned to him.

He left Anne talking to the patrolman with the scar, made his way toward Paula, and saw that the doorway led to the bedroom. Paula moved aside so he could enter.

A woman from the ME's office was hunched over the dresser, picking up something with tweezers and preparing to drop it into a clear plastic evidence bag. She was young, almost a kid. Straight blond hair, blue eyes, no makeup because she didn't need it. Looked like a cheerleader his daughter had known years ago in junior high. But she carried herself and did her work with a kind of confidence Horn liked.

He moved closer. She knew who he was and didn't object, even inched over to make room for him. He looked down at a pointed white tooth with gray matter dangling from it.

"Tell me that's an animal's tooth," he said.

"It's a human eyetooth," said the assistant ME, who'd probably never been a cheerleader. "I'd guess it was knocked out, or maybe caught in material or something and ripped out. People get in fights sometimes, try to bite the other guy, and their teeth get snagged in a shirt or whatever. A violent motion and the tooth gets yanked."

"Have you ever actually seen that?"

"Once. A bunch of teeth, all false. We got a good yuk out of it."

Horn pointed to the object in the delicate grasp of the tweezers. "So what's that hanging from it?"

"That's part of the gum still attached."

"You're sure?"

"I'm sure. But we can all be positive after some concurring opinion and basic tests to confirm."

Horn saw the chess piece near the base of the dresser mirror. Black plastic. An opposing knight to the red one he'd found on the brownstone's stoop this morning. Almost certainly it was from the same chess set.

He walked over to the bedroom window. There was the brass lock that connected top and lower aluminum frames. It was set, but that was meaningless; behind it, a neat crescent of glass had been cut away and was prevented from falling by a strip of masking tape.

There wasn't any doubt now.

Aaron Mandle had been here.

Horn remembered the hateful diatribes in court. The

dead-eyed, baleful stares. How Mandle must despise him! Must blame him for his capture and conviction.

And now he wanted to punish Horn by making Anne one of his victims.

Mandle wouldn't know about their separation. He must be assuming Horn had moved Anne out of the brownstone and was hiding her here for her protection until the Night Spider was once again captured and imprisoned.

And right now Mandle was moving freely and could take Anne whenever he chose. That was the message of last night. The chess knights, signifying that the game had begun. The opposing knight and the grisly souvenir, letting Anne—and Horn—know that Anne was alive only because the Night Spider didn't yet want her. Her destiny was in his hands. The knowledge would be toxic, working inexorably inside her. She walked the earth knowing her free will meant nothing if it existed only at his discretion. She wasn't free at all and never would be again. After last night, her every breath occurred only because he chose to let breathing continue.

And it wouldn't continue much longer.

The Night Spider was toying with her, and showing his disdain for Horn.

The intricate dance that would end in torture and slow death had begun.

40

"So you placed her under police protection?" Marla asked the next morning. Horn was waiting for Paula and Bickerstaff to arrive at the Home Away. She placed his plate of toasted corn muffins on the table. There was still some breakfast crowd in the diner, so their conversation had been sporadic.

"As much as possible," Horn said.

"Anne should be moved out of that place."

"That's exactly what she's refused to do. She says she won't be intimidated into living in terror."

"But she's *there* almost all the time, isn't she? I mean, she's not working right now."

Horn took a bite of buttered muffin and nodded. Chewed and swallowed. "We've got her apartment building and the apartment itself under close watch. And when she goes out, she has a shadow. But there's a limit to that kind of close scrutiny. The NYPD can't afford to guard individual citizens forever."

"And Mandle's waiting for it to stop."

"That would be my guess."

Horn finished one of his corn muffins and downed half a cup of coffee while Marla went to the front of the diner to wait on customers. He was hungry and exhausted. He'd caught only about an hour's sleep this morning before the scheduled meeting at the diner. It was probably the same for Paula and Bickerstaff; he could hardly blame them for being late.

When Marla returned, she topped off his coffee.

"He won't give up on her," she said.

"He should be thinking primarily of escape and going into hiding," Horn said, "instead of drawing attention to himself."

"Should be. And in his position most men would be holed up somewhere and counting themselves lucky."

"What's driving him?" Horn asked. He'd found Marla to be his wisest advisor in this case.

"The usual. Revenge, compulsion. And ego."

"Ego?"

"Anne's the most difficult of his victims. He deliberately made her even more difficult by telegraphing he was going to kill her. She's his ultimate challenge. In climbing terms, his Mount Everest. He sees her as a victory that can never be taken away from him, not even in death. Once Anne is dead, in the struggle with authority—with you—he's triumphant."

"He'll think he's triumphant even if it means his death? Instead of life in some distant city or country under another identity?"

Marla smiled. "You know the answer, Horn."

He nodded glumly. "Mandle would rather die a winner than live as a loser. He'll try to make Anne his next victim."

"Not necessarily his next. And my guess is there's a reason that nobody's mentioned yet that explains his entry into Anne's apartment. I don't think he's just letting you know he can have her whenever he decides to act. When it's over, he wants you to know for sure he murdered her and it wasn't the work of a copycat killer. That's also the reason for the chess knights, to make you aware this is a game you and he are playing, and when Anne dies, he's won."

"Winning is damned important to this fruitcake."

"Like Lombardi said . . . "

"Yeah. What about the tooth on her dresser?"

Before Marla could answer, the bell over the door jingled and Paula and Bickerstaff entered the diner. They both appeared tired, Bickerstaff especially. He was even more rumpled than usual and dragging his feet as he walked. This morning he looked like what he was, a man who should retire.

When they'd settled into the booth and Marla had brought them coffee and taken their orders, Horn said, "What have we learned?"

"That a human being might be able to go weeks without sleep," Paula said.

Horn ignored her.

"Nobody in adjacent buildings remembered anything of value," Bickerstaff said. "It looks like Mandle got up on the roof of the building to the east, got a line across a sort of courtyard between the two buildings and used it to cross over, then dropped down from the roof of Anne's building to her bedroom window. He did his glass-cutter-and-tape thing and got in and out."

"The doorman and neighbors?"

"Remember zilch."

"Like a ghost," Horn said.

"Huh?"

"Kray said Mandle was trained to move like a ghost."

"It was more than a ghost in Anne's apartment," Paula said.

"Ghost spider," Bickerstaff said. "Creepy thought. Almost enough to put me off my corn muffin."

"Horn's corrupted you," Paula said. "You're both going to have cholesterol like sludge." She looked across the table at Horn. "We do have some info on the tooth. It's human, an eyetooth, and the substance attached to it is human flesh—gum."

"So it was torn or knocked out," Horn said.

"Preliminary DNA tests and a dental match say it belonged to Don Perlman."

Horn put down his muffin and stared at her, waiting. Thinking Paula was developing a feel for drama.

"Perlman was one of the guards killed by Mandle when he escaped from the police van."

He wants you to know for sure he killed her . . .

"He took it as a souvenir?"

Paula shrugged. "ME says it's more likely it happened when he was beating Perlman's head and face with the butt of his handgun. Tooth dropped out of Perlman's mouth and got caught in Mandle's clothes, went inside his shirt or down one of his shoes. Maybe in a pants cuff; prisoners sometimes roll up those jumpsuit pants if the legs are too long. Mandle found the tooth later and thought of a use for it."

"Why would he put the tooth on Anne's dresser?" Bickerstaff asked.

"To make sure we know he was the one in her bedroom," Paula said.

"Ego-driven bastard," Horn said.

"Sick fuck," Bickerstaff said.

Marla with the coffeepot said, "They're not mutually exclusive."

Anne left her apartment and nodded to the uniformed officer with the scar on his face who was stationed at the end of the hall. He smiled at her then settled back in his chair. On the floor next to the chair was a folded copy of the *Village Voice* he'd been reading.

She took the elevator to the lobby and through the glass doors that looked out on the sunny street saw an unmarked car parked at the opposite curb. There were two men in it not doing a lot to dispel the notion that they were plainclothes cops. After all, they were on a preventive mission.

Anne used her key to open her brass mailbox. The mail

she pulled out didn't look promising. She shifted her weight to one leg and stood leafing through it. A Visa bill forwarded from her last address, a coupon for five dollars off a pizza from a nearby restaurant, a plain white envelope with her name typed on it.

She used a fingernail to raise a corner of the flap, then inserted a finger and tore open the envelope. She realized it was the sort of envelope cards came in.

And inside was a white card bordered in black. Centered on it was black lettering that said, simply, *Condolences in this time of your great loss.*

When she opened the card she found it blank except for four crudely inked letters separated by dashes: *A-N-N-E.*

Suddenly light-headed, she leaned sideways against the bank of mailboxes There was an ache in her stomach that she knew was fear.

She hadn't the slightest doubt as to who'd sent the card.

When finally she felt steady enough, she went outside and crossed the street toward the detectives in the parked car.

"It's part of his campaign of terror," said Dr. Ellen Nickels, NYPD psychologist and profiler. Horn was alone with her in her silent, monotonal beige office not far from One Police Plaza. It looked like a movie set and smelled as if all that leather and wood had been recently oiled and waxed. "Anne might receive more such mail, maybe anonymous phone calls."

"Or not so anonymous," Horn said. He told Dr. Nickels what Marla had said; the doctor was impressed. She was an attractive woman in her forties, with a no-nonsense, short hairdo and dead-serious brown eyes behind square-rimmed thick glasses.

"This person you're talking to," she said, "keep talking to him."

"It's a *her,*" Horn said. "A waitress at a coffee shop I frequent."

Dr. Nickels smiled. "She's dispensing wisdom with the coffee."

"Why just Anne's name on the card?"

The doctor appeared puzzled. "Because it was for her."

"I mean, why not a message?"

"Oh, I think the message was implied."

"And the dashes between the letters of her name?"

"Probably for emphasis. Detective Horn, this man you're hunting isn't always going to be predictable. In part because he's mentally unstable. And, in part, because his mental illness doesn't necessarily detract from his cleverness."

Horn nodded. *Tell me something new.*

The doctor must have read his thoughts. "You probably know the psychology of serial killers better than I do."

"They're not all the same," Horn said.

"No, they aren't. Usually they don't arm themselves in court then escape on their way to Rikers Island. This one seems deadlier than most. I think I can speak for every woman in the city when I say I want him apprehended as soon as possible. Has the lab had any luck with the card or envelope?"

"None. No prints on either, and no residue of saliva or DNA on the envelope flap. The card's for sale everywhere in New York, and the postmark's Brooklyn and means nothing."

"Cautious and diligent, your Aaron Mandle."

Horn looked at her. "No, not always cautious."

She smiled shrewdly and nodded, as if she knew exactly what he meant.

Not always cautious enough.

41

More than anything, Alice Duggan wanted to die, to escape the pain. Her entire body seemed to be on fire. She couldn't cry out, with the heavy tape over her mouth. She no longer even tried. Only lay still, listening to her own whimpers, praying for it all to end.

The bed creaked as the dark, lithe figure beside her moved to the side of the mattress and straightened up. She barely paid attention to it—to him—now. The pain was inside her forever, and he was merely a dark, moving shape in her nightmare. It was horrible, *he* was horrible, but even in horror, in terror, there was a saturation point. *There must be!*

And now there was the hope, the knowledge, that it *would* soon be over, that the nightmare the world had become would fade and disappear, as would she. Alice would no longer be Alice. Alice would be safe.

In the blurred lower edge of her vision she saw the lean figure standing before her dresser. Preening in the mirror?

No, picking up something. A statuette.

On Alice's dresser were two twelve-inch-tall plaster figures: one was Fred Astaire, the other Ginger Rogers. Alice had fallen for them as soon as she'd laid eyes on them at the

Twenty-sixth Street flea market. They'd adorned her dresser for more than a year. Sometimes, when she was in a role that required a hairpiece, she used Fred as a wig stand.

But the nightmare intruder had reached toward the right side of the dresser. It was Ginger he was holding, hefting it in his hand as if testing for weight.

He returned to the bed where Alice lay whimpering.

She saw him raise Ginger and closed her eyes.

The heavy plaster statuette crushed the bridge of Alice's nose. She felt blood spurt warmly from it and run down onto her neck. More blood began trickling at the back of her throat, then suddenly flowed heavily. She tried to spit it out, but the backwash from where it was blocked by the tape across her mouth made her swallow. She choked, gagged, frantically tried to spit out the blood again but couldn't. The mattress and springs began shuddering and making a low, fluttering sound. Her body began to tremble and rock so hard she momentarily levitated off the bed.

The blood flow continued. She had no choice but to inhale, to try desperately to breathe. It was instinctual, automatic, to inhale and expect air. To struggle to live.

Alice began to drown.

"I knew this one," Horn said to Marla. "Not personally. I saw her onstage. She was the stand-in for the star in *Leave Her, Take Her, She's Mine.*"

"Broadway?"

"Off."

"Uhm."

"Why did he beat as well as stab her?" Horn asked.

The Home Away had closed, and he and Marla were walking along dark streets to her subway stop. The media were alive with news of Alice Duggan's murder. NIGHT SPIDER ON THE HUNT AGAIN! the *Post* proclaimed in a gigantic headline. The story was above the fold in the *Times*. There were long-winded speeches in the state capitol and at

City Hall about reviewing procedures to transfer prisoners. Television pundit panels wondered how it could be—how it could *conceivably* be—that a serial killer so lethal hadn't been under constant guard and in direct view of law enforcement eyeballs. Was it incompetency or conspiracy that had led to Mandle's escape? Alice Duggan's parents in Pittsburgh were interviewed every time they ventured out of their house. "New York," Rollie Larkin had remarked dryly to Horn in his office, "is getting press like John Rocker's revenge."

Horn listened to the regular clacking of Marla's heels on the pavement as he strolled beside her. She hadn't answered his question immediately. It wasn't an easy one.

"If I had to guess," she said finally, "and I do, I'd say Mandle wanted to disfigure his latest victim for two reasons: He wanted to show you what he was going to do to Anne, to taunt you, and he wanted to further terrify Anne."

"I feel taunted," Horn said. "And I sometimes wish Anne were more terrified so she'd agree to go into hiding."

"She's confused right now as well as scared, and trying hard to establish her independence after years of marriage."

"She always had plenty of independence," Horn said a bit defensively.

"I'm talking more about her mental state than whether she pretty much did what she wanted."

They walked for a while without talking. Horn wondered if he'd irritated Marla with his claim of Anne's independence.

But no; she'd been thinking.

"Another possibility," Marla said, "is that Mandle is changed after his conviction and escape. That now there's an even stronger element of rage in his murders."

"He did beat one of the guards from the van in the face and head," Horn said. "I'd say he was enraged that night." A taxi swerved to the curb near them and the driver leaned down so he could peer out at them like a lonely puppy, offering to save them some steps. Horn shook his head no and waved the cab away, and was made slightly uneasy by how much he didn't want his stroll with Marla interrupted.

"Maybe Mandle's wounded and in physical pain," Marla said. "Exacerbating his anger."

"If he's wounded," Horn said, "it's minor and doesn't affect his strength or agility. His MO was the same as always, except for the battering he gave his victim."

"Was she alive at the time?"

"Yes. Losing blood fast but alive. The knife wounds hadn't killed her yet."

"Rage," Marla said.

"Or callousness. He might be a stone killer who simply doesn't care if his victim's alive or dead at the time of disfigurement."

"Stone killer?"

"Cop talk for somebody who'd just as soon kill another human being as munch a piece of toast. There's something missing in certain people. They don't relate to the rest of the human race. Like we don't relate to bugs and just step on them or kill them with insecticide, then forget about them within minutes. Stone killers sleep well at night no matter what kind of hell they've created during the day."

"Sociopaths."

"Yeah. And something more. Not all sociopaths are killers. Some become successful corporate raiders or great NFL linebackers."

"It must be truly liberating, being free of all human concern."

"It's probably addictive," Horn said. "And it leads to the kind of hubris that contributes to serial killers being caught." He reached into an inside pocket for a cigar, then decided against it. He understood the reluctance of many people, women especially, to endure cigar smoke indoors or out. Now wasn't the time to find out how Marla felt about it.

"You mentioned insects," Marla said. "It's interesting, Mandle's identification with spiders. And what came out during the trial, his history with his mother and the significance of spiders in her religion."

"I'm sure if we were to dig through history we'd come up with some ancient cult of the spider," Horn said. "Or maybe Mandle's mother saw an old movie and it set her off because she was on the edge to begin with. People are afraid of spiders, and fascinated by them."

"Fascinated because of their fear."

"Definitely."

"Spiders and snakes; religion and mothers. It's no wonder we have serial killers. They're created in childhood. The mechanism's probably wound and set when they're very young."

"I'm not so much interested in how or why Mandle ticks," Horn said, "as in stopping him from ticking."

"There's something else I think you should take into account," Marla said. "You have to concentrate on guarding Anne because Mandle might be watching her, formulating a plan. But he also might be watching you."

"What makes you say that?"

"The way he talked about you during the trial. He was full of hate for you. Obsessed."

"I noticed."

They were at Marla's subway stop. The night was warm and clear, but thunder was bumping and rolling in the distance somewhere over New Jersey. It was a celestial reminder that no one was ever really safe anywhere. Lightning was whimsical.

She looked up at him. "I worry about you, Horn."

He was surprised, not so much by her words but by the way they were spoken, like a confession. And by the look on her face. Horn didn't know what to say, but he found himself wondering what would happen if he suggested he take her all the way home. Home and inside.

"I'd like to tell you not to worry," is what he did say, "that I don't want you to. But I can't. A part of me's glad you're thinking about me that much."

And a part of me doesn't want to do this. A part of me still hasn't given up on Anne.

Marla seemed to know what he was thinking, sensing his hesitancy and the reason for it. And he saw something else in her eyes, some sudden fear of intimacy, not only with him but with anyone. *What's your secret, Marla?*

"I'd better get down to the platform," she said. "My train's about due. I've got them timed."

He nodded and touched her shoulder. She smiled but turned away abruptly to discourage any further contact, then started down the concrete steps to the token booth and platform.

Horn stood watching her until she was out of sight, thinking she was probably right about Mandle observing him, following him.

He wondered if it would occur to her that he might have been followed tonight.

As soon as Marla entered her apartment, she went to where a bottle was tucked away on a top shelf of a kitchen cabinet.

It had been a gift, Crown Royal in a fancy box. She pried open the box's flaps and removed the bottle, used a knife to slit the seal, then uncapped it.

She'd never intended to do this. The bottle was only on the shelf as a reminder, a temptation resisted on a daily basis. But she understood that self-delusion, even as she allowed it of herself. A part of her knew that she and the bottle might share an experience in a dark future.

She stood and poured the magic amber liquid down the sink drain, observing it swirl and disappear, growing more afraid as she watched.

Sociopaths, stone killers, serial killers, they knew about addiction.

So did she.

Years ago, one of her patients, an angry, middle-aged advertising salesman named Arnold Vernon, had followed her advice and calmly confronted his wife about her suspected infidelity. He'd progressed well in his therapy, and Marla was sure he was ready to manage such a situation.

She'd had the measure of her patient, but something unexpected happened—and continued to happen in Marla's dreams.

Mrs. Vernon responded by strangling their infant daughter.

Arnold Vernon responded by stabbing his wife to death, then slashing his wrists.

Marla responded by drinking her way out of her profession.

She'd finally gotten her alcoholism under control and kept it there. Under control enough, anyway. She could hold down a job, function in life from day to day.

She was afraid now of how she was beginning to feel about Horn. *Why the fuck did his wife have to leave him?* Now Marla was even more frightened by what she might be losing if she fell into the bottle again. Not just another waitress job. So much more.

The last of the Crown Royal was gone. She turned on the cold water tap and watched the residue around the drain become clear. She felt relieved now, safe from herself.

She suddenly remembered there was a half-full bottle of vodka in the back of the freezer, behind the plastic bags of frozen vegetables she never really considered eating.

Or had she known all along that it was there? She'd noticed the bottle when she moved in and acquired the refrigerator from the previous tenant, and she'd never thrown it away. Vodka never completely froze in such conditions, only thickened somewhat. Drunk at temperatures below freezing, the crystalline liquid was numbing.

Marla knew that tonight it could numb how she felt about Horn.

* * *

Letty Fonsetta had appeared on the financial channel that afternoon. She'd been sent to represent the firm of Helmont and Brack as their financial-sector analyst. If anybody could help to restore trust in stock analysts it was Letty, with her heart-shaped, honest face and genteel manner. How could anyone suspect ill of this petite, sweet-natured woman with the warm smile, who could strip a bank or brokerage firm's financial statement to its bones within minutes using her long experience as examiner with the Fed?

Letty had cheered up the financial channel staff and viewers with a rosy forecast of unchanging interest rates and a recommendation to buy three promising small savings and loans in the Midwest. Sleeper stocks, she'd called them. No, she didn't own them. No, Helmont and Brack had no sort of financial relationship with them. They were simply undervalued stocks with clean financial sheets and solid multiples. Buy 'em!

All three stocks had gained share price by the time the market closed.

Letty was feeling good as she left Helmont and Brack's new offices near the former site of the World Trade Center, looking forward to dinner at home and a warm bath before going over the numbers on a prospective New York bank merger.

On the subway ride uptown to her apartment, she studied her reflection in the dark window on the opposite side of the car. There she was, looking back at herself, much as she must have appeared on the TV screen. *Would you trust this woman? Have secret fantasies about her?* She cocked her head, then smiled slightly. She'd been professionally coached for her television appearances, but maybe she should practice more in front of a mirror. Who knew where TV spots might lead, especially if her stock recommendations panned out? Maybe to one of the regular financial panel shows.

What would her father think of her now, she wondered, after his admonitions and cautionary lectures about gambling in the stock market? Her own portfolio was flourishing and well hedged. She was even thinking of moving into another, larger apartment.

That is, if the television appearances worked out, if she struck a spark with viewers. Someone who knew one of the producers told her, in confidence, that ratings more than held up for her announced spots. The viewers liked her. Letty gazed steadily at her framed reflection across the aisle and let herself dream.

She had no idea she'd made a new fan that afternoon, who'd boarded at the same stop and was riding with her in the subway car, watching her watch herself.

"Why don't you come to bed?" Paula asked Linnert from the bedroom doorway.

He'd been sitting for over an hour at his computer. Paula thought he looked particularly handsome shirtless and in his boxer shorts, seated in his Aeron chair in the soft lamplight and working the keyboard. But she had other ideas about how he could use his nimble fingers.

"Almost with you," he said, without looking at her. Kind of miffed her.

Another few keystrokes and he turned to smile at her. "What was that all about?" she asked.

"Bought some stock on-line."

"I thought the markets were closed."

"The main ones are. But there are after-hour markets, or you can place an order anytime that'll be executed when the markets open the next day."

Paula grinned. "Are you one of those notorious day traders who lost their shirts? I look at you, I don't see any shirt."

"Nope, I'm an investor, not a trader. Done okay, too. How do you think I pay for you, Miss High Postage?"

"With your passionate love."

"Cheap at the price." He shut down his computer and stood up from his desk chair.

"What's the hurry?"

He looked puzzled. "I thought you were madly moist."

"I am. I mean, why did you have to buy stock tonight instead of waiting till tomorrow morning?"

He shrugged powerful tanned shoulders. "I was in the mood. And an analyst I respect recommended these stocks this afternoon on the financial channel. Small savings and loans. Sleeper stocks in the Midwest."

"Ah, and you want to get in before it's too late."

"Well, as early as possible. This analyst knows her stuff; she moves a stock for more than a day's pop. She's a solid researcher."

Paula's grin widened. "Come over here," she said, "and I'll show you some research."

Letty stopped at a newsstand a block from her apartment and picked up *Business Week*. Her eye fell on a tabloid's bold headline: CITY OF FEAR. Beneath it was a photo of the New York skyline. WHAT WOMAN IS SAFE? asked the caption of the lead story.

Ridiculous! Letty shook her head and smiled, paying for the magazine and turning away. *A city of over eight million people, and women are supposed to be afraid a serial killer will single them out.* Her smile stuck. *Hell, a serial killer might be preferable to some of the losers I've dated recently.*

Only kidding, she said to herself a little uneasily as she quickened her pace and pressed on toward her apartment.

Toward the security of home.

42

The uniform with the scar on his face was on duty in the hall when Horn knocked on Anne's apartment door. He looked over at Horn, gave a little half smile, and nodded. Horn nodded back, not smiling, as Anne opened the door.

"You've settled in nicely," he said, when he entered and looked around. The apartment didn't look so cold and modern. No cardboard boxes in sight. More pieces of furniture she hadn't put in storage were in place. Some of the wall hangings were familiar. A framed impressionist print she'd always liked was on the wall over the sofa. Horn felt like someone in a hotel room where he'd stayed before.

Anne looked good. She was wearing a beige blouse, dark brown slacks, and had her hair pulled back in a French braid.

"Going out?" he asked.

She looked at him.

"Never mind." Horn sat on the sofa and waited. She'd phoned him and asked for this meeting.

She didn't offer him a drink and didn't sit down herself. She said, "I'm going nuts here under guard."

"You'd be nuts not to want to be guarded."

"I don't have to be convinced of that. I even appreciate

what you're doing, Thomas. I'm well aware I'm receiving special treatment because of you. I'm also aware of the kind of danger I'm in. I can count on an anonymous heavy-breathing phone call almost every night."

"I know," he said. "They're from public phones around town. The receivers are always wiped clean of prints."

She smiled. "Yeah, I guess you would know." She paced a few steps this way and that—like an animal marking off territory—as if trying to locate the best position from which to speak. "I'm going back to work at the hospital, Thomas."

He didn't answer immediately, knew she was touchy and couldn't blame her. "Your old job?"

She nodded. "Finlay was by here today to talk to me. The Vine family's changed their minds. They've rejected any settlement and want more money, claiming the stress of their tragedy and the lawsuit have caused a regression to the severe depression Vine suffered after his military service. The main cause of stress is identified as Kincaid Memorial Hospital."

"So Finlay wants you back," Horn said. "All's forgiven, huh?"

"Not really. Neither of us forgives the other. But I need a job, and the hospital needs me back in my old position in order to mount its best legal defense."

"You mean they don't want to risk a whistle-blower out there unaccounted for."

"I suppose that's part of it. From my end, I'll have employment and an excuse to get out of this apartment."

"Which we tried to get you to leave."

"By *getting out,* I don't mean running away," Anne said. "I won't do that, won't give in to fear. It's my life, and I'm damn well going to live it as I choose. But I'm no fool. I recognize the danger better than anyone. I want to know what you think of my returning to work."

Horn sat back and extended his long legs, crossing them at the ankles. "I know you want something to do, but this isn't really the time—"

"It's exactly the time," she interrupted, "if I'm going to remain sane."

"And alive?"

"That's why I wanted to talk to you. Could you arrange . . . Would it make that much difference if I were guarded here or at my office? There's already some security at Kincaid anyway. I thought it might even be easier."

"You'd be working day hours?"

"I've been promised them." She smiled. "They do need me if they want to successfully plead their case."

"You almost sound as if you're looking forward to a court fight now."

She shrugged. "When your life's threatened you gain a different perspective on fear and stress. On what's important."

"And going back to Kincaid is important to you?"

"Very."

He looked at her standing there in the soft light filtering through the sheer curtains. Light like a time machine. She might have been the Anne of twenty years ago. They might have been—

Don't think it, you idiot!

He sat up straighter, then stood. "What you want can be arranged. But I want something in return."

"Oh?"

"When things get tight and really dangerous—and they will—I want your word that you'll follow my instructions."

"Instructions pertaining to what?"

"To anything. We're in a game with a psychotic killer who wants you as his victim. There might not be time for me to explain or try to justify whatever it is I'm asking of you."

"You have my word, Thomas."

"I'll talk to Rollie Larkin."

They looked at each other. She gave him a smile.

He waited for her to stop him and thank him as he left, but she remained silent behind him.

Oh, well, he'd demanded something in return.

And leaving her this time, walking away from her, the painful wrench he felt didn't rip quite so large a rent in his heart.

Horn spoke with Larkin later that day. Anne's return to work didn't really require that much extra security since she'd simply be office-bound rather than spending most of her time in her apartment. In fact, it enabled some of the security force to work closer to her, passing as hospital personnel. Ida, Anne's assistant, had been reassigned. The uniform assigned as Anne's last defense, who was usually the scarfaced cop Horn had seen several times stationed in the hall, could be outside her office door rather than noticeably hanging around outside her apartment.

"Police profiler can't understand why our man's staying in the New York area," Larkin said, while he and Horn puffed on cigars in Larkin's office. There was a small exhaust fan humming away in a window, tugging at the smoke. Horn had heard they'd made this a smoke-free building and wondered if it was true, if Larkin didn't give a damn. Might well be. Horn decided not to ask.

"Maybe he can't refuse a dare," Horn said.

Larkin exhaled a cloud of smoke and squinted through it at Horn. "You mean he sees it as a dare that we're bent on catching him?"

"That could be part of it. And I'm afraid part of it's me. He's making this personal."

"So why doesn't he go after you?"

"Might, eventually." *Killing Anne would be an initial step in murdering me, using her death to torture me before he finishes the job.*

Both men were thinking the same thing. Neither put it into words.

"I don't see why he doesn't simply try for Anne," Larkin said. "God knows, he's had plenty of practice."

"I don't know the answer to that," Horn said. "What's the police profiler have to say?"

"What you just said. She also said we might expect more murders after Alice Duggan's, with approximately the same amount of time between them as between Mandle's previous victims. That means we might have a couple of weeks, at least, to prevent the next killing."

And the next intended victim might be Anne, Horn thought.

Larkin flicked ash from his cigar. "If Mandle keeps killing, and it turns out there's some kind of pattern in the murders since his escape, it'll be clear he's toying with you and Anne, doing his sadistic act. But Duggan looks like the earlier random prey. High-rise apartments and windows difficult to reach, that encourage a kind of false sense of security and a carelessness, are what seem to dictate his choice of victims. There's no apparent similarity in physical type or in the work they did, and their ages varied. Some were divorced, some had never been married, and one was widowed." Larkin finished his cigar and snuffed it out in an ashtray. "Seems obvious Mandle's read the literature and knows how to avoid a pattern."

"So no woman can feel secure," Horn said.

"Yeah. So any woman in New York might be a victim and has to walk around terrified because of him. Loves power, does Mandle."

"Single women."

"Huh?"

"Mandle's victims were all single and lived alone," Horn reminded Larkin. "No live-in lovers, no roommates."

"True," Larkin said. "Like Anne."

"Like Anne."

And, as it turned out, like Letty Fonsetta.

Horn received news of her murder over his cell phone as he was driving away from his meeting with Larkin.

* * *

money she might not need if she had a man in her life. aybe this was the one, even though she wasn't a high-owered career-woman type. Or married. If you had a hus-band or kid you wouldn't work this kind of evening job. Not if you were a righteous woman.

Sitting there like a whore in a glassed, bright showcase, every man giving you a look as he drives past, sexy blonde showing off cleavage while she sells tickets to *f......* want to escape life for a while *i......... black*-and-white *....* Robinson, the tough-guy crime kingpin, trading snarls

It was like Alice Duggan's murder. Letty Fonsetta was lying on her back in bed, tightly shrouded in her blood-soaked sheets, a rectangle of duct tape slapped over her mouth. There was a depression in the center of the gray rectangle, from when she'd tried to draw her last, desperate breath, and even that was denied her. A clot of blood clung to her hairline. It was where she'd been bludgeoned. On the floor near the bed was a small, triangular marble clock with blood and a clump of hair stuck to one of its corners. Horn was sure it would yield no fingerprints.

"Only three days since the last murder," Paula said.

"And her apartment's only on the third floor," Bickerstaff added.

"Three's wild," Horn said. "Think that means anything?"

"Only if you're a numerologist or poker player," Bickerstaff said.

"The short interval between murders," Paula said, "might mean he's getting desperate. More driven by compulsion."

"More dangerous," Horn said. He wondered if Mandle might be sending a message to Anne and him: *Any night now. Sooner than you think.* Trying to heighten the terror. "The killer get inside the usual way?"

"He did," Paula said. "Dropped five stories from the roof, which he reached from an adjoining roof. I'm wondering why, though."

Horn looked at her. "Why what?"

"Where Letty's window is, he could have easily reached it from the ground without being seen. It looks out on an alley where he wouldn't have been noticed. So why didn't he choose the easy way in and out?"

"You said it yourself," Bickerstaff told her. "Compulsion. He's locked into a ritual. Gotta do it the same way every time."

Horn glanced over at the intense and somber techs gathered like visiting physicians around Letty Fonsetta's body. *Now you make house calls. Too late.*

"What do we know about this one?" he asked.

Paula tucked in her chin and consulted her notes. "Forty-one years old, divorced, a stock analyst and sometimes TV personality. She was on a financial channel just this morning, touting stocks."

"Anybody still pay attention to people who do that?"

"Sure it wasn't the comedy channel?" Bickerstaff asked.

Paula glanced up from her notes to nail him with a glare. "Neighbors said she pretty much kept to herself but was friendly enough. Didn't notice any men coming or going at her place. A career type. And successful."

"Like Alice Duggan," Bickerstaff said.

Paula had closed her notepad. "There's something else she had in common with Duggan. They were both public figures. Not exactly famous, but public. Duggan was an off-Broadway actress with her name and photo on a poster and playbills outside a theater. And Letty Fonsetta was recently on television."

Once again, Horn was glad he'd chosen Paula for his investigative team. "They'd be easy enough to find and follow," he said. "This is a media city. Lots of prospective victims like that. Mandle chooses his prey from public women who are most likely to be living alone, then finds out where they live, probably by following them from wherever they practice their professions. If his simple requirements are met, they're in his web."

"If they live alone in high-floor apartments," Paula said, "they're as good as dead as soon as he lays eyes on them. And there might be another reason he's choosing public figures. He understands that people feel they know them, maybe even identify with them. Women will think, *It could have been me.*"

"It might be simpler than that," Bickerstaff said. "Maybe he's murdering women in the public eye because he knows they're attractive and he's in a hurry. Instead of walking around looking at the buffet, he's choosing from a menu."

"Compulsion," Paula said. "Getting more powerful and controlling. More urgent."

"At least Anne isn't in the public eye," Bickerstaff said.

"She doesn't have to be," Paula said, knows where she lives, and probably where glanced at Horn, maybe regretting her w Bickerstaff exchanged a look.

Horn seemed not to have heard them. After glance at the carnage, he instructed them to follo usual procedure, then left Letty Fonsetta's apartment as as possible.

He already had his hand in his pocket and was clutching his cell phone. He wanted to get someplace where he

obvious in retrospect—would pop into his consciousness, something like a fact or a name from the past that he couldn't quite recall but knew was there. It was there all the time, inches beneath the surface where it could only be glimpsed . . .

By the time the cigar was smoked, he was tired and had thought of nothing useful.

But at the same time he had the feeling he was missing something important. *Something was there that he couldn't quite grasp* . . . His smoking and musing had resulted in that conclusion, anyway. A reason to prevent another decent night's sleep.

He snuffed out the cigar stub and poured himself another two fingers of scotch. He knew the alcohol would help him get to sleep but not stay asleep. Using scotch for a sleeping pill always caused him to awaken in a few hours with his mind awhirl.

It seemed there was a price to pay for everything in life.

Nadine, wearing jeans and carrying an umbrella because of unreliable weather forecasts, left the Projections Theater before the last showing of *Key Largo* was over. Bogart was just putt-putting away from the dock in his rickety boat, so why shouldn't she leave, too?

She was watched from across the street.

For a while the figure that moved out of a shadowed doorway paralleled her course on the opposite sidewalk, then fell back half a block and crossed the street at an angle to be directly behind her. Though there were other people out walking, the sidewalks weren't crowded. However, there were enough pedestrians that Nadine's follower could be reasonably sure she wouldn't notice him.

As she crossed another street, he followed, staying now about half a block behind her.

Suddenly he noticed they were walking past Kincaid Memorial Hospital, where Anne Horn worked, where she'd recently returned to work as if to defy him. Venturing out of the apartment where Horn tried to hide her. Would it be possible to act impulsively and enter one of the hospital's side doors, make his way to Anne's office, and then . . . ?

No. He realized that wouldn't allow for the ritual. And she would undoubtedly be closely guarded.

Anyway, it wasn't yet time. They both knew it wasn't yet her time.

He saw that a woman had turned the corner from the street where the hospital's main entrance was located and was walking toward Nadine. Since it was a warm night she wore no coat and in her nurse's uniform was stark white against the darkness. A bright thing seeking light. Maybe that was why she held the Night Spider's attention.

His gaze fixed on her and didn't stray.

A short, compactly built woman with a graceful walk, head held high, arms swinging freely. She and Nadine didn't acknowledge each other as they passed, and the nurse strode toward the man walking toward her half a block down the sidewalk.

He pulled his Mets cap down lower as she approached. A car was coming up behind him. Good. He'd be backlighted, and the headlights might temporarily blind the nurse. She wouldn't remember him.

She veered ever so slightly toward the curb to give him a wider berth, the way women do, just as the car drove past. Headlights illuminated her almost beautiful features and the hospital name tag pinned to her white uniform top. *Nora*.

The nurse didn't so much as glance at him as they passed. *Nora who works where Anne Horn works. The two women might even know each other.*

He slowed his pace, turning his head to see the retreating nurse's back, then glanced again at Nadine.

Suddenly changing his mind, seizing opportunity, he turned all the way around and began walking in the opposite direction.

Forgetting the girl from the ticket booth and following Nora the nurse. He was smiling, thinking what a sense of irony fate had, and how it sometimes dispensed opportunities like dark party favors.

He stayed well back of Nora, watching the repetitive switch of her hips beneath the tight white uniform skirt, the flash of white stockings above her soft-soled shoes. Motion marking off time. Made for the night. So easy and natural to follow. *She's the one.*

The *R.N.* on Nora's name tag stuck in his mind. As he walked he wondered what, besides Registered Nurse, the letters might stand for.

R.N. . . . ?

By the time she entered an apartment building about six blocks from the hospital, he'd settled on *Retribution Night.*

Two nights later, working the late shift, Anne took the call on the desk phone in her office. It was 2:12 A.M. exactly. She would remember that later when the police asked her.

"Anne Horn?" A man's voice. He'd called her direct number rather than go through the hospital switchboard, so he must know her. She should know him.

"Yes? Hello?" Her own voice sounded thin.

"I'm calling to ask about Nora Shoemaker. Do you know her?"

"Not personally. If you want to talk to her, you've dialed the wrong number. She's a maternity nurse in another part of the hospital. I can switch you if you—"

"No, no, I wanted to talk to you about her."

Anne felt a draft on the nape of her neck, an ache in her stomach. She knew it was fear that might be the beginning of terror. "Who is this?"

"I'm calling from Nora's apartment. I'm afraid something terrible has happened to her."

"Who is this?"

"I'm sure you know who. I called to tell you not to worry too much about Nora. You'll be seeing her soon enough."

"Are we talking about the same Nora?" Anne asked, having trouble breathing, getting her legs to work as she stood up from the desk and silently placed the receiver on the desk.

She ran for her office door and flung it open, motioning frantically and quietly for the guard stationed outside.

He wasn't the guard with the scar on his face. This one was middle-aged and Anne thought that with the right sort of mustache he'd look amazingly like Hitler. She frenetically pointed toward the phone.

His bright blue eyes narrowed, and he caught on immediately and didn't make a sound.

Of course, when he picked up the receiver it was dead.

Anne told him about the phone call, spilling out words that sometimes didn't make sense.

A tracer had been placed on Anne's office phone. The guard did some punching on the keypad and got the location of the phone last used to call in to it.

The call hadn't originated from Nora Shoemaker's apartment, but from a public phone on the other side of town.

"Is Nora Shoemaker in the building?" the guard asked.

Anne took the phone from his hand and checked.

"She worked the last shift and went home," she said, replacing the receiver in its cradle. Her face was pale. Fear was clawing at her guts. *What he wants! Exactly what the bastard wants!*

"Get her home phone number," the guard said. "Let's call her."

Anne complied, then watched the guard's impassive face as he stood silently for almost a minute with the receiver pressed to his ear.

He hung up the phone. "No answer."

"She should be in bed."

"Maybe she doesn't wanna answer the phone," the guard said. "Or has her answering machine turned off and the volume down so the ringing won't disturb her sleep."

"Do you really believe that?"

"I'm trying."

Anne's legs were too weak to support her. She took three unsteady steps and slumped into her desk chair, then glanced down and saw that both her hands were made into fists tightly clenched around her thumbs.

"It was probably a crank call," the guard said, obviously noticing how scared she was, "but it won't hurt to send somebody around to Nora Shoemaker's place and check on her."

Anne bowed her head, staring into her lap at the whitened fists she couldn't unclench, and was squeezed by a knowledge that had more to do with the heart and gut than with the mind. Ancient instinct. Signals from the cave.

It wasn't a crank call . . . It wasn't a crank call . . .

44

Horn got the call at 3:01 A.M. A woman named Nora Shoemaker, an off-duty nurse at Kincaid Memorial Hospital, was found dead in her apartment on the West Side. She was apparently another victim of the Night Spider.

Not only that, Anne had received a phone call from the killer intimating that he'd murdered the nurse.

A nurse in the same hospital where Anne worked. It could just as easily have been Anne.

Horn was sure that was the message Mandle wanted to say. And it could happen anytime. Nora Shoemaker's murder was only two days after Letty Fonsetta's. And where was the pattern? The nurse was in no way a public figure like Fonsetta and Duggan. Why had Mandle seen her as one of the chosen? Made her a victim?

Horn's mind was whirling with these questions as he began making calls, demanding that protection be stepped up for Anne.

Then he phoned Anne, who seemed more deeply shaken by the nurse's murder than by any of the others.

"He might have been *here*," she said. "In the hospital, making up his mind who to murder. And for no reason other than to terrorize me! That's why Nora Shoemaker died—to make me more afraid! In a way, I'm responsible for her death."

"That's what he wants you to believe," Horn said. "He wants to panic you. Not just for pleasure, but in the hope that you won't be thinking straight and you'll make a mistake. If he makes you feel guilty as well as terrified, that's fine. You'll be more vulnerable and he'll be able to get to you. Nora Shoemaker died because Mandle killed her. Period."

Her voice quavered but there was strength in it. "I know that intellectually, Thomas. I won't let this sick freak panic me. My thinking is clear."

Horn believed her. "For now," he said, "cooperate with your guardian angels, even if it doesn't make sense to you. They know their job."

"All right, Thomas. And you promise to be careful."

She hung up without waiting for his promise. *Only making conversation. The inane conversation of terror.*

He got on his cell phone and woke up Paula and Bickerstaff. Then he got dressed in a hurry so he could drive to Nora Shoemaker's apartment.

This one was like the others done since Mandle's escape from the prison transport van. A woman shrouded in her bedsheets, gagged, then tortured with stab wounds. She was killed by a blow or several blows to the head, with the killer using whatever bludgeoning instrument was handy and suitable for the task. This time it had been a cut-glass candelabra. It had been used with such force and viciousness that two of its six gracefully curved branches had broken off.

No fingerprints, as before.

Ah, but there were differences!

This time no sign of entry from the roof. The knob lock on the apartment door had been expertly slipped. The splintering of the door frame indicated that the chain-lock bracket had been forced not with a sudden, violent effort, but by someone leaning harder and harder against the door, several times in succession, until the screws flew from the wood. It was a method long used by breaking and entering pros who didn't want to wake anyone sleeping inside.

The method had worked with Nora Shoemaker, who was probably wrapped like a package and gagged before she woke up completely.

What happened to her next must have seemed to last forever, until finally the glass candelabra led her to true eternity.

"There was no doorman," Paula said over breakfast at the Home Away, where Horn had called a meeting to discuss what they knew before they all went home and caught some much-needed sleep. "There was a keypad outside that the tenants used to open the outer doors."

"The code changed recently?" Horn asked.

"Changed last week. Not that it makes any difference. After using the keypad to gain entrance to the outer lobby, tenants then use a regular key to open the door to the inner lobby and elevators. All Mandle had to do was wait on the sidewalk for somebody to enter the building, time his approach, then grab the door before it closed all the way. He could enter with them, as if he'd just walked up and was about to go in when they came along. Then he could wait politely while they used their key to open the door to the inner lobby, and ride up in the elevator to a different floor, as if he belonged in the building."

"Do any of the other tenants remember something like that happening?"

"Sure," Bickerstaff said. "Half a dozen. It happens all the time. People are lazy with their keys and too trustful, even in New York. It's like they go to sleep at night and forget everything that happened to them that day or what they've read in the papers, then they get up next morning not knowing again how many assholes are walking around out there. A guy edges in with them when they're buzzed up or unlock a door, they don't think much about it. They've done the same thing themselves."

Horn shook his head. "So much for building security." He sipped from a glass of ice water. He was staying away from coffee so he could actually get a few hours' sleep and be more effective the rest of the day. "Whatever's driving Mandle is getting stronger. He's stepped up the pace, killing with increasing frequency."

"Like most of those jerk-off serial killers," Bickerstaff said.

"What I don't understand," Horn said, "is why his method of entering Shoemaker's apartment was different."

"Another message," Marla said.

Surprised, the three detectives looked up at her where she was standing near the booth. There were several customers in the front area of the diner this morning. Marla had to work her trade.

"He wanted to let you know you had more than his usual MO to worry about," she continued. "That he was ahead of you in your game of wits." She might have been about to say more, but a voice called her name. She turned and strode toward an elderly man in a window booth who was animatedly motioning for her with his empty coffee cup.

"She's probably right," Paula said.

"Can we be sure the nurse wasn't a copycat murder?" Bickerstaff asked.

Horn and Paula looked at him.

"Not likely," Paula said. "Remember the phone call to Anne."

"Still possible, though," Bickerstaff said. "All someone had to do was find out how to get in touch with Anne at the hospital. The news media's been on this case like flies on a dead carp. Lots of information on TV and in the newspapers."

"There are too many similarities with the previous murders," Horn said.

"Not the method of entry," Paula reiterated.

Bickerstaff grunted and got his notepad from a pocket of his wrinkled suitcoat. He absently propped his reading glasses on the bridge of his nose and consulted his notes. Paula thought he looked ten years older with his glasses on, the way they slid halfway down his nose. And incongruously academic. Mr. Chips with a 9mm.

"We got the three victims," he said. "Alice Duggan, Nicolette—long for Letty—Fonsetta, and Nora Shoemaker. The first two were in their early thirties, Nora in her early forties. All at least reasonably attractive. The first two were public figures. They were killed after Mandle dropped down like a spider from the roof and entered through their bedroom windows. The nurse was killed after her apartment was entered through the door."

"Because Mandle wanted to send a message," Paula reminded Bickerstaff.

He grunted again and nodded. "Thirty-seven stab wounds in the first and second victims, thirty-five in the nurse. All three with their heads bashed in."

"He might simply have lost track of the number of stab wounds," Horn said.

"Or was scared away," Paula said.

"Or got bored." Bickerstaff dropped his notepad on the table. "I could go on, but it looks like the same killer to me. The nurse's death looks quite a bit different from the other two until you start listing similarities."

"Different nonetheless," Paula said. She yawned.

Made Bickerstaff yawn. He glared at her as if he resented it.

"Let's catch up on some rest," Horn said, "before we all drift off here in the diner."

Bickerstaff said, "You think he knows we meet here?"

The thought hadn't occurred to Horn or, apparently, to Paula, who was looking at him with a stunned expression.

"I mean," Bickerstaff went on, "Mandle knows who's working his case. And we've been using this diner like it was a squad room."

"It's always possible," Horn said, watching Marla bring

the impatient customer in the window booth a glass of orange juice. For a second, he thought about calling Larkin, getting protection for Marla. But he couldn't do that. How many women could he insist the overworked NYPD protect? And Rollie would ask, what was Marla Winger to Horn?

Horn had no concrete answer.

"Let's meet back here about two this afternoon," he said, sliding out of the booth and standing. He tossed enough money on the table to cover breakfast and a tip.

Both men stood aside and let Paula lead the way toward the door. They all paused to say good-bye to Marla, who was now busy behind the counter.

At the door, Paula stopped and stood still. "Wait a minute!"

"You're letting out the air-conditioning," said Mr. Impatient with the orange juice.

She realized she was holding the door open and went the rest of the way outside. Horn and Bickerstaff followed. Heat and noise wrapped around them like a blanket.

"You said Letty Fonsetta's first name was short for Nicole."

"Nicolette," Bickerstaff said.

"Think of the three victims in the order of their deaths," Paula said, keeping her voice down and moving back against the building so passersby wouldn't overhear. "Their first names."

"Jesus!" Horn said.

Bickerstaff looked from one of them to the other.

"Alice, Nicolette, and Nora," Horn said grimly. "The first letters of their names spell *Ann.*"

"Maybe a coincidence," Bickerstaff said.

"They don't exist," Paula told him. Something she'd heard Horn say.

"It's too much of a stretch not to be deliberate." Horn had removed a cigar from his shirt pocket when they left the diner. Now he put it back.

"Remember the note Mandle sent her," Paula said. *"A-N-N-E,* with the dashes between capital letters."

"I'll be damned!" Bickerstaff said. "The son of a bitch is leading up to Anne's murder, spelling out her name with his victims' first initials."

"If that's true," Paula said, "there'll be another Night Spider murder before he tries for Anne. The victim will be a woman whose first name begins with *E*."

Bickerstaff gazed out at the traffic, at the endless stream of vehicles and countless pedestrians. The expression on his face suggested he was thinking about all the Ellens and Emmas out there. "At least we have the note he sent Anne, so we know we've got a little time."

Paula stared at him. "What's that supposed to mean?"

Bickerstaff turned to look at her. "We can be sure he knows how to spell her name."

The two o'clock meeting with Paula and Bickerstaff had yielded nothing else new. Horn was wearing down. He didn't bother undressing or going up to his bedroom. He merely removed his shirt and shoes and stretched out on the sofa in the living room. Planes of sunlight dancing with dust motes sliced in through the spaces between shades and window frames. The chaotic but muted sounds of the city found their way inside and were oddly relaxing. *Four familiar walls, dimness, cracks of sunlight, sounds of human connection too distant to be threatening . . .*

Horn rested the back of his wrist on his forehead, blocking some of the light, and closed his eyes.

He woke in darkness.

Horn was hungry, but he was sure that wasn't what had woken him.

He straightened his right arm and worked it back and forth until most of the soreness was gone. Then he sat up on the sofa, managed to stand, and switched on a table lamp. He saw by the grandfather clock that it was past 9:00 P.M.

Great! He'd intended to check and make sure Anne's security had been increased and was in place. And he wanted to call Anne and reassure her. He rubbed the back of his hand across his lips. They seemed to be glued together.

As he staggered through the brownstone toward the bathroom, switching on lights as he went, he wondered if he should tell Anne about how Mandle was spelling out her name with victims before trying to kill her. A sadistic game played by an expert. If she knew about his latest gambit, she might feel all the more helpless.

By the time he'd relieved his bladder and was leaning over the washbasin splashing handfuls of cold water on his face, he decided Anne deserved to know. It was, after all, her life that was at stake. There might even be an odd comfort in the knowledge that probably another victim, whose first initial was *E*, stood between her and her encounter with the Night Spider.

But he'd also have to tell her that might be precisely what Mandle wanted the police to think, so he'd have an easier time getting to her.

After putting on his shoes and a clean shirt, Horn phoned Lieutenant Howard Burton, who'd been put in charge of Anne's security detail. From Burton he learned that two more undercover cops disguised as hospital employees had been placed in the hospital on Anne's floor, and another uniformed cop was stationed in the lobby. *Good. More visibility.* But the NYPD was aiming for an arrest, while Horn's top priority was prevention. Anne was working in her office at the hospital now, he was told, with her uniformed guard outside her door.

When Horn had hung up on Burton, he phoned Anne's direct line.

"You doing all right?" he asked.

"Only if you call worrying about getting sued and getting killed doing all right." She sounded tired. Discouraged.

"You should leave the city, Anne. Go somewhere you know you'll be safe until we find Mandle."

"That sounds so much simpler than it is. And how do you know I *would* be safe? Or that you'll ever find him? In the meantime, I've got a life to live."

"Mandle sees you as a life to take. You're running a big risk, choosing this as the time to assert yourself and prove your independence."

"The time chose me, Thomas. And this isn't political correctness or feminist dogma. I'm clear-eyed about the facts and who and what I am. And I've made up my mind. I'm not going to be a victim of fear."

"How about of murder?"

"I didn't say I wasn't afraid. I said I wasn't going to be a victim. Any kind of victim, including one who's willing in some indirect, perverse way."

"Were you ever?"

"A victim?" She took a few seconds to consider. "I don't think so, no. And I'm not going to begin because this evil freak is pushing my buttons."

"Mandle's changed his MO somewhat. He's not as predictable now."

"Are you trying to frighten me more?"

"For God's sake no, Anne! I want you to know the facts so you can take precautions. Mandle didn't come through the window of his last victim. He forced the lock and came in through her door."

He could hear her breathing loudly into the phone. "Okay, Thomas. I'm sorry. I'm strung out with this . . . with everything that's going on. But my nerves are holding. Damn it, they *are!* The more I know, the better off I am."

"Here's something else you need to know, or at least have a right to know. The NYPD's not releasing the information yet, so this is in confidence. It appears Mandle's using his victims' first initials to spell out your name." He explained to her what Paula had figured out. "It doesn't necessarily mean," he added, "that a woman whose first initial is *E* will actually be a victim before Mandle tries for you. The order of victims' names might only be his way of throwing us off guard so he can get to you while we're concentrating on someone else."

"You really think his fucked-up mind works that way, Thomas?"

"Why not? You just said yourself it was fucked up."

"He'd only be pretending to be locked into a compulsion. I'm no psychiatrist but nothing Mandle's done before has suggested he's anything other than a true obsessive-compulsive."

"The sad truth about serial killers," Horn said, "is that we really don't know how their minds work, what's missing in them. They aren't all locked into patterns. And some of them, for unknown reasons, change patterns. Some of them even suddenly stop killing, as if finally they've become satiated with death."

"Satiated with death . . ." The concept seemed to intrigue her. "God, wouldn't it be wonderful if Mandle suddenly decided he'd taken enough lives?" There was a slight note of hope in her voice, beneath her despair.

"Wonderful," Horn agreed, "but not the sort of notion I'd stake my life on."

Horn left the brownstone before ten o'clock to stroll down to the Home Away and have a late-night snack, hoping Marla was working. The evening was warm, with a breath of breeze, and reminded him of other warm evenings of his life: swimming illegally in a lake as a teenager; cruising in his first car, an old Ford convertible; romancing Anne; sweltering during summer stakeouts; helplessly watching a mugging victim bleed to death on a sidewalk in Queens . . .

Enough of warm nights.

He was a hard man who'd long dealt with hard facts; he'd never been able to afford a world of fancy. Now here he was feeling as if he were walking in a dream. Had he really awoken, or was he still home, lying asleep on the sofa? Was the warm evening a dream while he was suspended in the world between sleeping and waking? So many mornings he hadn't wanted to wake up . . .

But he knew he was awake and walking in the city of his younger days, away from his wife's voice and toward another woman. Looking forward to seeing the other woman. Feeling the stirrings of new beginnings.

Brakes squealed and rubber rasped on concrete.

"Watch where you're fuckin' walkin'!"

Horn backed away from the cab he'd almost stepped in front of and waved an apology to the driver.

He stood chastised and did not look back at his fellow pedestrians on the sidewalk, who were staring at him with blank cops' faces as they waited for the traffic signal to change.

Marla was off work until morning. Horn got his usual booth but had to settle for an omelet and decaffeinated coffee served to him by a new waiter named Leonard who spoke so softly it was hard to understand him. That seemed to work both ways because he brought Horn a cheese omelet thinking Horn had said "cheese" instead of "please" when he'd ordered.

Horn, who chose his battles carefully, said nothing, fearing more complication.

He'd taken only a few bites of the omelet when his cell phone beeped in his pocket.

Good. Someone I can understand.

But at first he wasn't sure who was on the other end of the connection.

"Waldo Winthrop," repeated the caller.

"Sorry, I don't know any—"

"Newsy. I used to be Nina Count's assistant."

"Newsy! Sure, I remember you. How'd you get this number?"

"Captain Horn, you insult my professionalism."

"Sorry, Newsy. So I take it you're still in the business."

"As an independent."

"You mean you sell information?"

"To news outlets. Not to you, Captain Horn. Nina wouldn't have wanted it that way. She liked you."

"I liked her." But Horn knew others in the information business, at her station, who hadn't been crazy about Nina and her news-diva ways. And resentment of her rubbed off on her assistant. After Nina left for Atlanta, it probably hadn't taken long for the corporate sharks to close in on Newsy and chase him out of his job.

"One of my informants in the NYPD told me the story's been leaked," Newsy said.

"What story?"

"About how the Night Spider's spelling out your wife's name with the first initials of his victims. And now it's *E*'s turn."

"I don't suppose it'd do any good if I asked how it leaked?"

"Hey, Captain Horn . . ."

"Okay, Newsy. Thanks for the information. I owe you."

Horn deactivated the phone and slipped it back in his pocket.

Leonard had been hovering in the distance with the coffee-pot, obviously waiting for Horn to finish his phone conversation. Now he closed in and topped off Horn's cup, spilling a liberal amount of coffee on the table.

Leaks.

45

Newsy was right to warn him.

The next morning's *Post* all but shouted the glaring headline *E-E-E-K!* superimposed over the gray silhouette of a tarantula. Kudos to the art department.

Horn bought a paper and continued his walk toward the Home Away, glancing at the text and stopping now and then to read more carefully.

The *Post* contained a painstakingly accurate description of the Nora Shoemaker crime scene, almost as if it were lifted directly from a police report.

No *almost* about it, Horn reminded himself. Sometimes he wondered if every large bureaucracy was so porous. But he knew the answer.

The fact that since his escape, the first initials of Mandle's victims spelled the first three letters of Anne's name was said to have been noticed by "several journalists." The media protecting their sources.

Horn removed his half-glasses, tucked the folded paper beneath his arm, and continued walking. The cool summer morning gave him slight respite from his worries. Breezes and rising exhaust fumes sent discarded advertising circulars and scraps of newspaper dancing over curbs and wide sidewalks. The sun's increasing heat drew a melange of odors both rank and delicate from uncollected trash. The morning traffic roared and blared, a cacophony of constant background noises.

All of it surrounded Horn and he was glad. The city was beautiful and wonderful in its own flawed way, always moving, always vital, a presence indomitable in fact and mind. Terrorist attacks, murders and muggings, mob families, insolvency, brownouts and blackouts, financial and political scandals, riots and racism—none of them could bring the city down. It was a sprawling organism of sight, smell, sound, fear, and hope, and it fed on crises. It gave Horn life and will.

"Horn."

He turned around to see Colonel Victor Kray standing behind him.

Kray was in mufti, wearing dark slacks, a gray pullover shirt with a red fleck design woven through it, and comfortable hiking shoes that didn't go with the slacks. His clothes looked like someone else's, and he looked like a warrior who was out of uniform yet still required a salute.

"We should talk," Kray said. "I tried calling you, knocking on your door, but neither you nor your charming wife was home."

"My charming wife and I are separated," Horn said.

"I'm sorry. It isn't a pleasant thing, as I know from experience. It isn't easy being a career military man's wife."

"Or a cop's. I was on my way to breakfast. Do you want to—"

"I'd rather talk here."

"On the sidewalk?"

"Over there." Kray pointed toward a low concrete wall running parallel to the walk and sectioning off a narrow area alongside an office building. There was gravel on the other side of the wall and a lineup of neatly trimmed yews that seemed to be at attention just for Kray. The top of the wall was tiled and about bench height. A man and woman who looked like tourists were sitting on it near the corner. The man seemed frustrated, trying to explain to the woman how the gadget-laden camera slung around her neck worked. Kray said, "We can talk privately enough there, I think."

"Probably with complete privacy," Horn said, thinking how difficult it would be even for sophisticated listening devices to separate their speech from other voices and the raucous sounds of the city.

He walked with Kray to the low wall, and they sat side by side a good hundred feet away from the man and woman with the perplexing camera.

"I'd appreciate it if you'd keep this conversation and my presence in the city a secret," Kray said.

"I'll keep it as secret as possible," Horn said, thinking Larkin, Paula, and Bickerstaff.

"Agreed." Kray settled back on the wall's top surface and seemed to relax slightly, crossing his legs and clasping his hands over one knee. "I came to warn you."

Horn felt the coolness of the hard wall penetrating the material of his pants. "I've had a lot of that lately."

Kray smiled. Not for the first time, Horn thought that he looked like a full-size military action toy that had aged gracefully. G.I. Kray, rising through the ranks.

"I figured out what Mandle was doing with his victims' initials before the media did," Kray said. "It would seem he's going to take one more victim before your wife, the *E* woman." Kray glanced at the paper still tucked beneath Horn's right arm. "I'm here, in part, to warn you he might not. That kind of sequential diversion is part of his training. Mandle might go directly to Anne."

"We've thought of that," Horn said.

"There are so many ways Mandle knows how to kill that you can't have thought of them all. He can kill all the conventional ways and dozens of unconventional."

"Like with a sharpened steel screw."

"Or his hands and feet. Another thing you should know is that Mandle's an expert with explosives."

Horn felt a sudden unease. That was one method Anne might not be sufficiently protected from. "What kinds of explosives?"

"Just about every kind. Both in using them and in making them. Plastique, black powder, liquid chemical . . . You'd be surprised how many common, easy-to-obtain substances can be mixed or transformed into explosive elements."

"Our profilers think Mandle's locked into compulsion, even though he altered his routine with his last victim. They think he'll take an *E* victim."

Kray unclasped his hands and brushed his fingertips over the silky material of his slacks, as if reminding himself he was in civilian clothes. "You know serial killers," he said. "I only know soldiering. And I know what kind of soldier Aaron Mandle was. I can't impress upon you strongly enough how difficult it will be to stop him."

"Even with your help?"

"I'm not in a position to help you directly. The army doesn't know I'm here. And of course we don't know what approach Mandle will take." Kray reached into the breast pocket of his shirt, felt around behind a pair of sunglasses, then drew out a folded slip of white paper and handed it to Horn. "That's the phone number where I'm staying at the Rion Hotel."

Horn accepted the paper and glanced at it, then slipped it into his own shirt pocket. He knew the Rion, a midsize, overpriced, and discreet hotel near Gramercy Park. Foreign dignitaries and celebrities who wanted privacy often stayed there.

"I'd appreciate it if you'd keep me somewhat informed," Kray said. "And call me if you need any sort of question about Mandle answered. Or anything else. I mean that. I'm partly responsible for what I've created through his training. I want him caught and this time put away for good so he can't harm anyone else."

Kray stood up from the wall and briefly and adeptly brushed off his clothes, front and back, as if sitting on a wall were as untidy a proposition as yard work.

"This conversation never took place," Horn said, before Kray could.

Kray smiled. "Actually, I was going to say you never saw me. I guess serial killers aren't the only ones locked into compulsion and routine."

"There's a difference."

"And thank God."

Kray shook hands with Horn, remembering to reach for Horn's noninjured left hand. Horn watched the colonel put on his sunglasses, then nod, turn, and stride away. He niftily dodged a few people walking toward him on a collision course, then within a few seconds, was lost from sight in the stream of pedestrians.

Horn stood up and tugged his pants legs free from where they were stuck to the backs of his thighs. As he continued his walk to the Home Away, he repeated in his mind his parting words to Kray: *There's a difference.*

And if only we understood what it is.

What's missing in people like Aaron Mandle? Or what dark demons possess them? And when? And how?

If only we understood and could stop them before they begin.

Horn picked up his pace and redirected his thoughts, reminding himself his job was to deal with such human anomalies only after they *had* begun.

And specifically, urgently, his job and his personal mission were the same—to stop Aaron Mandle.

As soon as Horn entered the Home Away, he was struck by a sense of dread.

Several customers were eating breakfast in booths, and Marla was taking the food orders of a couple with two small children at one of the tables. She glanced at Horn and couldn't avert her gaze, though she appeared to want to look away.

Toward the back of the diner, Paula and Bickerstaff were seated in a booth. Bickerstaff's back was to Horn, but he was twisted around so he could see toward the front of the diner. He and Paula were looking at Horn; Horn didn't like the expressions on their faces.

When he approached them, and before he could say anything, Bickerstaff said, "Did you get it on your cell phone?"

Horn realized he'd turned off his phone while walking toward the low wall with Kray, thinking it might be the kind of conversation he wouldn't want interrupted. He reached into his pocket and switched on the phone by feel.

Without waiting for Horn to answer Bickerstaff, Paula said, "A woman named Emily Schneider was found dead in her apartment this morning, shrouded in her bedsheets. Multiple stab wounds. Everything about the murder fits."

"It had to be Mandle," Bickerstaff said.

They watched him absorb the news, Paula with a concerned little frown.

Horn stood motionless and uttered one word: "Anne . . ."

Anne!

In his pocket, his cell phone began chirping urgently, like a live thing trapped.

46

Patrolmen Lee Sanford and Amos Prince of the One-three precinct didn't need lights or a siren as Sanford drove their radio car toward a Lower East Side address in response to a *Crimes in the Past* signal.

Sanford, a fifteen-year veteran of the NYPD, was a tall, thin, taciturn man with the solemn demeanor of a grave digger. The much younger Prince was a stocky African-American who, as far as Sanford was concerned, smiled too much and too broadly and was maybe a little too hip to be a cop. They'd been partners in the patrol car for a little over a month. It had taken three weeks before Sanford decided Prince might be a good cop despite his runny mouth and devotion to rap music. Prince was beginning to suspect his partner Abe Lincoln might just do when it came crunch time. Might.

Sanford pulled the car to the curb in front of one of a row of almost identical brick six-story walk-ups.

"This is it," Prince said, seeing the crudely painted address next to the building's door. "Let's do it."

"Wanna make sure," Sanford said, sitting motionless behind the steering wheel and studying the notes he'd scrawled when the call had come through.

Prince squirmed. "C'mon, Lee. Time to get outta Car Fifty-four."

Sanford gave him a sideways morose look, then put down his notes and opened the car door. Relieved, Prince reached for the door handle on his side.

"Had to be on the sixth floor," Prince said as they climbed rickety wooden steps that led from landing to landing. Barely enough light made it through the landings' dirty windows for them to see where they were going.

They were both breathing a little raggedly when they reached the door with a painted-over brass 6-B on it. Prince knocked on the age-checked enameled wood.

The door opened almost immediately and a worried-looking stout woman wearing jeans and combing her long dark hair looked out at them. "It's you," she said simply.

"Us," Sanford confirmed.

"You put in a call for the police," Prince reminded the woman.

She looked agitated, dark eyes narrowing. "I hear this shit, I gotta come home early from work."

"What kinda shit?" Prince asked.

"Teenage, is what. I got two sons, fourteen and fifteen. You got teenagers, Officer?"

"Git outta here!" Prince said.

"Rafe and Georgie, only four days since school let out and they already found trouble."

"What kinda trouble?" Prince asked.

Sanford gave him a disapproving look. He knew they should let the woman run her mouth; she'd get around to it in her own time. What she had to say might be hard for her to get out.

"I get a call at work from Georgie—"

"The fifteen-year-old?"

"Fourteen. He tells me Rafe's got a gun. I say is Rafe there and let me talk to him and Rafe comes to the phone. You got a gun? How'd you get it? Where'd you get it? Jesus! I tell Rafe to put down the gun and the two of them stay right where they fuckin' are and stay away from the gun. Okay?"

"You did right," Sanford said.

"Not that they listened to me one little bit. They came home with the gun."

The woman suddenly realized Sanford and Prince were still standing in the hall. She stopped combing her hair and moved aside so they could enter her apartment. The messy living room was unoccupied except for a grungy 9mm handgun lying on the coffee table next to a soda can.

"That it?" Prince asked unnecessarily, pointing to the gun.

"Course that's it."

"Where are the boys?"

"In their rooms. I didn't send them there. They don't like cops."

"At their age? They should still love us, the way we give them directions and help them get across the street and such."

Sanford had crossed the magazine-and-newspaper-littered floor and was leaning down looking at the gun. Besides being grimy, it was just beginning to rust and its barrel was clogged with dirt. It was also exactly the same model as the 9mm semiautomatic in Sanford's holster. A cop's gun. "Where'd the boys say they got this?"

"Off a dead body."

"*Really?*" Prince asked. "That must have been some wild experience for the little shit-kickers."

"Where?" Sanford asked.

An hour later Horn, Paula, and Bickerstaff were standing with Sanford and Prince in the basement of a condemned and boarded-up building off First Avenue in lower Manhattan. They were about ten feet away from the body, trying to avoid the smell that was made even worse by the usual musty and stale-urine stench of abandoned urban buildings. If the ancient basement had ever had anything other than a dirt floor, it was no longer evident. Lights had been carried down, the ME was in attendance, and techs were buzzing around the half-buried and badly decomposed body that had loose earth scooped over it. They weren't the only things buzzing around it. The dead man was stripped to the waist and wearing what looked like the filthy remnants of work pants.

Paula saw that the ME was the little redheaded geek. Harry Potter.

"This guy's been shot," Harry Potter said to Horn.

"Fatal wound?"

"I haven't checked his pulse yet."

"Do I have to ask again?"

"Mighta killed him eventually. Gotta examine a stiff like this in the morgue to make sure of anything, what with all the decomposition, insects, and dirt. Guy shoulda known we were coming, used some underarm deodorant."

Paula felt her stomach kick. She could do without the sick cop humor. It was difficult enough trying to breathe only out. The techs were wearing surgical masks. Paula wished she had one but didn't want to ask. She got one of those looks from Bickerstaff, even though he was standing with his hand cupped loosely over his mouth and nose.

"What the hell were two teenage boys doing down here?" Paula asked. "The place looks ready to fall down around itself."

"Their mom said they came here to look for antique bottles," Sanford said. "They collect them. The basements of these old buildings are a good place to hunt for them. One of the kids noticed a hand sticking up outta the dirt, so they dug and right away found the gun, found some more of the dead body, and got out fast."

"I'll just bet," Bickerstaff said. "You say they took the gun with them?"

"Would a boy leave behind a gun?"

"Wouldn't be natural," Paula said.

"Mom oughta whip their asses!" Prince said. "Least the dead guy's not a cop."

"Probably not," Horn said. "We've got no missing cops, but we do have a few missing guns."

"Fucker mighta stole one from a cop," Prince said.

Horn's cell phone beeped, and he walked away a few feet to answer.

When he was finished with the call, he motioned for Paula and Bickerstaff to come over, leaving Prince and Sanford out of the conversation.

"We've got the computer match on the gun," he said. "It's NYPD and registered to Sergeant Donald Perlman."

It took Paula and Bickerstaff a moment to recognize the name.

"Holy shit!" Bickerstaff said. "One of the guards Mandle killed when he escaped from the van taking him to Rikers. And Mandle got away with the guards' guns."

"He did," Horn said. "And only about three blocks from here."

Paula stared over at the grisly sight of the half-exhumed body. *Wouldn't it be something . . .*

"Naw! Can't be Mandle," she said. "Might be somebody he shot, then he threw down the gun. Buried it with the body."

"Probably the dead guy was one of the homeless," Bickerstaff said. "Or a doper using the building as a place to cook and shoot up. Mandle surprised him and had to get rid of him."

"Most likely thing," Paula agreed.

"I can't see Mandle leaving the gun behind," Horn said. "Earlier that night his only weapon was a screw. So now he's got a couple of guns and he tosses one away? He sure as hell wouldn't care if it linked him with the crime, considering his position."

"Panic?" Bickerstaff suggested.

"Not *our* boy," Paula said.

Horn glanced over at the techs carefully excavating around the dead man. "Another gun lying anywhere around there?"

"There was just the one," called back a tech. "We used a metal detector to look before we started digging."

The toe of one of the dead man's shoes had been unearthed and shone dully with reflected light.

And that's when Horn realized what had been skittering along the edges of his consciousness for days, the piece he couldn't recall and fit into the puzzle. The photograph of the faint footprint in the heat-softened tar on the roof of Alice Duggan's building. Horn closed his eyes and conjured up an image of that footprint, the gentle curve of the impression in the tar.

And he was sure: the footprint on the roof had been made by the sole of a shoe on a right foot. *A shoe.*

But that would mean! . . .

He walked over to where Harry Potter was stooping near the body. "I need to look at the right foot," he said.

Puzzled, the little ME pointed. "Right there it is, sticking up out of the earth."

"I mean take off the right shoe. I need to know about the foot."

The ME stood up. "That'd be better done in the morgue, when we remove the rest of the clothes."

"I need to know now," Horn said, and something in his voice made the ME step away and nod his assent.

While the shoe was being carefully removed, Horn looked over at the confused Paula and Bickerstaff, standing and waiting.

"We got us one weird-looking big toe," Harry Potter said behind him.

Horn turned and looked.

One weird looking big toe.

The decomposed body in the shallow grave was Aaron Mandle's.

Which meant Mandle had died before Alice Duggan. *The second gun! The missing second gun!*

It took Horn another ten seconds to figure out what it meant.

He strode past Paula and Bickerstaff and barely glanced at them. "Let's go! Fast! I'll explain later."

"Go where?" Bickerstaff asked, picking up the pace and catching up with Horn.

"To Kincaid Memorial Hospital. Where Anne is."

"But that right foot," Bickerstaff said. "If this is Mandle's body . . ."

"Since the escape from the van," Horn said, "we've been hunting a different SSF member. A second Night Spider."

As they sped through crowded streets toward the hospital, Horn got back on his cell phone. First he called the hospital and told them to be on high alert. Then he phoned Rollie Larkin. He needed something sensitive done quickly by someone with pull.

He explained to Larkin what had happened and what was needed.

Larkin called back even before the car reached the hospital.

"Public records," he said to Horn. "Easy enough to get, and fast, if you have the clout. Joseph Arthur Vine joined the army in late '94, did his basic training at Fort Leonard Wood in '95. The odd thing is, no posting after basic training is listed for him."

"That's when he began his SSF training," Horn said.

Bickerstaff, driving the unmarked, had to swerve to avoid a double-parked cab. Paula, in the front passenger seat, cursed loudly.

"What was that?" Larkin asked.

"Just New York. Can I ask another favor? Will you check with your sources again and find out if Aaron Mandle and Joe Vine ever crossed paths in the service?"

"We're going beyond public records, Horn. It would have to be just between us, whatever I told you."

"That's how it'll be."

Larkin said he'd get back to Horn and hung up.

Horn saw that Paula had both hands on the dashboard, squeezing it.

He looked down and saw the fingers of his left hand digging into his thigh.

A woman about to cross the street almost fell backward. She screamed at the speeding unmarked. A delivery van screeched to a halt coming out of a building garage, braking so hard that several cartons bounced from an open front door. The driver leaned on his horn and shouted at Bickerstaff, who ignored him.

Paula glanced back at Horn, wide-eyed. Horn shrugged.

He decided Bickerstaff had been away long enough that his driving skills were rusty. But they'd reach their destination. With luck.

They were in the hospital elevator when Larkin called back. Horn stood listening with the cell phone pressed to his ear. Reception wasn't great in the elevator, but he knew it wouldn't be good at all when they got to Radiology, Anne's department.

"Aaron Mandle and Joseph Vine trained in the same unit at Fort Leonard Wood in the spring of '95," Larkin said, "after which they don't appear in official army records. Like they never were. When we reached that point I lost my source. He sounded scared."

"Thanks. The information means a lot."

"I hope so, Horn. I hope it takes us where you think it will."

The elevator lurched to a stop. Horn thanked Larkin again and broke the connection.

Larkin's information meant Mandle and Vine knew each other before volunteering for their special units.

And maybe later.

Anne was at her desk. She knew what Horn would want and was already cleaning out some of her drawers, stuffing things into a large brown valise.

When she saw Horn enter, trailed by Paula and Bicker-staff, she had to smile. She felt a bit like a princess in a fairy tale who at any cost mustn't be harmed by a dragon—or a spider. Right now, she didn't mind the feeling.

She said hello to the trio and closed her desk drawers.

"I thought I'd have to do some work at home," she explained.

Paula looked into her blue eyes and saw fear but no panic. *So cool under this kind of pressure.* Paula could understand why Horn had married her, why her marriage to a cop had survived so many years.

"Not exactly at home," Horn said.

Anne paused and looked at him. "You're calling in that promise I made to you?"

"It has to be that way." He explained the situation, watching her expression change as he did so.

Paula watched, too. *Almost panic in those eyes now. For only an instant . . .*

"That makes it intensely personal," Anne said.

"And intensely dangerous."

"What about the dead guard's tooth that was left on my dresser?"

"Mandle's grisly souvenir, but to his killer it looked like a calling card he could leave to establish the false impression that the Night Spider was on the hunt again."

Anne rested a hand on the desk as if for support but didn't actually lean her weight on it. "I'll do what you say. Where am I going?"

"I'm thinking your brother's cabin in upstate New York. He only uses it in the winter, for hunting. If we can get you there without anyone following, you should be safe. You'll be heavily guarded there, too, of course."

"I can call him," Anne said, "find out where he hides the key."

"Don't call him. Don't tell anyone where you're going. We'll get you into the cabin even if we have to force a lock or break a window. We'll explain it to your brother later; he'll understand."

"Jim's in Philadelphia. And he'd never tell anyone where I was."

"He would if they started snipping off his fingers."

Anne looked ill. "Jesus, Thomas . . . Can I go to my apartment and pick up some clothes?"

"Of course. Paula and Bickerstaff will drive you. Then they'll take you to the cabin after making sure nobody's following. Do you have your Ladysmith thirty-eight here, or at your apartment?"

"Neither. I left it. I didn't want to live with guns anymore."

"Swing by the brownstone and get it," Horn said to Bickerstaff. "She's qualified and can shoot both eyes out of a gnat."

This seemed a bad idea to Paula: maybe the gnat had to be sitting still: maybe one of the cops guarding Anne would be mistaken for a gnat.

Anne started to hoist the big valise down from the desk, but Bickerstaff hastily stepped forward and took it from her. He wheezed and was obviously surprised by its weight.

"When you leave the brownstone," Horn said to Bickerstaff, "give me a call."

He watched them leave, Anne walking between Paula and Bickerstaff, who was leaning sideways, the heavy valise bumping against his knee with every step.

When they were gone Horn talked to the security cops at the hospital, then called Lieutenant Burton to arrange for reassignments.

Then he took an elevator to a floor where he knew there was a large waiting area with public phones in insulated stalls, where people had privacy to inform friends and family of joyous or tragic news. Either way, they could shed tears without anyone watching.

The carpeted area lined with sofas and chairs was almost

unoccupied. No one was near the phones, and the TV mounted on the wall was showing a muted *Law and Order* rerun with Jerry Orbach as Detective Lenny Briscoe. Horn's favorite.

He used one of the phones to call Victor Kray at the Rion Hotel.

"There's news?" Kray asked, when Horn had identified himself.

"The news is your list of SSF members was incomplete. You left off Joe Vine."

"What's Vine got to do with Mandle?"

"Why did you leave him off the list?"

"Ah, a question in answer to a question."

"Cop stuff," Horn said. "We also demand answers that aren't questions."

"I knew Vine lived in the area, and I learned about his family situation. His son's in a coma and might not recover. He has money problems. In fact, I think he's suing a hospital, or is being sued. I liked Joe. He was one of our best. I was sure he was above suspicion. Still am. I simply didn't want to involve him in this and add to his problems."

"He's suing the hospital where my wife works," Horn said. "He's suing my wife personally."

Kray was silent while he processed the information. Then: "Where is this conversation going, Horn?"

Horn told him what he thought. After escaping from the police van, Mandle contacted his old SSF buddy Joe Vine and asked for help. Vine helped him by killing him with one of the guns Mandle took off the dead guards. Then, as the Night Spider, Vine could continue Mandle's string of killings, and Anne Horn, wife of the Night Spider's public nemesis, would be considered another Spider victim. Vine would never be suspected of executing the woman he held responsible for his son's permanent near-death state. If Mandle's body were never found, or if enough time passed to make it possible to ascertain only an approximate date of death, Mandle would be blamed for Vine's killings as well as his own crimes.

"That doesn't sound like the Joe Vine I knew," Kray said. "Are you sure Mandle is dead?"

"I saw the corpse's right foot."

"Oh . . . Christ!" What sounded almost like a sob came over the phone. It was strangely shocking to imagine Kray as its source, like a tear shed from Mount Rushmore.

"I'm not accustomed to telling people I'm sorry," Kray said. "That's not often done in my line of work. Maybe not in yours, either. But I am sorry, Horn. If there's any way I can make it up to you, anything I can do . . ."

"Tell me about Vine. Is he as capable as Mandle?"

"Almost. Not as adept a climber. He's an explosives expert and a skilled sniper and knife fighter."

"Great."

"He didn't like killing as much as Mandle," Kray said. His tone of voice suggested that was something Horn needed to know.

Horn imagined Vine dutifully stabbing four women over and over to emulate Mandle's murders, then bashing in their heads to make sure they were dead and couldn't identify him.

He likes killing well enough.

So Mandle had waited around for his victims to suffer and bleed out, but Vine wasn't having as much fun and wanted to leave the party early. Horn didn't see that as much of a distinction.

"If I can help . . ." Kray offered again, a plea for forgiveness.

"I'll let you know," Horn said, and hung up.

As he stood and turned away from the phone, he saw that *Law and Order* on the waiting-room TV had been interrupted for a news flash. The condemned building on the Lower East Side where Mandle's body was found filled the screen except for the crawl at the bottom:

NIGHT SPIDER SQUASHED? IT'S REPORTED THAT LESS THAN AN HOUR AGO POLICE FOUND . . .

Horn thought of Newsy and everyone like Newsy only worse. And the people who supplied their information. *Damned leaks!*

His cell phone chirped and he yanked it from his pocket. *Oughta get a belt clip.*

It was Larkin. "A SWAT unit's on the way to Vine's apartment," he said. "You wanna be there for the collar or whatever?"

"You know it. I'm at Kincaid Memorial, but it won't take me long."

"I'll see you there," Larkin said. "Just make sure you don't arrive before we do."

As he hurried from the waiting area, Horn glanced over and saw that *Law and Order* was back on above the crawl. Lenny, questioning a suspect in the interrogation room, gave his patented hopeless smile and weary shrug. The world kept turning, the truth would seep out, justice would find its way to the surface. It was in the script and took about an hour.

47

The apartment building had been quietly evacuated. SWAT leader Sergeant Lou Marcus led half his team down the narrow hall, while a lanky blond man Horn had heard addressed as Newman led more of the team up the fire stairs in back.

Marcus and three other SWAT members had come up in the elevator. It would take Newman longer in back, so their timing had to be right. There was no telling what was inside the Vine apartment, so there was no more communication over the two ways that might be overheard. The working assumption was that no one inside the apartment knew it was just them and the SWAT team in the building. When Newman and his men were positioned at the back door, the door would be taken down and a diversion device would be fired into the apartment.

Diversion device was bureaucratese for a flash-bang grenade that would be harmless but made an ungodly amount of noise when detonated. This was designed to do two things: for a few seconds, freeze with shock whoever was inside the apartment, and cause their attention to be focused toward the rear of the apartment and sound of the explosion.

During this brief suspension of time, Marcus's part of the team would batter down the front door and stream inside.

When the stun grenade went off, everyone had precious few seconds to operate in with comparative safety. So all hell would break loose. While SWAT members were invading the apartment from both ends, NYPD uniforms would be entering the building and pounding up the stairs, as reinforcements arrived by car. Five, maybe ten seconds, while the element of surprise applied.

Everything might depend on making the most of those seconds.

Marcus checked behind him. The two men with him were ready with the battering ram that would swing forward on thick leather straps and make short work of the ancient wood door. While the door was still flying open, they would enter with Heckler and Koch MP5 automatic weapons at the ready.

It sure made the mouth dry, Marcus was thinking, when a tremendous roar shook the building. Even here in the hall his ears were ringing. Anyone inside had to be paralyzed with shock.

Marcus waved his right hand and the battering ram slammed into the door, shattering wood and crashing it open on the first attempt. He gulped down his fear and led the way inside, smelling the burned stench left by the grenade.

And within seconds, with mixed emotions of relief and disappointment, he saw through faint smoke that the room he was in was empty.

A dark, bulky figure appeared in the hall. One of Newman's men.

Quickly the SWAT members moved from room to room, dancing with nerve and purpose, swinging their MP5s in arcs. Shouts of "Clear," "Clear," sounded shortly after each room was entered.

Then: "In here! East bedroom!"

Marcus went.

The small room was suddenly filled with equipment-laden, menacing figures in dark uniforms. They stood leaning forward tensely, guns like extensions of their bodies, alert as prey though they were the hunters.

Their attention was focused on a small, huddled figure wedged between the bed and the wall. A woman in what looked like a faded red robe pulled tightly around her as if for protection, though her bare legs were exposed. Her entire body was shaking so violently that beads of perspiration flew from her wild damp hair.

Guns were trained on her as the bed was pulled farther away from the wall.

Two of the SWAT members gripped her beneath the arms, yanked her upright, then forced her facedown on the bed while handcuffs were snapped around her wrists.

"Cindy Vine?" Marcus asked in a loud voice.

The woman managed to nod.

Cindy Vine couldn't stop trembling and sobbing while she was informed she was under arrest on suspicion of being an accessory to murder. She began gnawing her lower lip as her rights were read to her.

"Where's Joseph Vine?" Marcus asked her.

Cindy merely shook her head and continued sobbing. Her hair, which was made even wetter by her tears, was stuck across her eyes. One of the SWAT team gently brushed it aside. She continued to sob.

"Do you know the whereabouts of your husband?" Marcus asked again in a voice neither threatening nor soothing.

But she was sobbing too hard to answer.

They waited patiently until she'd calmed down, then asked again, but she would only tuck in her chin, clench her eyes shut, and remain silent.

Marcus knew that for the time being he'd lost her. Cindy Vine's stunned psyche had carried her somewhere else. She wasn't going to talk. He might as well have been questioning a piece of the room's furniture.

*   *   *

As Horn turned the corner of Vine's block, he saw half a dozen police cars angled in at the curb, and beyond them a police van. The street was blocked except for one lane that let traffic siphon through. There were knots of pedestrians at each end of the street. Uniforms held everyone back at both ends of the block unless they were residents or police.

Horn showed his shield out the car window, then he parked near one of the cruisers across the street from a run-down stone and brick apartment building that had a skeletal steel framework but no awning over its entrance. A tall uniform was standing directly in front of the entrance with his feet planted wide and his arms crossed. *Somebody or other at the bridge.*

Horn showed his ID again to the uniform at the door, the large man with the scarred face who'd guarded Anne at the apartment and hospital. The man told him the Vines' apartment number, on the sixth floor.

A few minutes later, as Horn stepped from the elevator and made his way down the hall toward the open door, he could hear voices, all male, drifting from the Vines' apartment.

When he entered, there was Rollie Larkin, a plainclothes detective Horn didn't know, and three dark-uniformed SWAT guys with automatic weapons. Dwarfed by all the good-sized men in the small living room was a thin woman curled in a corner of a sofa with her legs tucked beneath her. Her head was bowed and her lank brown hair was plastered to most of her face, leaving only her nose exposed, reminding Horn of a character left over from *Cats.*

"Cindy Vine," Larkin said to Horn, and motioned toward the woman.

"No Mr. Vine?"

" 'Fraid not. And the missus isn't talking."

The plainclothes detective, a middle-aged chunky guy in a better suit than most cops would wear, leaned down so his head was near Cindy Vine's. He had his shield out of its wallet and pinned carelessly to his suitcoat's lapel, and when he bent over, its weight tugged at the dark gray material.

"Mrs. Vine?" he said. "Cindy? You do understand you'd be helping your husband if you told us where he is?"

The hair mask moved and it looked like she might have shaken her head no, but she made no sound.

The detective stood up. "She's been like that, silent. Probably still in shock from when the SWAT team did their thing. Percussion grenade and all."

"Hell of a thing to have happen in your home," Horn said. He moved over and stooped down so he could see Cindy Vine's pretty but haggard, tearstained face beneath all the hair. She continued her empty staring at the carpet. "Mrs. Vine, has anyone apologized to you for breaking in the way they did?"

She raised her head slightly and glanced at him, then looked back at the floor, or maybe at his shoes.

"Would you accept my apology?"

She sat up suddenly so her back and cuffed wrists were pressed against the sofa, then threw her head back so she didn't have to look at him and was staring at the ceiling. She closed her eyes.

He took that for a no.

Horn straightened up, feeling it in his knees and hearing cartilage crack.

"We're getting old," Larkin said behind him. "Fucking shame." Then to the detective with the dangling badge, "Take her in. Do her a favor and call Legal Aid."

Cindy Vine moved like a zombie as she was led from the apartment.

"Any idea of hubby's whereabouts?" Horn asked Larkin.

"No. And so far there's nothing in the place by way of a clue. SWAT team says that when they broke in, the bedroom TV was on."

"We have to assume Joe Vine knows about Mandle's death," Horn said.

"That's where Cindy could help us, if she would."

"When she gets a lawyer and rejoins the real world, she might be more willing to cooperate." Horn knew that Cindy Vine would have little choice, once her attorney filled her in on the facts and told her she herself was in trouble with the law.

"A blood sample was taken from Mandle before his trial," Larkin said. "The DNA from it matches that of the corpse found in the building. Mandle probably didn't get far after his escape, with the bullet wound in his chest. Got to a phone somehow and called Joe Vine for help, then hid out in the condemned building's basement and waited for Vine."

"Who found him dead or shot him with the other guard's gun," Horn said. "And decided he'd be useful in murdering my wife."

"You're half right," Larkin said. "ME said there was only one gunshot wound and it wouldn't have been fatal. Mandle was stabbed in the back."

Horn looked hard at Larkin, taking in what he'd just heard. It made Vine all the more dangerous. "In the back, huh? Cold-blooded even with his friends, and cautious enough he didn't want anyone to hear a gunshot."

"Yeah. Pretty chicken-shit. You'd think the sonuvabitch would have some kind of code. Just about everybody does."

"His code," Horn said, "is whatever's in his best interest."

"Shoulda gone into politics, or to more John Wayne movies as a kid. We also gotta figure he's in possession of the other dead guard's gun."

"He'll have more than that to work with by this time. Kinda guy that can make a weapon out of Jell-O."

"Did Anne get to the cabin okay?"

"I haven't heard yet from Bickerstaff and Paula," Horn said. "It's a long drive."

"Plenty secluded?"

"Surrounded by woods. Anne's brother's a dedicated hunter, only uses it for that."

"I sent along a detail so security will be in place shortly

after Anne arrives. It'll be impossible for Vine to get to her even if he somehow figures out where she is. You can check it out later and be in overall command."

Horn walked over to the window to watch Cindy Vine being loaded into the back of a patrol car for her ride to captivity and interrogation. A woman in a jam not of her own making, with a difficult time ahead. But maybe that was wrong. Maybe she'd urged her husband on, driven just as he was because of their son. It sure wasn't a perfect world.

"There was a human hair stuck beneath the duct tape over Emily Schneider's mouth," Larkin said. "It turned out not to be hers. We took some hair samples from Vine's comb to see if we come up with a match. We will. There's going to be a solid case against Vine. We have no worries on that account."

Horn nodded, but he didn't think evidence would make much difference.

They were going to have to kill Vine.

Paula was standing at the bureau in Harry Linnert's bedroom and packing a blue vinyl club bag. Toothbrush, deodorant, gun . . .

"You're going to spend nights on a stakeout?" Linnert asked behind her, still not quite believing it. That she was a cop hadn't really hit home until now. Not like this, anyway.

"A security stakeout," Paula said, continuing with her packing. "It will probably only be for two or three days and nights."

"You're guarding some big shot? Some Mafia witness or something?"

She laughed. "Nothing like that."

"I couldn't stand for you to be in any danger."

"I'm not, usually, except for being surrounded by too many doughnuts."

"They haven't ruined your figure."

He came to her and kissed the nape of her neck, then

turned her around and kissed her on the lips. The world, everything, slowed down and became better when she was in his arms.

She confided in him, explaining the situation.

He gave her another kiss. "You be careful, you hear?"

She nodded. "For you and for me."

When Horn used the cell phone to call home from his car parked across from the Vines' apartment building, there was a message on his machine to contact Kray at the Rion Hotel.

He turned the air conditioner on high, sat back, and punched out the Rion's number then Kray's extension.

Kray picked up on the first ring. "Horn?"

"Yes."

"I've been reading the papers, watching TV news."

"Spending a lot of time in your room."

"It's my information center, such as it is. After Emily Schneider was killed, this operation really started to bother me. Then when you told me about Joe Vine. Jesus, you can imagine."

Horn wasn't sure he could. "You're not the one killing women," he said. "You're being too hard on yourself."

"It's just that I know what someone like Vine can do. How he can be impossible to find, then how deadly he can be. I know his moves. More than that, Horn, I know his counter-moves. Because I taught them to him. The kind of training he had, that *I* was trained to provide, I had to get inside his mind. I know his mind. I can help you like no one else can."

He was probably right, Horn thought.

"My advice is to get Anne out of the city, out of an urban environment. Vine is trained to be his most deadly in cities, where we ran night strikes and did certain difficult . . . jobs for the government."

"She's in a secluded wooded area, in a cabin owned by her brother."

"That's good. Urban and mountain terrain are where you don't want her. Is there lots of underbrush?"

"I'm not sure."

"Don't take it for granted that Vine will make noise moving through dry brush. There are ways not to. Thick woods?"

"I was there once. The woods are plenty thick. Gently rolling hills."

"Water nearby?"

"I recall a creek. Maybe a couple hundred yards beyond the place."

"Not big enough for a boat or canoe?"

"Definitely not. Probably even dry this time of year."

"Dry creek beds are like highways through wooded areas," Kray said. "Vine knows how to travel them."

"We've got that covered," Horn assured Kray.

"Whatever you do, don't let Anne accept any package, delivered or mailed. The same goes for any strange object placed outside the cabin, especially one virtually calling for a woman to pick it up. It should be checked before she touches it. She should stay away from windows, especially at night with a light on inside. The thing to remember is he can kill from a distance. There are ways you wouldn't imagine."

"We won't underestimate him," Horn said.

"Good luck, and if you want me there when and if you get him cornered, please call on me. I might be able to help you in unexpected ways, and at the same time atone for my sins."

"A church is the place for expiation. A priest rather than a cop."

"You understand what I mean, Horn. I know you do."

"Yeah, you're right," Horn admitted. "But I don't think I can help you. I'll keep what you said in mind, though. And thanks."

"Good luck," Kray told him again, in a way that left no doubt that he meant it.

Horn sat in the car with the engine idling, wondering if maybe he was being overconfident. Vine was trained in methods beyond those usually dealt with by the NYPD. And the truth was, Horn hadn't really thought of everything, not so far, and that disturbed him.

He started the car, but before driving away used the cell phone to call an old friend named Morris Beiner on the bomb squad. Men like Mandle and Vine knew how to get their hands on explosives, or they could make explosives themselves.

As the phone on the other end of the connection rang, he remembered Kray's cautionary voice: . . . *he can kill from a distance. There are ways you wouldn't imagine.*

All those years in the NYPD, Horn thought. Maybe he hadn't seen it all. Maybe nobody ever saw it all.

He thought about Anne, hidden away and heavily guarded, and in more danger than she knew. Vine's motivation might be more understandable—raw, irrational vengeance—but he was no more an ordinary killer than was Mandle. They were both practitioners of the same rare trade. Death's craftsmen, even artists, in a world of dilettantes.

Maybe there are ways I need to imagine.

48

When they'd left her alone in the cabin, Anne stood in the center of its main room and looked around. It was a small structure, not much more than the single room in which she stood, with a tiny kitchen area, a bathroom, and a crude staircase that led to sleeping lofts. At least it had indoor plumbing, though her brother told her it sometimes didn't work all that well. She made a mental note to check it as soon as she got unpacked. Maybe before.

Though the construction was crude—stained cedar planks on the outside and on one of the inside walls—there was a certain coziness about the way the place was furnished. A large nubby sofa faced the big stone fireplace. Antlers and stuffed fish were mounted on the walls, along with a few unframed prints of hunting scenes. The floor was rough-hewn cedar, with an oval red and gray woven rug in its center. There was a smaller woven rug in the same colors in front of the fireplace. Framed photos of her brother holding up fish he'd caught over the years were propped on the mantel, and above them an old rod and reel were mounted on the wall. There was a mustiness about the cabin, made somehow pleasant by the underlying acrid scent of all the cedar.

Anne looked over at her suitcase, placed just inside the door, then up at the sleeping lofts. *Is this really going to be home for a while?*

She hadn't been here in years and didn't even recall if the place had a generator and electricity. But she was relieved to see a light switch on the wall, and that there was a ceiling fan mounted high on the beamed ceiling. Electrical cords extended from the oversized lamps on tables at each end of the sofa. It would be dark soon. At least she'd have light.

There was a knock on the warped plank door as it creaked open. Anne felt a thrill of terror, then relaxed.

It was only Paula, who'd driven her here.

Paula smiled. "Sorry if I spooked you. I forgot something."

Anne was spooked, all right. She wondered how secure she really was in the cabin.

Cindy Vine was finally talking, but hestitantly. Horn and Larkin watched through the one-way glass of the precinct interrogation room as a detective named Millhouse, whose specialty was sly interrogation, questioned her in the presence of her Legal Aid attorney. The attorney was a handsome, stern woman in her forties named Vicki Twigg, who, in private practice, had almost been disbarred five years before for her romantic involvement with her client. Rumor had it she'd also been doing drugs but had cleaned up that act before it destroyed her personally and professionally. Horn knew Twigg could be her old clever and unprincipled self from time to time. Cindy Vine hadn't done badly in the luck of the draw.

"You're the only one in any sort of position to help your husband," Millhouse was telling Cindy.

She glanced at Twigg, who sat motionless and might have been thinking about a Macy's sale.

"And help yourself, of course," Millhouse added. "Unfortunately your husband's crossed a threshold into a lot of serious difficulty. I sincerely believe he wouldn't want you to follow him, but I'm afraid that's what you'll do if you continue your refusal to cooperate—"

Cindy squirmed. Twigg remained unmoving, maybe wondering how crowded Macy's would be.

"Damn her," Larkin said, on the other side of the thick glass.

He punched out a number on his cell phone. The phone in Millhouse's pocket vibrated soundlessly, and Larkin broke the connection.

"I'm authorized to offer a deal," Millhouse said.

Twigg looked over at him without moving her head.

"If your client is completely truthful and cooperative—"

"She walks," Twigg finished for him. Twigg knew the score, the inning, the pitch count. "It's her husband you want. My client has done nothing actionable."

"Being an accessory to murder is actionable," Millhouse said. "But even so—"

"She walks."

Millhouse glanced over at the glass behind which Larkin and Horn stood unseen. Twigg made it a point not to follow his gaze, but she smiled slightly.

"Okay," Millhouse said. "Charges won't be brought as long as she's truthful. I'm authorized to make the offer. You have my word."

Twigg looked over at Cindy and nodded. Cindy began to sob.

"Agreement in writing," Twigg said.

"Sure," Millhouse said. "I'll set it up."

49

Afghanistan, 2001

SSF trooper Joe Vine used a polymer line and belayer to rappel down the rocky mountain face to the cave entrance they'd spotted from the ground. The main cave was still being explored. The Taliban had been driven from the area, or deeper into the caves, so there shouldn't be much danger in Vine checking out this cave by himself. Judging by the contours of the mountain, it was probably small and shallow and not much more than a grotto. This region was full of such minor caves, sometimes man-made, with dark entrances that usually led nowhere.

The mission was to mop up any remaining Taliban resistance, then search the caves for records and munitions. That could, of course, be extremely dangerous.

Vine stopped his descent about a yard to the side of the cave entrance. He saw now that the cave might be reachable by using a narrow path below, but it would be difficult, and, in places, the rocky path disappeared.

He would have tossed a grenade into the cave before entering, only the unit didn't want to make its presence known.

The sound of the grenade explosion would echo around the mountainous terrain, and the resultant smoke might be visible for miles.

So Vine readied his automatic weapon, gathered his guts, and pushed off from the mountain face to swing in through the cave entrance and take anyone inside by surprise.

From sunlight to dimness. It took a fraction of a second for Vine's vision to adjust.

Which was a good thing, or he might have squeezed the trigger.

Inside was his fellow SSF unit member Aaron Mandle. He was stooped over a bundle of some sort and staring up at him in surprise.

"Shit!" Vine said, relaxing. "You beat me to this one."

Mandle didn't answer, didn't move.

And Vine looked down at the bundle at Mandle's feet and knew why.

It was a young Afghan girl, wound tightly in her burka, which was darkly stained. Vine knew the stain and the faint metallic scent in the cave. Fresh blood.

"What the fuck did you do, Aaron?"

"It doesn't matter," Mandle said, standing straight now and smiling, his automatic weapon slung beneath his right arm, the knife in his left. "I found her in here."

"Like this?"

Mandle actually smiled. "Not exactly, Joe."

Vine sat down on the hard earth. "Fuck! Oh, fuck!"

"I didn't do that to her."

"What I mean," Vine said, "is that you can't get by with something like this, Aaron. It's murder."

"It's war, Joe. Total fuckin' war. The small and the crawl—that's us, Joe—we get fucked in total war. Any goddamn thing goes."

"Not *that!*" Vine said, pointing to the dead girl, marveling at how pale and angelic her face looked in the dim cave. She must have lost most of her blood before she died.

"Yeah, that," Mandle said. "It's what we trained for, Joe. Don't shit yourself, it's what we trained for."

"That kid's not the enemy!"

"Sure she is, just like all those Kraut and Jap civilians we bombed in World War Two. You ever read history, Joe?"

"Yeah, history . . ." Vine was feeling a little sick. The heat, even in the dim, shallow cave. The dead girl and the smell. *Jesus! . . .*

"I want you to do me a favor, Joe."

"I know. Forget about this."

"For a while, is all I'm asking. Until we can both think some more. Talk some more. Maybe straighten this thing out. Will you do that for me? I'd sure as fuck do it for you."

Vine worked his way to his feet, still feeling woozy. He glanced at his watch.

"We gotta rejoin the unit," Mandle said.

"Yeah, Aaron."

"Thanks, brother," Mandle said. "I owe you big."

Vine wasn't quite sure if he'd agreed to anything. He had to get away and find some time. Think about this.

He led the way out of the cave.

Closer to the base of the mountain, at the mouth of the main cave, they heard gunshots.

Mandle and Vine looked at each other. Then training took over. Crouched and fast, they moved into the cave with weapons at the ready.

The firefight was over when they reached the bend in the cave. Three al-Qaida lay dead in limp bundles like the girl in the other cave. Colonel Kray had a brown metal box tucked beneath his left arm.

Vine almost said something to him then, even though it wasn't the right time. The girl in the cave. Probably no more than twelve or thirteen. *She was a kid . . .*

Mandle was staring at him.

And for the first time Vine felt afraid of Aaron Mandle. And felt his resolve waver.

After all, Mandle could simply deny Vine's story. Might

even say he, Vine, killed the girl. Simply reverse their roles. There were no witnesses, only a dead Afghan girl. Dead in a country of death.

Gotta think about this, Vine told himself, and held his silence.

Think about it.

". . . time we shag-ass outta here," Kray was saying. "We got what we wanted. Looks like it could be a schematic for some kinda biological weapon or some such shit. We get it back to base, no matter what. Understood?"

"Understood, sir!" answered twelve voices almost in unison, heavy on the *sir.*

Kray motioned with his right arm and led the way out of the cave, toward sunlight and heat.

Vine spat on the cave floor and fell in behind Mandle, knowing he'd turned a corner in his mind, trying to convince himself he hadn't.

Think about it . . .

50

New York, 2004

Ten minutes after Cindy Vine had agreed to talk, Horn and Larkin were in the interrogation room with Millhouse, Twigg, and Cindy.

It was warm in there. Horn could feel the body heat and smell the sweat and fear emanating from Cindy. Getting mixed up with the wrong man was every woman's potential pitfall, he thought. It worked the other way, too, but not as often and not as severely. Not a lot of wives turned out to be serial killers.

"Joe had a lot of pressure," Cindy began, with the recorder running. "So did I, so maybe that's why I didn't notice how odd he was behaving. He was full of hate, and something else. Then, a couple of months ago, he told me about Aaron Mandle killing those women."

"The Night Spider murders?" Millhouse asked softly.

"No, the ones that happened while they were in the SSF, when they were on missions in various trouble spots around the world. Mandle was sick, dangerous. In Afghanistan, Joe walked in on him right after he'd killed a girl."

"Did Joe tell his commanding officer?"

"No, he couldn't. Their unit was separate from the main force, like usual when they were on a nearly suicidal mission. That's how Joe described it. So he waited before saying anything. He figured out that the girl Mandle killed wasn't the first and wouldn't be the last. Then, after a while, he realized it was too late to speak out. It would have looked bad for him if he'd said something, maybe ended his career in disgrace. He said that until now they never told their wives or anyone else about the murders. Joe thought Mandle was dead, until he was arrested for the Night Spider killings. He watched the news and followed the trial, the conviction . . ." Cindy started to sob again but bit her lip. She held in her distress like a great pressure, without breathing for a long time.

Finally she sighed, in control of herself, but seeming to become smaller as she exhaled. "Then came the phone call the night Mandle escaped. We were in bed, but I heard Joe on the phone. I knew he must be talking to Mandle. Joe hung up and started getting dressed in the dark. It surprised him when I asked where he was going. He'd thought I was asleep."

"What did Joe say?" Millhouse asked casually, isolating and emphasizing the answer for the recorder.

"That he had to go out. An old friend who was in trouble had called. I asked him what old friend, but all he said was not to worry about it. He kissed me good-bye and went."

"When did he return?"

"I'm not sure. I'd taken pills. We'd both been drinking. The stress of our son . . . what was happening in our lives. When I woke up at about nine the next morning, Joe was next to me in bed." Cindy couldn't hold back her tears now. She dropped her head onto the table, hid her face in the crook of her arm, and began to sob uncontrollably.

"Enough for now," Twigg said.

"Joe's not an evil man!" said Cindy from the shelter of her bent arm. "Joe is *not* an evil man!"

Horn kept his teeth clenched. *Oh, really? Is this the Joe who wants to torture and kill my wife?*

But he said nothing, glancing at Vicki Twigg.

She nodded slightly, as if to say, *I understand. We both know about evil.*

Horn was again humbled by the realization that what was profound in life usually lay unspoken.

And what needed to be said was usually spoken too late.

51

Afghanistan, 2001

The next evening at base camp, Aaron Mandle spoke to his commanding officer in private in the captain's tent.

Kray listened silently, rubbing his chin.

When Mandle was finished, Kray said, "You're telling me you and Vine killed this Afghan girl without provocation?"

"Vine was only the accessory, sir. I administered the fatal wounds."

Kray stared at him in disbelief. "Why the fuck are you telling me this, Aaron?"

"Because I knew you'd understand."

Kray studied him carefully, the pockmarked face, the creepy dark eyes. It was a face that was impossible to read. Kray often thought Mandle would make a hell of a poker player; he wondered if he might be playing poker now.

"Why might I understand?"

"Because we're all brothers, here or in hell. You've said so yourself, over and over. And we have to look out for each other no matter what. You, me, Vine."

Kray felt himself tighten inside. "I don't quite follow." But he did follow.

"I mean," Mandle said, "what would it do to your military career, two of your men doing murder under your command? What would it do to our unit and others like ours? Those pussy politicians in Washington get hold of this information and we'll all go down hard. Nobody'll be without blame. They'll go right up the line far as they can, chopping off heads, one right after the other, and not much worrying about whose heads they are."

"That's the way it works," Kray agreed.

"The word gets out," Mandle said, "it'd ruin a lot of careers, a lot of lives. Have an adverse effect on everybody it touched. It wouldn't be fair."

"Those things never are."

"So I figured I'd keep quiet about this, and I thought you'd see it the same way. It's not really like we have much choice, 'less we want to be brothers in the brig or gas chamber. We all owe each other, sir. It's like combat—if we're gonna survive we have to care for each other. Brothers all the way."

"You're saying we're in the same boat," Kray said carefully. "But the fact is, your end of the boat has a bigger leak in it."

"Whole boat sinks, though, sir. Who's even to say you didn't know about the murders from the beginning?"

There was the whole boat. "Yes, Aaron, I suppose you have a point."

"I figure we all three keep quiet, everything'll be fine, sir."

"That would be my suggestion, Aaron."

"Joe Vine, he's a good man but he needs to understand."

"I'll talk to him."

"He waited too long already before saying anything. And hell, it mighta been him killed the girl, if push comes to shove."

"It won't come to shove, Aaron. I'll speak with Trooper Vine. He'll understand that in time of war—in the world we live in—some things should be left unsaid."

"Thank you, sir."

"I suppose we should thank each other, Aaron."

"Yes, sir."

Mandle about-faced and was gone from the tent.

Kray had to fight himself so he wouldn't go after him and kill him.

Mandle, Vine, and Captain Kray never mentioned the matter again.

Four days later, on the outskirts of an Afghan village they were clearing of Taliban, Kray led Mandle, Vine, and a trooper named Reever into a mud-brick dwelling at the end of a narrow street.

At first the place looked empty. Then they saw that what looked like a rag pile in a corner was actually three huddled Afghan women in burkas.

They stood up slowly. Two of them raised their hands. The third flipped her wrist and expertly tossed a knife that stuck in Reever's throat.

The women went for the door.

Kray, Mandle, and Vine stopped them.

And didn't stop themselves.

The counterattack on the women turned into a gory struggle and then a sadistic bloodletting.

Crossing the river Styx, Mandle thought, watching life leave the women one by one. Their eyes. It was wondrous what happened to, what happened *in*, their eyes. The mystery just beyond grasping. *Crossing over, crossing over, passing . . . The small and the crawl . . .*

It was a bonding in blood for the killers.

They dragged Reever's body outside the mud dwelling, then Kray tossed a grenade in through the doorway.

Artillery and rocket fire were coming in on the other side of the village. In the hell and panic of the greater din, the muffled sound of the exploding grenade was barely noticeable.

52

The night after Cindy Vine's statement, Will Lincoln rotated the valve to extinguish the flame of his welding torch. A wisp of smoke and the stench of hot metal lingered.

He'd come out to his garage studio to work, thinking it would take his mind off what he'd just seen the TV news saying: that the police suspected Joe Vine of killing the last four Night Spider victims.

When he'd heard that, Will set down the Budweiser he'd been drinking. Kim had bitched, telling him the bottle would leave a ring on the table, he should use a coaster. Didn't he see the stack of coasters right there on the table?

At first Will hadn't even heard her, then he calmly told her he didn't care if the bottle left a ring. She was yelling at him as he stood up and walked out of the house. He heard her for a while after he shut the front door, even after he entered the garage, until he'd turned the air conditioner on high.

Then he set to work on *Flying Vengeance*, the steel American eagle sculpture he'd been working on.

But it hadn't helped. He hadn't been able to shake his concern for Vine.

Joe Vine . . .

Will remembered Vine very well. He could recall his face in minute detail: tense going into action; relieved and looser around the eyes and mouth afterward. He was never really afraid enough for it to show. Watching Vine had helped Will steel himself for the things they'd had to do, the things he never talked about and that no one would believe. Not in their worst nightmares.

Will stepped away from his workbench and peeled off his tinted welder's glasses. He didn't feel like working anymore. Not after the news and the memories that had been stirred.

He felt like having another beer, but not at home.

He felt like talking to someone, but not his wife.

Joe Vine and Kray were in Kray's black rental Ford Explorer, driving north. They had everything they needed. Kray had seen to it.

Vine was slumped against the door in the passenger seat, staring intently ahead into darkness. His gaze didn't seem to carry, as if he were concentrating on the bugs occasionally flitting in the headlight beams and smacking against the windshield. Kray didn't like the way he looked.

"We can pull it out, Joe," he said, shooting glances sideways while paying attention to the highway. "We've been in deeper shit."

"I'm not in any shit. I'm gonna get what I want."

"We're trained for the impossible," Kray reminded him. "Don't change your mind and go pussy on me, Joe."

"You know I won't. I want to kill her more than you do."

"Closer than brothers. That's how the unit survived."

"Those of us who did."

"Fuckin' right!" *Those of us who did! The winners!* "We survived because in situations like this we toughened up. There's nothing new for us here, Joe. We deal with it or it buries us. And we can deal with it if we've got the guts. You got the guts, Joe?"

"I'm fine in the guts department. Anyway, like I told you, there really isn't a choice. Not for me. I'm on my way to kill the cunt who ruined my son."

"There's always a choice. You throw up your hands and get fucked, or you become the fucker."

"I don't have a choice."

"Truth is, I know that, Joe. In this, you don't have any *real* choice. It's why I'm here with you, helping you in what you have to do."

Vine pulled himself up to sit straighter, though he continued his intent stare out the windshield at the headlight beams and rushing highway. Kray hoped Vine was going to be okay. Vine was at the edge. His blood lust might overwhelm his reason, or worse, his madness might shut him down, paralyze him.

"Closer than brothers, Joe. That's how we got it done. That's how we'll get this done. You ready?"

Vine didn't answer for a while. The intermittent *splat!* of insects on the windshield was the only sound other than the hum of motor and moan of wind.

Finally Vine said, "Fuckin'-A. I'm better than ready. I'm eager."

Kray smiled tightly. Confidently. Those words from Vine had been good enough before. They'd be good enough again.

Horn got the call that evening at his brownstone. He'd just snuffed out a cigar and was getting ready for bed when the phone rang.

Rollie Larkin.

"We don't have the DNA yet," he said to Horn, "but I thought you'd like to know that microscopic analysis matches the strand of hair found stuck beneath Alice Duggan's duct-tape gag with hair taken from Joe Vine's comb. Vine killed her, not that there was much doubt."

"No doubt at all," Horn said, "but thanks for calling. Everything in place for Anne?"

"I'm in tight communication with the operation. Everyone's in place. Men in the woods and in the creek bed, sentries watching the road. An officer is sitting guard while the cabin sleeps."

"I guess I can sleep then."

"Go ahead, Horn. Drink some of that scotch of yours, if it'll help."

Horn smiled. "I might do that. Then I'll drive up to the cabin in the morning."

After hanging up the phone, Horn was glad the conversation hadn't been on the cell phone. It would have been more likely overheard.

On the other hand, given the capabilities of Joe Vine, the phone line to the brownstone might be tapped.

Horn decided he probably wouldn't sleep very well, scotch or no scotch.

But he did—for less than an hour.

Then he was wide awake and fumbling for the phone.

Larkin said a thick hello, as if Horn had woken him.

Horn didn't care. "Rollie, I've thought of something!"

"I'm thinking of something right now, too," Larkin said sleepily.

"Cindy Vine," Horn said. "I remembered something she said during her interrogation, about when her husband confessed the murders to her. She said, ' . . . they never told their wives or anyone else about the murders.'"

"Yeah," Larkin said.

"Vine said *they.* And he said *wives.* Mandle never had a wife.*"

"This means? . . ."

"Joe Vine was telling her about more than one other killer besides himself. He must have been referring to Victor Kray. The three of them—Mandle, Vine and Kray—

took up murder together during the SSF's black operations."

"It's possible," Larkin said cautiously. He sounded all the way awake now and somewhat skeptical. "But why Kray?"

"Mandle stayed in the SSF and was never called on the murder Vine witnessed, so Vine must not have talked."

"True," Larkin said.

"Unless he did go to his commanding officer, and it went no further."

"Makes sense."

"And it went no further because Mandle must have had something on Kray."

"So why didn't Vine go over Kray's head?"

"My guess is by that time he was in too deep," Horn said. "All that's important is we know he *didn't* go higher than Kray in the chain of command. Then, when Mandle escaped from the prison van, Vine picked up where the Night Spider had left off, after killing Mandle. All so he could avenge what happened to his son and kill Anne; her death would've been blamed on Mandle."

"So why is Kray trying to help us nab Vine?"

"He doesn't want us to nab him; he wants to make sure we kill him, so he can't talk and implicate Kray. He wants to stay close to the investigation so he can control it, make sure Vine dies before talking, even if he has to kill him himself. Kray probably helped his old military buddy Vine kill Mandle after he escaped from the van, then thought the situation was contained. He had no way of knowing Vine would go on a killing spree of his own. Something else: I mentioned to Kray that Anne was going to be hidden away in her brother's cabin."

"You mention where the cabin was?"

"Do you really think Kray couldn't find out?"

"I get your point. You say Kray's at the Rion Hotel?"

"Yeah."

"I'll send around a detail to bring him in."

"No," Horn said. "Just put a tight tail on him. No need yet to let him know we're on to him."

"Chess game, huh?"

"I hope we're still at that point."

"Where's Bobby Fischer when you need him?"

"I'm driving up to the cabin."

"I'll go with you, soon as I arrange for the watch on Kray. That's where this is all likely to come together. I want to make sure everything up there is being done right."

"No need for that. Can you call Army Records in St. Louis this time of night?" Horn asked.

"I know a way to get through."

"Get any information they might have on Colonel Kray. It might help us string him along while he thinks he's stringing us along." Horn glanced at his watch. 11:35 P.M. "I'm leaving in five minutes. I've gotta make another phone call."

"I'll be on the road in ten minutes."

Larkin was determined. Horn decided to give up trying to talk him out of it. "Okay. Meet me off the highway on the county road that leads to the cabin."

"Take your cell phone," Larkin said.

"Always."

As Horn hurriedly got dressed, he wondered if Larkin really knew how much the NYPD leaked.

After leaving the brownstone, Horn's first act was to call Bickerstaff and Paula on a public phone three blocks away.

At about the halfway point of the drive to the cabin, Larkin called Horn on his cell phone.

"Just got the word," he said. "The detail sent to the hotel to observe Kray says he checked out only hours ago. Desk clerk said he was in a hurry."

Horn felt his stomach go cold with apprehension. Things were moving ahead of them; they weren't in control and might not possess the necessary knowledge. Losing at chess, and the stakes were unbelievably high.

"Something else," Larkin said. "Army Records tells me

Colonel Victor Kray resigned his commission and left the
service over two years ago."

Horn was silent, trying to drive and comprehend all of
this at the same time.

"Whaddya think, Horn?" asked Larkin's voice from the
cell phone. Horn could hear the constant snarl of Larkin's
car engine in the background. Larkin wasn't worried about
speeding tickets.

Horn said, "Drive faster."

Harlington Sheriff's Deputy Albert "Sass" Collier settled
deeper where he sat in darkness among last year's leaves. He
was alongside the dry creek bed. Like the others guarding
Anne Horn, Sass had strict instructions to hold his position
and not go near the cabin unless ordered to do so. The
NYPD guys were farther in toward the cabin, one of them
inside with the blond Anne Horn. Sass had seen her photo in
the New York papers. Nice looking lady from the big city.
He wondered what she'd be like to talk to. He smiled. *Talk
to, hell!*

Collier was on loan from the sheriff's department because he was a local and a hunter. He knew the woods. If the
wind was right, he could hear a deer move a hundred yards
away. He could hear a squirrel chatter and know its direction
almost well enough to fire at it blind and hit it with a shotgun
blast. Rumor had it Sass was half Cherokee Indian. He wasn't,
but he should have been.

Nothing, nobody, was going to pass him in or on either
side of the creek bed without him knowing.

He was called "Sass" because of some wildness in his
younger days, and a stubbornness that had matured into genuine toughness. Sass was six-feet-two and two hundred
pounds of solid cop. He knew the skills of his trade and beyond that held a black belt in Tae Kwon Do. If he did hear
somebody moving through the woods toward the cabin, he'd
know what to do. He'd be able to do it.

But he heard nothing other than the soft breeze playing through the leaves, even as dark forms above him moved through the forest canopy. If he'd glanced up, they would have been still, merely shadows among shadows.

One of the dark forms dropped straight down on a slender line to a point about three feet behind and above the seated Sass. The dark figure made a sudden, silent movement that tipped his body forward and down. In the same abrupt but smooth motion Sass's hair was gripped, his head yanked back to expose his throat, and tempered sharp steel sliced through his neck deep enough to sever both carotid arteries.

It had all happened in a few seconds, and the only sound had been the gush and soft splatter of blood on the dry leaves—like a gentle summer rain that passed quickly.

Sass's face barely had time to register surprise.

53

When Horn turned off the highway onto the narrow country road and killed his headlights, he saw by the faint moonlight that Rollie Larkin had already arrived.

Larkin was standing by a uniformed NYPD cop Horn didn't know, a stocky young man who looked like a serious weight lifter. Horn wondered if some of these young guys were taking steroids. He wondered if he would have when he was young, to be a better cop. Only animals took steroids when Horn was the young cop's age.

"This is Officer Wunderly," Larkin said, when Horn had gotten out of the car and walked off the road and into the tall grass where Larkin's car was parked.

Horn looked at Wunderly and gave him a nod.

"No sign of anything since we've been here, sir." Wunderly had a narrow head, made pinched-looking by the sidelighting of the moon. It was a head that didn't go with his muscular frame.

"Been in touch with the sentries?" Horn asked.

"Every hour," Wunderly said.

"How long since the last time?"

Wunderly glanced at his watch. "Twenty minutes."

"You doing it on the hour?"

"Yes, sir. Easier to remember."

And predict, Horn thought. "Contact the nearest."

Wunderly went to the patrol car and got out a black, leather-cased walkie-talkie. "These are from the sheriff's department. Regular two-ways don't work worth a damn out here," he explained. "Local yokels don't have 'em anyway."

Horn and Larkin looked at each other while Wunderly tried to contact the sentry, keeping his voice low.

"Wunderly to Deputy Collier . . . Deputy Collier . . . Sass, you there? . . ."

Wunderly's brow furrowed. He looked at Horn and Larkin. "Can't raise him."

"Got a map?" Horn asked.

"Sure. Sheriff's department gave us a dandy."

"Sounds like the sheriff's department is running the whole goddamn show," Larkin said.

"You relay my order for the sentries to maintain position?" Horn asked Wunderly.

"Yes, sir. Made it plain so everybody understood."

"Get the map and show me where Sass is," Horn said.

In the blackness of the night, Vine and Kray silently moved from limb to limb, overhead in the forest canopy, then dropped straight down on lines and garroted or slit the throats of the police guarding the cabin where Anne was staying.

Vine spotted one sentry, a local, sitting halfway up a tree in a deer seat, a contraption hunters used to stake out spots during deer season so they could fire down on the unsuspecting animals when they approached. The seats were held fast to the trees by the tension of weight and leverage against metal frames or straps.

Vine dropped silently along the other side of the tree's trunk, made a slight sound on the sentry's left so he'd turn his head in that direction, then deftly reached around the trunk from the right and slit the man's throat. He knew that Kray, watching, must approve.

This was the third man they'd killed. They wanted to be sure that when they finally did enter the cabin, they'd be alone with Anne.

Then Kray would be alone with Vine.

Then Kray would be alone.

Kray knew the aftermath would be awkward. He could say he knew how dangerous Vine was because he'd trained him, that he'd taken it upon himself to make sure Anne Horn was protected and Vine was captured or killed. Unfortunately, he'd been only partly successful.

Still, he'd be a hero. And he knew PR and how to cover his ass. He'd be first to get out his version of what happened, take advantage of all the media morons and cable news channels that would want to interview him.

Who could prove his story false other than Anne Horne and Vine?

The dead didn't testify in court.

Paula knew the way better, and she could see better at night, so she gave Bickerstaff directions as he drove.

The dusty unmarked car, running without lights, pulled to a stop behind Wunderly's patrol car just off the county road.

Bickerstaff leaned forward over the steering wheel and looked around. "Where the hell is everyone?"

Paula didn't answer. She got out of the unmarked and right away noticed two other cars. They were parked in the shadows of a copse of trees. Moving closer to them and squinting in the dim light, she saw that they were unoccupied. But she knew the cars.

She took a few steps back to where Bickerstaff was climbing out of the unmarked.

"Horn and Larkin are here," she said. "Somewhere."

Bickerstaff looked in the direction of the cars, then all

around him. Nothing but night. Not even the sounds of crickets or nocturnal animals. Maybe something moving, far away. A bear or cougar? He wondered, uneasily, if they were still to be found in upper New York State. He looked over at Paula in the faint moonlight.

"We seem to be alone," Bickerstaff said.

"Yeah."

"So whadda we do?"

Wunderly had gotten Horn and Larkin Kevlar vests from the trunk of the patrol car. The three of them had gone about two hundred yards into the woods, walking as quietly as they could. Still, they made what Horn considered to be a lot of noise as they strode through the dry underbrush and occasionally blundered into unseen branches that snapped back, sometimes scratching their arms and faces.

Two middle-aged Caucasians and a big-city white boy, Horn thought, trying to act as if they knew what they were doing in the wild.

Finally they came to the creek bed on the sheriff's map. Horn saw no more than a shallow depression full of dry twigs, vines, and uneven stones. The detritus of winter that hadn't washed away.

"Easier going that way," Wunderly said in a soft, knowledgeable voice that would have made an Indian guide proud. He spat off to the side. "Creek bed's like nature's path."

"Where you from, Wunderly?" Horn asked.

"Brooklyn, sir."

"Nature's path, huh? We go crashing along through all those rotted leaves and dead wood, we'll make a hell of a lot of noise."

"You got a point, sir. "

"How far till we get to this Sass character?" Larkin asked.

" 'Bout a hundred yards that way, sir." Wunderly pointed in the direction of the cabin.

"Let's approach at an angle," Horn said.

He led the way, moving more confidently, The woods still obscured what faint moonlight there was, but his eyes were accustomed to the dimness.

The three city animals were making less noise now, but still too much.

"This Sass guy won't lose his cool and shoot us, will he?" Larkin asked.

"Not the type, sir." Wunderly's feet suddenly slipped out from under him and he was on his back on the ground. "Jesus!" He was staring at his hand.

It was black. No, red.

"It's blood!" Wunderly was staring to his left, scooting backward away from what he saw.

Wunderly'd had his direction right but his distance wrong. A man Horn assumed was Sass was sitting with his back against a tree, his head dangling to the side. So saturated were his clothes with blood it was hard to recognize them as a uniform. The expression on his pale face suggested he was leering at a dirty joke. He wasn't, though. His throat was slit so deeply he was nearly decapitated.

"How far ahead is the next sentry?" Horn asked.

"Not far. Over that way." Wunderly pointed, then abruptly leaned to the side and began to vomit.

Horn and Larkin waited. Larkin stood staring at Sass, his face almost as pale as the corpse's. "Think you ever get used to this kind of shit?" He was talking to Horn.

"I hope not," Horn replied.

Wunderly was struggling to stand up straight. He wiped his bloody hands on his pants, then spat off to the side as he had when he was the seasoned trail guide.

"You okay?" Horn asked.

"Yeah. Not the first body I saw. I don't know why I let go like that."

"Lead on."

They walked with guns drawn, afraid of what they were going to find, afraid they might be making enough noise to draw attention.

The second sentry was lying on his back. More blood. But this time Horn saw that he'd been garroted with a length of wire so thin it had sliced flesh and arteries. Both men must have been killed soundlessly, and somehow were taken by complete surprise. Horn remembered Kray's words: *He can kill in more ways than you can imagine.*

The third sentry was seated halfway up a tree in what reminded Horn of the sort of harness phone company linemen used when they wanted to sit and work high on telephone poles. Both his arms were hanging limply. He wasn't moving.

Something was making a soft *pat . . . pat . . . pat* sound that was unmistakable.

"He's still dripping blood," Horn said. "Killed not long ago."

"Jesus!" Wunderly said. "Maybe they're *all* dead."

"Goddamnit!" Larkin said. "This wasn't supposed to fucking happen! What in God's name are we dealing with here?"

"Cabin straight ahead?" Horn asked Wunderly.

"Not exactly, sir. We just stay parallel with the creek bed and we'll come to it, though."

"Only one more sentry between us and it, right?"

Wunderly swallowed. "Yes, sir." He was looking again at the blood he couldn't wipe off his hands. "We gotta call in some help."

"You and Larkin go back to the cruiser, call the state patrol."

"Maybe get a chopper with a spotlight in here!" Wunderly said.

"Wunderly can notify them," Larkin said. "I'm going with you."

"You can't, Rollie. You're an assistant chief of police."

"Doesn't mean shit at a time like this."

"Sure it does. You want to be promoted someday, I'm asking you to trust me here. I don't have time to explain."

"You real sure you know what you're doing, Horn?"

"State police'll get us reinforcements fast," Wunderly said. "I know what I'm doing."

Larkin studied Horn as if there might be some kind of code written on his forehead. Then he nodded and turned away, Wunderly following.

Horn had to resist an impulse to join them.

Then he began moving fast through the woods. He was breathing hard and his heart was a drumbeat in his chest. Kray and Vine couldn't be far ahead.

For some reason, the dead sentries, methodically killed one after the other, reminded Horn of a phrase from his Bible-school days, something about the Grim Reaper gathering sheaves—or maybe it wasn't from the Bible. Wherever he'd heard or seen it, it sure applied tonight.

What in God's name are we dealing with here?

Horn knew the cabin was in a clearing. Vine and Kray would have to cross open ground. If he could catch up with them before they did that, and before they separated and slipped into the cabin, he'd be able to spot them in exposed positions. There was enough moonlight for him to see that well.

If the clouds cooperated.

"Christ!" Horn muttered, and lengthened his stride, ignoring the brush trying to snag his ankles and the branches that scratched his face and arms. He scraped his bare left elbow on the rough bark of a tree trunk but ignored the pain. He was carrying his service revolver in his left hand, but when it came time to fire the gun, he'd transfer it to his right, trading pain for accuracy.

Lately it seemed he was always trying to get something in exchange for pain.

Vine and Kray had heard the sounds of their pursuers in the woods. They paused now in shadow, just inside the line of trees, two dark-clad figures like shadows themselves. About a hundred yards ahead, the tiny, crude cabin shone in the moonlight like a prize in the middle of a clearing.

"They know we're here," Kray whispered. "And we have to cross open ground."

"We gotta go in anyway," Vine said.

Kray grinned in the night. "You really want to waste her, don't you?"

"I do. And if she's gone, I'll get outta here and try again. If there's a policewoman in the cabin taking her place, we got us a hostage."

"Makes sense," Kray said. It was daring enough to work, if Kray would let it. "In fact, I like it."

Vine looked over at him and smiled. "Like brothers?"

"I'm with you all the way," Kray said. "Wherever all the way goes."

Horn saw movement through the trees. He hurried his pace, trying to keep quiet. He wanted to get close. As close as he could . . .

But the two dark figures were already moving across the clearing, keeping low, almost but not quite running.

Horn decided to run toward them, not worrying about the noise. Shoving branches away with his free arm, he raced through the woods.

Amazingly, the trailing figure heard him from that distance. The figure hesitated, turned, then dropped flat to be almost invisible, even in the level clearing.

Horn was at the line of trees marking the end of the woods. He stayed halfway hidden and snapped off a shot with his revolver, knowing he was way out of range.

Both figures had disappeared now.

"Only one so far," Vine whispered to Kray, lying low in the tall grass about ten feet away.

"So far," Kray said. "Spot him?"

"Maybe in line with that tall pine tree, right at the fringe of the woods. I'll see him if he moves. Think we should take him out?"

"Might not make the cabin if we don't. Sounded like a handgun, but we can't be sure what else he has."

"Or how soon help'll come his way."

"Still got your sniper's eye?"

"We'll find out," Vine said, shifting his body slightly and bringing his automatic rifle around. He kept the rifle low and parallel to the ground; its barrel flattened an arc of tall grass as if it were a scythe.

Horn saw the slight movement of grass in the moonlight. He knew where they were and wanted to flush them out. Had to flush them out.

He decided on another useless pistol shot. Might as well use his strong but inaccurate left hand since he wasn't going to hit anything anyway.

He shifted the pistol back from his right hand and moved to where he could fire around a tree.

A sledgehammer hit him high on his chest on his right side.

He was on his back on the ground without remembering falling. He did recall the short burst of automatic rifle fire and knew he'd been hit. *Even at this distance, the small, brief target I presented* . . . He was amazed by the accuracy of the shot.

He felt his chest with trembling fingers and found the depression in the Kevlar vest. Felt around some more. Apparently, only one of the burst of about four shots had struck him.

They're human after all. Only human!

He located his revolver—the hard lump he was lying on—and held it in his right hand.

There was no way Vine or Kray could approach to make sure they'd killed him without being outlined against the moonlit sky.

Unless they circle around! Come through the woods.

I'll hear them! They'll make noise in the woods. They have to make some noise!

He didn't allow himself the slightest movement, knowing they might see it.

As he lay there calculating his chances, the dark clouds scudding across the sky obscured the moon.

Now, against an unbroken black backdrop, they could come at him, unseen!

It took all of Horn's willpower not to move. Let them think he was dead. Maybe he could get a shot off, kill one of them.

Suddenly, the moon was clear and the sky was a pale purple rather than black—like curtain time, last act.

And there they were, faint dark shapes against the sky, only about ten yards away.

Pistol range!

Knowing they might be wearing flak jackets, Horn aimed for the knee of the closest and squeezed off a shot.

Heard a yelp of pain as he rolled to the side, into shadow, into the woods.

A burst of automatic weapon fire rustled and picked at the leaves in his wake.

He fired his pistol again, then rolled to his left. He had to fire with his right hand to have a chance of hitting anything, and his arm was aching more with each shot, with each roll. "The area's sealed off!" he shouted. "State police have you surrounded!" *Lie to the bastards!*

Another burst of fire, over his head and to the left.

"You don't have a chance unless you surrender!" He moved again. *Fifty-fifty, right or left. They're gonna guess right.*

No blind shots at the sound of his voice this time. Neither one of these guys wasted ammunition.

Not like I'm doing.

Staying as low as possible, he reloaded.

* * *

"Hit bad?" Kray asked in a whisper.

Vine's voice was tight with pain. "Fucker got me in the thigh. Lucky it wasn't my knees."

"Will the leg take your weight?"

"I think so. You figure we're really surrounded?"

"Hell, yes. We knew they were here when we arrived." Kray scooted over closer to Vine. He could see blood glistening on his left thigh. Goddamn moonlight.

"Let's go for the cabin," Vine said.

Kray couldn't help feeling a rush of pride. His men were the finest. "You know she might not even be in there."

"God help whoever is!" Vine said.

Several shots came from the direction of the dark woods.

"Prick must have reloaded," Kray said. "Give him something to chew on and let's move!"

The woods came alive around Horn with the crackle of 9mm slugs snapping through leaves and branches. He knew it was covering fire, and as soon as it ended he raised his head and saw them making for the cabin. One of them was lagging, limping from the shot in the leg.

Not the knee, though. Running too fast. Tough fucker.

Horn moved beyond the edge of the woods and got off a shot, feeling the recoil up his bad right arm. The arm started to pulse. "You don't have a fucking chance! Give it up!"

He began to give chase. One of the fleeing figures turned slightly and rattled off a few shots, obviously not caring if he hit anything. They were making for the cabin.

To finish their mission. That's how they think. To make the kill.

"Me first!" Kray said to Vine as they ran. *Planning while on the run. Attacking! No questions. Attacking!* They were closing fast on the cabin. "I'm right!"

"Left!" Vine replied through clenched teeth.

* * *

Behind them, Horn stopped running and stood watching, firing his remaining rounds into the night sky.

Holding his breath.

Kray was up on the plank porch, automatic weapon slung low, getting off a burst at the knob and lock as he went.

He stopped firing the moment before he lowered his shoulder and slammed into the door, forcing it to fly open.

As soon as he was inside he rolled to his right, then sprang to his feet, weapon at the ready.

Vine was a second behind him, rolling left, and regained his feet shakily because of the wounded leg. He knew instantly that the cabin was unoccupied.

Kray scanned the cabin's interior, sweeping the gun barrel in an arc. In a crazy way it felt wonderful. *Doing business again. But something. Something . . .*

And he realized his right ankle had met resistance as he'd burst into the cabin.

Trip wire!

His last act was to turn to see if Vine had somehow realized the danger. If he could get out in time. Like brothers . . .

Not a chance!

It was all in slow motion, like the opening moments of a space shuttle launch. Horn saw the cabin lift off its slab foundation. From the moment Vine and Kray entered the cabin, he knew they had three seconds to live before the bomb he'd planted exploded.

The sides of the cabin flew outward, unable to contain the expanding orange fireball that rolled and rose into the dark sky. An instant later came the roar, and a shock wave surged across the meadow, bending tall grass and pressing Horn back a step, making him stagger.

Neither man had gotten out.

Paula had followed Horn's instructions to the letter in rigging the trip wire for the bomb Beiner had given him, the bomb Horn had secured beneath the cabin's floorboards.

Just inside the door.

A quarter of a mile away on the county road, Paula and Larkin heard the explosion and glanced at each other in the night. In the corner of her vision, Paula was aware that Bickerstaff and Wunderly were climbing out of the cruiser where they'd been sitting and waiting.

Paula knew what had happened wasn't exactly police work. In fact, unless Horn revealed that she'd set up the trip wire, the police weren't exactly involved. After all, Horn was a civilian acting as an advisor.

After delivering Anne to the cabin, letting her believe, so everything would look real to anyone observing them, Paula had returned and spirited her away. Most of the trip back to the city Anne lay in the backseat out of sight. She'd been sent safely away and was with her brother in Philadelphia.

Horn had acted alone as much as possible. Paula knew he'd take the responsibility but wouldn't talk—couldn't be made to talk. And Larkin, he'd learned of Horn's plan too late to do anything about it, even if the truth did leak out somehow, which it wouldn't. This time, no leaks. Bickerstaff was retiring again this week or the week after, and Wunderly still wasn't clued in. If he needed clueing in, Larkin would see to it. Wunderly might find himself promoted to sergeant with a promising future. Maybe Paula would even find herself promoted.

Paula smiled. *Fucking politics!*

"We probably won't be charged with anything other than disturbing the peace," Larkin said beside her. "The noise."

"Yes, sir," Paula said. "Should we go find Horn? See if he's okay?"

Larkin looked genuinely confused. "Horn? Is he here?"

54

Eighteen months later, Paula was eating dinner with Harry and some of their friends on the West Side, when she thought she spotted Horn sitting alone on the other side of the restaurant. She had to look twice, being patient until a waiter had moved, to make sure she wasn't mistaken.

She excused herself and wove through the crowded restaurant toward his table.

When she got closer, she saw that he looked slightly grayer but not a year older. He was wearing a tan tweed sport coat over a black turtleneck sweater. A wrapped cigar stuck out of the coat's breast pocket. She was pleased to note that he hadn't diminished even slightly with age; his bulk made the table look like a miniature.

She noticed something else. Though he was sipping a glass of white wine and sitting alone, the table was set for two.

He looked up at her and gave her his slow and genuine smile. *The one he sometimes gives to suspects.*

"Paula Ramboquette. You look wonderful!" He stood and grasped her in a firm hug. "Sit down, please."

"No, I have to get back. And you're waiting for some-one."

"Sit, Paula."

She grinned. "That sounded like a command." She sat down across the table from him.

"You're plainclothes now," he said. "Lead detective, with a recent commendation. A rising NYPD star." He winked. "The one to watch."

Paula was surprised and pleased that he'd followed her career. "You seem to be doing very nicely yourself. You look terrific."

"Just another old cop, Paula. Heard anything from Bicker-staff?"

Paula nodded. "He phoned last Christmas Day. He had a bad cold, but he was going ice fishing anyway." She could imagine a heavily bundled Bickerstaff sitting and sniffling, hunched over a hole in the ice, maybe a dead fish or two next to him. Fun. Really fun.

"Paula?"

"Sorry. Thinking about Bickerstaff." She suddenly felt ill at ease. "How is—" Remembering the impending divorce of last year, she bit off her words.

"Anne? She's fine. Still working at Kincaid Memorial. She's engaged to a corporate attorney."

Paula sensed someone beside her and looked up to see Marla Winger. Marla looking glamorous and sophisticated in a simple navy blue dress with a pearl necklace.

"Paula," Horn said, "you remember Dr. Winger . . ."

"Damn it, Horn, you know I do!" Grinning widely, Paula stood up and she and Marla hugged. Paula caught the scent of expensive perfume.

"It's wonderful to see you both," Paula said. "Really!" She couldn't stop grinning and was beginning to feel awk-ward about it. Like Frankenstein's bride with the giggles. "Listen, I'm interrupting . . . I'd better get back to my table."

She muttered a few more polite inanities and turned away, wishing like crazy that Bickerstaff were there. She was unable to control what she was thinking:

Corn muffins!

ABOUT THE AUTHOR

A multiple Edgar and Shamus Award–winner—including the Shamus Lifetime Achievement Award—John Lutz is the author of over thirty books. His novel *SWF Seeks Same* was made into the hit movie *Single White Female,* and *The Ex* was a critically acclaimed HBO feature. He lives in St. Louis, Missouri.

Praise for John Lutz

"John Lutz is a major talent."

—John T. Lescroart, *New York Times*
bestselling author of *The First Law*

"I've been a fan of John Lutz for years."

—T. Jefferson Parker, *New York Times*
bestselling author of *Cold Pursuit*

"*The Night Spider* is compelling, suspenseful and—dare I say
it?—creepy. John Lutz knows how to make you shiver."

—Harlan Coben, *New York Times*
bestselling author of *No Second Chance*

"Shut the phone off, don't answer the door . . . and spend the
the day reading *The Night Spider*. Author Lutz offers up a heart-
pounding roller-coaster of a tale, whose twists and turns are
made all the more compelling by the complex, utterly real characters populating his world."

—Jeffery Deaver, *New York Times*
bestselling author of *The Vanished Man*

"Some writers just have a flair for imaginative suspense, and we
all should be glad that John Lutz is one of them. *The Night
Spider* features elegant writing enveloping exotic murder and
solid police work during the nightmarish aftermath of 9/11 in
New York City. A truly superb example of the 'new breed' of
mystery thrillers."

—Jeremiah Healy, Shamus Award-winning
author of *Turnabout* and *Spiral*

"Compelling . . . a gritty psychological thriller . . . Lutz's details concerning police procedure, fire-fighting techniques and
FDNY policy ring true, and his clever use of flashbacks draws
the reader deep into the killer's troubled psyche."

—*Publishers Weekly* on *The Night Watcher*

"John Lutz is the new Lawrence Sanders. *The Night Watcher*
has enough twists to turn you into a raging paranoid by page
thirty. What's new is the sleek presentation of the detectives, the
nocturnal underworld of NYC, and most of all the most original
character I've seen in crime fiction in years (she brings out
Lutz's Chekhovian side). This is a very smooth and civilized
novel about a very uncivilized snuff artist, told with passion,
wit, carnality, and relentless vigor. I loved it."

—Ed Gorman in *Mystery Scene* on *The Night Watcher*

ALSO BY JOHN LUTZ

The Night Watcher
The Night Caller
Final Seconds (with David August)
The Ex

From Kensington Publishing and Pinnacle Books